THE BITTER RIVAL

LM FOX

THE BITTER RIVAL

THE BITTER RIVAL

Editor: Readers Together

Proofreader: Cheree Castellanos, For Love of Books4 Editing

Formatter: Shari Ryan, MadHat Studios

Cover/Graphic Artist: Hang Le

Cover Photographer: Wander Aguiar

Cover Model: David Turner

To TL Swan, who brought light when there was only darkness.

Ask, believe, receive and be immensely thankful
for all is possible when we live in gratitude and joy.

CHAPTER ONE

Isabella

"Here's to a much-needed girls' night, Bella. Cheers."

Clinking our frosty margarita glasses in celebration of an overdue girls-only evening, I take a much-anticipated sip of my drink and smile at my sister over the salty rim. "Oh, Bailes, I really needed this. The only thing I need more is a little hot and dirty. But if I can't find a man, I'll happily accept the next best thing."

"Ha. Well, given my poor history with the male population, I haven't completely ruled out women. However, sleeping with you might be taking it a step too far." She giggles. "I know you're juggling a lot with school and your internship, but we need to put a stake in the ground, B. Girls' night is mandatory from here on out. It's been way too long," she shouts over the dance music behind us.

Growing up in a big family, we rarely enjoy time alone. Bailey, the youngest of my three siblings, is also the loudest. She's never been treated like the *baby of the family*; that could be because our older brothers looked out for the two of us equally. Dominic and Damian, along with our cousin, Donovan, watched over us like they were self-appointed bodyguards. We grew up knowing we had their protection, whether we wanted it or not. Needless to say, dating was not easy. Prospective suitors needed to pass inspection from each of the 'Potter Boys' before being granted access to us. Bailey and I have worked hard to keep our relationships private, out of the scrutiny of our overbearing family.

"Oh, I love this song. Come on, Bella, please?" Bailey begs, grabbing my arm as she wiggles her hips toward the dance floor. As "Wobble" by V.I.C. begins to play, we squeeze through the many patrons on the small dance floor of this downtown club to find a spot big enough for the two of us to move. Normally, this go-to club is a favorite, even if the clientele seems to get younger and younger. The atmosphere is eclectic, the bartenders hot to peruse between drinks, and the music is always good.

Richmond, Virginia, wasn't always a huge town for tourists. Yet, in recent years the amount of travelers has picked up. It has started to develop a name for itself amongst foodies, with all of the new restaurants popping onto the scene. Even Guy Fieri has visited with several eateries starring on his *Diners, Drive-ins, and Dives* Food Network show. But this weekend has become quite crowded with the Richmond Bike Race in full swing. The central Virginia area is rich with outdoor activities this time of year between cycling, BMX, the Flying Squirrels double-A baseball team, outdoor festivals, and hiking and boating along the James River. Quite honestly, it's hard to know how many of this club's current patrons are local or out-of-town trekkers to the city.

I watch as my little sister swings her arms over her head with wild abandon to the rhythmic beat of the music. Bailey's such a free spirit. She's the creative sibling while my older brothers joined the fire academy, and Donovan, went to medical school, Bailey pursued a career in art. She accepted into Virginia Commonwealth University's competitive art program and has continued to cultivate her talent.

I'm the late bloomer to higher education. I'd embraced domestic bliss after graduation, supporting my young husband in his pursuit of a medical degree. It wasn't until I turned thirty-four when post-high school instruction became a priority. Although attending college and managing my home responsibilities has been difficult, I'm proud of all I've accomplished. Even if that means Bailey and I haven't had many opportunities for a night out.

Taking in the contagious smile on my sister's pretty face, I feel a warmth in my chest. I'm proud of her. Proud of us. She, much like myself, has been single for a long while. While I've spent the last twelve years a divorcée, my younger sister has admittedly not found *The One*. Watching this willowy, brown-eyed beauty spin and sway before me, fills me with pride. She's protected her heart. While she's dated her fair share of men, she's not settling. She's awaiting *The man God created just for her*. I'd given up on that notion long ago. Yet, I still miss the company of an attractive man, particularly when I lie alone in my bed, night after night.

As if cupid has been on standby, I hear a masculine voice over the thumping base behind me. "Hi. Would you like to dance?"

I glance over my shoulder, and a tall man with closely trimmed brown hair stands a foot away from me, staring at me with a hopeful look in his brown eyes, framed by wire rim glasses. As I turn to acknowledge his presence and hopefully let him down easily, I reassess his physique. He's not what most would describe as tall yet, at my petite five-foot-three frame, everyone appears to tower over me. He's not unattractive, but this is a girls' night, and he's clearly not female.

"Hi," I shout over Post Malone's sultry styling. "I'm here with my sister." I point my thumb over my shoulder before turning back to her.

I watch as Bailey shrugs her shoulders, questioning the interruption, but I have no time to fill her in before the relentlessly needy dancer pushes for more.

"Can I buy you a drink?" His voice is a little closer now.

"I already have one, thanks." I toss my rejection his way before turning my back to him. *Please take the hint, buddy.* I inch a bit closer to Bailey, hoping the closer proximity will offer protection from any further interruption. Rolling my eyes at her in frustration with his unwanted persistence, I suddenly feel a hand on my elbow. *For fuck's sake.*

Spinning on my heel, ready to give him a piece of my mind, I stop in my tracks. There's no disputing *this* man is tall. He's tall, dark, and holy hell is he handsome.

"I'm sorry I'm late," he offers before sliding his hand from my elbow to the small of my back, pulling me into him for a quick peck on the cheek.

Um, what? Stunned at the change in scenery, I try to play this cool. Leaning back, I take in the rogue before me. He must be the most attractive male specimen I've ever seen in the flesh. His dark brown hair is styled to perfection, and as I gaze into his piercing deep blue eyes, I notice a spark of humor. There's a trace of a five o'clock shadow on his square jaw that commands attention—and that deep dimple is hard to miss, even under the slight facial hair.. He's an imposing presence, not due to his height or attractiveness, but the air of superiority rolling from his confident stance.

"I'm sorry, man. This one's taken," he directs to the ever-persistent male who still lingers on the dance floor.

Glancing to the menace who's volleying between us for clues, I watch as he turns and walks toward the bar without another word.

"Thank you," I utter quietly in the direction of the gorgeous man. He's wearing an expensive gray suit and crisp white shirt. The top buttons are undone, revealing tantalizing bronzed skin and just a hint of dark chest hair.

"Don't thank me," he replies. "I'm kicking myself for letting that guy slither over before I could get the nerve to talk to you."

Unable to help myself, I roll my eyes at this statement. Like this guy would ever need to 'get the nerve' to talk to anyone. I hope he doesn't think I'm falling for that line.

"Awe, come on. You need to dance with me, at least. To keep up the rouse." He winks.

Craning my neck toward the bar, I notice the man in question has already found a new source of entertainment. "I don't think that's necessary." I point a finger in the gentleman's direction, making my point he's completely forgotten about me. I rotate slightly and realize Bailey has slipped back to our table. "Thanks again," I acknowledge before heading in her direction.

"Really? Not even one dance?"

I stop in my tracks, trying to come up with some clever anecdote when it dawns on me. *Why am I in such a hurry to distance myself from the hottest man I've ever encountered?* Everything about this attractive man screams 'Run.' But it's just one dance. I spin on my heel and look up at him. *God, he's one tall drink of water.* "Okay, one dance then."

His expression shifts from a seductive smirk to a warm grin. His bright blue eyes twinkle in my direction, like constellations painted across a clear, dark sky. They could easily hypnotize me if I wasn't distracted by that flirty dimple sending me morse code. Not wasting any time, he steps forward and wraps his strong arms around my back, pulling me into him. An immediate hum begins to stir in my belly. *Just one dance, Bella.*

Shocked at his invasion into my personal space, as well as my reaction to it, I attempt to retreat a step until the warmth of his strong hands caresses my lower back. I instantly feel goosebumps pimple my flesh and try to take a cleansing breath to calm my nerves. This action has the opposite effect, as now I've inhaled the most intoxicating scent. I relent and place my palms flat upon his chest as we move in beat with the music, all the while trying to decipher the incredible notes of his cologne. There's a woody, floral scent with a strange touch of spice. I lean into him, continuing to draw in the heady aroma. I quickly determine I should discontinue this investigation before his scent completely inebriates me.

As I attempt to pull back, his strong arms pull me closer. I can feel him slide his body down the length of mine in time with the music, placing his pelvis entirely too close to mine. One firm rock against this incredibly well-built man, and I might start entertaining ways to satisfy my much overdue craving for some hot and dirty sex.

Taking an opportunity to change positions during a transition in the chorus, I twist to dance with my back to him. His hands move to position themselves, not on my hips, but my lower abdomen. As he rocks my body back against his, I can feel his steely erection against my back. *Good lord, is that his arm or his dick?*

The song comes to an end, and I seize the opportunity to make my exit. As tempting as it might be to consider a one-night stand with this man, he's way out of my league. Truth be told, I think I'd be nervous considering anything with the likes of this one. He seems a little too hot for me to handle.

"Thank you," I blurt before offering a smile that feels forced. Before he can offer a reply, I make haste to my table to find Bailey. Dropping into my chair, I grab the remains of my margarita and chug it down. *Hell, who am I kidding? I'm going to need an ice bath to cool down after that hot piece of—*

"Uh, Bella? Why on earth would you come back here with me when you could keep dancing with tall, dark, and *fuck me, is he sexy*? Jeez, he's the hottest man I think I've ever seen. I almost had an orgasm watching him move his hands all over you. That look on his face. Gah," she utters, fanning herself.

I can't possibly find an answer that will appease her, so I simply shrug my shoulders.

She gives me a blank stare, mimicking my ridiculous motion by drawing her shoulders up toward her ears in question. "What is wrong with you? That man is beautiful."

"Yeah, a little too beautiful."

"Huh?"

"The way he was looking at me, Bailey, and touching me... I was starting to feel like shark bait," I reply as I swiftly look toward the bar for a waiter. I need another drink.

"Well, hell, Bella. I'd let him bite me," she scolds, waggling her brows in my direction.

"Bailes, something tells me if a guy like that takes a bite out of you, you won't recover."

The much-needed waiter arrives at our table, and I order refills. I turn my gaze back to the dance floor, not wanting to make eye contact with the shark but to interrupt this conversation. Even if only for a moment.

"How long has it been, Bella?"

The question catches me off guard. Not sure why it should, as I've never kept anything from Bailey. I make eye contact with her but avoid answering the question. I'm embarrassed to admit it's been way too long.

"Bella? You said earlier you needed some hot and dirty. Well, I bet it doesn't come any hotter or dirtier than that guy."

The conversation stops as the waiter returns with our drinks. I slide him enough cash to cover the cocktails, including a generous tip and quickly take a sip. *Oh, that's good.*

Bailey takes a sip of her drink and leans across the table to whisper-shout over the dance music. "He looks like the kinda guy who'd go down on you without asking for anything in return. Like the unicorns you read about in romance novels that'll eat you out because they're hot for it."

"Oh, good lord, Bailey." I feel my cheeks turn pink at the statement. As long as it's been since I've had sex with a man, it's been too long to remember when I've had oral. Sure, I've given a blow job or two, but no one has reciprocated in a very long time. I shake my head briefly before diving into my delicious cocktail once more.

"Look out now, B. It appears the shark is circling the water." Bailey giggles over her glass.

My eyes flick over my shoulder, making direct contact with the predator in question. His stare is intense. It's as if he's trying to send a message through his penetrating gaze. I feel the familiar tingle on my skin from earlier, and arousal stirs between my legs that I haven't entertained in quite some time.

Realizing I need to get my body under control, I stand to look for the restrooms. "I'll be back, Bailes. I just need the little girls' room," I say before looking in the direction of the front of the club. Maybe splashing some water on my face and neck will put out the fire that wimpy margarita couldn't douse.

Turning the corner of the dark hallway, I discover the usual line that extends from the ladies' room. It doesn't appear long, so I decide to wait a few moments and pull out my phone to check for any missed calls or texts. I haven't investigated this long before sensing an unmistakable aura behind me, causing me to pull the phone into my chest in alarm. My breath catches and my eyes flutter closed as the feeling of warm air dances over my left shoulder, neck, and ear. Again, I feel my goosebumped flesh betray me.

"Yes." I feel the heat of the exhale tickling along my nape as a deep, masculine voice floats down my ear—the rich tone of his speech causing everything to tingle. No longer limited to the skin of my arms, my pimpled flesh alive with excitement, it now appears my nipples have joined the party.

I dig my heels in, keeping my back to him. "I'm sorry. I don't remember asking you anything." I try to deliver my retort with a flat affect, knowing full well there's a tremble to my voice.

"You didn't. But I believe your friend did."

Unable to decipher this riddle, I rotate to stare up at this intoxicating man. "Friend?"

"The pretty girl you're with tonight," he croons. Avoiding eye contact, I attempt to focus on his strong jaw. *Big mistake. That dimple is going to need a nap for all the effort it's put forth this evening.*

"Ah, you mean my sister," I correct. Not sure why I've shared this, as it's none of his concern who I'm with.

"So, yes. To your sister's question, then."

I shoot him a blank look, baffled by this conversation.

"Yes. I'd love to eat your pussy."

I feel my legs wobble and discover he's intuitively reached down to steady me. Looking up at him, stunned by such a bold statement, I'm greeted with a sultry smirk.

Leaning into me, his hand still at the small of my back, he continues. "What's the matter, good girl? Afraid of the big bad wolf?" His deep voice coats me like a sensual oil. My body feels aglow, provoked by his daring words and his dreamy scent. "It's one night. Let me please you for just one night," he probes with a hushed, gravelly tone.

Trying to gather my wits, I stare up at this brazen man. Hell, I'm sure he could please me like no one else ever has. Yet, the cockiness of his pursuit has me on edge. I'm not sure I'm willing to release all control to a man like this, even if it is only for one night. And that I'm sure of. There's no doubt who will be calling the shots if I go home with him.

Unable to string two words together, I purse my lips, spin on my heel, and head back to the table and the safety of my sister.

"What on earth? What's going on, B? You look flushed. Are you okay?"

"Yeah," I belt out, finishing off my margarita in one toss. "I thought I was going to the restroom, but instead, I ended up in the shark tank."

Bailey's eyes spring wide in recognition of my statement. "Oh my gosh, spill. Did he put the moves on you?"

"Did he? Lord, that man's something else." I briefly eye Bailey's cocktail glass to see if she has anything remaining I can steal from her.

"What could it hurt, Bella? One night? You're both adults. So long as you're safe, why not go get you some hot and dirty?" She laughs, looking over her shoulder in a nonchalant attempt at locating the overconfident playboy.

I admit it's tempting. I've been alone for a long time. My divorce was a wake-up call. I was completely blindsided by his decision to end the marriage. There was no attempt at counseling. No infidelity I'm aware of. He simply said he *couldn't do it anymore*. As if being married to me was a chore. I'd stood by him for years, allowing his dreams of a future in medicine to best any of mine, and yet I was the chore.

It took a while to recover from the devastating blow. If my radar was that off after the years we'd spent together, I knew I wouldn't be able to trust someone new in my life. And there wasn't room for anyone else anyway. I've focused on becoming independent and pursuing a degree. I've had a few relationships with men over the years, but none of which were in any way serious. Honestly, the liaisons felt more like a friends with benefits scenario. Yet, I wouldn't let anyone get close enough to hurt me again, so what did I expect? At least I had occasional company with the opposite sex so I wouldn't dry up completely.

It's been over a year since I've been in any relationship with a man where sex was involved. Usually, I'm too busy to reflect on the absence of male company, but it appears my desperation is a prime hunting ground for the lethally finned prowlers in the water tonight. And this one scares me every bit as much as the one in the movie. The shark that would devour its victims whole. I couldn't shake the feeling, one night or not, I'd befall the same fate.

"Excuse me, ladies," the waiter interjects, redirecting my thoughts. I watch as he places two fancy cocktails on the table.

"Did you order more drinks?" I ask Bailey, not realizing she was looking to get hammered tonight. Although my sister is taller than I, she's a tiny wisp of a woman. More than two drinks, and I'd have to take her home personally.

"No," she answers, appearing as stunned as I am.

"These are from the gentleman at the bar," the kind waiter instructs.

Bailey and I both turn simultaneously to find the arrogant playboy tipping his scotch glass in our direction. Looking back to the table, I notice Bailey inspecting the two cocktails carefully.

"What are these?" she asks.

"This one's a Dark 'N Stormy, and this one is a Screaming Orgasm."

Bailey doesn't even pretend to hide her laugh. I, on the other hand, turn and cock a distasteful brow in the waiter's direction before pushing the drink closest to me away with my index finger. I'm surprised at the juvenile attempt of this haughty man to needle me. This is more the act of an overgrown frat boy than an overconfident playboy. I turn back to Bailey, confident in my decision to end my evening alone.

"Okay, call me crazy, Bella. But I think you're making a mistake. That man is hot as sin. A guy like that doesn't come around often. Who knows, maybe he's in town for the bike race, and you'll never see him again." She lifts the Dark 'N Stormy cocktail and takes a sip, making a face of approval as she lowers it back to the table. "Look at it this way. If you're looking to get an itch scratched, well, I bet he has really good hands." Bailey begins to laugh but abruptly comes up short.

Wondering what's changed her facial expression, I follow her gaze to see a striking blonde saddle up to the bar in front of the man in question. She's tall, thin, and appears several years younger than I am. Well aware of my curvy, petite frame suddenly has me feeling a bit dejected. This is silly. I didn't want anything to do with him anyway. What should I care if a blonde bombshell is flirting with him? I observe the two of them as they appear to make conversation and sit stunned as I see his arm slink around her waist, laying his hand on the small of her back. My body tenses in response to his familiarity, and I'm immediately incensed at the effect this is having on me. *What is wrong with you, Isabella? He's a player. Let that shark take a bite out of some other unsuspecting female.*

Sebastian

"Fancy seeing you here, Sophia," I greet cautiously as she slinks closer.

"I could say the same for you, Sebastian. This isn't your usual haunt. Looking for some fresh meat?"

Truth or not, hearing this fall from her well-glossed lips stings a little. Thirty-six years old, and this is my life. Finding a new woman to fuck for the night who won't want to get her tentacles into me. I instantly feel tense. Not sure if it's having this reality acknowledged by another person or the fact it's from Sophia that has my hackles drawn.

I take in the stunner in front of me briefly as I sip my scotch. She's statuesque with curves in all of the right places. She's well-groomed and carries herself like an heiress. Sophia is the eldest daughter of an upper-middle-class family. While not a pauper, she's far from the socialite she carries herself to be. Yet, in my experience, her life's mission appears to be climbing the economic and social class ladders by sleeping her way to the top. And I should know. I narrowly avoided falling into her trap.

Sophia's unquestionably gorgeous. We'd met years ago when she came on to my best friend, Nick. Nick and I were classmates in medical school and spent most of our free time together. We determined quickly we had a lot more than our curriculum in common. We were driven, top of our class, and addicted to the hunt. We both strived to be number one in school and extracurricular activities, particularly women. He had no more interest in a long-term relationship than I did until Sophia came along. I'll admit, if I were to entertain a relationship with a woman, it would've been with her. She was all the things I was attracted to in the gentler sex. She was beautiful, intelligent, and sweet. I was disappointed she'd chosen Nick over me. But she'd charmed him into marrying her, and

I was in no way ready for that type of commitment—even with Sophia.

As the years passed, Sophia's true colors emerged. Yet, not before pulling me temporarily into her web. Nick and I had become focused on our careers. Unaware there was discord in their marriage, Sophia had come to me crying that Nick had rejected her. She suspected his career was his true mistress but hadn't ruled out another woman. He'd supposedly tossed her out, and she was devastated.

In my efforts to comfort her, I made one of the worst decisions of my life. Thinking their marriage was over and Sophia left devastated in its wake, I slept with my best friend's soon-to-be-ex. Not only did I break Bro-code, but I destroyed my relationship with Nick. In a moment of weakness, I let this woman come between us, just to find out later it was all a lie. She'd been having affairs with other men, looking for her next victim on her way out of Nick's life. Apparently, his lifestyle wasn't enough for her. I'm sure I was just one more unsuspecting asshole she was trying on for size. Someone with a bigger bank account and a pocket-sized heart to match. A rich, arrogant preoccupied man who'd be happy to have her on his arm and let her live as she pleased.

I was in a bad place when Sophia called crying that night. Otherwise, I might've seen her for what she was sooner. But, the more time we spent together, it became clear her only allegiance was to herself. It's taken a lot of repair work to get my relationship with Nick back on track after my involvement with her. As much as I'd like to resent her for the situation, I'm a grown-ass man. I made my own choices and have to own up to them.

Sophia has tried to make amends to me in her own way for lying about the situation and straining my relationship with Nick. She's agreed to help me in a few instances when I found myself in a bind— completely platonic instances. We only slept together once, and I plan to keep it that way, just like every other woman I encounter.

Taking another sip from my scotch, I peer over the rim of the crystal tumbler to observe the dark-haired minx sitting at the table with her sister. The drinks I'd delivered were sitting between them. While her sister's cocktail was near empty, her screaming orgasm sat untouched. I shake my head at the stubborn temptress. *What is it about this woman that has me so intrigued?* Normally, I never give a second thought to any female, whether I've slept with them or not. There are plenty of other beauties in the sea for me to enjoy. I don't need to chase someone who isn't interested. Yet, I have to admit this particular rejection stings a little.

"I see someone's got your eye," Sophia tosses in my direction, following my gaze to the petite brunette.

"Just leave it, Soph."

"What, did someone reject the sexy surgeon?" Sophia cackles as she accepts her Manhattan from the bartender.

"Just drop it. She's no one," I grunt as I take another drink, hoping I can convince myself of the statement. This mesmerizing woman strikes me as a good girl. One you'd take home to meet your family. Not the kind you pick up hoping to bend her backward with your dick buried in her every orifice. My cock twitches within the confines of my pants at this delicious notion.

My dalliances are very impersonal. I avoid sharing any details with the women I meet. I give them my surname instead of my first, avoid career conversations, and never bring anyone home. Most rendezvous are either at their abode or a hotel. I don't do sleepovers. Even in college, I learned quickly. An attractive man with money and a promising future drew women like flies to honey. I have no interest in such entanglements. A healthy relationship was alien territory for me.

I hadn't enjoyed a life raised by loving, committed parents like my friend, Nick. My mother was a self-absorbed socialite who didn't have the self-respect to divorce my cheating father for fear of what she'd lose. Growing up in this environment was less than pleasant, to say the very least. I didn't need to make that lifestyle a generational reoccurrence.

There were only two times in my life I'd even considered a long-term relationship with a woman. One I'd put behind me years ago, and the other stood before me. *Never going back there.*

"If you say so," Sophia returns. I watch as she casually glances over her shoulder at the table in question. "I've got to say, Bas. Neither of those two looks like your usual conquest. One looks like a hippy chick, and the other is… well, she's a little old for you, isn't she?"

What the hell? "What are you talking about, Sophia? I have no idea how old she is, but she's certainly not any older than I am."

"As I said, a little old for you. But I guess you've always been an equal opportunity offender."

Before I can snap back a witty retort, the bartender returns.

"Ah, thanks. Dr. Lee will take care of that, won't you, honey?" Sophia answers the bartender, rubbing her well-manicured hand along my arm. The comment and her touch making me equally irritated. "Thanks for the drink, Sebastian. I'll catch you later," she adds, just before sauntering off toward the other end of the bar. I'm sure she's already made her mark on some poor sap. Better him than me.

Unable to help myself, I allow my gaze to drift back to the brunette. Yet, it appears they've left for the evening. The table is clear of any evidence of their existence. I toss back the last of my scotch and wince. I guess I'm calling it a night. While I'd still love the company of a sultry woman for the evening, I have to admit anyone I'd pursue now would feel like a consolation prize. If I'm going to end the night disappointed, I might as well do it alone.

CHAPTER TWO

Isabella

What on earth is wrong with me? I'm out having a good time with my sister. I shouldn't even be considering anything with this man. He's arrogant, brash, and just the type I'd normally roll my eyes at. *Oh, yeah, I did that already.*

Yet, all I want is a one-night stand. And everything about this man screams self-assuredness. I can only imagine the orgasms he could bestow. But, could I walk away unscathed from a guy like this?

"You okay, Bella?"

"Yeah, Bailey. I'm fine. I'm just tired. Sorry for deciding to head home early. I have a lot on my plate with clinicals right now. But, you're right. We do need to get back to our girls' nights. I'll get better about making them a priority from now on."

"Okay. I'm holding you to that," Bailey adds, leaning in for a hug before turning back to the Uber at the curb. "Call me soon."

"You've got it." I look down at my phone, trying to determine why the Uber driver I hired is still so far away. Tapping my fingernails on my phone screen, my mind wanders as I stand awaiting my ride home.

I can't believe I considered using that ridiculous drink as an excuse to approach that guy. Well, until I saw that gorgeous blonde at his side.

Honk, honk.

Jumping back, startled by the intrusion, my eyes flick upward, wondering if my car has finally arrived only to see two girls, at least a decade my junior, grabbing for the door handle. Looking up and down the sidewalk, I feel conspicuous standing here. These clubs are teeming with young people, adding to how old and lonely I feel lately. I've been on my own so long, you'd think I'd be used to this by now. At thirty-six years old, I'm standing alone in front of a nightclub, leaving early because I'm too tired to party.

My shift will come early tomorrow. I'm easily the oldest radiology student on staff at St. Luke's. Most mornings, I shake my head at the antics of the young students and technicians, retelling their adventures of the evening before. Truth be told, I'm probably a little jealous. I missed the opportunity to live the type of existence they're embracing. Now, I feel I'm too old to consider such things. I want success in my newfound career. Being older brings certain responsibilities. I'm paying for my education, not my parents. I need to get the most I can out of it.

Breaking from my mental ramblings, I look back down at my phone's Uber app. *What the hell? The car is driving away from here?* I look at the time and consider whether the two intoxicated young ladies may have inadvertently taken my ride. Hell, they probably needed it more than I did. Maybe I'll just call a cab. I move back from the curb toward the overhead light, allowing me to search for the number.

After hunting on my phone briefly, I hit the call button for Yellow cab and look up to see one tall, dark, and incredibly handsome shark at the curb in front of me. His back is to me, standing with his feet shoulder-width apart as if he's awaiting a ride as well. My mind briefly taunts me. I could always ask if I could catch a ride home. *What the hell, Bella? Have you lost your mind?*

Taking him in unawares, he's wearing dark gray dress slacks and a matching suit jacket. I can't see his ass, but the broad expanse of his shoulders makes my mouth water. He's got the most stunning inky hair. It's a little longer on top, and I can almost imagine how soft it would feel sliding through my fingertips.

Speedily, a sleek black town car pulls up to the curb. I watch as he looks up from his phone and strides casually toward the back door. As he reaches for the handle, he appears to catch sight of something out of the corner of his eye. I observe as he turns his head briefly in my direction and our eyes connect. There's instant recognition, instant heat. I have to gulp to propel the breath that's currently lodged in my throat to move. It's at this moment I realize I've completely forgotten about my call. While I'm still holding the phone to my ear, it seems they disconnected when I turned into a vegetative zombie, staring at the man candy in front of me. As I end the useless phone call and bring the device down from my ear, I stand wordless as this god of a man walks toward me.

"You're still here?" His warm, scotch scented breath coats me with his greeting as he towers over me. His expression is one of hopeful delight. I'm sure this is my libido's wishful thinking.

"I am."

"Can I offer you a ride?" As he grins down at me, I suddenly hear the theme from the movie *Jaws*.

"Um, no. I don't think so," I reply, unsure if he'll believe my rejection any more than I do.

"Which is it, good girl? You don't want to bring me back to your place, or you don't want me?" he asks while reaching out to stroke my jaw with his thumb.

All of a sudden my mouth is parched. Maybe I need to go back inside for another drink? What the hell am I doing?

"The first one." I feel my voice crackle in the air between us.

He steeples his left brow at me, a slight grin curling his mouth. "So, you do want me?" *This cocky son of a gun.*

"You keep talking like that, and all bets are off," I toss back.

I watch as he lifts his hands in surrender. "Then, my place it is. Shall we?" He flashes his gorgeous smile at me as he extends his arm toward the awaiting car. I peer up into his sparkling deep blue eyes. His hypnotic dimple seems to soften at my hesitation.

Steeling my nerves, I take in a fortifying breath and walk past him toward the sexy, black town car. I cannot believe I'm doing this. Should I text Bailey and let her know where I am? She'd probably just blow up my phone. I'm a big girl. I can handle this. *This isn't the first one-night stand you've had, Bella. Grow up.*

But this guy is all kinds of different, and I know it. The other men have all been incredibly average. When those transgressions occurred, I was drunk and needy or just plain lonely. They were always disappointing afterward. Like breaking your diet for French fries or a sweet treat when you're starving, just to reconcile what a poor choice it was before you've finished the last bite. So long as this meal satisfies, I'll give myself a break. I deserve a hot night. I'm a responsible adult. I'm not hurting anyone.

Climbing into the back seat of the car, I watch as the door closes behind me and see him through the rear window as he approaches the opposite door. Sliding into the seat beside me, he raps his fingertips on the glass partition between the driver and us.

"Yes, sir?"

"Home, Charlie."

"Home, sir?"

I watch as he clears his throat, looking a bit flustered all of a sudden. "Yes, home," he says, with a bit of a bite to it. Wanting to avoid staring at him, I peer out the window as the car pulls forward.

We continue en route to 'home' with no words exchanged. It's hard to believe this is the same charismatic man I fell prey to moments ago. The silence is maddening. *What is he thinking?*

Sebastian

What am I thinking? Home? I never take anyone home. Never. I've made a point of always staying at their place or a hotel, so I can leave as soon as I'm good and ready. What's more, now I have to contend with the awkward morning after, as I doubt she'll appreciate me throwing her out immediately after I've fucked her. Hell, I don't know if I can relax enough to fall asleep with a woman. Plus, now this chick will know where I live. I should've had another scotch. Or maybe that's what's gotten me into this predicament.

But that wasn't it, and I knew it. I wasn't drunk. There was something about this woman that made me act out of impulse. I didn't want her to walk away.

I'll be the first to admit, I haven't made the best choices when it comes to women. Beyond sleeping with my best friend's ex-wife, I've often succumbed to lust in inappropriate places. It was not uncommon to take a willing partner in a dark corner, a bathroom, or in an alley by the exit door of an establishment back in the day. I've grown a lot. Well, I've grown to understand I cannot risk my job and professional reputation by continuing to act in a manner unbecoming of a highly sought after, highly paid reconstructive hand surgeon.

While the choice in the setting has been narrowed down to locales much more private, I've still taken a no-questions-asked approach to the women with whom I bed. I don't provide my personal information and have little interest in theirs. It's one night, for fuck's sake. They're all big girls. If they're married or living with someone, it's none of my concern so long as their significant other doesn't come after me. Or they aren't looking for a threesome. Not really into that kink.

The two things I always insist on are anonymity and a condom. Those are an absolute must. But apparently, the voice of reason is slipping tonight, as I'm bringing this woman into my private domain.

Looking in her direction, it's apparent she's as wary about this evening as I am. She's been studying the town's terrain through that window since we pulled away from the club. Normally, I'd have my hands down her panties by now. But my anxiety about my first co-ed sleepover, revealing my home, and with it, my obvious wealth, and not to mention, the morning after awkwardness is starting to tear a hole in my mojo.

"Um, you can drop me off up here, and I can get a cab or something if you've changed your mind." I notice she's pointing out the window toward a darkened street corner, her face expressionless.

What? What the hell is wrong with me? "No," I quickly reply. The thought of this woman leaving again brings me back to the here and now. Sliding closer to her, I place my arm behind her, resting it on her back. Nuzzling my nose against her dark tresses, I try to get this night back on track. "I can't wait to get you home, beautiful girl."

I sense a shiver from my companion and move to pull her against me while I tuck her silky hair behind her ear. Placing soft, teasing kisses along her nape, I can't help but grow hard in my pants at the thought of kissing her lower.

"Do you have any idea how much I want you?" I exhale onto her skin, dropping my mouth lower onto her neck and down toward her collarbone.

"No." Her voice is barely a whisper. Is she nervous? Or is she afraid of me?

"I thought I made it abundantly clear at the club," I tease. I await a retort and become more alarmed when I'm met with silence. "Do I make you nervous?"

"A little. I don't usually behave this way. I mean, I've had a one-night stand before, but this feels… well, reckless. I don't know a thing about you, and no one knows where I am."

Pulling back from her, I see her point. She's as anxious about coming to my place as I am to bring her there, just for completely different reasons. "Would you like to go to your place—"

"No," she blurts quickly. "I'm sorry, I can't. This is fine."

Giving her a questioning look, I choose to ignore her wariness. Even though the thought some other man may be home waiting for her is now causing a strange pull in my chest that I'm unaccustomed to. "Well, let's start over. Shall we?" Picking up her hand, I gently kiss the palm. "I assure you, I won't hurt you. You can leave whenever you like. I'll even have Charlie take you home, no questions asked. Just say when," I console, trailing soft, closed-mouth kisses from the soft skin of her palm down to her wrist. "I just want to make you feel good, bella."

I hear a gasp escape her lips and notice her eyes have widened. Does she think I've called her someone else's name? "It means beautiful, in Italian," I assure her, making eye contact to ensure she knows I haven't blundered her name with another's.

"Oh," she answers, placing her free hand over her heart.

"One night, good girl. I only want to make you feel good for one night. No one has to know." I smile.

"Yes, one night." Her eyes darken.

Fuck, I want to kiss her. I rarely kiss anyone, as it always feels so personal. I need to keep control of this situation, so there's no mistaking this is one night of hot sex, and that's it. But the more I look at her puffy, red lips and those molten brown eyes, I wonder who I'm trying to convince. She seems fine with the one-night scenario. I'm the one struggling to be anything but distant.

Sucking in a breath, I decide to ignore these novel feelings and treat this girl as I would any other. "I can't wait to taste you," I moan into her ear. "I'm going to make you come all over my tongue."

Another audible gasp, this one not as loud as the last. I'm choosing to believe it's a moan. I can practically feel her pulse thrumming under my lips as I continue to nibble and lick at her neck. Sliding the pad of my index finger down her throat, I stop at the swell of her breast. She's wearing a tight little black dress which exposes plenty of leg but only a hint of the soft mounds I'm dying to see. This petite beauty is not my usual type. As irritating as it was to be reminded, Sophia was right. The women I spend time with are usually young, blonde, tall, and thin. This lovely lady is almost the polar opposite. She's probably about five foot four, dark hair and eyes, and curves galore. I supposed she was my age or slightly younger, but I found her confidence and maturity a lot more alluring than the women I've enjoyed of late.

"Would you like that?" Kiss. "Do you give as good as you get?" Kiss. "I'd love to see those dimples in your cheeks pop out when your mouth and throat are full of my fat cock."

"Oh, god." She exhales above me.

Okay, that was definitely a moan. It appears she doesn't mind reciprocating. Reaching up to her neck, stroking my knuckles across her cheek, I realize the car is coming to a stop and peer out the window. "Ah, we're here."

I watch as her face snaps swiftly toward the window, her mouth falling ajar at the sight of my home. *Yeah, it still has that effect on me too. And I live here.*

Sliding out my door, I quickly stride around the rear of the car to meet her. Reaching for her hand, I pull her into my chest and place a gentle kiss on her head before pulling her along behind me. Normally, I'd enter through the garage, but I admit, I'm feeling a sense of pride in showing off my home to a woman for the first time. This is a bit ridiculous given the extremes I take to avoid bringing women here. I prefer to keep my wealth and personal identification under wraps, and yet, I head up the stairs to the front door nonetheless, my hand resting gently on the small of her back.

The home is a stately brick three-story with a three-car attached garage which houses my rarely used McLaren and a separate enclosed garage for my toys. I house my gear for water sports, jet skis, my Ducati Panigale V5 motorcycle, and my snow ski equipment there. My pride and joy, my Sea Ray 540 Sundancer speed boat, is docked at the Marina. This thought has me wishing I could introduce this little minx to her. Picturing her in a cherry red string bikini, sprawled out on the lounger as I steer, has my dick pushing firmly against my zipper. *What the hell, man?* First, you bring this woman to your home, and now you're picturing her on your boat?

Grasping for what's left of my sanity, I open the front door and usher her inside. There's no mistaking her awe as she takes in the place. It's a whole lot of house for one person, but it's a good investment. I have an in-home gym, a study, a media room, a library, and a pool. It's my all-inclusive sanctuary. I'd offer to give her the tour, but that's exactly what I want to avoid here. I'm unsure why I'm tempted with this woman. I need to get control of whatever this is. She doesn't need any encouragement that this is a date. Or that she'll be back.

We round the foyer to the den. Taking her little black purse from her, I place it on the oversized marble kitchen island as I continue walking her down the hall to my bedroom. She doesn't pull back to look more closely at my abode. She's cool as a cucumber. Maybe she assumes she'll see the details later as the sun comes up.

As we enter my bedroom, it isn't lost on me the scale is over the top. I don't make eye contact with her but can imagine what she might be thinking. This room is practically the size of my three-car garage. There's a large, king-sized, four-poster bed along one wall with an oversized couch at the foot of the bed. Along the opposing wall is a row of bookshelves flanking a large wood-burning fireplace. Rich, mahogany shelving with a built-in bar sits adjacent to the right of the fireplace.

Sliding my suit jacket from my arms, I drape it carefully over the wing-back chair in the center of the room before turning back to my gorgeous guest. As I unbutton and roll my shirt cuffs, I rake over her tantalizing form. She's standing, quietly watching me, arms hanging loosely at her sides. She seems pensive. Her dark hair falls loosely about her shoulders. Her soft breasts appear to be straining against the smooth material of her dress, begging to get free. I can't wait a moment longer.

"Strip for me, good girl."

CHAPTER THREE

Isabella

"Strip for me, good girl."

My heart rate is beating at the speed of light. I admit, I'm incredibly turned on, but extremely nervous. I've never been with a man like this. He's so confident and self-assured. What's more, this home looks like something you see in a movie or read about in a romance novel. Who is this guy?

"Uh, hm."

Hearing a throat clear, breaking my trance, I instantly make contact with his deep blue eyes. They're every bit as intoxicating as his scent, and his voice, and his—

"Do you need some help?"

Looking back to him, his lip curled in another smirk, I realize my mind is completely overwhelmed. *Stay on track, Bella.* I slowly start to lift my dress overhead, enjoying his heated gaze as I stand before him in my lacey black bra and panties. I remove my heels and reach back to unhook my bra. His right hand is rubbing the front of his pants as he devours my breasts with his eyes. Placing my thumbs in the sides of my panties, I slowly drag them down my legs and stand for him. I'm on edge. I hope he gives me some direction soon, as standing here in this way is unnerving.

"Beautiful," his husky voice groans. "Get on the bed, right on the edge, on all fours. I want your ass in the air and your cheek on the bed for me," he instructs, a little more gentle than his previous command.

I turn to comply, feeling as if my heart will beat straight through my chest. Allowing this man to control the evening's festivities is both thrilling and threatening. Not knowing what to expect causes anxiousness and arousal in equal measure. I can only imagine what I look like, perched on the edge of his bed, fully exposed.

"Jesus, your pretty pink pussy is making me crazy," he says in a throaty moan. *Well, I guess that answers that question.* Feeling him come closer behind me, I can't help but peer over my shoulder in curiosity. He hasn't removed one stitch of clothing. It's hot as hell, really. Being naked before him while he remains fully clothed. *Lord, what's wrong with me?* The only exposed skin present is his hands and forearms. I look about the room and wonder briefly if he's some famous artist or musician to have hands like that. Immediately my thoughts are cut short as I feel his hot breath skate across my backside. *Good lord.*

My mouth drops open at the exquisite feel of his searing, wet tongue dragging from my clit to my opening in one rapid swipe. *Holy hell.* I've never had oral in this position before. There's no time to compare my current position to those who've given me oral pleasure in the past. My attention is immediately drawn to the feel of his talented tongue back on my clit, rubbing back and forth before dragging back through my folds again. Try as I might, I cannot contain the groans of pleasure he's eliciting. There's no getting away with playing coy here. I'm intoxicated by the feel of his skilled fingers spreading my sex wide just before his tongue darts into me. He thrusts his hot, wet tongue back and forth, in and out of my quaking core. I'm lost in sensation until his finger lands on my clit and starts to rub as he fucks my opening with his tongue.

"Youre swollen little pussy is so sweet. I want to feel you come on my tongue for me," he directs as if he's speaking directly to my girl parts. He continues to lick, flick, and suck my overly aroused sex until I feel I'm close to the edge. But, as much as I love what he's doing, I don't want my orgasm to be on his face. I want to feel this man inside me.

"You're holding back, good girl. I can feel it. You're right there. Give it to me," he barks out, his face buried in my most private area as if he's starving for it. He unabashedly eats and sucks, causing my limbs to shake. He's right. I'm right there. But, I'm not someone who has multiple orgasms. I'll settle for one good one. I want to hold—

Thwack.

The sting on my backside registers before the realization he's slapped my right ass cheek. Unexpectedly, I feel a tug on my clit with his fingers, his tongue pushing deeper into me, and I know I can't hold back much longer. I might as well face it.

Thwack.

I don't have time to consider the slap to the other cheek before my orgasm hits me like a sledgehammer. Crying out, overwhelmed by the force of this climax, I try to stay upright as this man still has his face buried in my pussy. This is a true act of agility on my part as my legs are wobbling beneath me.

I've barely come down from what's just happened before I feel tender kisses along my backside and a wave of cool air float over my overheated skin. Knowing he's retreated from me, I slump onto the bed, awash with post-orgasmic oxytocin. Turning to look over my shoulder, I meet the intense stare of the talented man behind me, an inquisitive expression on his face. Rolling over to better understand what he wants, I sit up on the edge of the bed.

"On your knees, good girl."

Oh hell. Yes, please. I scamper to the floor in front of him, feeling overly aroused at the sight of him fully dressed before me. I'm dying to finally see all he's kept covered. I don't have to wait long before he shares his intent.

"Take it out."

Reaching up for his zipper, I slowly slide the teeth down. The metallic clicks of the fastener adding to my eagerness. Unsure of how he envisions this going, I tread carefully. I want to make this as good for him as he's already made this night for me. I slowly pull the waist of his pants down low enough I can reach into his snug black boxer briefs and withdraw the most incredible cock I've ever encountered. Completely enthralled by the long, steely hard erection, I examine it closely. It's not just long but thick and veiny. *No wonder I thought it was his damn arm behind me.*

"If you lick your lips like that again while you're holding my dick in your hands, I'm going to come all over your face," he growls down in my direction.

Darting my tongue out to his tip, I tease the droplet of precum awaiting me before swirling my tongue around the broad mushroom-shaped head. I glide my tongue back and forth across the underside of his cock, feeling it jerk against my hand. Sliding my hand up and down the length, I trail my tongue along the veiny expanse. Not desiring to leave any part of him wanting, I continue to stroke firmly as I suck one of his large balls into my mouth and then turn to the other. I can feel his groan vibrate down the length of him, encouraging my continued lavishment. His hands come to rest upon my head, gently stroking my hair as I move back up to suck on his long, thick cock. Jeez, I'm so turned on I'm going to need to finger myself if he lasts much longer. I've never gotten this aroused giving someone a blow job before. If his dick is this magical in my mouth, what could it do to the rest of me?

Sebastian

Watching this little vixen go down on me is otherworldly. I can honestly say I've never gotten head like this before. From the minute she pulled my straining, rigid dick out of my pants, it was on. I'm starting to wonder if she's forgotten I'm still attached up here.

The sensation of her slick, hot tongue along my cock and balls has me tied up in knots. I've been hard for her for what seems like hours, and this might push me over the edge if I'm not careful. But, I refuse to come in her mouth. I have to get inside her.

I begin unbuttoning my shirt as she continues to take me into the back of her throat. I'm telling myself this is to quickly move to the next step in our evening, but truthfully, I'm trying to gain her attention.

Don't get me wrong. I'm thankful for my DNA. However, I've never had anyone so focused on my boner they forget about the man joined to it. Hell, my dick might be impressive, but I'm no chump to look at —*enough of this.*

"Up on the bed, flat on your back," I direct. My voice is a little gruffer than I intend yet, I'm feeling a little jealous of my own damn cock right now.

As I watch her steady herself on her feet and turn toward the bed, I begin removing my shoes and socks. I'm an asshole. I love feeling dominant over the women I meet and keeping clothed while they service me is a heady turn-on. I finish unbuttoning my shirt and watch her gaze as I remove it, placing it with my suit jacket. She's back to licking her lips again. I can't control the grin that's taking over my lips. Striding to the nightstand, I grab a condom from the drawer before removing my pants and boxers in one smooth motion. Once I've placed the rubber onto my aching dick, I crawl onto the bed to loom over her.

"Fuck, you're beautiful," I share, honestly. And she is. There's something so alluring about her. I'm not sure what makes her so different. I can't put my finger on it. Distracted by the creamy soft mounds beckoning me, I place my face between them before turning my head to lick and suck from each peak. For a tiny woman, her tits are generous.

Reaching down, I lift her legs around my hips before teasing her folds gently. She's gloriously wet for me. I hear little whimpers escape her as I drag the head of my dick back and forth across her clit and her pretty pink opening. Unable to take this torture any longer, I press inside carefully. I realize how big I am, compared to her tiny frame. I have no interest in causing her pain to gain my pleasure.

"Oh, god," she pants out. I echo the sentiment. Her tight, wet heat is gripping me deliciously. I've seriously never felt anything this good. I'm dying to be completely inside her, yet I notice I'm only halfway, and her whole body is shaking at the invasion. I still, waiting on her to accommodate me before proceeding any deeper. Holding myself up on my forearms, I groan as her tight pelvis slides back and forth as if making room for me.

Trying to take cues from her, I slowly press forward. Inch by delicious inch, I thrust and retreat until I'm fully seated. Holy hell, this woman is tight. Her body is straining around my cock, sucking me back in with every withdrawal from her wet center. The wet sounds of our bodies' intimate dance pushing me ever closer to the edge of release.

"Oh, please." I hear escape her.

I stop abruptly. "What is it? Am I hurting you?"

"God, no. I'm right there. I can't believe I'm going to come again."

"Oh, baby, you're coming twice before I'm letting go, and I'm right on the edge." I pull back, angling my hips to stroke her clit with each thrust. I can feel her tighten further, unsure how that's physically possible. This sensation is indescribable.

"Oh, I'm—"

Looking down at her, I manage to see the moment her rapture has taken her. Her eyes roll back in her head, her mouth slack. She throws her head back just as her entire body starts to shake. Her rosy skin is covered in a sheen of sweat as she starts to convulse around me. As if the sensation of my cock being milked by her tight channel isn't enough, the sight of her surrendering to her orgasm is. I've never seen anything more fucking erotic in my life.

Her climax is barely complete before I've withdrawn. There's no way I'll last another second if I continue to see that look of ecstasy on her face. Flipping her over, I pull her hips back to meet me, thrusting deeply into her. Holding myself steady, I relish the sensation. Teasing her back, I lightly drag my fingertips through her hair and down her silky smooth back several times while my dick sits nestled inside her tight heat. I can tell my resolve is quickly dissolving as I start to unconsciously rut into her.

Reaching around her, I start to tease her swollen nub as I growl into her ear. "I'm going to get a little rough with you, good girl. I've been hard for hours just thinking about spurting inside your tight little snatch. I can't hold back anymore," I warn.

"Oh, god, please," she exhales back in my direction.

Her response gives me the green light to proceed, and I spread my legs wider, on either side of hers, bending my body over the top of her.

Leaning on my left arm, I continue to tease her clit with my right hand as I pick up the pace. I can feel her bucking back against me. I know she's with me. It won't be long for her either. Altering my position, I lean onto my outstretched arm as I pound into her. I can hear choppy little grunts escaping. It takes a moment to realize that's me and not her.

"Oh, my god, I'm going to come," she practically squeals.

Her shocked utterance signals my balls it's showtime, and I practically pound her into the bed. I can barely hear anything over the sounds of the blood rushing in my ears until she belts out a scream I pray is pleasurable. There's no way I can stop to check on her now.

"Fuck!" I pant out, bracing myself for the storm that is about to strike. One last push into her tight body, and I still, feeling the hot seed rip through my balls and into the condom. The first spurts are practically painful, but as the white dots dance across my vision and the continued waves of my climax crash over me, I'm overtaken with a sensation I've never experienced. The heady euphoria of this orgasm is like nothing I've ever known possible. And hell, I've had a ton of sex, in every imaginable position.

It feels like an hour has passed since I emptied into her, yet I realize it's purely the adrenalin talking. Slowly, I withdraw from her and immediately miss her warmth. As I sit back on my heels, my breaths still ragged, I watch as she rolls to face me. I'm straddling her well-used body, awash with endorphins.

Our eyes lock, and for a moment, I can't breathe. The most dreamy smile crosses her face as she looks up at me. Reaching up, she affectionately pushes loose hair from my face. It's the only physical act she's initiated. She's practically angelic. God, I want to kiss that sweet mouth. But I've already been hit by something with this enchanting wench. I can't risk what the feel and taste of her lips on mine could do to my resolve. I've still got a night and awkward morning to get through with her.

I place a kiss to her forehead, grinning back down at her before rolling off to dispose of the condom. As I wash my hands, I look in the mirror. Just go to sleep and tell her goodbye in the morning, Bas. Don't start any uncomfortable conversations. Don't entertain tours of the house or 'I'll call yous.' Just tell her Charlie will take her home when she's dressed and ready, then make yourself scarce. *God, I'm such an asshole.*

Returning to the bed with trepidation, I take in what appears to be her already sleeping form. She's lying with her back to me, completely still. Carefully skulking around the foot of the bed, I observe the scene before me. She's lying with her hands clasped beneath her cheek, like a cherub. There are a few stray hairs tucked under her cheek that have escaped the now tousled mane about her pillow. I watch as they dance against her soft skin with each exhale. Her gorgeous breasts are barely covered by the thin white bed linens.

Coming closer, I gently pull the covers up and reach down to kiss her head. Stroking her hair gently, I marvel at how natural this feels— having her here with me. Shaking this crazy thought from my head, I return to my side of the king-sized bed and climb in. I'm fatigued by the vigorous exertion of the evening. Yet, lying here staring at the ceiling, I can't give in to sleep. It's ridiculous at thirty-six this feels so alien to me. Peering over at the beauty beside me, I give in to temptation once more.

Oh, what the hell? I roll onto my side, nestling into the warm backside of this enchanting woman. It's just one night.

It's early. I sense this immediately by the darkness surrounding me and the fact I haven't needed an alarm clock in over a decade. I rise every morning at 4:30 a.m. to hit the gym, shower, eat, read the paper, and make it to the hospital to round on my patients before clinic each day. It may be Saturday, yet, my body rises at this hour seven days a week.

Suddenly, it hits me. I'm not alone. Well, if I'm going to endure the awkwardness of *the morning after,* I should at least get morning sex out of the deal. Recalling the events of last night, my morning wood is much more excited about the prospect of this woman's body than the fist that usually greets it. Morning sex. In all my years, I've never experienced this. Let's see if it lives up to the hype.

Turning on my side, I discover quickly these plans have been thwarted. I'm alone. Sitting upright, I lean forward to inspect any signs of movement or sounds emanating from the master bath. Nothing. I place my hand on the sheets beside me, but they're neither cool nor warm. Instantly, my ire stirs. She probably got up to go to the bathroom, and her curiosity got the better of her.

Irritated that I didn't make provisions for this scenario, I grab my boxer briefs and head down the hall in search of my wandering guest. As I come around the corner of the kitchen, I note there's no one in the dining area or the great room. There's no one on the lanai. I investigate a little further before returning to the bedroom. Then it dawns on me. Her clothes are no longer where they were lying last night, and her little purse wasn't sitting atop the kitchen island where I left it. This brazen beauty did her walk of shame in the dark, no note, no awkward conversation.

Lying back on the bed, staring up at the ceiling, I mull over how lucky I am. I'd avoided the very things I'd had such anxiety about. My dick has softened at the realization morning sex is no longer on the table. Yet, as visions of our escapades return to my mind, I feel my cock begin to stir. Hell, I'll have spank bank material for days. I chuckle to myself, noticing my laugh feels hollow. Placing my folded arms behind my head, I exhale. *If I'm so lucky, why do I feel so disappointed?*

CHAPTER FOUR

Isabella

"The part of the day is the clavicle," Jeff instructs.

I've been in my radiology clinicals for some time now. My comfort level has increased, but there are still some items I need to complete on my checklist. There are a few skeletal x-rays I haven't had the opportunity to check off as well as a few procedures I haven't accomplished independently. A clavicle x-ray has eluded me for months. Hopefully today is the day.

The radiology technicians assist with more than just performing x-rays. We assist the interventional radiologist in procedures as well as operate the C arm during surgical procedures. The C arm is a machine that requires skill to operate, allowing the surgeon or provider the ability to see immediate high-resolution feedback to assist in completing their repair with precision. These cases are often high stress. Although I've had a lot of practice, I worry about the first time I have to operate this unit alone. Luckily, today is about checking off the remaining skeletal films I need to obtain. And we're apparently on a hunt for clavicles.

"I let Kat know to call me if they have anyone who needs a clavicle or shoulder x-ray so we can get you checked off," Jeff advises.

"You're always looking out for me. I couldn't have asked for a better person to show me the ropes during my hands-on training, Jeff. I know I don't thank you enough."

"Oh, you thank me plenty. Besides, that smile is all the thanks I need. It's nice seeing you happy. What's going on with you? You seem different."

"Oh, I got to spend some time with my sister a few weeks ago. We hadn't had a girls' night in a while. Boy, did I need it." I'll leave out what I really needed and how I was satisfied beyond anything I knew imaginable.

I've replayed that magical night in my head repeatedly. I still can't wipe the smile from my face when I think about how good I felt. How sated I was for the first time in years. I would've been happy with one good orgasm, but multiple? I've never been with anyone so capable. He was confident and with good reason. The whole night was over the top sexy, but at times, bordered on the fringe of ridiculous.

He was so cocky and arrogant. Normally the type I'd quickly run in the opposite direction from, yet, he was so flipping handsome I couldn't turn away. And unlike many of the men I'd met, he was able to follow through. He wasn't all pomp and circumstance. He could deliver. He wanted to please me for one night. And that's exactly what he did.

"Hey, there's a few of us going out to grab a quick drink after work tonight. You want to come?"

"Oh, Jeff, I'd love to. But I can't. I have to get home. Maybe some other time?"

"Hope so. My birthday is coming up. Maybe you can make that one."

Jeff is an incredible man. He's about my age with two young daughters. He'd lost his wife a few years ago to cancer, and according to the other techs, he spends his time devoted to the girls and his job. He doesn't date much, but he's a catch. He's quite attractive, smart, funny, and so kind. Any girl would be lucky to have him in their life.

I'll admit, from time to time, I wonder if his attentions are all work-related. I'm not the best person at picking up signals. The dissolution of my marriage highlighted this particular weakness. There's a certain twinkle in his eye I find appealing. However, Jeff is the 'all in' kind of guy. He'd want to date and marry a woman who could love his daughters. I'm not saying I couldn't open my heart to someone else's children. But with school and my current responsibilities fighting for space on my overcrowded plate, I have no room for anything else right now. Plus, there isn't a spark there. Sadly, the only current I've felt in years was with that overconfident shark from the club the other night.

I'd dated a few men over the years, but there was never anyone I felt serious about. I'm sure part of the disconnect was the nosedive my self-confidence took post-divorce. I want to protect my heart from any further mistreatment. It's a vicious cycle, I've found. Once you erect those protective walls, they're hard to tear down. They're like my security blanket. But, again, not sure I'm missing much right now. Until I graduate and secure a job, I need to maintain my focus on the important things.

"Hey, B. I didn't know you were working today."

Looking up, I take in Donovan's broad grin. He, quite honestly, feels more like an older brother than a cousin. He and my two older brothers have been inseparable since I can remember.

"I'm putting her through the paces, Dr. Grant. If you see anyone who needs a clavicle x-ray, give me a shout. She still needs that one checked off of her list."

"Yeah, Donovan. I can't not graduate because I didn't get a clavicle." I laugh.

"Ah, Bella. If it comes to that, I'll snap Damien's for you." He chuckles.

"Oh, lord. Can you come up with a clever way to break his collarbone? If it comes down to that? Like take my brothers to the park and play football or something? I can't let my parents find out we sacrificed him so I could get my diploma." I shake my head, knowing the joke's on Donovan. Damien may be the younger, smaller brother, however, he was a state champion wrestler. That guy is scrappy. Anyone getting into a tussle with him has no idea what they're in for. "Are you just getting here?"

"Yeah, you know me. I'm a night owl. Even on my days off, I tend to be up 'til 4:00 a.m. and wake at noon. I've been that way since residency."

"Hey, Donovan. A respiratory distress patient is coming by EMS to room fourteen. You got it?" Dr. Silver asks from the hallway.

"Sure, man. I got it." Donovan returns his attention to us and squeezes my arm. "Catch you later, Bella. I'll call you if I see any clavicles come in. Jeff," he adds before heading toward the front of the ER. My chest fills with pride, knowing how delighted my aunt would be if she could see Donnie now. God rest her soul. He's worked hard to get where he is. He's so handsome and successful. I have yet to figure out why that one isn't married.

We take a few portable x-rays in the ER before heading back to the radiology department. I hope I can manage to get the last items on my checklist complete and a bit more experience in the OR before my time here is up. Graduation is only a few months off.

"Hey, Erin. What's up?" Jeff asks one of the part-time radiology techs.

"Ugh. I just got back from the OR. That was a shit show," she huffs.

"What happened?"

"Well, let's see. I was using the C arm to assist Dr. Lee in the repair of a severed finger, and he was less than impressed with my skills."

"It couldn't have been that bad," I reply, trying to reassure her.

"Oh, he had no problem voicing his disdain for my incompetence in our surgical suite today."

"Oh, god. I know you haven't worked here much. I should've offered to take that one. Dr. Lee is normally at Mary Immaculate, but Dr. Morgan's been on an extended vacation. So, Dr. Lee's been covering hand and wrist surgeries here in his absence. He can be a bear when things don't go exactly to plan."

"Well, I'm used to arrogant surgeons, but this guy…" Erin shakes her head, her face still reddened by her lingering anger. "One of the surgical assistants didn't hand him a piece of equipment the right way, and it fell on the floor. You would've thought they threw it at him, the way he reacted. Hell, she didn't do it on purpose. From then on, no one could do anything to his satisfaction."

"Man, he sounds like a real treat," I mutter.

"Yeah. I'll say. At least he didn't single me out or anything. I mean, he was an equal opportunity offender. He pretty much sneered or barked at everyone in his path. Afterward, I heard some of the nurses talking about how they put up with him because he's such a gifted surgeon. Well, and because he's hot as fuck."

My ears perk up at this. Maybe it was just Erin dropping the F-bomb. I don't normally find even the most handsome men attractive if they display behavior similar to the picture Erin just painted. I've been divorced by one of the worst of them. A handsome, skilled cardiologist who went from high school sweetheart to cold as ice asshole in a matter of years. Rick could come crawling back on his hands and knees, and I wouldn't care less. Burn me like that once, and I'm not dumb enough to let you into my world again.

"Hot or not, I wouldn't want anything to do with a guy like that," I blurt. The memory of my ex-husband's flat dismissal is now fresh in my mind. I can still hear him telling me he was leaving because *he can't do this anymore.* I hear a groan escape my lips and realize everyone is looking in my direction. "What? I find that behavior completely repugnant."

"I'm with you, Isabella. But unfortunately, it's part of the job. You'll run into physicians and surgeons in this line of work with a God complex. You have to ignore it, do your job, and stay out of their way. It sucks, but it's the reality of the situation. They make this hospital a shit load of money. No one's ever going to do more than slap them on the wrist for treating people that way."

"I can't believe in this day and age Human Resources can't put a stop to that kind of behavior," I rebuff, shaking my head.

"I think they have to choose their battles carefully. If it's sexual harassment or something that clearly crosses the line of professionalism, they'll pursue it," Jeff adds.

"Well, they'll never get Lee on sexual harassment," Erin interjects.

"Why is that?" I ask, baffled.

"Hell, have you seen him? I can't imagine a woman alive that would turn him down. Whatever he offers, they'll easily take."

"Not me. I don't care what the guy looks like. No one's going to treat me like a second-class citizen in the OR and think I'm going to bow down to him once the gloves come off."

This conversation has me more determined than ever to focus on completing my education and avoiding temptation. If I could manage to get another rendezvous like I had with my dirty talking one-night stand, I could probably avoid the whole lot of them. I'm too old for shenanigans. I'm going after what I want and avoiding the rest. I have commitments that need my undivided attention.

"You coming out with us tonight, Isabella?" Mike asks from the doorway.

"Nah, I asked her already," Jeff answers.

"Sorry, guys. I can't do a lot of spur-of-the-moment activities. But I'll try to make it to your birthday celebration, Jeff."

"I understand, Bella. It's okay," Jeff replies, rubbing my arm in consolation.

I gather my things in preparation for the drive home. It'd be fun to relax with my new friends and hopefully soon to be co-workers after a long day. But my man is waiting for me, and I can't disappoint him. He wouldn't understand the need to relax with a drink when I could be home with him. As complicated as the situation is, I'm completely committed to him. He comes first. All of my decisions revolve around him.

"I'll catch you guys tomorrow." I wave as I head for the door.

As I reach the car, I pull out my cell phone. Opening the door and sliding inside, I listen as the phone rings on speakerphone.

"Hello?"

"Hey, Austin. I'm on the way home."

CHAPTER FIVE

Sebastian

Jesus, I need a drink. It's only day three of Dr. Morgan's two-week vacation, and I've already had it. My job has been stressful enough lately without covering his patients on top of mine. It's one thing having to drive an hour to St. Luke's to evaluate and treat patients on top of my Mary Immaculate ones, but the added caseloads don't seem to be worth the added income.

It's hard to complain about my job. Working as a reconstructive hand surgeon has been a dream come true, for a number of reasons. Meeting the constant need to test myself while heavily padding my bank account being at the top of the list. I've always craved a challenge. I was never a big sports fanatic. I was raised with more of a focus on the arts, music, and education than sports. A game of pool or darts is more my speed. However, I could go toe to toe with the best of them when it comes to wit and women.

My friend Nick and I were well paired in medical school. While I was raised with a silver spoon, I had absentee parents and prep school as my nurturers. Nick was raised an only child by devoted parents with a lower middle-class income. Yet, he had the same drive to meet any challenge given him I did. He'd had dutiful parents whose lives revolved around him until his mother passed away at age sixteen. He channeled his heartbreak into excelling at soccer, grades, and women. While I hadn't suffered the losses he'd endured, I had my own chip on my shoulder.

My parents inherited a local vineyard from my grandfather when I was young. The winery was successful when they acquired it. They put very little into the family business to warrant the monetary gain they collected. It was expected my brother, Samuel, and I would take over the business as soon as we graduated college so we could continue to make the vineyard profitable while my parents lived a life of luxury on someone else's back.

My mother and father had spent most of their adult life living large. I was unsure why they even chose to have children as little as we saw them. Even when we were young, we spent more time with nannies than our parents. What's more, their ridiculous sham of a marriage was far from the loving relationship my best friend Nick's parents enjoyed.

Nick's father, Garrett, remained single after his wife's death, completely faithful to her even in her absence. Yet, my father made no bones about the fact my parents' union was only cemented on paper. He made frequent 'business' trips without my mother. He didn't bother trying to hide the fact that many of these sojourns were unabashedly with other women. My brother and I were made painfully aware of this fact after witnessing the many screaming matches between my parents upon dear old Dad's return. He'd assured Mother dearest some of his business jaunts had occurred on his own. This was usually met with scornful laughter as she accused him of taking those opportunities to find 'fresh meat.' Unlike many of my classmates, I found living at preparatory school wasn't such a bad thing.

To this day, I don't know which is worse. The years of unapologetic cheating by my father or the fact that my mother stayed in spite of it to ensure she had access to the largest amount of cash possible. I'm assuming my grandfather was smart enough to place legal stipulations on what they can and cannot do with the vineyard, or they would've run that place into the ground with their greed years ago.

While Sam has remained part of the family business, I couldn't stomach the thought of staying in that miserable environment. Sam's a different breed than I. He's always seemed to be happy to live off of the family money and settle for whatever the vineyard could provide. He's a smart guy, though. If he kept our parents out of the business, he could probably turn the place into a real success story. Yet, he seems to be happy to live every day like a party.

My brother and I haven't been close in some time. He's more family to me than my parents will ever be yet, I always feel like he's hiding something. Maybe it's just suspicion on my part. Yet, he tends to live life by the seat of his pants most of the time, and his choices are often suspect. Plus, there's that whole spending time with my girlfriend when I was away at college thing. They both claim it was innocent. They were just friends. But I can't help but wonder. Particularly when I came home from school unannounced to a *not so happy to see me* girlfriend of over two years. A girlfriend who proceeded to dump me and move away without a look back.

"Can I get you another drink?"

"Sure, another scotch," I answer the bartender. I'm sure he's starting to question why a thirty-six-year-old has been spending every weekend at this club full of young people—probably looking like quite the perv in here with all of these sorority girls living the *girls gone wild* life on the dance floor behind me. I'm starting to question my own sanity.

The first few weeks after meeting my mystery girl, I was living off the high that night gave me. My work was on par, my stress level the best it's been in years. Yet, her disappearing act was starting to really bother me. Correction. It was the fact that it bothered me what was causing me anxiety. She'd left with no note or number. I didn't even know her name. That's usually how I liked it. Hell, I was bordering on having a panic attack about bringing the woman home to my place at all. Now, I can't get her out of my damn head.

I've become obsessed. I've returned to the scene of the crime every Friday as of late. All on the off chance I might see her again. What the hell is wrong with me? Sure, the sex was incredible. But I had to admit, it was more than that. There was simply something about that spunky, secretive, sex kitten that had me tied up in knots. As if the way her tight little body responded to me wasn't enough, that dreamy smile she gave before she fell asleep has tortured me.

"You mind if I ask you something?" The bartender's question breaks through my mental torture.

"I'm sorry, what?" I respond, unsure if I've heard him correctly.

"You've been here every weekend I can recall recently. But all you do is drink at the bar. You know there are quieter places for a drink than this place. Plus, there are these things called liquor stores."

I glare back at him, unhappy with being called out. And here I was afraid he was going to accuse me of wanting to pick up girls almost half my age.

"It's just…" he leans in closer, dropping his volume.

Here it comes.

"You must be blind, man."

Confused at the direction of this conversation, I watch as he points his chin to my left. I turn to take in a beautiful young blonde, sipping her cocktail through a bright red drink stirrer. She's smiling at me playfully over her glass. Flicking my gaze back to the bartender, I can't help but shake my head.

"Every week, it's the same thing. They all swim up to the bar, trying to get your attention. But you're lost to your glass. They aren't your average girls. These chicks are smokin'. What gives?"

"I'm not an alcoholic. And I haven't come to drown my sorrows or anything." I defend, giving him a quick glance before spilling the truth. "I don't know. I met a girl here a few weeks ago. I'm not usually one for collecting personal info. More interested in one night and moving on. But I can't get her out of my head. I don't even know her name. Guess I figured this was as good a place as any to grab a drink, on the off chance she strolled back in." Taking a sip of my scotch, I continue, "No one else has really held my attention." I've officially lost my mind. I've turned into Norm from Cheers, spending my free evenings saddled up to the bar, spilling my private life to a bartender. *What the fuck? I'm a God-damned middle-aged stereotype.*

"Ah, I get it," he consoles, leaning onto the bar in my direction. "I met this girl here awhile back. She came in a few times with her friends. I tried flirting with her at the bar whenever I could. I'm sure she thought I was bucking for a bigger tip. It's harder than you think to meet women working here. Anyway, I look around the bar for her almost every night. Maybe one day she'll stroll back in here, and I can get my shot. I won't make the mistake of waiting for next time again."

I nod, mulling over his words. I know full well that if that little minx came strolling in, I'd do the same. I'd admit I want to get to know her better. Is she married? Or was she rushing home to a live-in boyfriend? I admit the latter was more appealing, but for the first time, I didn't like either scenario. I've never cared who the women I slept with had waiting on them. They were big girls. So long as neither the women nor the scorned lover came looking for me, we were good. But I was irritated by the notion some other man had a committed relationship with the woman I've been fantasizing about, when I didn't even know her name.

"Thanks, man." I wave to the bartender after closing out my tab. This weekly venture has proven worthless. Yet I know I'll be back. It is my only link to her. I have no idea what my intentions are. I just want more. I want her name, details about her living situation. I want to know what makes this good girl tick. Fuck, I want her. I want her riding me, my name on her lips. I want her underneath me, her name on mine. I want her to belt out my real name as she shudders all over me. I'm not looking for a relationship. I just want more.

I await my driver at the curb and recall I need to sober up quickly. The conversation with the bartender got me halfway there, not to mention limiting any further alcohol intake. I'm on call starting at six a.m. With covering both hospitals, my days are getting more tiring and demanding. This has contributed to more stressful experiences in the operating room. Sadly, this seems to be happening more as of late. Perhaps I need another sojourn.

Over the last few years, I've noted that as my schedule became more hectic or the surgery I was involved in was particularly nerve-wracking, more mistakes seemed to occur. I'd always had a steady hand and clear head once I stepped foot in the OR, yet, my circumstances were affecting my precision. These complex patients come to me because I have a reputation for taking cases others won't touch. I have a duty to follow through.

I stay physically fit. I work out daily and run several times a week. I've never over-indulged in vices. Only women. Yet, I'd never embraced meditation or yoga until these little errors started to transpire during surgery. Grabbing surgical instruments too quickly, sending them to the floor. Straining to suture a tendon where this was commonplace years before. I'm sure part of this is to be expected with age, but I'm thirty-six, not sixty-six. It dawned on me I needed to consider offering my mind and soul a similar workout routine that I gave my body.

I've started to meditate and include yoga into my workout regimen. This is usually all I need. Yet when the stressors mount, taxing my mental fortitude, I've found stepping back to recharge works best. I've made a habit of feeding my love of travel with my need to detox my brain. Several times a year, I pull back from work and find somewhere new to trek. It has to be a peaceful environment, with options for the utmost in self-care. I indulge in massage, meditation, relaxation and will often explore the religions of the culture I'm temporarily residing. Whatever it takes to center me before I return to the high-stakes environment of reconstructive surgery.

Charlie pulls to the curb, and I immediately grab the door and gain entrance. There's little conversation, as he has become used to my routine as of late. Drop me off and return to find me alone and disappointed. Jesus. Why didn't I just give that little blonde sorority chick a ride she'd never forget? Hell. I couldn't remember the last time I'd gone this long without sex. I need to get laid before I leave the country.

This thought has me scrolling through my phone, wondering where my journey will take me. I haven't been to Bali. That would be a great place to embrace my Zen. The trip to Costa Rica a few months back was exactly what I needed. Pulling the phone away, I open the calendar app, trying to calculate the timing of these trips. They seem to be occurring more often than the twice-a-year voyages I'd taken in the past. *But times have become more stressful.* At least that's what I'm telling myself. Where were the days of centering myself within the tight, warm walls of a woman? I guess we all have to grow up sometime.

Walking into my home, I feel unsettled. I need to get to bed as I have an early morning with rounds and a few clinic patients before my scheduled surgeries begin in the OR at St. Luke's. Any elective surgeries Dr. Morgan will perform upon his return. But there were two patients who I treated in the ER that required surgical intervention that shouldn't wait another week. Neither needed to be admitted to the hospital. Their preoperative tests have been completed and they've been cleared by their primary care providers for surgery.

Walking into my immaculate white marble kitchen, I put on a kettle of hot water. Growing up, my favorite nanny would always have a cup of herbal tea and cookies before bed. She'd pour apple juice into teacups, and Sam and I would join her in the nightly routine. Leaning against the counter, my mind wanders to years past. Sam and I knew our lives were different from our friends. Their parents would accompany them to their activities, cheer them on after piano recitals. Instead, we had Cheryl. She was the comfort we ran to when my parents' arguing became frightening to young ears. I was never having children. I'd never be so selfish as to put my needs above theirs. Thus, it was best to leave happy families to people like my friend, Nick, and his wife, Katarina. They have a daughter through an open adoption with the child's biological mother, but I know they'd love to have more. Then there's me, who won't look at a naked woman without a condom in my pocket.

Jumping, startled by the sound of the kettle's whistle, I pour the boiling water over the jasmine tea in my mug. I'll take a quick shower, grab my book, and hopefully retire at a decent hour. Bringing my steaming cup to the master suite, I carry the hot beverage to the wing-back chair and reach for the novel I've been enjoying, A Gentleman in

Moscow. As I grab the spine, I look up from the shelf it was occupying and notice an unfamiliar title. *I didn't know I had a copy of this.* Jane Austen's Pride and Prejudice. *How the hell did that—* Suddenly, I recall receiving a box of books from Cheryl's family after her passing. She had bequeathed a similar box to Sam. I remember as if it was yesterday, the pride I had in that gift. That her reading to us had meant so much, she'd want to share her treasured books with us.

Placing A Gentleman in Moscow back where I'd found it, I reach instead for the Jane Austen classic. I'd faintly remembered reading it in high school, but not enough to tell you much detail about Mr. Darcy and Elizabeth Bennet. Attempting to take a sip, I place my still scalding cup of tea and the novel down to revisit after my shower. Hell, I have no idea why I'm entertaining this read, but maybe I could learn what not to do... if I should get the chance to see my mystery girl again.

Isabella

"Austin, I'm home," I shout, juggling two large grocery bags against my chest as I attempt to close the front door behind me. Rounding the entryway toward the kitchen, I place the paper bags onto the counter and head in the direction of the bedrooms.

The home we shared was an older brownstone with high ceilings and small, dark rooms. These dwellings were not constructed during the open floor plan era of today's homes. The kitchen was closed off from the den. I'd paid a pretty penny to open up the space. The two bedrooms were down a dark, narrow hallway. The building was actually a duplex in the fan district of Richmond. My older brothers lived nearby and could offer help at a moment's notice if needed. It was also close to the VCU campus where Bailey had attended college. She'd often stop by for lunch on her breaks, but alas, she's working full time at the Richmond Art Museum, and those luxuries are few and far between.

I quietly push open the door to Austin's bedroom, never knowing what to expect when I enter. Today, the wall shared between the two residences of the duplex is covered in a variety of earth tones. This piece is in the beginning stages of construction, so I don't tax my brain too hard to consider the direction the piece is headed. My son is hard at work, ensuring the entire wall is covered in one color or another. A cream-colored, well-used, drape cloth is on the floor beneath him, spattered in multicolor paint.

"I got us a rotisserie chicken and some macaroni and cheese for dinner. You hungry?"

"Not right now, Mom. I need to paint this some more. Maybe later, Mom," he replies flatly.

"Okay, Austin. But don't get so focused on your new project you forget to eat. Okay?"

"Okay, Mom."

My gifted son is the love of my life. While Rick and I married for love at the ripe old age of twenty, it didn't take long for Austin to pop onto the scene. We'd apparently conceived on our honeymoon, having a newborn before my twenty-first birthday.

We were nervous about raising a small child while Rick worked through a demanding pre-med curriculum. Yet, Austin was an easy baby. He slept through the night quite early, and he never cried. Initially, despite the fear of being young parents, and Rick having a stressful college program, he seemed excited to be a father. He spent every free moment with Austin. Rick and I had dated all through high school and had plans. He'd go to school first, and then, once he'd fulfilled his dream of being a cardiologist, it would be my turn.

My focus was my family. I didn't mind at all. I loved Rick and Austin. They were my whole world, and I'd do anything to make them happy. I thought Rick felt the same way until he started pulling away. He was a smart, caring man. I thought if anyone could handle the pressures we were facing, it would be Rick. Yet once Austin was formally diagnosed with autism, our family began its slow and steady demise.

Austin was a quiet child. He was incredibly smart, but his inability to maneuver social interactions created difficulty for him as early as age three. Initially, I thought he was just an introspective toddler. I assumed he liked to investigate the world around him at his own pace. But the older he grew, the more I noticed his lack of eye contact, even with me. Once the pediatrician confirmed his diagnosis, I went into overdrive. I looked for any available service to aid in his progression. The more I immersed myself in Austin's therapy, the more Rick engrossed himself in his studies. He gradually found studying on campus much easier than doing so in his quiet study.

Austin never interrupted. He rarely required direction of any sort. He was quick to learn how to be self-sufficient and preoccupied himself with creating visual works of art. My oldest brother, Dominic had given him some drawing pencils, a sketch pad, and an easel for Christmas one year, and Austin's talent gradually revealed itself. He loved all forms of creativity, be it paintings or sculpture, but gravitated most toward sketching vibrant, abstract pieces of art.

The older Austin grew, the larger his artwork became. By age six, it was apparent he could not limit his enthusiasm to paper. I began applying large sheets of butcher paper to the walls to allow him the room to create without constantly having to repaint the walls of the home. He'd begin constructing his masterpiece in his sketch pad but would not quit until the work was translated into the form of a mural on his bedroom wall.

Rick barely made it to age four before checking out of our family. Initially, he'd pick Austin up for the day, every other weekend. Yet, the excuses became more frequent for his absences until he eventually just stopped coming. I secretly wondered if he took Austin over to his mother's home for the day while he returned to his studies. But Austin didn't seem to miss his father when he wasn't here. So, why make a big to do about the situation? I only worried about him when he was gone anyway.

Heading to the kitchen, I put away the groceries and decide I'm not really hungry at the moment. My walk down memory lane having depressed my appetite.

"Austin, I'm going to take a quick shower."

"Okay, Mom," I hear from the bedroom. My standard reply. Austin can be tough for some newcomers to handle. He's very tall and well built for a seventeen-year-old. He's nearly six feet already, taking after his father's side of the family. He interjects very little into any conversation, and most of his answers are succinct. Dating during the early years was difficult. I chose to be cautious about bringing new men into our lives. This was warranted as very few had any interest in taking on a special needs child like Austin.

While he didn't have outbursts or put people in uncomfortable situations, he was overwhelming to someone not accustomed to his behavior. All of his focus was on art. I had help from my family and a lovely neighbor, Mrs. Robinson, who looked in on Austin while I worked. Yet, I'd frequently come home to find he'd fallen asleep on the floor, covered in paint. There would be random, multicolored footprints scattered about the hardwood of our home. I'd given up on trying to attack each stain with vinegar or paint remover as soon as it was spotted. I now saved and hired someone to come in and paint and strip the floors once a year.

As I find clean night clothes to don after my shower, I decide to relax with a glass of wine and a good book after dinner. Sure, I would've loved to have joined my new friends from work for a drink. But there's no reason I can't enjoy my evening just the same. Sliding my fingers along my modest library, I grab a book and place it by my nightstand for later. I'm sure Austin will take his dinner back to his room to eat as he paints. If I can't enjoy my evening with Jeff, Mike, and Erin, I'll at least get to spend it with the likes of Elizabeth Bennet and her sisters. Not sure if tonight is the night to deal with the haughty and arrogant Mr. Darcy. May have to save him for another evening when I can deal with that scoundrel better.

My mind suddenly shifts to the last haughty, arrogant scoundrel I met and blush. Hell, now I'll be picturing the shark as I turn the pages of Jane Austen's masterpiece. One thing's for certain with the real-life Mr. Darcy. There's no happily ever after coming in that scenario.

CHAPTER SIX

Sebastian

"Good morning, Dr. Lee," the lively nurse greets as we scrub up for surgery.

I'm sure I should know her name, as her voice sounds familiar. With her face covered in a surgical cap and mask, I cannot place her. Admittedly, there hasn't been much of an attempt on my part to learn names at this hospital. "Good morning," I reply. The first surgery scheduled this morning isn't complex. Hopefully, we won't have any issues today.

"I heard you're operating on Mr. Hansen after this," she continues.

"Yes, he had an unfortunate encounter with a table saw." The patient is in his late sixties and has neuropathy, damage to the nerves in his fingertips. I suspect the neuropathy is from years of diabetes and may have contributed to his accident.

"Well, he's a local celebrity around here. I hope you can get him back to his old self," she replies, her eyes appearing to smile in my direction over her surgical mask.

"What kind of celebrity," I coax, wondering how this fact wasn't revealed during his examination in the ER.

"He's a painter. He has his work in all of the local art shows. It's incredible. He's been creating landscapes and seaside paintings for years."

Would've been nice if he'd volunteered that little tidbit before now. I feel my agitation begin to stir at discovering this new information. Perhaps the nerve issues in his fingers are from years of repetitive use. I frequently attend art functions in the surrounding area. How was I unaware of this man? "I'm surprised I haven't heard of him. I attend Arts in the Park and the art museum in town regularly."

"Oh, he paints under a different name. He goes by R.B. Garland. I'm not sure why. Maybe he was getting more attention than he wanted in the grocery store." She laughs.

Holy shit. R.B Garland? There was a thirty by twenty-foot seascape canvas of his hanging at our family vineyard. I could feel my blood pressure rising. How had no one felt the need to enlighten me regarding his identity? Dealing with the unknown just before surgery is not helping my headspace.

"We're all set, Dr. Lee." I hear someone beckon from the surgical suite. I follow the remaining members of the team into the operating room and find my patient is sedated and ready to go. I need to focus on who is in front of me and put R. B. Garland's surgery out of my mind.

Well, that was a shit show. How did a simple procedure become so out of control? Dr. Morgan had operated on this patient the week before he left. Since that time, the woman had developed an abscess at the surgical site. This should've been an easy technique. Go in, drain the infection, irrigate and clean the area, and place her on antibiotics. Yet, the handoff of instrumentation by the surgical assistant was less than adequate, causing the repeated clank of metal against the hard tile as the tools struck the floor. Each time this occurred, the procedure would come to a halt as we waited for new sterile instruments to be delivered, the sounds still echoing in the otherwise quiet room. I tried desperately to hold my tongue, but the third time something hit the ground, I lost it. The total time in the OR nearly doubled what was scheduled.

There's less than an hour left to decompress before the next surgery begins. *The surgery on the town celebrity,* I groan so no one else can hear. I normally crave challenges of this sort, but I'm mentally and physically exhausted by covering Dr. Morgan's patients as well as attending to my own. Hell, how much longer until he returns? I need that trip to Bali, like yesterday.

Walking down the hall from the surgical suites toward the physician's lounge, I grumble to myself. *Get your shit together, Bas.* I've handled far more complicated procedures than the fracture and tendon repair of R. B. Garland's finger. Just forget who he is and what he does. *You're letting it fuck with your head.*

Pushing the door to the modest-sized break room open harder than necessary, I walk in and lock eyes with my friend and orthopedic surgeon, Nick Barnes.

"What did that door ever do to you?" He jibes.

"Yeah, yeah. I just had a rough morning in the OR and have half the allotted time between cases now. Just irritated. How are you? It's been too long." I walk toward him, grabbing his shoulder. I consider this man my closest friend. But then again, he may be my only true friend.

"You're right. You need to come out to the lake. We can take the boat out and have a few beers," he encourages.

"I'd love that, man. Can we go now? This extended vacation of Morgan's is killing me." Shaking my head, I walk to the coffee machine and grab a pod of the strongest brew they have. I'm grateful to have this man back in my life. I can't believe after giving in to temptation and sleeping with his ex-wife, I almost lost this. My closest confidant for years, and I almost let a woman come between us. *I've got to stop thinking with my pecker.*

Suddenly, the door swings open, and a stunning brunette in black scrubs saunters in. Her long dark hair is braided, trailing down her right shoulder.

"Dr. Barnes," she greets with a knowing smile.

"Mrs. Barnes," he returns, beaming proudly at her. I never thought I'd be jealous of some poor sap who's married with a kid. Nick had fought hard for his relationship with Katarina. The two met working here at St. Luke's. Kat works as an ER physician assistant, and Nick admitted he fell harder each time he came to the emergency room to see a patient. Neither was looking for a relationship, but they couldn't fight their overpowering attraction. It took overcoming some serious obstacles to have the relationship they have now. They've grown into the strongest, most grounded married couple I've ever known. Maybe it's in his genes.

"How long until you have to get back to the OR?" Nick asks, taking a sip of his coffee as his beautiful wife wraps her arm around him.

Looking at my watch, I grimace. "Twenty minutes."

"Don't be a stranger, Bas. Once Morgan gets back, you need to come by the house," Nick repeats. "Little Grace is turning one soon. Can you believe it?"

"Man, time flies. You're right. As soon as I get back, I'll call you, bud. I just need some downtime first. The last week alone has racked my nerves."

"What exotic destination are you headed to this time?" Kat asks.

"I'm thinking I might go to Bali. I've never been, and this two-week stint calls for somewhere mind-blow—" The buzz of my cell phone interrupts my conversation. Retrieving it from my pocket, I peer down at the incoming text. "Oh, well, looks like they're ready and waiting. Need to get back to the OR."

"It was good to see you, Sebastian," Katarina says, leaning in to kiss me on the cheek.

"You too. I promise I'll call when I get back." I wave. Heading back toward the OR, I try to take some relaxing breaths. *You've done this procedure hundreds of times, Bas. Shake it off.*

~

Isabella

"Nice job, Bella," Jeff encourages as I push the large portable x-ray machine toward the radiology department. "Unfortunately, trying to get films when a patient is in pain is a daily struggle in the ER. You handled that quite well."

"Thanks. I felt like it was a no-win situation. Whatever I did, she groaned."

"I know. Sometimes they get medication on board before we get there, and it isn't so bad, but we can't put off getting the x-rays the providers need to treat their patients. It's tough maneuvering around their pain, but you did well. I think you're going to do great once you graduate and start your first job."

"Thanks, Jeff. I owe a lot of it to you. I couldn't have asked for a better mentor."

"Do you think you'd consider working here?"

"Heck, I'd love that. I didn't think there were any openings," I state excitedly.

"Well, there may not be anything here full-time, but you could start part-time and be the first considered when a spot opens. Or do you need insurance? For Austin?" I see the grimace hit Jeff's face. He's probably realizing I'm older than most of the students he normally works with, bringing a host of responsibilities most of the twenty-somethings don't have to contend with yet.

"No, we're covered on health insurance. Austin's father is a cardiologist in New York. I have no problem accepting the money he sends each month. He decided to leave our family and not look back. It's the least he can do."

"You're right. Sorry if I brought up a touchy subject," Jeff says, looking a bit embarrassed.

"Not at all. I think a lot of people assume the ex-wife of a doctor would want to take him to the cleaners. I simply want what the courts determine is fair. I put my dreams on hold to support Rick and Austin while Rick was in school. It's only fair he contributes."

"You're absolutely right. I think it's amazing you've raised Austin on your own, and now you're going after the career you always wanted. You're a very determined lady." He smiles.

Again, I can't help but wonder if these compliments are purely motivational or if there's something more there. Jeff's an incredible guy. Any girl would be lucky to go out with him. Sadly, I find he's more akin to the Mr. Collins character in Pride and Prejudice than Mr. Darcy. You'd think I'd learn to find comfort in someone like William Collins. He provided for his wife, Charlotte, and didn't make her crazy like arrogant, bad boy Mr. Darcy did Elizabeth Bennet. But after all of these years alone, I want to feel a spark. I can take care of myself. I don't need a Mr. Collins. And if someone the likes of Mr. Darcy comes along, a man who cannot commit or treat me with the utmost respect, then I'll simply use him for sex.

"Bella?" I hear Jeff interrupt my crazy tangent.

"Oh, I'm sorry. My mind trailed off. What were you saying?"

"I just said it would be great to have you on the team. Hey, we decided on going to The Zone for my birthday. The girls in the department wanted to dance, and I don't care where we go. We're going the week after next. Think you can come?"

"I wouldn't miss it."

As we walk into the radiology department, I park the portable machine and follow Jeff into the dark area where we normally sit. It's a small hallway behind the two rooms we use to obtain x-rays. The dim lighting allows us to verify the quality of the pictures before uploading them into the system for the radiologist to read.

"Jeff, please tell me you'll switch with me and take the next OR case. I *really* need a break. It's been a long morning taking x-rays on the hospital floor," Erin grumbles.

"Sure, babe. I can do it. Bella can get more experience with the C arm, too," Jeff replies.

I've worked with this device multiple times, and while it was intimidating the first time I operated the apparatus, I feel quite comfortable with it now. The most difficult thing I've found about operating it in the OR has been my height. It's fine when I have someone with me. Jeff tends to slide a stool over so swiftly I usually step up without even thinking about it. I can maneuver the device easily. I've been told my shots are always good quality. Sure, there's some fear about how things will go once I'm on my own. But, I'm certain every student has some concerns about working independently.

"Thanks, Jeff. You're a doll. I haven't sat down since I got here. I'm going to run and get something to eat. You guys don't have long. That OR case starts in about thirty minutes," Erin states as she practically sprints for the door.

"You have any questions before we get there, Bella?" Jeff asks, placing his warm hand on my shoulder. He's so kind. *Gah, why can't I ever feel chemistry with kind?*

"No. I think I have it. Doing this should allow me to sign that skill off of my checklist once and for all." I hesitate, realizing I have no idea what type of case this is. "Do you know what type of surgery it is?"

"If I remember right, I believe it's a finger fracture with tendon repair. It shouldn't be a long surgery. Dr. Lee's pretty fast."

Lee? Why does that name sound so familiar?

"Boy, I'm glad you're here." Tiffany greets Jeff with a haggard look on her face.

"Well, *now* that makes one of us," he replies sarcastically. "What's got you looking so flustered? I thought this was a simple finger fracture with tendon repair?"

"Let's just say, I was here the last time Dr. Lee operated, and Erin was operating the C arm. It didn't go well." She shakes her head in memory of the event. "And that's putting it nicely."

Oh, that Dr. Lee. Now I remember. Erin was going on about a surgeon who was less than pleasant to work with. Could she have shirked this case because of him? My confidence from earlier is suddenly waning. *What have I gotten myself into?*

"Okay, Bella. Get out of your own head," Jeff scolds. "I can see it written all over your face. Don't let the opinions of others impact your ability to do your job. You've had no issues with handling this C arm in the past. There is no reason to think you will today."

"But—"

"No buts. We have a job to do. Dr. Lee has a job to do. So long as you focus on your part of the procedure today and ignore the rest, you won't have a problem. You need to get used to this now. Surgeons are a different breed. Many of them have a God complex. I've never had an issue working with Dr. Lee. But I don't tend to let his antics bother me. You're a tough cookie. Look how well you managed to get those x-rays of winey Mrs. Walsh earlier. You never let her behavior rattle you. Don't let his."

I know he's right. What's more, I'm not a woman who cowers in fear of a man and his bravado. After Rick discarded Austin and me, I developed a thick skin. I have no problem demanding what is fair from him or anyone else. I'm a strong woman in my personal life, so why should this be any different?

CHAPTER SEVEN

Isabella

After scrubbing in, I don my surgical gloves and gown and follow Jeff into the operating room. We always stand over to the side so as not to get in anyone's way. I've tried to learn from Jeff's actions. He watches the team closely and seems to pick up on subtle cues on when to intervene. I know I'll get there eventually, but I hope one day to be able to read the room as well as he does.

Slowly, additional team members trickle in. I still find this whole experience exhilarating. To be involved in even a small way in something as profound as repairing an injured body part is incredible to me. I know I'm only here to obtain pictures for the surgeon. Shots that will guide them toward making the patient whole again. Snapshots that will enlighten them on how they're doing and where they may need to adjust. I need to focus on my part of this elaborate jigsaw puzzle and not respond to the actions of those around me. Jeff is right. I have a job to do, and I plan to do it well.

Light chatter invades the room as the patient is prepared. This surgery will be different than those I've attended in the past. This patient is only receiving what Jeff called a Bier block. That means they'll only numb the hand, but he'll otherwise be wide awake. I'm not sure if this is why the room feels more tense than usual. Dr. Barnes performed a rotator cuff repair on an older man's shoulder and had nineties music playing in the OR suite throughout the procedure. Dr. Morgan's cases occur without music, but he interjects bad jokes throughout the procedure. From what Jeff tells me, he has like ten kids or something, so maybe 'Dad jokes' are all he knows.

A hush abruptly falls on the room, jolting me from my internal musings. I look up to see who I assume is the surgeon walking in. He appears formidable. He's tall, broad-shouldered, and there is a definite air of confidence about his stature. He's wearing some type of headset with glasses attached, allowing visualization of the bone fragments and tendons more easily, I suppose. It's eerie how silent the OR has become. Is it always this way when he operates? The utter quiet alone is unnerving. If he was condescending to Erin after standing in this intimidating environment for too long, it's no wonder she didn't want to come back.

Watching his every move, curiosity getting the best of me, I notice he bends down to speak with the patient and greets the nurse anesthetist briefly. He turns back toward the bedside and stands alongside the patient's right hand. There is no additional conversation or introduction to the remaining surgical team members. But I'm probably the only one new here.

I hear his deep gravelly voice as he announces the time and begins the surgery. My heart is beating so fast. Is it just as Jeff had warned? Was I too *in my own head* about what Erin had said? Why was I so on edge with this case?

Sebastian

Thank fuck. Jeff is here. My stress level can't handle another case like the ones lately. I need to be surrounded by capable team members. I cannot afford to be distracted by the lackluster performance I've seen in this hospital as of late.

Greeting the patient and nurse anesthetist as I approach the table, I confirm the patient is ready to go. This procedure will not be performed under general anesthesia, adding to the stress level a bit, given the patient is a local celebrity. Focus is the name of the game. Hopefully, we can keep chatter to a minimum today.

"I can't believe I'm getting to meet you, sir." Jason, the nurse anesthetist, whispers to the patient. *Well, so much for that thought.* "My wife gave me one of your paintings as a wedding gift."

"Oh, that's very nice to hear. Thank you, son," the older patient replies.

I glare over my mask at Jason, trying to get my point across. Pausing for enough time to pass that he might realize something's amiss, he eventually looks up. Instantly aware of my ire by the expression on his face, I'm hoping everyone at the table follows suit and keeps their comments to themselves from here on out. *Jesus, I need this one to go well.*

I test Mr. Hansen's hand to ensure it's numb before beginning the procedure. The room is now quiet, and I zone in on the task at hand. The index finger of his dominant hand is broken, and the tendon is lacerated from the use of that table saw. Why anyone would use a table saw when they knew their art was at stake is beyond me. I wouldn't contemplate such a thing knowing it would destroy my career. I remove the stitches temporarily placed in his finger to hold the wound together and find the exposed bone. Only one end of the torn tendon is visible. After the wound is well irrigated, I look toward Jeff, giving him the signal that I'm going to need a visualization on the C arm soon. I need to verify no other bone shards are farther down and verify alignment before I secure the fractured pieces.

Sensing a presence beside me, my skin starts to heat. I'm unsure what this is all about, as I've never felt this in an OR before. Glancing to my left to investigate, I realize someone small is stepping onto a stool beside me. *What the ever-loving hell?* Every time I think I'm gaining control of the situation in here, someone tries to throw another wrench in the system. "Jeff, this isn't preschool career day. I want you operating this C arm so I can proceed, not someone needing a booster seat."

A voice clears beside me.

"Bella has this, Dr. Lee. I'm right here. But she's got this," Jeff says calmly. I can tell he's right behind us, but I'd prefer to have one fucking surgical case that doesn't turn into a train wreck today. Why on earth does he think this girl should be assisting me with this instead of a fully trained professional? Couldn't she learn on a hip replacement? Was he sleeping with this girl? What's his need to involve her in a case of this magnitude versus taking over as I'd requested? The more I question his motives, the more agitated I become.

"Jeff, I want someone who doesn't have training wheels on today," I bark.

"Dr. Lee, she's got this," he repeats. Not an ounce of emotion in his voice.

My anger is beyond a simmer. The day... hell, the last ten days is catching up with me. I still have a ways to go to repair this finger. I need to get my temper under control before the whole town learns there are no more R. B. Garland seascapes because Dr. Lee couldn't get the job done.

I glance toward the petite radiology tech, now standing on the stool beside me. I can see her narrowed eyes between the blue surgical cap and mask. There is a fire there. A dark, brown blaze beginning to rage. *Who does this girl think she is?* No one dares look at me that way, much less during surgery. And a student no less. I'm the maestro of this complicated concerto. She needs to learn some respect. Maybe *that's* what this case will teach her. "Bella, is it?" I hiss.

She responds with a curt nod, no words. Just a quick dip of the chin and that piercing glare.

"Can I have a shot of the finger so I can repair this patient's wound?" I sneer.

Snapping her head back in the direction of the machine, she meticulously adjusts the unit in an attempt to gather the shots I need to proceed.

I'm so angry now, everything feels as if it's moving in slow motion. My pulse is beating in my ears, my head starting to pound. There's a familiar tingling sensation settling into my fingertips as I stand waiting as if I've been holding my surgical instruments for so long my hands have fallen asleep. Feeling out of control has become a definite trigger for the poor outcome of many surgeries of late. I need to wrap my head around how to quelch this feeling while I'm in Bali. Unfortunately, I don't have a technique in place for that now.

"We don't have all day." Pause. "This is pain—" The shot appears on the screen, interrupting my rant. As my eyes flick back in the technician's direction, I'm met with a smug glower. Her pupils are so dark I can barely find where they stop, and her deep brown irises begin. They're practically smoldering. *Hell, I'd be turned on right now if I weren't so fucking mad.*

"I think you're done here, Bella," I toss in her direction, emphasizing her name in annoyance. I dive into the completion of the delicate task in front of me. Feeling her retreat, I let out a quiet exhalation and refocus. As I reach for a surgical instrument, I shift my stance slightly and nearly trip over the stool which remains by my side. "Jeff!"

"Yes, sir. I apologize, Dr. Lee. That was completely my fault."

Standing there, momentarily trying to calm my nerves, I take in my surroundings. The surgical team at the bedside all look like they want to dive under the table for cover. Jason is looking down at Mr. Hansen. I've completely forgotten he's been awake through this entire procedure. *Fuck!* No one should ever hear their surgeon behave this way. Looking across the room, I notice Jeff whispering into the ear of the small-framed radiology tech I shamed moments ago. Yet, she doesn't appear defeated. She doesn't look the least bit intimidated. *She looks pissed.*

Get your head back in the game, Sebastian. Find the pieces of severed tendon, sew him up and get the hell out of here before you do anything else you'll regret. I'm already going to have to come up with a suitable apology for Mr. Hansen when I see him in the recovery unit. I need to do some serious soul searching in Bali. This behavior cannot continue, even if *I am* surrounded by incompetence.

I manage to repair the tendon and close the wound without another incident occurring. My heartbeat thundering in my ears has been the soundtrack to the second half of this painful surgery. I don't care what else is on the books after I get out of this OR suite, I'm getting Dr. Morgan's PA to handle it. I have to get the hell out of this hospital before I lose it. As soon as I can make it out of here, I'm changing clothes, apologizing to Mr. Hansen, then going home for a swim and a bottle of Scotch.

Walking away from the tension-filled operating room, I pull off my gown, gloves, and mask and dispose of them in the appropriate bin. I need to get my fury under control before I make more of a scene than I already have. I'm fully aware of my reputation here. Apparently, I'm an overbearing, condescending asshole when I'm not trying to score my next lay. Since my stress level has climbed to monumental heights, my behavior at Mary Immaculate has begun to slip as well. I have to face it. I chose this profession. Stress or not, I need to get my act together or find a different line of work. Maybe I need to consider concierge medicine. There I'd only see high-paying clients who practically have me on retainer. *Hell, that might be more stressful.*

As I turn, I see Jeff standing down the hall and cannot stop myself from venting. I know I should just walk away. Making eye contact as I get closer, I notice he's still wearing his surgical cap but has removed his gown and gloves. "I thought I could count on you. We've worked alongside one another for years now. If I say I want you, that's exactly who should be manning the C arm. Got it?"

"Yes, sir. I apologize. I really wanted Bella to have this experience, Dr. Lee. She's due to graduate soon—"

"Do I look like the kind of guy who should be helping some little student get her wings in the OR to you, Jeff? My surgeries are intricate, high-stress cases. Let her cut her teeth with Dr. Morgan or even Nick. Someone who won't have the whole town wondering why the surgeon couldn't repair the *painting* hand of the county's award-winning artist!"

About that time, I see his student behind him. She's pulled off her gown and is glaring at me through the remainder of her surgical garb. Her audacity strikes the final match of annoyance within me, setting me ablaze. "And you." I storm over to her. "I appreciate that Jeff placed you in this position however, I don't need the continued disrespectful glances my way. If you can't play with the big dogs, Bella, maybe you need to stay home."

"Got it," she barks, surprising me with the venom in her tone. Still not backing down, this one. *She's got a fucking lot of nerve.*

I return toward the bin to remove my surgical cap, my hair falling onto my forehead, reminding me I need a trim. Reaching back to rub the spasm from my neck, I try to calm my nerves before attempting to dictate my surgical note and giving Mr. Hansen an apology for the unprofessional behavior he witnessed. As I turn to head for the door, I'm stopped in my tracks. My heart clenches inside my chest at the sight. Bella's mask is off, and the oddest feeling of déjà vu smacks me in the face. *Where do I know that face? Have I slept with her? No. I'd remember—*

Bella reaches up to remove her surgical cap, her luscious brown locks tumbling down about her face and neck as she stares directly at me with complete and utter disdain. I take her in. Those gorgeous eyes. That beautiful hair. The dimples I can almost picture hidden beneath her furious features. *It's her.*

Holy fuck! What the hell have I done?

CHAPTER EIGHT

Isabella

I think I'm going to need surgery myself after this. I've nearly bitten a hole through my tongue, trying to keep my thoughts to myself so I don't get chastised for voicing my opinion of that asshole. That sexy as fuck, arrogant asshole. *Why? Why did I have to have nightly naughty dreams starring this man? Him?* Well, I bet they'll stop now. *Yeah, right.* That was by far the best sex of my life, and there's no way I can forget it. I'll just chop his head off in all the replays. I'd say I'd sew his mouth shut myself, but I have first-hand knowledge of his skills with that body part, and I'm not sure I want to forget that either.

"You okay?" Jeff interrupts my internal ranting.

"Yeah, I'm okay. Just part of the job, right?"

"No, Bella. That was beyond anything I've witnessed before. I'm so sorry. I would've never put you in that position if I thought for a second, he could've been so unprofessional."

"Unprofessional? He was downright mean," I spit back. So I guess I'm done holding back. "But I can handle it. Just chalk it up to a learning experience. I can safely say I feel like I can handle anything anyone could throw at me now."

I realize I'm still walking, but I've left Jeff a few paces behind me. "Are you okay?" I ask.

"You might be the most incredible woman I've ever encountered. Well, besides my late wife, of course. You took all of that in stride and with your head held high. I hope I can find a way to instill that in my daughters one day. I'd hate to think of them being treated the way you were and not standing up for themselves. Is it okay to say I'm proud of you? Hell, I don't know if I could've handled that better myself."

"Thanks, Jeff. I grew up with two older brothers and Donovan around all the time. They taught me well. Then when Rick left, I guess I learned how to stand up for myself because of Austin. I'll never let him see his mom disrespected. I want him to realize it's not okay to treat other people the way his father has treated us."

If only there was *any* chemistry here. Jeff is such a nice man. He's attractive and smart and obviously a great father. I haven't dated many men since my divorce. Once Austin was older, and I felt ready to put myself out there again, I found it was hard enough to find a man if you were single. Once I announced I had a son, the return calls frequently ended. The ones who stayed only did so until they met Austin. It appears the incredibly unique things I love about my special child are not as attractive to outsiders. I've already lived through his father's rejection. I don't want to continually expose Austin to men who'll disrespect us or leave because we don't fit their cookie-cutter lifestyle.

As much as I'd like to find a partner to share my life with, I want the fairy tale next time. I want someone who'll love and cherish me as well as my son. Someone who'll make me weak in the knees and wet between the sheets. If I can't have it all, I'll settle for our family of two and get my needs met the way I've done it for years. I'll enjoy a quick romp and move on.

Walking into the radiology department, I try to shake it off. There's no point in perseverating on this. I was never going to see that guy again anyway. So, my dirty dreams are going to be missing a handsome head from now on. Dreaming about the 'headless' hot guy from the club will still be the best sex I've ever had. I'll manage.

"How'd it go?" I hear Erin ask as we walk into the darkened hallway.

"Um, you owe us big time, missy," Jeff scolds. "You knew full well you didn't want to work that C arm for Lee again. And I fell for your shenanigans. Hungry and tired, my ass." He snickers.

"That good, huh?" She gives a lopsided grin.

"Well, there are about fifty new orders for x-rays in the ER, it appears," I interject. "I think I'm just going to jump in here and start on the first three. Mike, are you coming with me? I think Jeff deserves a break."

"Sure, Bella. I got you," Mike answers. "You still missing a clavicle?"

"Yeah, who knew finding a patient with a possible broken collarbone would be this hard?" Heck, it doesn't even have to be broken. I just need a picture, broken or not.

"We can make a loop around the department again and ask the docs to keep you in mind if they see someone with a shoulder injury. Wouldn't want it to get past you by mistake."

We walk down the hall toward the main physicians' workspace, and I smile when I see Donovan.

"Hey, B. How much longer do you have?" My cousin greets me.

"Only about a month, and I'm done. I can't believe it."

"I can believe it. You can do anything you put your mind to." He winks. God, I love that guy.

"Bella still needs a clavicle x-ray. Let us know if you have anyone who might need one," Mike advises.

"Sure thing." Donovan waves as he walks to the ambulance bay doors to greet a paramedic pushing a gurney through the doors with a very pregnant female on the stretcher. I instinctively place my hand over my belly, feeling forlorn that those days are over for me now.

Sebastian

I still cannot believe it. Week after week, I sit talking to a bartender like a stereotypical middle-aged man looking for the meaning of life. Yet, all the while, she was here under my nose. What's worse, my stressful OR life has just become ten times worse.

I can't believe I couldn't get my head out of my ass to control my temper while the patient was awake and listening to me rant like a spoiled brat. No surgical tools had hit the floor. Other than almost tripping over that stool, the case had gone better than most of late. My fear of what could go wrong has turned me into a tyrant. I know my behavior is escalating. The concern over the success of my surgical cases while tired and stressed has me so on edge, I would've snapped at one of the chaplains if they'd been there. I've clearly become unhinged.

I rub the back of my neck, still sore from the stress of my morning, as I walk to the recovery room. As I approach the nurses' station, the women on duty all instantly stop speaking. This isn't new. Yet, this occurrence doesn't appear to be an attempt to win my attention. None of them is smiling. *Shit. I guess everyone knows how I behaved earlier.* I need to face the music.

"Hi. Is Mr. Hansen doing okay?' I ask. I don't anticipate he'll need to remain in the recovery room long. Unfortunately, he'll need to stay in the hospital to receive intravenous antibiotics but likely will be home very soon.

"Yes, sir. He's doing fine," a blonde nurse wearing navy blue scrubs answers. There isn't the flirty smile I've received in the past. But then again, I probably look like I've been hit by a truck after the day I've had.

Walking over to the patient's stretcher, I greet him and sit down beside him. Gathering my thoughts for a second, I decide to go all in. "Mr. Hansen. I need to offer my sincere apologies for my behavior earlier. It was completely unprofessional, and there is no excuse for the way I acted."

"You're right, son. There isn't."

Hanging my head in shame, I try to find words to salvage this shitty situation. But before I can open my mouth to speak, I'm interrupted.

"You have a reputation," he states, making me wince. "Let me start over. You have a good reputation. I knew I was in good hands today. I know your job is stressful, so I tried to explain away your behavior. However, there's more to a man than his work and reputation." He pauses, looking at me with the eyes of a loving parent instead of a patient. "Please forgive an old man for butting in."

"No forgiveness needed. You have every right to voice your opinion. You were a witness to my unprofessional behavior. As I said, there's no excuse for it. I've piled too much on my plate, covering for another surgeon while he's away. Several of my recent cases at this hospital haven't gone smoothly. Don't misunderstand. They were all successful, but it hasn't been smooth. I, unfortunately, brought my concerns into the surgical suite today. Then on top of that, I didn't find out until this morning who you were."

Mr. Hansen looks at me mystified until he realizes I'm speaking of his pseudonym. "Ah, you found out you were operating on R. B. Garland. I'm sorry. I've told my story to so many people. Between the EMTs, nurses, and ER physician, I just assumed you knew."

"Oh, it's not your fault, Mr. Hansen. If it weren't for recent events, I would've laughed it off afterward. But with the tension so high already, it was just one more thing on my shoulders." I pause for a moment, wondering if I should proceed after what he already thinks of my behavior. I'm surprised he didn't dismiss me immediately. "Do you mind my asking why you use R. B. Garland?"

"Haven't been asked that in a while," he answers sheepishly. "I'm a bit of an introvert. I've always fancied myself a creative type. But that wasn't respected in my family. I grew up in a long line of businessmen. It was expected I'd graduate college and work in the family business. Yet, I didn't enjoy that line of work. Worse, I didn't enjoy talking to people about business."

Sitting taller in the chair beside him, I'm awestruck by our commonality.

"It was made clear to me that if I pursued a career in the arts, I'd be doing it of my own accord. I was essentially shunned by my family from that moment on. They said I'd never make anything of myself."

"Well, it appears you showed them."

"They don't know," he answers.

"I'm sorry. What do you mean? Everyone in town knows who R. B. Garland is," I answer, shocked.

"My family doesn't know that I'm R. B. Garland. My success or failure is none of their concern. I did this for me. Once they made their decision to disassociate themselves, I changed my name."

"Wow. Thank you for sharing that with me. I have a similar situation with my family. They wanted me in the family business, but when I chose to walk away and follow a career in medicine, they cut me off financially. They haven't shut me out of the family. That was more my doing, given their toxic lifestyle. But I'm glad they know I've done well without them." I pause, reflecting on my situation more than I've allowed in recent years. "I guess I had a chip on my shoulder."

Looking over to this kindhearted man, I see one eyebrow raised at me. "Okay, so I still have a chip on my shoulder."

"You're learning. You need to make peace with that situation. Don't let others define you. You have enough riding on you with your work. Do you want to know how I chose R. B. Garland?"

"Yes, I'd love to."

"RB Garland is short for Ralph Bernard Garland. Ralph, Bernard, and Judy coined three of my favorite quotes. I always appreciated the motivation they provided. They stuck with me."

I glance at him inquisitively, silently hoping for more.

"Ralph Waldo Emerson said, 'To be yourself in a world that is constantly trying to make you something else is the greatest accomplishment.' I thought he was on to something. Bernard, oh, he's one of my favorites. 'Be who you are and say what you feel, because those who mind don't matter, and those who matter don't mind.' Haha. You may have heard that one before. But Bernard M. Baruch said that. Then lastly, there's Judy Garland."

"The 'Somewhere Over the Rainbow' Judy Garland?" I ask, shocked by all this self-proclaimed introvert is sharing with me.

"That's the one. Her quote is one of my favorites. It's always stuck with me. 'Always be a first-rate version of yourself and not a second-rate version of someone else.' I've tried to live my life that way. When I decided to put my dream of painting out there, I wasn't trying to hide behind a false name. I wanted to have the freedom to create without interference. So I found a new name based on my favorite quotes. Having the 'pen name,' if you will, also provided a little more privacy through the years, living in a small town." He chuckles. "I don't judge you for wanting to stick it to your family that you became successful in spite of them. But, your successes or failures should mean the most to you. To hell with what others think."

"You're right. You've given me a lot to think about. I appreciate your kindness, despite my horrific behavior. Again, I hope you can forgive me. I plan to use this as a real wake-up call."

"Well, don't worry about me, son. It's that young lady you should be apologizing to."

My head, again, drops in shame. "I know. I can't believe what's become of me." I shake my head, baffled at how I've treated the people I work with. *This really is a wake-up call.*

"Listen, no more lectures. I appreciate you trying to heal an old man. I admit this was of my own doing. I've had a good run. If, after this surgery, I'm not able to paint again, it's on me, not you. I've made peace that whatever life sends my way, I'm going to accept it graciously. I've enjoyed creating art for many years. I could've been slaving away at my family's business, miserable. Whatever happens, I'm grateful."

"Why would you risk it? There are a lot of things I can't even consider doing for fear it would ruin my career. I can't use power tools, knowing it can end me."

"I was trying to make a bookshelf for the sweet lass who lives next door. She's really into her books, and I thought if my art didn't impress her, maybe making a home for her prized possessions would. Hell, what you do for love." He laughs. "But one last thing before you go. Your career is only one part of who you are. Don't miss out on things in life because you are protecting one part of yourself. Don't let it consume you as it did me. Otherwise, you could end up a lonely old man like me."

I sit stunned, staring at this amazing man. I came here hoping to salvage my career with a half-hearted apology. Instead, he completely opened up to me and shared his wisdom. It's a conversation I'd imagined a father might have with his son—if only I'd had a *different* father.

"Thank you, sir. This conversation has meant a lot to me." I pause, shocked at how emotional I've become. "Would you mind... well, if I kept in touch?" I could see by the expression on his face, he understood my request.

"I'd like that. Now, go apologize to that young woman and do a little soul searching—"

"Sebastian. Please. Call me Sebastian. I'll let you get some rest. I'll be by early tomorrow morning to check on you."

Standing from my chair, all of a sudden I feel a bit overwhelmed. This day had already taken a toll, but I feel like I'm leaving my first therapy session. *It's long overdue.* I didn't realize how much baggage I'd been carrying around. Maybe I *should* be more grateful. In a million years, I wouldn't have predicted this day could end this well.

Walking toward the physicians' parking lot, I make an abrupt turn toward the emergency room. I need to use this turn of events to do the right thing. I just hope I can find the right words to say to her once I get there.

Swiping my badge, I gain access to the ER. Radiology is tucked in the back of the emergency department, between the ER and an outpatient testing center. As I head in that direction, my mind is still blank. What do I say? *Just say you're sorry, asshole. I know those words don't come out of your haughty mouth often, but just say it.* I need to forget there was ever anything between us physically. It was one night. This is simply about apologizing to a colleague that I've wronged. *Forget that she's the hottest colleague I've ever—*

"Dr. Lee."

I turn toward the voice unexpectedly shouting my name and see Donovan Grant running in my direction.

"Hey, you operated on Mr. Hansen this morning, right? How'd it go? I took care of him last night when he came in."

Boy, now there's a question. "I think the surgery went well." *Liar.* "I'm hoping for a good outcome." *That's a little closer to the truth.* "He's an amazing man." *Okay, that one's at least on the mark.*

"You're right. But so are you for taking that on? That had to be incredibly stressful, knowing what was riding on you," he generously offers.

"Dr. Grant, a stroke patient is coming to room twenty-four. He's in CT now," a nurse shouts as she continues down the hall.

"Ugh. The ER never sleeps. Got to run," he adds before running back in the direction he came. Turning back toward the radiology department, it dawns on me that I don't give a lot of the ER attendings as much credit as they deserve. *Jeez, who am I right now?*

Feeling more confident in my task, I stand a little taller as I walk down the hallway. I enter the first x-ray room, see no one on the table, and head to the door connecting to where the technicians usually sit. As I open it, I see multiple technicians present in this small dark space. In the far corner, standing next to an attractive young male tech with colorful tattoos climbing up his left arm, is Bella.

"Hi," I greet them meekly. This tone feels alien to me. Yet, there's no mistaking my name is mud around here after my last few run-ins with the staff. I notice Erin is also here. I acknowledge the need to right that wrong as well. Almost everyone in attendance has made eye contact with me, but no one's uttering a word. I have this coming. *Just grow up and do what you came here to do, Bas.*

"Um, Bella. Could I speak with you a moment?"

You can hear a pin drop. I watch as the entire group turns to look at her.

Glancing up from the stack of papers in her hand, her eyes connect with mine. She must not have recognized my voice, as the sweet smile and deep dimples present moments ago have abruptly disappeared. "No."

CHAPTER NINE

Isabella

"Um, Bella. Could I speak with you a moment?" I hear from the doorway. Looking up from the x-ray orders I'm sifting through, hoping for a potential clavicle order, I lock eyes with Dr. Lee. I cannot hide the exasperation I feel at his presence. *Do I really need to endure anything more with this man today?*

"No," I respond flatly. I hear a gasp from the corner of the room and quickly determine it's Erin as she sits with her hand covering her mouth in shock.

"No?" Dr. Lee returns, seeming astonished. Why would I want to intentionally put myself through any more of his abuse?

"Anything you need to say to me, you can say in front of my coworkers. You had no problem speaking in front of everyone earlier." Lifting my chin, hoping he realizes I'm not taking any more of his crap, I let my eyes briefly drift about the room. Yet, instead of finding looks of solidarity, I find utter shock. All of them are staring at me, mouths wide open. Have I just committed professional suicide? Could this affect graduation if he goes to the administration? He could say I was insubordinate. Even if *he* is in the wrong here, I'm a nobody to them.

He brings in big money, I'm certain. Suddenly, I'm not feeling quite as confident I've made the right choice here. But how do I change my position without coming off weak? To him and to my colleagues? Before I can come up with an alternate plan, Dr. Lee floors me.

"You're absolutely right. My behavior earlier was unprofessional and uncalled for. You did your job and did it well. There's no excuse for the way I treated you," he says, appearing sincere.

Again, I hear gasps. This time there are multiple. I have to admit, I'm a little shocked by this turn of events. I'm not even sure I know how to respond. Feeling tongue-tied, I try to gather my wits.

"Do you accept my apology?" he asks, looking at me with what I want to believe is true remorse. I've never been spoken to the way this man chose to speak to me today. Not in private, much less in a crowded OR suite. I'm not going to just roll over and accept this and act like nothing ever happened. But I only have another month here. I'd like to have a chance at working here once I graduate, and I doubt that'll happen if I'm on the outs with one of their top surgeons.

"Bella?" Dr. Lee interrupts my scattered thoughts. *Oh, yeah. He's waiting on an answer, you goof.*

"Sure," I volley back and return to the printer to continue on my hunt for a clavicle. He's done what he came here to do. Now, let's move on. Nothing more to see here.

He clears his throat, causing me to look back in his direction. I see he's pulling at the collar of his shirt. *Maybe he forgot how big his head was and tied his tie too tight.* "Erin. I owe you an apology too," he directs her way.

Out of the blue, it occurs to me. Did someone complain about his behavior, and he's been forced to go on this apology tour? Not that I think his apology is less sincere now that he's offering one to Erin. Yet, given how he acted earlier, I admit I have my suspicions.

"Again, there's no excuse for my behavior. I've been under a great deal of stress recently, and I took it out on you. I'm sorry."

Glancing toward Erin, I notice she, and quite honestly, everyone else in the room but me, is sitting in stunned silence, all of them with their mouths open like baby birds waiting to be fed. Yet, unlike me, she quickly responds to her offender.

"Thank you for saying that, Dr. Lee." She actually looks like she's going to cry. *What the hell?*

"Jeff? Are we good?" Dr. Lee asks, stepping further into the office to offer his hand.

"Yes, sir. We're good."

Oh, brother. What a bunch of sellouts we are.

From the corner of my eye, I see Dr. Lee look my way once more before turning to exit the department. After the door shuts behind him, we all look at each other, eyes wide in amazement.

"Holy shit. I never thought I'd see the day," Mike says.

"Me either," Erin adds.

I look toward Jeff. He has an odd look on his face.

Coming closer, he pretends to look at the stack of orders I'm holding as he whispers, "I'm glad he said it, but I'll never forget how he spoke to you. It'll take a lot to change my opinion of him now."

"Yeah. I want to be able to work with him without animosity, but I'm going to have my guard up from here on out."

Jeff and I head toward the front of the ER to room thirteen. As we pass the physicians' workstation, I notice Dr. Lee is still here, sitting next to Donovan. As our eyes connect, I feel a twinge of concern for the illustrious Dr. Lee. He doesn't look well. *Maybe eating humble pie has upset his stomach.* About that time, Donovan sees me and jumps up from his chair.

"Hey, B. I almost called you." Draping his arm around my shoulders, he laughs. "I thought I had a clavicle for you, but the guy looks like a shoulder dislocation." Feeling him squeeze me like he did when we were in grade school, he chuckles, looking down at me with those big beautiful green eyes. "Maybe next time."

"Whatever," I tease, catching up to Jeff as Donovan returns to where he was sitting.

Deciding to take my lunch outside, I sit in the courtyard behind the cafeteria with my sandwich and chips. Sipping from my bottle of water, I have to admit, I feel much better now that Dr. Lee has apologized. Whether forced to do it or not, he appeared sincere. Popping a salty chip into my mouth, in this quiet space, I'm able to reflect. I'd been too overcome with rage to adequately consider the fact that the shark that rocked my world a few weeks ago is a surgeon. And not just any surgeon, but a well-regarded, talented surgeon. Granted, after Rick, it takes more than a title to impress me. Yet, I know what it takes to achieve his level of accomplishment. It's no easy feat.

I'm not sure why, but unexpectedly, the delicious way he ravaged my body is even more delectable, knowing someone of his status had been so into me. *Lord, how pathetic am I?* He's probably had more women than I can count. If it hadn't been me that night, I'm sure he wouldn't have gone home alone. Plus, he's a pompous asshole. Why would either of these qualities make that night with him more appealing?

"Uh-hm."

Looking up, I discover the man himself, standing above me. Shielding my eyes from the bright sunlight, I glance at him wordlessly.

"Can I sit down?"

"I'm almost done here—"

"Please?" I feel his warm hand on my arm as he lowers himself to the seat beside me. Feeling the heat of his body next to mine has momentarily distracted me from the frisson of current coming from his hand. "I wanted to make sure you knew my apology was sincere. It felt less so when I had to address the others in the group I'd wronged."

I look at him, puzzled. *So, were their apologies not sincere?*

As if reading my mind, he quickly interjects, "I needed to apologize to everyone, but my behavior toward you was much more appalling. I've never spoken to anyone that way. It's despicable. You deserve more than I can offer in words. You did absolutely nothing wrong. I was an ass." He stops, momentarily running his hand through the dark strands of hair that have fallen onto his forehead. As pissed as I am with him, I can't help wanting to touch him. Just to feel those inky strands between my fingers again. "Please know this is a tipping point for me. I'm going to find a way to deal with my stress and hope to prove it through my actions in the future."

Feeling a little snarky, I toss out, "Well, I only have my training wheels for a few more weeks. Then I'm done here." I watch as a pained look crosses his features. Unable to hold back any longer, I reach over to grab his hand. "I'm kidding. I accept your apology, Dr. Lee."

Looking toward our hands, he mutters, "Feels odd, you calling me Dr. Lee."

"What do you mean?"

"Until today, I only thought of you as this beautiful, nameless, naked woman who—"

"Okay, okay," I interrupt, looking about to make sure we're completely alone. "I'm sure I'm not the first person you've slept with that you happen to work with."

"No," he answers sheepishly. "But, I knew that when I acted on it with them. You surprised me."

"Ah. I see. So, you have a lot of women here, calling you by your first name?" I ask, pointing my finger at the hospital behind me to make a point.

"No. They call me Dr. Lee."

"Well, then why is it odd, I call you that?"

"I don't know." I watch as he appears to examine my I.D. badge more closely and shifts in his seat a bit. Attempting to change the subject, he states, "So, Isabella, if I offer to let you punch me in the chest, will we be even?"

Almost choking on my sandwich, I lean forward as I cough. I feel that warm hand caressing my back and look back at him, stunned. Taking a sip of my water to clear my throat, I lift a brow at him, hoping he'll explain himself.

"Donovan told me you needed a clavicle x-ray." He chuckles, shrugging his shoulders.

I can feel the corner of my mouth lift at his offer. "As tempting as that is, I'm hoping to not be the cause of any more stress on the job." Standing, I grab my lunch tote and water bottle. "I have to get back now. Thank you for the apology, Dr. Lee."

"Sebastian."

"What?"

"My name is Sebastian."

"Oh." I'm stunned. Not sure what to say to this, "Well, goodbye."

Heading back to work, my head is spinning. *What the heck just happened?* This has been one rollercoaster of a day, that's for sure.

Closing the door behind me, I practically collapse on my couch. Thank heavens Bailey has Austin tonight. I need some 'me' time to unwind after this crazy-ass day! Pulling off my shoes, I shuffle over to the kitchen to grab a bottle of wine. Finding the opener, I pop the cork on this puppy as if its contents are needed for my very survival. Carrying the glass of crisp Pinot Grigio to the bath. *This day calls for a quick rinse, then a hot soak in the tub.* The sushi I picked up on my way home will just have to wait.

After stepping out of the shower, I decide to make a plate of sushi as the tub fills with water. Sitting at my kitchen island, I devour the delectable rice-covered rolls as I sip my wine. This day feels like it lasted a week. It's hard to wrap my mind around the chaotic events. From the belittling dressing down in the OR, the heart-to-heart with Jeff, then the surprising apology from Dr. Lee... it barely seems real. But the kicker was his appearance in the courtyard on my break. If I hadn't seen and heard it with my own eyes and ears, I would've thought I imagined the whole thing. He seemed like a completely different person. Not only had the condescending surgeon from the morning transformed into a genuinely remorseful man, but the overconfident arrogance from the night I met him seemed to have also vanished. What could've possibly happened to have changed him in only a few hours?

Popping the last California roll into my mouth, I refill my wine glass and return to my steamy bath. Placing my drink down, I reach for a eucalyptus mint bath bomb and drop it into the water. As the bomb disintegrates into the hot water, I watch the greenish-blue hue dissolve and equate it to the way my emotions have felt today. Before my break, my body felt like a turbulent sea, reacting to everything in my wake with a harsh, edgy recoil. Needing that clavicle x-ray for my checklist was both frustrating, and at times, funny. Being in the operating room while a surgeon operated on the town celebrity was exhilarating, 'til it wasn't. Having a man who I'd dreamt about scold me in front of my peers was humiliating. Having said man apologize in front of my colleagues, felt gratifying. Yet, his private confession in the courtyard had me baffled. I've never had a man speak to me that way. It felt real.

Rubbing my thumb along my lower lip, I let my mind wander to the man I'd replayed in my dreams. He's even more attractive than I remembered. Maybe the haze of the alcohol that night had clouded my memory. Or the overconfident shark persona had me more focused on his skills in the bedroom versus his physical appearance. He's more than attractive. He's downright beautiful. His dark hair is a little longer than I remembered, but just how I like it. He wears a five o'clock shadow like no one I've seen. His dimples aren't as deep as mine, but there's a playful quality to them. Maybe I only notice them when he's flirty. But his eyes, now they're the showstopper. The deep blues had teased me in my dreams but didn't compare to the technicolor irises I witnessed today. Beyond the coloring were their depths. Maybe he simply knows how to lure a woman, but there was a tortured look about him. With each smile in my direction, I could see the regret lingering there.

Lying my head back against the tub, I inhale the calming scents as they waft from the water. I'm not a pushover. I will not be won over with a simple apology and the offer to snap his clavicle like a twig. Biting my lip as I giggle at the recollection, I reach for my glass. *You did well today, Bella. You learned a lot. You kept your head held high. And you offered forgiveness when you didn't think you had it in you. Now, don't let your guard down if he comes sniffing back around.*

What had he said? "If you can't play with the big dogs, Bella, maybe you need to stay home." I play the words in my head, again and again. Getting out of my bath, I towel off and put on my sleep clothes before grabbing my phone. I'd grown up watching old black and white movies. I was such a fan of the bygone era of Hollywood. The days where celebrities were a bit of a mystery, unlike this day and age where you can become famous for a reality tv show stint or going viral on YouTube or TikTok. One of my favorites was Marilyn Monroe. She was an incredible beauty but so troubled. It was fascinating to read how someone that looked like her could still struggle to find love. It made my plight feel more normal.

Scrolling through the phone, I locate the quote I'd remembered Marilyn Monroe saying. I found it some time back, and it hit me as poignant then, and even more so now.

"Dogs never bite me. Just humans."

CHAPTER TEN

Sebastian

It's been an incredible few days in Bali. I can't believe I've never come here before. The tranquility of this place enveloped me the minute I stepped off of the plane.

I'd found an exclusive beach-front resort in Bali with a breathtaking view of the Indian Ocean. The tropical paradise sits on the south coast of Bali Island, on Nusa Due beach. My bungalow has every amenity I need to relax and recharge. Yet, somehow this jaunt feels different than the previous escapes I've made.

Nick had likened my excursions to those he'd read Richard Gere making to Tibet. The actor shared his adventures with journalists who observed his emersion into the Tibetan lifestyle and Buddhist religion. I could relate to the desire to find my true self. Yet, looking back, I think I was more caught up in the uniqueness of the different cultures I visited than I was at being introspective. However, that short talk with Mr. Hansen has opened my eyes. I need to release that chip on my shoulder once and for all. If I can't find a way to make peace with my past and regain control over my career, I'll become just as he warned. Old and alone.

After witnessing my parents' marriage, I had to acknowledge, the odds were against me ever having a healthy, committed relationship with anyone. Hell, I'm about to turn thirty-seven and have only slept with one woman more than once. Boy, was that a colossal mistake. My high school sweetheart had been my first and only love. Well, what I thought was love. I never told her that I loved her, but that wasn't a sentiment I witnessed shared between two people. The only time I could remember hearing it was from my nanny. After my girlfriend and I split, I heard she moved on to some college kid. In hindsight, I'm not sure why our break-up had caused me to avoid getting close to anyone.

Maybe it was the rejection. Perhaps the lingering questions about her relationship with Sam. Or possibly it was simply that I failed at something. Who knows? I admit I've never completely recovered from that experience. Between that and the stellar association my parents modeled for me, why would I want to chance a relationship with someone?

Yet, Bella had me considering things I hadn't before. As much as I was anxious about her coming to my home and waking with me the next morning, I had to admit, I was disappointed when she was gone. More unsettling than her leaving was not being able to find her afterward. For all the times I'd shielded my identity to protect myself from a woman latching on, I was the one that was left reeling. And the whole time, she was right down the hall. *Was she possibly in a relationship with Donovan? They seemed awful chummy for a physician and student.*

These sojourns have taught me one thing over the years. I no longer believe in coincidence. I have to face the fact that there's some purpose in completely humiliating myself. If I've lost my chance with her, maybe the universe is giving me a chance *with me*. I've been traveling the world, appreciating its splendor, yet couldn't be bothered to appreciate the beauty surrounding me every day. Sure, I could appreciate a hot piece of ass. But not the amazing people I was fortunate to meet. Had that humbling event not happened with Bella, I don't know that Mr. Hansen's words would've sunk in. I would've offered him a flat, professional, take it or leave it apology and been on my way. But, facing what I'd said to the woman I'd been pining for had made me feel raw. Exposed.

As I sit here on the balcony of my bungalow, looking out onto the Indian Ocean, I feel gratitude. While I normally look for ways to incorporate a sense of inner peace on these trips, suddenly, those activities seem superficial. I acknowledge it'll take more than one trip to Bali to get myself centered enough to stop acting like an egotistical maniac, but it's a start.

Standing from my sling-back chair, I walk toward the teak table in my room. The list of superfluous adventures seems silly now. I'll still visit sites I want to see, hike, and connect with mother nature, but I need to focus on the things that'll help me find peace. I still plan to surf, hike, and take in the local culture. But visiting local temples, a yoga retreat, and a spa for meditation, relaxation, and soul searching are the mainstays of this trip. I'm shocked to find I'm no longer interested in rounding out my trip with a nameless lay. That would no doubt leave me feeling more empty than rejuvenated. Particularly after my night with Bella.

Grabbing my backpack, I head for the beach. There's an area for snorkeling not far from here and a local restaurant offering fresh seafood by the water. Perhaps I'll plan my next day trip to a local temple and waterfall over dinner.

Only a few days remain on this trip before I have to head home. I've built a cushion into my time off, allowing me to make some adjustments to my schedule once I return home. I've definitely come to the realization I can't handle another stressful two weeks like the one before arriving in Bali. I'll advise Dr. Morgan I can only cover a week at a time and will adjust my schedule to allow for the combined workloads from here on out.

Walking toward the tranquil spa before me, I take in my surroundings. The posh resort I'd booked had a spa with amazing amenities yet, I wanted something more. I'd found this retreat had been recommended by the concierge as a place of healing. There was a sparkle in her eye when she spoke of it. I've decided to try acupuncture and a therapeutic deep tissue massage while I'm here.

The more time I spend in Indonesia, the more magical the place becomes. I don't know which is more welcoming, the climate, the unbelievable scenery, or the gracious people? What I do know is that eventually, I'll need to head home, and I need to bring back the serenity I've found here. I cannot return to the stress-filled life I was living. Maybe these treatments can send me back in a better headspace.

As I rinse off in the narrow open-air shower facing the ocean, I breathe in the tranquil space. Turning off the water, I towel off and head to the massage table as the attendant had instructed. Lying face down, I attempt to stretch my shoulders. I'm not sure what I was expecting to happen with the acupuncture technique, but maybe its effects will be more obvious later. I'd read it could help release pent-up aggression and stress. At this point, I'm willing to try anything.

Hearing a door open behind me, a woman's voice greets me as she comes closer. We go over the usual questions regarding massage, and she advises she'll be placing a warming lotion on my skin. As the droplets hit my aching trapezius muscles, an instant sizzle is present. There's no concern for burning my skin or allergic reaction, but a true warming sensation that's quite different than I've experienced with past massage oils. Her nimble fingers dive into the overstressed muscles and tissue of my upper back, and I start to feel more relaxed than I've felt in weeks. Not since lying in bed with Bella had anything felt this good. *Fuck. Where'd that come from?*

As the woman's skillful hands stroke my skin, I can't help but recall how my body had reacted to Bella. I've been with hundreds of women, and no one had ever made me feel that alive. What's more, I'd never felt so satisfied afterward. Curled up against her sleeping frame, I felt truly sated. No trip to Bali or the Maldives could touch what she'd done for me.

My surgeries had gone amazingly well the weeks following. While I blamed the poor surgical experiences of late on the team at St. Luke's, I had to admit there'd been some less than pleasant procedures performed at Mary Immaculate as well. The common denominator here is me.

I'd felt so at peace after that night with Bella. Is that what had me chasing after her every Friday night at the club? Do I want more of the magic she possesses? Her black magic that soothes my nerves and allows me to perform at my best? Or is it her I crave? Maybe after all of these years, I've met my match. Why else did I give her my first name in the courtyard? Hell, she now knows my place of employment and my home address. I barely know her name. Her name tag said Isabella Potter. I take it Bella is a nickname?

Advising me to roll onto my back, the masseuse lifts the blanket for me to turn, and I catch the appreciative look she gives. Her eyes trail up my body to my face, and I realize it's my dick she's smiling about. Normally, this would be the point where I'd insinuate a *happy ending* would be welcome, yet, today, this feels wrong.

My thoughts are redirected to the skilled woman above as I again feel the warm, sizzling sensation of massage oil connecting with my skin. I observe the dark-haired beauty. She's tall, thin, and undeniably gorgeous. She's very much my type. As more oil is applied to my lower belly, a smile crosses her features at my perusal of her.

"You like?"

Unsure if she is asking about the massage oil or her, I simply answer, "Yes." I witness a familiar glimmer in her eyes as she looks back toward me, and I quickly decide to clarify. "What is that?" Tipping my head toward the brown bottle in her hand.

"This? It's warming oil. To loosen your body," she answers, her voice thick with her native accent. She suddenly dips her head down to my navel and traces her tongue from my abdomen to my chest before looking up at me. "It's organic," she says with a wink.

Startled, I sit up, holding the sheet against me to prevent further unwanted *licks*. "I didn't mean to give you the wrong impression. You're beautiful, but I'm not—"

"It's okay. I saw you had responded to my touch," she says, pointing to my dick which is still at half-mast. My thoughts of Bella had apparently gotten me hard, not this woman. Why did this feel so wrong? Was it because I'm here for a different purpose? I'm looking for peace instead of pussy, for once. It couldn't possibly be about Bella. *Hell, that's never going to happen now.*

"Thank you for this." I reach for my clothes, hoping she'll realize this tantric massage has come to an end. "I'll settle up in the lobby once I'm dressed." As she turns to leave, I quickly dress. What the hell has happened to me? I haven't gotten laid in over a month. She was mine for the taking. Granted, I'm committed to getting myself to a better place. But I never committed to becoming a monk. Grabbing for the door handle, I stop momentarily. Grabbing the brown bottle of warming oil, I take it with me to the front desk.

Exiting the spa, I rub the back of my neck. I'm not as relaxed as I'd been a few short moments ago. Maybe that acupuncture session will kick in by the time I'm back home. *Lord, I need to get my life back on track.*

Home, sweet home. Dropping my bags by the door, Charlie wishes me well and heads out the way he came. The place feels better than I remember. Not sure why. Normally I'd come home from these trips, missing the locale almost before I landed. Yet, this trip was entirely different. Don't get me wrong. I loved everything about Bali. But, try as I might, I still feel unsettled.

Limping toward the den, I stare out over the pool. Maybe that'd be good. A nice soak in the hot tub and a swim in the pool to ease the achy muscles now in spasm after such a long flight. I strip out of my clothes and walk toward the jacuzzi. As the jets pummel my back, I rub at my aching left leg. I can't believe after the failure of that massage, I managed to fall on the rocks of the Gitgit Waterfall. At least I hurt my leg and not my hands. Plus, there's been no major change since the acupuncture. Not sure I'm giving that therapy a second chance.

Starting to overheat, I gingerly climb from the hot tub and dive into the still waters of my pool. This overindulgent home has its benefits, beyond the fact there's no need for clothes when I live alone.

As I come up for air, I look up to see a blonde standing at the side of the pool. She's wrapped in a towel, blue eyes dancing with mirth. "Who are you?" I bark. It's in this moment I remember I'm completely naked. Swimming closer to obstruct her view with the side of the pool, I notice she's biting her lower lip. *What the hell? Have I slept with her before? Is she some weird stalker?*

Things instantly become clearer as Sam comes into view. Walking up behind her, he wraps his arms around her waist before placing his chin on her shoulder.

"You're back. Welcome home, big brother. Candy, this is Sebastian. Sebastian, this is—"

"What are you doing here, Sam? This is *my* home. You can't keep dropping in uninvited."

"Chill, big brother. I called and found out you were away and didn't think you'd mind. I can see you're back and need your space. We'll get out of your hair."

"How long have you been here?"

"Only a few days. Don't worry, we left you some food."

Jesus, I'm not worried about the damn food. I watch as Candy wiggles her fingers at me as she walks away. Hopefully to put some damn clothes on and leave. I'm starting to feel as tense as when I left.

The following morning, I manage to swim about 100 laps in the pool before settling in for a leisurely breakfast when my cell phone pings. Looking at the screen, I see it's Dr. Morgan.

"Hey, man. What's up?"

"Hey, Sebastian. Glad you're back. I hate to ask, especially after everything you did while I was away, but is there a chance you could swing by St. Luke's? Donovan Grant called. He has a patient there that could potentially need to go to the OR. I'm not asking you to take him. But, if there's a chance you could evaluate him to see if he needs to be operated on today versus scheduling outpatient, I'd really appreciate it. I just started a case that's going to take me hours. I hate to leave the guy sitting there if he could go home."

Rubbing my neck, I shake my head at this unwelcome intrusion. At least I won't have to operate. "Sure, I'll go." I admit I like Donovan. Even if he is sleeping with Bella. He only calls when it's necessary. I know he typically works nights, so this patient has probably been there a while.

"Thanks, Bas. Just text me once you've seen him. I'll be free this afternoon if he needs to go to the OR."

"Got it. It's no problem," I say as I end the call. Taking a sip from my coffee, I decide to call Nick after this ER visit. Maybe I can arrange to spend time with him at the lake. A few beers with him might finally take the edge off.

Walking into the ER doors, I head for the nurses' station. Once directed on where I can find the patient in question, I head down the long corridor to the back section of the ER. St. Luke's has one of the larger emergency rooms I've ever worked with. It's not a trauma center yet still has enough traffic to keep almost fifty ER beds full most days.

As I get closer to room twenty-seven, I notice movement in the hallway to the left. Unable to keep moving forward, I'm shocked to see two people in a tight embrace in this environment. I become even more shocked when I realize it's Jeff. He doesn't strike me as someone who'd act this way on the job. As he steps back, the other party in this equation comes into view. Bella.

CHAPTER ELEVEN

Isabella

"I need more pencils, Mom." The words trail along behind Austin like billowing smoke from a train as he blasts from the front door back to his room. An order for his favorite charcoal sketch pencils was placed yesterday, and he's practically worn out the carpet walking back and forth from his room to the mailbox in anticipation. This isn't new. This is his normal display of impatience.

"Austin, you still have one left. That should hold you until the package arrives." My attempt at consolation has, I'm sure, fallen upon deaf ears. He has a one-track mind when it comes to art. Checking my cell phone, I verify the order is due to arrive today. Upon quick reflection, I realize the orders for sketching material have morphed from monthly to weekly. We spend a great deal of the stipend we receive from his father each month on Austin's art supplies. Knowing the money Rick earned is supplying the very habit which probably sent him running for the hills brings me joy. Most fathers would be proud their child has such love and dedication to their art. Yet, Austin's creativity didn't fit inside the carefully constructed box Rick had placed him in. Rick would never admit his leaving was connected to Austin having special needs. I mean, how could a physician shun his flesh and blood because they have autism? It was easier to blame it on me. Yet Rick had no patience for Austin's behavior. His son's lack of engagement when we met people out in public only furthered the strain. I, for one, am thrilled my child doesn't color within the lines.

Wandering into the kitchen, I almost drop the teapot as the phone's chirping breaks the now silent space. Grabbing a dish towel to sop up the spilled water from the counter, I notice Bailey's name flash across the screen. "Hey, Sis. Whatcha doing?"

"Hi, B. I only have a few minutes, but I wanted to verify you still need me to hang with Austin this Friday."

"Oh, yes. Thank you. I feel like I've been leaning on you a lot lately. I should hit up the boys. A guy I'm working with is celebrating his birthday at The Zone, and I really want to join them."

"Bella, you know it's never an imposition. Heck, if I ever find someone worth spending a Friday night with besides you and Austin, I'll ask Dominic and Damian to help out."

I know my brothers love Austin and don't mind spending time with him. Yet, I'm hoping to get my drink on and let loose a little and don't really want the grand inquisition from them if I'm home late. "Well, it's only a matter of time before some hot guy figures out what he's missing and starts chasing after you, Bailes. But I'll enjoy your free Friday nights as long as I can have them."

I hear giggling dancing through the phone line as she continues, "So are we talking all night, so at least one of us can get lucky?"

"I don't foresee getting lucky hanging out with work colleagues. I'm hoping to get a job there when I graduate, not a reputation. But I'd appreciate it if I could swing by and get him in the morning. I plan to have a few margaritas and cut loose with my co-workers. Don't want to worry about how late I'm out or waking you and Austin when I stumble in."

"It's really no trouble. He's a joy. I honestly feel like I learn from him when we paint together." Bailey has set up a room in her home for Austin to express himself and feel as comfortable there as he does here. "I sit with a glass of wine, watching him paint, and it's otherworldly.

How he creates... it's magical, Isabella. We need to get him into a class that can help him fine-tune some of his skills."

"I'm still looking into it. Richmond has some services available for people on the Autism spectrum, but I haven't found anything specifically related to art that wouldn't make him feel more uncomfortable. I don't think he'd be able to relax if the class size was too large or someone was judging him as he worked."

"I understand. Hey, I have to run. Just drop him off Friday evening anytime. I'll have his pizza ready."

"Plain cheese." I shake my head.

"Yep, plain cheese."

"You coming this Friday, Bella?" Mike asks as we walk down the ER hallway.

"What, to Jeff's birthday celebration? Definitely!"

"Great. It should be fun. I've never been to The Zone. From what I hear, it's a lot of fun."

"I'm looking forward to it." I park the portable x-ray unit outside door four and verify I have the right patient. After introducing myself, I verify we're obtaining an ankle x-ray. This routine is starting to feel standard. As nervous as I am about graduating in a few weeks, my confidence is growing that I can do this.

After the x-rays are obtained, I grab ahold of the handle and begin to maneuver the beast to our next patient. The thought of shedding the student scrubs and finally working after all of these years has me standing taller.

"Hey, I heard through the grapevine that Angie's leaving," Mike whispers. "Maybe if you get your application in right away, they might bring you on before they list the opening. You'll have great references. We all love working with you."

I feel my face light up with the news. "Mike, that'd be fantastic." I clap excitedly. "And thanks for offering the reference. I appreciate it. It'd be great to transition from student to an employee here," I practically squeal.

"Well, someone looks happy." Donovan approaches, smiling down at me. How did Donovan and my brothers get the tall genes while I practically need a booster seat to see out of my windshield? *Booster seat...*

My internal dialogue has churned thoughts from weeks gone by. *Shake it off, Isabella.* We've all moved on from there. Dr. Lee seemed sincere. It's okay to have your guard up but put it behind you. He was just angry... *or was it something else?*

"Keep it on the down-low, but I told her I'd heard there might be a full-time opening in radiology. I think she needs to jump on it," Mike continues to keep his voice low.

"That'd be great, B. I'd love to see you here full time." My dear cousin smiles.

"Oh, me too."

"Donovan, a patient with chest pain just came in. We're putting him in room twelve. He doesn't look good," the concerned nurse advises.

"Got it, Jess. Gotta go, B. See ya." Donovan strides over toward his newest patient, and pride fills my chest. Who knew that smart-mouthed Irish boy could've turned out to be such a capable physician?

"Austin, I'm home." Shutting the door behind me, I place the takeout from Luigi's on the kitchen counter. I'll take a quick shower and then get dinner ready. As I turn to head toward my bedroom, a bottle of unopened chianti beckons. *Hmmm, this should do just fine.*

As I walk the narrow corridor toward my room, I stop by Austin's door. He's fully engrossed in his sketch pad.

"Your pencils come today?"

"Yes, Mom," he answers, not breaking eye contact with his pad.

"What did Mrs. Samuels bring you for lunch?"

"Chicken tenders." Another flat reply bounces off the black and white sheet of his latest creation.

"I'm heading to shower, and then I'll get our dinner ready. I got us baked spaghetti."

Austin's face suddenly pops up. "With extra cheese?"

"Yes, Austin. Just how you like it."

"Thanks, Mom," he replies, no smile or emotion evident. But I know it's there. The only time I can recall seeing a smile was when it appeared he was trying to mimic the faces around him. The grin was not a reflection of his joy. My boy has other ways of expressing that sentiment. Others may miss it, thinking his flat facial features indicated a withdrawn life of depressing solitude. Yet my special man has a unique way of expressing himself. He shares his love through his creations, his presence, and his mannerisms. I know my boy is happy. I pray Rick's absence doesn't bother him much. But I honestly feel, deep down, he's happy.

Turning on the water, I step into the shower and attempt to wash away the workday and relax into a nice evening at home. My shoulders begin to sag under the hot spray, and I consider how very much I have to be thankful for. This is a habit for me. I say my morning prayers of gratitude before opening my eyes fully each morning and repeat this when I'm in the shower after work. Surrounded by people in the hospital who are sick or hurt continues to remind me of how blessed I am.

I'm fortunate to be healthy and surrounded by friends and family who care for Austin and me. Bailey has been a godsend as well as Mrs. Samuels, my kind, retired neighbor. She's been so thoughtful to look in on Austin when I work and make sure he eats. He feels comfortable knowing she's next door, and I know if he needs anything, he won't hesitate to ask her.

Margaret Samuels is a kind, beautiful woman who seems to have a soft spot in her heart for Austin and me. She's been divorced for many years, and her only son lives out of state. I often feel I can see her mind drift to a time where it was just her and her son when she watches Austin and me together. From what I can gather, her ex-husband left the picture soon after her son was born.

She often declares that her son, Declan, and I would make "a cute couple." However, I've lived next door to Margaret for over ten years, and to this day, I've never met him. The only pictures I've seen are faded snapshots about her home from when he was young.

The first time I saw them, I had to do a double-take. It was like looking at the childhood photos of my brothers. The similarity was uncanny. I guess Irish boys all look alike at that age. But this isn't an avenue I'm interested in pursuing. I've suffered enough rejections from the men I've dated after my divorce to last a lifetime. I certainly don't want to do anything to cause my relationship with Margaret to sour.

There haven't been many relationships with men since Rick. The few men I dared introduce to Austin didn't stick around long. I no longer bring anyone around him. I don't need Austin questioning where they went or why we aren't friends any longer. My dating life isn't worth the risk of affecting my son in a negative way. We're doing okay as we are. I get my needs met and can focus on my work, my friends and family, and my son.

Rinsing off, I contemplate the last time I *got my needs met*. It's been difficult to not let my mind wander there often. It was the most passionate night of my life. Although I'd love to have another meaningless encounter that left me completely sated for weeks on end, knowing the potential for seeing Sebastian in the hospital has made this seem all sorts of wrong. There are way more negatives on this checklist than positives. Mind-blowing orgasms aside, he's a cocky, rude, arrogant playboy. I've already survived one run-in with him, I'm not chancing a second. If only he hadn't made me feel so—

"Mom, I'm hungry."

"Oh, Austin, I'm sorry. I'm coming out." Leave it to me to get lost in dirty thoughts in the shower.

Quickly toweling off, I throw on my robe and head to the kitchen. Plating baked spaghetti for Austin and myself, I inhale the rich blend of tomatoes and herbs. I can smell the delicate aromas despite being covered in two pounds of mozerella. One day, Austin is going to end up constipated with as much cheese as he consumes.

"Okay, dig in. Thank you for waiting for me," I add. On occasion, I allow Austin to serve himself when I bring home takeout. Yet, with Luigi's baked spaghetti, I learned the hard way. He practically ate the entire pan, leaving me a handful of pasta and a salad the last time. He has a limited palate. He enjoys chicken tenders, fish sticks, and anything covered in cheese. But Luigi's is his favorite, and his eyes are always bigger than his stomach.

Twirling my decadent pasta around the tines of my fork, I watch as Austin pops up from the table toward the sink. "You're done already?" *He must have inhaled it.*

"It was good, Mom."

I can't help but laugh. "Okay, I'll finish up here and join you in a bit." This is our customary routine. When he doesn't eat in his room, he tears through his meal so quickly I'm unsure how his tastebuds are in contact long enough for him to enjoy it. He's in such a hurry to return to his drawing. I often finish my meal with a good book, perusing my phone for any fun posts on social media, or just enjoying the silence after a long day.

Placing my dishes in the sink and putting away the leftovers, I grab my chianti and head down the dark hallway toward Austin's *studio*. We live in an older home along Monument Avenue in Richmond, Virginia. There's no way I could afford this without the money Rick provides each month, but it's there to provide for Austin and me, and I've loved this home from the day I laid eyes on it.

The home is considered Colonial Revival in style. It's a dark red brick with red-tinted mortar and round arches over the windows on the third floor. The exterior has two classical columns on the entrance to the porch, mimicking many of the other brownstones along the popular midtown location. The building was turned into a duplex some years back, and we rent the lower unit, which has a sitting room, a dining room, two bedrooms, and one bath. It's small, but all we've ever needed.

Entering his modest space, I take a seat in the sling-back chair in the corner across from Austin's twin bed. Looking from the bed to my overgrown child, I realize I probably need to upgrade. He's pushing six feet already. He'd probably rather I stick to an extra-long twin versus a wider bed, as he has it pushed against the wall in the corner of his room to leave as much space as possible for his studio.

The walls of our entire home are painted an eggshell white with the exception of one. The wall directly in front of me, which abuts the door to Austin's room, is more than likely several inches thicker than any other in the house. It isn't a firewall or built to provide soundproofing but has too many layers of paint to count. Early on, it was evident Austin was not a fan of canvas and easel. I suppose it's too restricting for him. He gravitates to painting directly on the wall. This made Rick crazy and honestly took me years to come to terms with, but it's only a wall.

Sometimes he creates a portrait in the center of the wall. Occasionally, he groups a collection of different paintings. But most often, he creates a mural covering the entire wall with brilliant, rich color. After witnessing the uninhibited bliss that shone from my beautiful son's eyes when he was in the throes of a new creation, my earlier frustrations faded away. Why on earth would I stop him from doing something that gave him such joy?

It saddens me when we paint over something he's worked on so tirelessly. Austin seems to find peace in the process, having let go of his attachment to the production almost from the moment he lays down his brush. Pictures of his masterpieces hang throughout our humble abode. Reproductions. How I wish I could keep an original to cherish. Yet, this is how he works best, and I refuse to cage him. Bailey can occasionally get him to sketch or paint onto canvas, but this is usually if she takes him to the park or along the water. For now, I accept his gifts in the form they're given.

Taking another sip of my wine, I close my eyes as the fruity chianti tickles my tongue and warms my throat. My cheeks warm, and I smile as I watch my son, curled up in his beanbag chair, sketching like his very existence depends on it. Glancing up, I tilt my head, trying to decipher the current work in progress. Austin's work is vibrant. If I had to give a likeness, I'd probably say Van Gogh. Particularly the landscapes. There's a movement to his work that draws the eye, wanting to learn more. It'd be wonderful to let others see what amazing talent my son possesses, but Austin is content to create. My pride shouldn't make him uncomfortable. Instead, I bask in the glow of my private art show.

"It's Friyay!" Erin calls out as we sift through the current x-ray orders awaiting us. This week has dragged on and on. I'm ready to get my party on.

"Man, I'm so jealous. You guys get to live it up, and I'm going to be here with Cliff all night," Rhonda says, pointing to an older radiology tech who only arrived an hour ago and has already fallen asleep in the dark corner, light snores emanating from his overweight frame. "I can tell who's going to be doing all the work around here." She huffs, pointing her thumb to her chest and shaking her head.

"How do you put up with him?" Mike asks.

"Awe, he's a good guy. He'll step it up once I prod him or bribe him with food." Rhonda giggles. The two have worked the same shift for years. Although she protests regarding missing out on the party, I have it on good authority she never joins the group out, opting for spending time with her family instead. "Oh, Jeff. I got you something. It's in the bag over there on the counter."

"Awe, thanks. You didn't have to do that, Rhonda."

"I know. It's not much, but I wanted to help you celebrate."

Everyone has their eyes glued to Jeff as he opens the bright red birthday gift bag and withdraws a card and a mug. He turns the mug for everyone to see a picture of Sammy Davis, Jr. with a balloon over his head that reads "The Candy Man can." Everyone laughs, but I think my laughter is more at the realization only Jeff, Rhonda, Cliff, and myself are probably old enough to know who Sammy Davis, Jr. is.

"Only two more hours between me and clocking out. I can't wait to get ready for the big night," Jeff states with a huge smile. "Come on, Isabella. Let's knock out these x-rays, so the time goes by faster."

"You got it." I grin at him.

"Hey, Kat. How are you?" I greet my favorite ER physician assistant.

"I'm good. I wanted to see if you were available to make a birthday cake for Grace. She's turning one soon, and I'd love for you to make her cake if you're up to it. My niece and nephew loved the last one you made."

"Sure, I'd love to. Just let me know when."

"It'll be in a few weeks. We're having her party at the lake house. Nick and I would love it if you and Austin could come and join us."

"Oh, Kat. That would be awesome. We'd love to come. Boy, I'm getting invited to birthday parties all around lately. I feel like a kid again."

"Oh, yeah?"

"Jeff's birthday is today. We're heading to The Zone later."

"I'd love to crash that party. I love it there. Maybe I'll meet you guys." She smiles.

"I bet Jeff would love that."

"Okay, I better get to work before Dr. Silver sees me here talking to you and asks me to do a pelvic exam for him." Kat laughs.

"Got it. Hope to see you later." I wave, walking back into the x-ray department.

"Bella, come here a second." I hear from around the dark corner of the suite. I recognize Jeff's voice and wonder what he's up to.

Stepping through the door he's opened for me, I notice he cannot contain the grin on his face. We're in a hallway just outside of the x-ray department that extends from a wing of the emergency room.

"I have a surprise for you," he states, handing me a familiar-looking red birthday gift bag.

"Um, did you forget it's *your* birthday?" I chuckle.

"Nah, just regifting the bag."

Reaching inside, I find a folded piece of white printer paper. *Hmmm, what is this?* Looking up at him, he's beaming at me now. I'm unable to stop laughing at his pure joy. Unfolding the document, I quickly realize it's an x-ray order. *What on earth is so funny about—*

"I got you a clavicle," he bellows like I just won the lottery.

The ridiculous excitement over this long-awaited order instantly causes my cheeks to ache with their stretch across my face. I throw my head back in glee. Jeff pulls me in for a hug, and I can't help but hug him back. I'm so thankful to have met such great friends here.

"Let's knock out that elusive last item on your checklist and celebrate tonight," he whispers into my ear.

Pulling back with a wide smile draped over my face, I turn and lock eyes with a very stern surgeon. *What's that look for?*

Sebastian spins on his heel and walks with determination toward the front of the emergency room, stopping briefly to pull Kat in for a hug.

Doesn't he know she's married? Or perhaps, he doesn't care.

CHAPTER TWELVE

Sebastian

"Bas, wait up!"

Turning abruptly, I note my buddy, Nick, running across the physicians' parking lot in my direction.

"Hey, glad I caught you. You got any plans tonight?"

"No. What've you got in mind?"

"Well, Kat is going to The Zone with some friends. I'd much rather drop her off and grab a beer with you before we head back home."

"Who has Grace tonight?"

"Ha, Gavin."

"Your Big Brother Association smart-ass little brother, Gavin, is watching your soon-to-be one-year-old daughter?" I laugh sarcastically.

"Well, Gavin and my dad. Gavin's actually good with her. Watching the two of them together, I think he wanted a sibling. I can relate, having been an only child."

"Tell him he can have Sam," I quickly interject.

"Ha. Well, Gavin would never admit it. When I asked him if he'd watch Grace tonight, he just asked, 'How much?'"

"I've always liked that kid. He kinda reminds me of... well, me."

"Fuck, there's not enough room in this world for two of you." Nick shakes his head. "You up for dinner and a beer?"

"Sure. Why don't you swing by the house? We could have dinner and drinks there. I'm not up to going out."

"Yeah, that'd be great. I'll give you a call after I talk to Kat. See ya, man."

I turn toward my car and feel better about the direction my evening is going. Seeing Isabella in Jeff's arms had rattled me. Other than a fascination with my one-night stand, I have no claim to her. What's more, Jeff is a good guy. If that's who she has her eyes on, I should leave her be. He could treat her far better than some asshole with commitment issues.

"Hey, Nick." I greet on speakerphone as I take inventory of my grocery items.

"Bas, is it okay if Kat comes with? I'm not dropping her off at the club until later. Just didn't want us to have dinner after ten."

"Hell, of course. I'll have dinner waiting. Steaks okay?"

"Sebastian, are you kidding. Steaks would be great. You need us to bring anything?"

"Nah, man. Just yourselves. It's been way too long."

Having hit my gym and showered after arriving home, I set about getting the steaks ready for the grill. I'd picked up a few things on the way here, anticipating leftovers for the weekend. There'd be plenty for the three of us. I had a personal chef that would leave items in my fridge each week. I'm not much for cooking, but I enjoy grilling on occasion.

Bzzz. Bzzz.

Glancing down, anticipating Nick had forgotten something, I instead find Sam's name flashing across the phone screen.

"Hello?" I practically sneer into the line. After his unwanted visit to my home the night I returned from Bali, I can only imagine what this call might be about.

"What a greeting," he chastises.

"What do you want, Sam?"

"Well, I was hoping I could crash at your place to—"

"No."

"Wait, what? Why not?"

"Because you have a home. Are you suddenly renting it out? Why do you need to crash here?"

"Well, I've gotten myself into a bit of a bind."

"Sam, you need to be a little more careful about who you're fucking. I can't have your women and their scorned lovers coming here after me."

"Oh, you're one to talk."

"I've never had to hide out from anyone. I don't bring women here. You're a grown man. Get your shit together."

"Come on, Bas. Just tonight," he pushes.

"No. Figure it out," I bark, hanging up the call. Shaking my head at the intrusion, I have to admit my life hasn't been that different from my party boy brother's. It was clear our upbringing affected our ability to enter a committed relationship. We both bounced from one woman to another. It was simply our approach that was unique. While I'd made a conscious decision not to date anyone twice or let them into my world, Sam would string them along until he was ready to move on. I'm sure he frequently juggles more than one woman on his dance card.

Feeling my ire rise, I make my way to the bar for a drink to shift my mood. *Damn, Sam.* Looking over the oversized kitchen island at the steaks, I add some seasoning and place them back inside the fridge next to a salad my chef had previously prepared to await Nick and Kat. Reaching for some foil, I wrap the potatoes and head toward the grill.

Sipping my scotch, I relax into the Adirondack chair by my outdoor kitchen and look around. I'm damn lucky to have this life. I have everything a thirty-seven-year-old could ask for. A nice home, a nice car, a great job, and the ability to travel wherever I like. So why had this recent sojourn to Bali left me feeling more flat than the trips of the past?

"Anybody home?"

Jumping to my feet, I turn and see Nick and his bride at the front door. "Come on in. You guys never need to knock." Greeting Kat with a kiss to the cheek and a slap to Nick's shoulder, I usher them inside. Walking behind them toward the great room, I notice they're holding hands. *Could anyone really have that kind of relationship with someone, still wanting all of that after the honeymoon ended?*

"Spuds are on the grill. There's a salad in the fridge, and I'll throw the steaks on in about ten to fifteen. You want a beer?"

"Sure, I'll take one," Nick answers. Turning behind him to peruse the fridge, he asks Kat what she'd like.

"Oh, I'm sticking with water. I think I'll have enough alcohol later."

"Just don't overdo it," Nick scolds. "I don't need to hear tales about the Dirty Librarian at work next week.

Almost choking on the sip of scotch that has just landed on my tongue, I look to the two in front of me for clarification. "Um, what's that?"

"Let's just say the nickname Katarina's friends have given her for the way she dances isn't that far off the mark," Nick explains to Kat's chagrin.

"Okay, okay. It's not that bad." Kat crosses her arms, bright pink cheeks reflecting her embarrassment. "How was Bali?"

"Ah, I see what you did there," I tease. "It was beautiful. It was exactly what I needed. You'd love the resort."

"Well, after hooking us up with the resort in Antigua and Barbados for our honeymoon, I'll take your word for it. You know how to travel," Nick replies.

"So, Sebastian. When are you going to start taking someone with you?" Kat asks coyly.

"What do you mean?"

"These places are gorgeous, tropical destinations. So romantic. And you go alone."

"I go to relax and get myself centered. If I brought a woman, I have a feeling I'd feel the complete opposite."

"Why is that?" She prods.

"Katarina. I'm not relationship material. And the older I get, the more set in my ways I am. I haven't been in a relationship with a woman in twenty years."

"Don't you ever get lonely," she asks, leaning into Nick and resting her cheek against his shoulder.

"Sure, sometimes." I take another sip of my scotch, wondering how this conversation became about me. "I get what I need and move on. It's all I'm capable of. Besides, who needs to ruin a relaxing, tropical getaway worried about entertaining someone else? I can find the cure to loneliness anywhere." I wink.

Kat rolls her eyes and shakes her head before reaching for her water.

"I don't think you give yourself enough credit, Bas. You're not your parents," Nick bites back. There's a hint of irritation in his tone. "I hate to see you give up before you've even tried."

"Has there ever been anyone you thought you could date?" Kat asks, taking a sip from her water and watching me with bated breath.

"Maybe when I was young. But, that ended badly, and so I chose not to repeat that mistake in the future."

"Awe, come on, Sebastian. You said it yourself. It's been twenty years. Don't you think you could give it another try?" Kat pushes.

How had this conversation even started? "Sure. If I find someone worth taking the risk, I'll let you know," I toss back cynically. "Now, do me a favor and grab those steaks, will ya?"

Fortunately, the evening's conversation moves away from my love life, or lack thereof, and instead on lake living, Grace's development, and my idiot brother. Apparently, Nick and Kat had unknowingly met him when visiting my family's vineyard on a date some time back. Kat laughed at the memory of that evening, explaining how she thought I'd picked up a side hustle when she saw him. "The resemblance between the two of you is unbelievable."

"It's getting that time," Nick announces, looking at his watch. "I've got to get Kat to the club. You still up for another beer?"

"Hell yeah. Why don't I get Charlie to drop Kat off so you can kick back?"

Nick looks to Kat, who shrugs her shoulders in silent approval before he turns to me and says, "Nah, man. I'll take her. I don't want her riding there alone in your fancy car."

"You two are something else," I say, shaking my head. "When does the honeymoon end?"

"With this one? Never," Nick answers, pulling his wife's palm to his lips for a kiss. Lucky Bastard.

"Come on, we'll all go. We can have a drink once we get back. Maybe hit the pool." Standing from my stool at the kitchen island, I grab the leftover steak and place the plate directly into the fridge. "But you're helping clean all this shit up when we get back, loverboy."

"Deal," Nick says, grabbing Katarina's hand as they head for the door.

~

"You look happy, man. Really fucking happy," I say to Nick as we're sitting in the hot tub, cold amber bottles of ale in hand.

"I didn't think it was possible, feeling this way. I fought it tooth and nail, but I've never been so grateful to have lost at something."

Shaking my head, I tilt back the bottle, letting the cold lager coat my throat. "It couldn't have happened to two nicer people," I say, holding out my bottle to clink with his.

"Thanks, Bas. But if it could happen for me, there's no reason—"

"Let me just stop you right there."

"Sebastian. Has there ever been anyone? Well, besides her?" Nick knows better than to mention her name. I don't let myself consider her any longer. It's no longer anger, simply a reminder of a significant failure I don't plan to repeat.

"No. Just haven't let myself go there. My life is full. My career is demanding, and any increased stress has a direct impact on my performance. I don't need any distractions. Things have been tough enough lately. I'm sure it comes with getting older, but my precision and reaction times are slipping. I need to keep my focus on my work."

"I used to say the say damn thing. Knowing she's waiting at home for me has lowered my stress level. My job performance is better. Plus, having someone supportive to listen and give you space to decompress is nice. Hell, sometimes after a tough day, I just want a hard fuck without words, and she just gets it." Nick takes another pull from his bottle, and I consider all he's said. His words aren't without merit. Jesus, just the last point alone would be worth considering a relationship if I didn't have to contend with all the other issues.

"That's all fine and good if you can find the right one. But I don't want to let my guard down simply to end up with someone like Sophia. Hell, or worse yet, my mother."

"We both dodged that bullet." Nick laughs. "I'm just saying, it might not be such a bad thing after all of these years to give it a try. You might be surprised."

"If after all of these years I manage to find someone who isn't a money-hungry bitch wanting to control me… then yes, I would be surprised."

"Fuck, Bas. You're so damn derisive. Your parents have really done a number on you. I'd try and set you up with Kat's sister, Rachel, but she's got kids, and I think that's probably way more than you'd be ready for."

"Hell, you can say that again. I need kids like a fish needs a bath towel."

"Don't knock it 'til you've tried it. You and Gavin get along well."

"Ah, I love that kid. He cracks me up. Just says what he's thinking. Never gives a shit."

"You're right. He is just like you." Nick chuckles as he finishes off his bottle. "The kid even looks a lot like you, now that I think about it."

"You think so? Lucky bastard." I laugh into my beer. "I can't believe I'm telling you this. But, if it's possible, I think I found a woman who might be just like me." Shocked at my honesty, I tip back the last of my lager, place it on the edge of the hot tub, and reach for another.

"Jesus, that's scary. In what way," Nick guffaws.

"A lot of ways. I've only spent one night with her, but she's as private as I am. Best fucking sex of my life, and that says something.

She left the next morning before I woke up. I only learned her name recently."

"Wait. So you spent the whole night with her?"

"Worse. I brought her back to my damn house. I don't know what I was thinking other than I didn't want her to get away."

"Man, this girl must be quite the looker."

"It's more than that. There's something about her. I could sense it before I took in her appearance. She's not the usual young, thin, blonde type I hook up with. She's our age. A tiny, curvy brunette with a sassy mouth and an attitude to match." I take a larger pull from my beer, letting the hops cool down my overheated body.

Pulling myself out of the hot jets, I realize it's been silent for longer than I'd expect given my admission. Turning questioningly to Nick, I find he's smiling at me.

Shaking his head, he laughs. "That's how it fucking starts, Bas. That's how it fucking starts."

An hour later, we're dried off and are heading to The Zone to pick up Katarina. I have no idea why I've joined him other than this is the most relaxed I've been since... well, since Isabella was in my bed. Shaking that thought from my mind, I look through the windshield as the car begins to come to a stop. I send Charlie a quick text letting him know I'll need him to slide by and pick me up after a quick drink. I have no plans to stay here long. Maybe I should pick up a sweet co-ed while I'm here. I'm relaxed enough I could probably enjoy a leisurely romp without letting my mind wander to women I can't have.

Nick finds a spot and points toward the line of college-aged kids extending from the front doors.

"Hell. I'm not waiting in that."

"No, Kat's going to meet us. She said they're all done for the night."

Retrieving my phone from my back pocket, I text Charlie that it appears I won't be having a drink after all. I barely hit send before raucous commotion bursts from the doors. Lifting my head, I recognize Katarina, Erin, and another guy I think works in the radiology department at St. Luke's. This has barely registered before I see Isabella coming out of the doors, face flushed and beautiful in a short black dress, on the arm of none other than Jeff. My shoulders stiffen as I take in their casual familiarity. His proximity is closer than one would expect a coworker to stand. *Are they intoxicated? Is this who she was running home to?* As the question taunts me, I notice Isabella has stopped moving and is staring directly at me. I can't read her expression. This night's taken a nosedive. Fuck this. I'm going home.

Isabella

What on earth is he doing here? Attempting to keep some semblance of control, I've been careful not to have too much to drink tonight. I'm still taking an Uber, so I don't have to risk driving, but I need to remember these are potential work colleagues. I don't need to do or say anything that could get back to the job. As well, I can't let Jeff think I'm interested in anything more than a friendship. Loneliness fueled by alcohol can be a combustible combination.

Yet, the last thing I expected to see when we came out of the club was smoking hot Sebastian Lee standing in the parking lot. And talk about flammable. I've never seen him looking this casual. Don't get me wrong, he's a smoke show in his expensive suits and scrubs. But standing tall with his legs spread shoulder-width apart, one hand tucked into his dark jeans, his black long sleeve button down clinging to the firm muscles of his chest and arms is more tantalizing than I was prepared for. His dark inky hair has fallen over his forehead, almost appearing damp. I just want to run my fingers through the tousled strands.

Trying to allow the cool night air to bring my mind into focus, I look over to Kat, who is wearing a strange expression. *What is that all about?* There's no time to continue considering her morse code when Nick swoops in, wrapping his arms about her.

"Did you have a good time, kitten?"

"Yes."

"Did you save the Dirty Librarian for me?"

A giggle escapes me before I can stop it, contemplating this saucy little conversation I've eavesdropped on.

Katarina flicks her eyes over to me and answers, "Yes. Only for you."

My cheeks pink, and a warm sensation tickles my senses at the voyeuristic moment. Unable to stop it, I allow my gaze to drift back to Sebastian, only to find he's gone. I can feel my face fall at this realization. Unsure how to interpret the disappointment I now feel, my eyes reconnect with Kat, who is now wearing an unmistakable look. It's a knowing look. *Don't be silly. You've probably had more to drink than you thought.* One of Katarina's well-manicured dark brows lifts in question, and there's no doubt. She knows.

CHAPTER THIRTEEN

Sebastian

Well, that didn't last long. Something tells me getting back into the Jacuzzi and having another beer won't bring back the relaxation from earlier either. To think I thought I might try to get laid, just to have the star of my wet dreams walk out on the arm of someone I have to work with day in and day out.

This is the longest I can ever recall going without getting any pussy. It would anger me if it weren't so ridiculous. I've never let a woman get to me like this. I could probably get Charlie to take me to any bar in town and find a willing partner. But, I already know it won't matter. Any sex would be lackluster after her. The masseuse in Bali practically threw herself at me, and I turned her down spectacularly.

It's probably some weird mid-life crisis. Questioning my life choices. Either that, or Nick and Kat have put some sort of hex on me to join their honeymooners' club.

The drive is short from the club to the house. I throw open my door, heading up my front steps without so much as a 'goodnight' to Charlie. Nothing new to him, I'm sure. So long as he gets paid, I doubt he cares. I stomp up the stately steps to the double front doors and instinctively turn the knob, realizing I left the door unlocked. The home is set back from the main road with security cameras marked along the drive, so I've never truly worried about a break-in. More so, an invasion of my privacy from my ludicrous brother.

Recalling his recent phone call, I shout into the empty space. "Sam? You here?" Satisfied I'm alone, I grab a scotch from the bar and flop myself onto the couch. This is depressing. How did I go from such a phenomenal evening with my friend to this? I let the burn of the scotch grab my attention ever so briefly before the conversation from earlier returns to my mind. What would it be like to have a partner waiting at home for me? To have something akin to the relationship Nick and Kat enjoy.

Shaking my head at this nonsense, I take another sip of the mind-numbing amber liquid. "Fairy tales," I utter aloud. I need to face the music. It's me and the hand again tonight. I'll finish off this scotch, pound one out, and try and get a good night's sleep. I need to embrace a brighter outlook tomorrow.

Swirling the remaining alcohol in my crystal highball tumbler, I can't help but recall the way I felt when I saw Isabella come out of the club with Jeff. For the briefest of moments, our eyes connected, and I felt she wanted me too. But I need to face it. That's twice I've seen them entwined. He'd be much better for her anyway. *You're not your parents.* I hear Nick correcting me.

Throwing back the last drops of scotch, I stand from my leather couch. Placing my glass into the sink, I unbutton the top few buttons of my shirt and pull it overhead as I make my way to the bedroom. Removing the rest of my clothes, I get into bed and exhale. What the fuck has become of my sex life where I'd rather jack off to visions of this woman than get pussy with a pulse?

Reaching down, I find I'm semihard just thinking about her. It doesn't take long, replaying the dirty pictures of our hot night together before I'm stiff. I can almost feel her soft skin against my chest as I remember how her body felt wriggling underneath me. The memory of her scent makes my mouth water. My tongue dips over my lower lip, yearning for the taste of her. Her warm, flushed skin. Her nipples. Her swollen, wet folds. Her arousal was like honey on my tongue. I jerk my engorged dick harder, imagining my fingers teasing her opening, wet and willing for my entrance. Everything about that night is burned in my memory. The way she arched her back as I thrust inside her. Her heady moans comingled with the sounds of our flesh slapping together. Our union was animalistic and raw but different than the nameless encounters of my past. It felt as if I could just fuck her hard enough, there'd be more. *But more what?* It was like she held the key to something elusive.

Fisting my cock harder, I strain to feel the electricity present when she was here in my bed. *I should have never washed these sheets.* Saved a pillowcase or something. Maybe the scent of her would give me what I need to cross the finish line.

I picture how she looked, kneeling at my feet, taking me down her throat. She was focused on her pleasure, which only added to mine. It was something to behold. Her cheeks would hollow with the glide of her mouth up and down my length and push me closer and closer to release. But watching her succumb to her carnal desires had me holding back for more. It was all I could do to keep from emptying down her throat, but I had to feel her wrapped around me.

Tugging harder on my dick, I can tell I'm getting close. There's a familiar sensation building in my balls, and while it won't consume me as she had, it'll be enough for tonight.

Picturing her sweet, dusky pink nipples sitting proudly on display for me, I cup my balls and prepare for my release. Only a few more strokes and—

Ding. Dong.

What. The. Fuck? I'm going to kill him. Maybe if I lie here for a minute, Sam will give up and go away. *Fuck. Did I lock the door?*

Ding. Dong.

Sitting on the edge of the bed, I contemplate going to the door as is until I remember the state I'm in and decide to don a pair of lounge pants. Seeing my brother at my door will piss me off enough without hearing any shit for the state of my dick.

Grumbling the entire way to the door, I consider investing in a few dogs to guard my home. Sam would run like a frightened cat if I had two Dobermans guarding the house. I'd laugh if I wasn't so fucking pissed off right now.

Swinging the door wide with vitriol on my tongue, my eyes widen in shock, and I clamp my mouth shut to prevent the ire from escaping. I was in no way prepared for this.

"You lost, good girl?"

CHAPTER FOURTEEN

Isabella

"You lost, good girl?" The haughty tone of his voice caresses my oversexed libido as I take him in. He's wearing gray lounge pants, which do very little to mask the firm bulge beneath. His chest is on full display, all of the rippled abdominal muscles fighting the distinct V of muscles for attention. Try as I might, I can't keep my eyes from trailing the sharp lines of corded muscle into his low-slung pants.

Walking past him into his home without invitation, I attempt to keep my cool. I don't know what's come over me, this brazen behavior. Maybe it's my sixth sense? The feeling he wants more every bit as much as I do. This is reckless, returning to the scene of the crime. Reckless for any number of reasons. The very least of which could be total humiliation if he's already entertaining someone new or shuns me for coming here unsolicited. Now that he knows we work together, he likely doesn't want to continue anything with me. I take a deep breath, gathering strength as I saunter down the hallway.

"Shut up." I turn my head to make eye contact with the egotistical playboy. "Things will go much better for you if you keep your mouth shut."

"As I recall, you quite liked my mouth."

"I prefer it when you're mute," I toss back. I'm walking directly to his bedroom like I own the joint. As I take a left into the massively large room fit for a king, I get to the edge of his bed and spin to face him. I need some sort of acknowledgment this is happening so I can exhale.

He approaches, looming over me. "I'll try to use my manners then. My nanny always said not to talk with my mouth full." He smirks as the rich timbre of his voice fans the flames of my desire. His arrogant playfulness is all the affirmation I need.

Reaching for the small hook at my side, I unsnap the black cotton wrap dress I'm wearing and allow it to pool to the floor at my feet. Standing in front of him in black three-inch heels, black lace panties, and a matching bra, I pop my hip in question. *You joining me, big boy?*

There's no need to question his interest. The bulge present in his gray loungewear earlier is now tenting directly at me. Choosing to keep control of this night for as long as he'll allow it, I slowly saunter forward and drop to my knees. I think I hear a heavy groan above me, but this could be wishful thinking. *Hell, it could be my nerves shouting in my head right now.* I've never been so bold in all of my life.

Extending my arms to the waistline of his pants, I slowly draw them down his bronzed, muscular legs. *How the hell can anyone be this tan and work in a hospital all day?* There's no time to consider such nonsense as his impressive erection juts in my direction, stealing all of my attention. I've replayed his physique in my mind time and time again after our one night together, but nothing beats the sight of him in living color. He's long and thick, and dare I say it, beautiful. Gazing up his torso, I take in the corded muscles of his neck, shoulders, and pecs before trailing down to the smattering of dark hair about his chest. I'm completely overcome with the sight and smell of him. He's all man. I'd beg for anyone to show me a more perfect specimen.

I hear his throat clear, impatience growing at my ogling. Deciding not to give his urging any undue attention, I open my mouth and drag my flat tongue across his balls before gripping his shaft and stroking upward. This delicious groan is unmistakable. I give a few more licks before taking him as deep into my throat as I can. There's no sense teasing him. He's hard as a brick. And the sight of him in this state could bring me to orgasm with just the slightest rubbing of my thighs.

"On the bed." I hear him growl above me after only a few slow glides of my tongue. *Well, that didn't take long.*

Getting to my feet, I reach down to remove my shoes before feeling his strong arms scoop me up and place me on the coverlet. Leaning over me, he gently slides his thumbs into the sides of my panties and lowers them over my shoes. *I guess those are staying on.* Sebastian takes his thick erection in hand and strokes slowly, his tongue darting across his lower lip as he gazes at my core. Bending over me, I await the feel of my bra being unsnapped only to find he's reaching in his bedside table for a condom.

"Take it off, good girl." He dips his head in the direction of my bra as he rolls the rubber over his shaft. Unlike our first night together, where he pleasured me to a climax before entering me, he's in no such mood to delay gratification tonight. I barely get the clasp of my bra undone before I feel him grab my hips, pulling me toward him, the wide head of his cock nudging my opening.

I'm wet and wanting, but I recall how wide he stretched me the last time. Before I can consider this further, he's thrust himself fully into me. My body arches at the delightfully painful intrusion, and I attempt to calm the pulse racing in my ears. A familiar burn is seeping into my sex, and I slowly shift my pelvis back and forth as I adjust to his size, appreciating his stillness at this moment.

"Fuck, you feel good," he moans. "So fucking good."

Needing something to cling to, I reach for his firm, muscular ass and press my nails into him. My pelvis is starting to rock with the need for more. Unsure if he's reading my cues or taking what he needs, he begins to steadily withdraw and plunge back in, burying himself to the hilt. This only lasts for a few steady strokes before his pace becomes frantic. It's so good. The fullness, the sensation of being savagely taken by such a virile man.

"Shit."

My hackles sit up a little. Is something wrong? That didn't have the same enthusiasm behind it the prior utterances possessed.

He's lost complete control, and I hold on for dear life as he pounds into me. It's so good, but there's no friction—

"Oh, Fuck!" His shout bounces off of the dark walls of the room like a silver sphere in a pinball machine. Looking up, I find Sebastian with his back arched, muscles taught, a sheen of sweat clinging to his masculine form. But the pièce de résistance is the look on his face. It's a rapture I've never encountered before that's painted over his features as he pulses inside me. I've seen men and women make faces of extreme pleasure in response to their unbelievable climax in porn with such an expression. *Sure, I've watched. I'm no saint. I've been single forever, for god's sake.* But none of them ever looked like this. It's breathtaking. I dare say it'll give me spank bank material for the rest of my life.

As his breathing settles and he starts to move, I decide, beautiful or not, I'm not wasting this opportunity to goad him. His head drops down, tousled inky strands dropping over his beautiful face, and I make sure he sees my smirk on full display.

"Fuck. Sorry," he says, slowly withdrawing from me.

The disappointment I feel is immediate. *That's what I get for teasing him. Karma is a bitch.*

"I was halfway there before you got here," he mutters.

"What?"

"Never mind." He stands from the bed and walks into the adjoining bath. I know this from my last visit to his stately abode. I couldn't tell you much about the room, given my nervousness and need for quick departure. The room was dark, and I did what I needed and ran.

Suddenly feeling self-conscious, I adjust myself in the bed and consider whether I should grab my clothing and head for the hills. As I reach down for my bra, I see Sebastian return to the bedside, and I look up at him in question.

"Now, where do you think you're going?" he teases. Placing a large, firm hand on my chest, he pushes me back into the luxurious bedding and climbs over me. "It's rude to leave before dinner is served."

He drops down to my waist, and my heart rate begins to hasten.

His large, flat tongue dances across my opening, and I practically shout my appreciation. He's right. I do like his mouth. He continues to tease my swollen opening, darting his tongue teasingly around my clit time and time again until he abruptly withdraws from me. The cool air of the room replaces the warmth of his talented mouth, and I nearly whimper. Taking a deep inhalation, I try to calm my racing heart as I feel a warm, almost sizzling sensation dripping onto my flesh. *What the hell is that?* The sensation is so sensual. Unexpectedly, the dripping stops, and his tongue returns. Was that his saliva? *Leave it to this devilish man to have spit that sizzles.*

Stepping up his delicious assault on my core, I feel two thick fingers thrust into me as he clamps his mouth around my bundle of nerves and sucks. My body quakes at the edge of sanity, my thighs tightening around him. He returns to swirling his thick, warm tongue over my quivering nub and strokes me more aggressively. I'm teetering on the edge of this orgasm, and he knows it. With a final flick of his fingers dragging along my sweet spot as they curl inside me, he sucks from my clit, and I detonate.

"Oh, god!" I cry out my release as my body shakes in response to my overwhelming climax. Feeling Sebastian move about, I lie still, hoping to regain control of my limbs. Opening my eyes, I glance up to see my earlier smirk mimicked back at me. *Yes, I like this bitch, Karma.* The man may be full of vibrato, but he's earned the right with his performance in bed. I'd never let him know it. But I have to face facts. There's sex, and then there's Sebastian sex. I'd never have imagined an orgasm could feel like this. This arrogant, dirty devil has ruined sex for me with any other man.

My thoughts are interrupted as the sizzling sensation returns. Dipping my chin to my chest, the sight of a dark maroon oil drips onto my taught nipples. I expect to see steam erupting as the warmth intensifies, but any chemical reaction is doused by the feel of Sebastian's hot, wet tongue and teeth clamping around the sticky peaks. He laves them equally, giving each a tight tug before releasing them to look down at me.

There's a heat in his deep blue gaze. It's as if he's trying to tell me something. But I can't risk reading too much into this just to leave disappointed. I've learned the hard way what getting your hopes up can do to you. I'm simply going to enjoy this moment for what it is. A ravenous release between two hot and hungry individuals. A need being sated. Nothing more.

My world immediately turns topsy turvy as I'm flipped onto my stomach, and my hips are pulled back into him. His strong, capable hands grip my ass firmly just before I feel his teeth bite into my right cheek. I feel the wet flick of his tongue over the wounded flesh before a growl escapes him.

"What I'd give to fuck this sweet ass." I feel him grip my bottom firmly with both hands before another groan escapes.

"Nothing the size of my arm is going back there," I quickly rebuke over my shoulder.

"We'll see," he says before gliding his now hard cock between my ass cheeks. Abruptly, I feel his warm, strong hand press between my shoulder blades, pushing my chest down into the bed. His stance shifts above me as he reaches for another condom, and I can feel my sex start to pulse in want. Hearing the rip of the foil wrapper, I bite my lower lip in anticipation of what's to come.

He presses the wide head of his cock into me, and the familiar sensation of the oil he applied earlier returns. Lord, I'm not sure I'll live through this orgasm. He slowly ruts into me, and I'm keenly aware it's not to be gentle. This motion is purely to tease my swollen flesh with this powerful sex oil he possesses. As if he's made his point, he begins pistoning inside me with deliberate strokes.

"Oh, please," I beg. I don't even know what I'm begging for, but the intensity of this sensation is too much to bear. The sounds coming from my mouth are desperate, obscene. I turn my head, attempting to bury my sounds in the pillow, when his voice rises above me.

"Turn your head back to me, GG. I want to hear it. I want to hear you shatter for me, good girl," he commands.

Doing as I'm told, I trade embarrassment for sensation and give in to the lust he's stoking. As hot as he's making me, I feel I'm just inches away from where I need to be to orgasm. I can hear his balls slap against me as he pounds into me, his grunts making me more and more wet for him. I'm so close.

His hot body drops lower, still slamming into me before I feel his hand fall away from my hip. Concern grows that he may be close to release, and I'll be left wanting, still chasing this sensation when his hand returns, cupping my sex as he thrusts me deeper into the bed. The warmth of the oil is on his fingers as he places them over my clit, the friction of the pounding setting off my climax like dynamite.

Screaming utter nonsense, I give in to the most powerful release I've ever experienced. Lights dot my eyes, and I worry I'll lose consciousness until I'm jolted back into awareness by the harsh chanting above me.

"That's it. Come all over my cock, good girl." Grunting resumes. "Fuck. Fuck. Fuck." More grunting. "Your tight pussy is going to make me..." The grunts are suddenly replaced with a hard thrust and a decadent growl as his body jerks his release into me.

His panting slows, drifting down from above. It coats my skin, adding to the bliss that is Sebastian.

"Fucking beautiful." His ragged breath comforts me. "So fucking beautiful."

It feels like forever before he withdraws from me. The sensation of having his body cover mine, still buried within me, is one I don't want to forget. There's a warmth, a comfort I've never felt from a man. This is dangerous. I can't entertain such things, particularly with a playboy like him. This is purely physical. I can remember the sensation, but I need to separate it from thoughts of comfort or emotion.

Turning on my side, our eyes connect momentarily, and there's a longing reflected back at me that makes me question whether I'm alone in my precarious thoughts. But that would be crazy. *Don't let yourself even go there, Isabella.*

He stands to dispose of the condom, and I instinctively pull the sheets up. Realizing I'm still wearing my black heels, my head drops back onto the pillow in amazement. I'd completely forgotten they were still on. I consider removing them until I remember where I am. I may be leaving shortly.

Sebastian's back by my side, sliding under the sheets and pulling me into him. I feel him pull my leg toward my chest, running his strong hands up and down my thigh before gliding down to my calf and fumbling for the clasp of my shoe. A soft kiss is placed on my left shoulder before he adjusts to reach for my other heel, making clear his intention. I'm not going anywhere.

Rolling in his arms, I look at his beautiful face. For all of his bravado, he *is* stunningly handsome. The man should be on magazine covers. His strong, chiseled jaw covered in a perfect dusting of scruff has me reaching for him. I dip my fingertip into the deep dimple in his left cheek as he gazes down at me with smiling, bright blue eyes. His lips are full and soft, and I drift the pad of my index finger from his dimple to his big, sensual mouth. It swiftly dawns on me, he's never kissed me. Well, not on my mouth anyway. Is it intentional? I'm sure it's his way of keeping women distant. I shouldn't be offended. I know the score. But I can't help wondering how they'd feel on mine, just the same.

A giggle erupts from deep in my chest as he mimics my actions, placing his fingertip in my pronounced dimples one at a time, twisting to demonstrate the depth. The smile he gives me makes my heart rate speed up, reminding me of the danger I'm in if I continue to entertain these thoughts.

"So, what was that stuff?" I ask, trying to steer this ship toward something more concrete.

"Stuff?" He repeats, tapping the end of my nose.

"The magic sex potion?" I prod.

"Ah, you liked that?"

"Liked? I didn't know anything could feel like that."

A soft chuckle escapes him as he buries his face in my neck. "Maybe I need to take you back to Bali with me. We'll buy them out of every bottle," he says, his face quickly morphing from playful to stoic almost before the last word has left his mouth. The change in his expression resembles a curtain falling at the end of a boisterous musical. You sit watching, not wanting it to end, but too tired after the long night to fight its conclusion. "It's late. Let's get some sleep," he adds, rolling back to turn off the bedside lamp.

What just happened? The awareness of considering *a next time*, a trip of all things, must have broken through his post-sex haze, I suppose. This realization jolts me away from the tender moment we just shared, back to the space I need to stay firmly planted. Safely in the single mom zone.

Lying on my side, wrapped in his strong arms, surrounded by his delicious scent, I await his heavy breaths. It'd be tempting to give in to this and stay, but my body will yearn to be back here enough without the added torture of what my heart might consider. I don't need to make this any harder than it already is. *You enjoyed two ravenous nights of sex, the likes most women could only dream. Don't be foolish and let emotions get in the way of this. This is the very last man that would want to build a life with you and your incredibly unique child.*

CHAPTER FIFTEEN

Sebastian

Stretching my arms overhead, I relish the delicious pull of my overworked muscles. Last night was one of the best evenings I've enjoyed in a long while. From the dinner with Nick and Kat, beers with my best friend while relaxing in the hot tub, and a surprising night with Isabella, I couldn't have planned a better evening. Rolling to my side, I already know before confirming it with my eyes that she's again flown my bed before dawn.

Rubbing my hands down my sleepy face, I question why this bothers me. Is it the curious nature of who she's rushing home to? Is it the unfamiliar desire to know more about her? The craving to have more of her? Or is it the lack of control I'm used to possessing over everything in my life?

And what the hell was that maybe I'll take you to Bali shit? I'm growing more and more certain Nick and Kat have placed some voodoo hex on me. That would've never escaped my lips if they hadn't planted that thought earlier in the evening. I'm sure of it. Hell, I even gave her a damn nickname. I usually didn't have any need for identification, real or otherwise. It was a quick romp and go. I didn't need anyone calling out my name, just to look me up and find out I was loaded. Between my family's vineyard and my surgical practice, it wouldn't take long to track me down. But I had to admit, hearing Isabella scream out my name would be hot as fuck.

Placing my hand over the wrinkled sheets where she slept, it's evident they're no longer warm. How long had she waited to run? Who was she running to? The question instantly tugs at the afterglow I'm enjoying, and I decide to focus on the positive. I got laid. I got laid spectacularly. I got laid with the one girl I thought was beyond my reach. I'm going to replace any negative thoughts with those of my incredible night. There's no sense in entertaining questions I'm not willing to pursue. There's no room in my life for a woman. Especially a woman full of hellfire and brimstone like that one. She'd take no prisoners in getting what she wanted. Hell, she marched in here last night like she owned the place. And I let her.

I've enjoyed a leisurely weekend. It's been nice not having to be on call, allowing the chance to unwind following my trip. I've enjoyed some heavy workouts, tried some new meditation music, done laps in the pool, and even purchased some new cigars. If anyone had seen me drinking my scotch, stogie lit, reading Pride and Prejudice in the hot tub, I would've told them Sam had broken in again.

I hate to admit I feel a little kinship with Fitzwilliam Darcy. There's an arrogance I'd be a fool not to acknowledge. Yet, mine has been directed at everyone at large versus Mr. Darcy's disdain for the lower class. I'm not truly an arrogant prick. As Mr. Hansen so eloquently identified, within ten minutes of meeting me no less, my issue appears to be the oversized chip on my shoulder.

I concede I need to work on my people skills. My interactions with Bella and her colleagues in radiology brought that issue to the forefront. It's difficult when the stressors of the surgical suite collide and cause catastrophe in an otherwise controlled environment. These are delicate procedures requiring intense concentration. Yet, it's up to me to act like a professional. After much thought, I'm aware I can't continue to blame these events on those around me. I need to take stock of what's contributing to the decline in my performance. The common denominator is me.

My stomach growls, reminding me I've had little to eat today. There are plenty of leftovers from the other night, so I open the fridge to decide what to prepare when my phone dings. Looking down, I discover the answering service number on the screen.

"Dr. Lee," I answer questioningly. I'm not on call, so I'm unsure what this could be about.

"Hi, Dr. Lee. This is Gail with the answering service. I'm aware you aren't on call tonight, but the on-call orthopedist, Dr. Morgan, asked if I could reach out to you.

This seems odd. Dr. Morgan also does hands. Why would he need me?

"It appears the patient in question is a patient of yours. He's in the emergency room with what appears to be a post-operative infection. Dr. Morgan said he could see him if you were unavailable but wanted to reach out since it's your patient."

Hell. This wasn't on the docket this evening. "Sure, Gail. I'll head in. You said, Dr. Morgan. This patient is at St. Luke's, I take it?"

"Yes, sir."

I grab a protein shake and decide to put off dinner until I can enjoy it. Hopefully, this will just require a consult and not irrigation in the operating room. Collecting my keys from the table near the garage, I make my way to the emergency room.

Fuck. Mr. Anderson has an infection that'll require a copious amount of irrigation and IV antibiotics. Trying to reassure myself this is a product of diabetes and poor life choices, I pray this isn't a reflection of my recent lackluster surgical cases. Regardless, it's a few extra hours in the operating room on a Sunday night I hadn't planned on.

As I make my way toward the OR, I pass an exam room door and stop in my tracks. "Mr. Hansen?" *Hell. Why is he in the emergency room? Is his wound infected also?*

Standing to his full height, he reaches his uninjured hand out to me in greeting. "Hi, Dr. Lee. How are you?"

"I'm well. I hope you are too. Is your hand doing okay?"

"Oh, I'm not the patient. I brought my lady friend. She slipped and fell, and I wanted to make sure she was okay. Our hips aren't made like they used to be," he jokes. "She's getting an x-ray."

"I get it. I've suffered more injuries approaching thirty-seven than I've had in twenty years."

"Getting old ain't for sissies. How have you been? You seem to be in better spirits than the last time we spoke."

I can't help but grimace at the recollection of my unprofessional behavior. My treatment of Isabella quickly comes to mind.

"I'm sorry. I didn't mean to bring up a sore subject," he apologizes.

"No, no. Don't apologize. It was an astute observation. I have to admit I haven't quite gotten over my behavior that day. I'm making a conscious effort to never allow that to happen again. I appreciate your candor that day, as well as your forgiveness." Beginning to turn away, I find my feet refuse to move. "Mr. Hansen? When are you scheduled for your follow-up? Did I miss that?"

"I saw a PA. Ava, was it? Beautiful girl. So kind. She said you were away."

"Ah, I was. Is everything doing all right?"

"It's great, son. No worries. You did a great job. Time will tell if I can use it the way I did before. And if I can't, it's no fault of yours."

"Well, make sure when you make your next appointment, they schedule you with me."

"Certainly."

"It was good to see you, sir. I'm headed to the OR. I hope your lady friend is okay."

"Thank you. I'm hoping it's just a bruise. But, I won't mind an excuse to dote on her a little." He winks. *Sly old dog.*

Giving a quick wave and a smile, I continue toward the OR. I'm not sure what it is about that man that makes me want to be a better person, but I'll take it. Let's just hope his hand fairs better than Mr. Anderson's.

Three hours later, and I'm finally heading to the car. I guess I can skip the steak and potatoes at this point. I'd settle for a quick burger and fries. And I don't eat that shit. Hopefully, there's a charcuterie tray in the fridge. My personal chef knows I can eat my weight in cheese. Dragging my weary body toward the physicians' parking, I realize it must be change of shift for many of the hospital staff. There are multiple nurses and technicians dressed in a variety of scrubs and lab coats exiting the building.

As I approach my car, I catch a glimpse of a petite brunette in the overhead lighting. She's parked in an adjacent lot, but there's no doubt in my mind it's Isabella. I watch as she waves to a colleague, opens her driver's side door, and slides in.

Getting into my vehicle, I start the engine. What is it about her that steals my breath? Is it all of the unknowns that pique my curiosity? I have an innate need to know more. Don't ask me what I'll do with the information once I have it. But the lack of control is starting to war with me.

Before I can think better of it, I've pulled out of the parking area with deliberateness. My pace is controlled, allowing me to follow her from a distance. *What the fuck am I doing? Jesus, I've turned into a damn stalker.*

I watch her SUV closely, trying to keep a safe distance as she takes the onramp onto the highway. Hell, I hope she doesn't live an hour away. *I can forget eating at this point.* She drives a Lexus. It appears to be in good condition. This is a rather expensive vehicle for a radiology student, I surmise. Maybe she bought it used. Or maybe her husband has a good job?

As we approach the midtown area, she gives her signal she's exiting the highway. Continuing to follow her, leaving several car lengths between us, I try not to question my sanity as she drives closer to the historic section of Richmond. There are fewer vehicles on the roadway now. It's late, but this area is still populated enough she wouldn't realize anyone is following her. Holy hell, the last thing I want is for her to think I'm… what? Stalking her? *What the hell is happening to me?*

Her vehicle starts to decelerate. There's no way. We're on Monument Avenue. It's a large roadway with a center median that is dotted with incredibly expensive homes, many dating back to the early 1900s. While many of these residences were converted to multi-family units after the second World War, there are quite a few in the Monument Avenue historic district that have been lovingly restored and value in the millions. Regardless, there's no way someone on a radiology tech salary could afford to live here. There has to be a significant other. Does she have a sugar daddy? She seems a little old for that, but maybe they've been together a long time, and she's looking for someone to rock her world. Could she be in an open marriage?

Pulling into a vacant space about five cars from where she's parked, I sit and watch. I'm not sure what intel I think I'm going to glean from observing her unlock her door, but I'm here now. Might as well see this through. She exits her vehicle, slinging her purse and some type of carryall over her shoulder. As she locks her car, she ascends the steps of the dark red brick brownstone, and as she reaches the top step, she drops her keys. I have a hard time making out much from this distance, particularly with the large porch columns beside her.

My breath suddenly catches as the door swings open. I cannot see who it is but suspect he's tall as she gazes up to see them. My heart sinks at her expression. She may be looking for a romp on the wild side, but there's no denying the way she feels about whomever she's greeting. Her smile is genuine and stretches from ear to ear.

As the door shuts behind her, I sit feeling more confused than before. I need to let this go. Let her go. Nothing good can come from pursuing her. It seems clear she rushes home to someone she cares deeply for. And as much as I can't stop thinking about her, I'm certain of one thing. If I tried again after all of these years, as Nick and Kat have encouraged, I'd only fuck it up for both of us.

CHAPTER SIXTEEN

Sebastian

"Ouch."

I yelp as the scalding hot coffee sloshes from my cup and lands on my hand. Unsure if it slipped or if I slammed it onto the counter harder than I should have due to my irritable mood, I acknowledge I need to turn my day around quickly, or things will continue to descend into an unproductive spiral.

While the first surgery of the day wasn't as explosive as those of late, my focus remains off. *I'm sure it had nothing to do with my lack of sleep.* Unable to shake the image of Isabella smiling up at her housemate, I had a fitful night's sleep. I don't know what possessed me to follow her home. Why had this morbid curiosity about her taken hold? What was it about her that had me wanting to break all of my rules?

I need to consider this a wake-up call and move on. As much as I'd love to know the reasons why she went home with me, much less returned, I need to walk away. She's obviously in love with whoever greeted her at the door. She couldn't escape my bed fast enough. I'm unsure a couple of hot nights of sex could lure her away from that. And why do I want to?

This simply has to be the relentless need to win. Wanting something I can't have. I'm not stupid. My competitive obsession is worthy of a support group. Pursuing her only to have her lose everything for her indiscretions would be beyond cruel. I've had not one but two incredible nights with her. I should simply face the fact that it's a dead-end and return to my habit of meeting women for a one and done. The last thing my stressful career needs right now is adding a relationship to the mix. That's one challenge I can admit defeat.

If only I could stop thinking about her. She's everything I could want in a woman if I were to try. *Well, minus the live-in lover.* Who knew this five-foot-nothing dynamo would rock my world and leave me questioning everything? But if there was the chance for more, would my actions leave us both shattered when I discovered the challenge had been met, and I was no longer interested? How many people would I destroy in this quest? *Just walk away, Sebastian. Put your energy into your work and leave that girl be.*

Isabella

"Hey, B. It's been too long," Dominic practically shouts into the phone.

"I know. It's been a juggling act managing school and Austin. At least I see Donovan if I can't see you and Damien."

"Well, I'm glad one of the Potter boys can keep an eye on you," he jests. "So, what's up? How long 'til you graduate and are a working girl?"

"Watch it. You make me sound like an escort. It's getting close. That's why I'm calling, actually. I hate to ask, but could you keep Austin in a week or two? I'm trying to line up several evenings when I'm off to study for finals, so I don't make myself a nervous wreck. Bailey's been a big help, but I'm hoping you and Damien can watch him a night or two as well."

"Of course, B. You don't even have to ask."

"I won't be interrupting a hot date?"

"Yeah, not likely. We've both been sticking to very casual after watching Donovan and Ashley. That chick is a stage ten clinger."

"I don't know why he puts up with her. I don't see it." According to Katarina, Donovan's current girlfriend even drives the nurses in the ER nuts with her demanding phone calls and rude behavior.

"Well, I have a pretty good idea why he puts up with her. She's hot as fuck and probably sucks—"

"Okay, okay. I don't need that mental imagery," I interrupt sharply.

"Yeah, well, that's the only reason I'd keep her around. Not sure even that'd be worth it for long."

"Well, I appreciate your help. You and Damian," I say, trying to get this conversation away from that unpleasant topic. "I feel like a terrible mother. Pawning my poor child off on all of my family. I can't ask Mom and Dad. They're getting older and set in their ways. I love them, but Austin's little quirks are harder on them. Mom's forever trying to get him to do things he isn't interested in and cleaning up after him. It's hard when you combine OCD and Autism in the same dwelling." I laugh. I know my mother means well, but her need for order will never mesh with Austin's need for freedom of self-expression.

"Isabella Potter. You're the best mother I know, short of our own. You went years without asking for help from anyone. Needing a lending hand to help reach your goals isn't a sign of weakness. You're getting the job done. I never know how much Austin sees, but I believe you're setting a good example for him. Our place isn't set up like yours and Bailey's, but he can bring his sketch pad and go to town while Damien and I watch the game. If he sneaks away, I've got an extra can of paint in storage. I just hope he gets Damien's room this time." His hearty chuckle warms my heart and brings a broader smile to my face. "Besides, I've been looking for an excuse to make five cheese nachos."

"Oh, good lord. Please make sure you give him some fruit. I'm sure a salad has never seen the light of day in that house. If he gets constipated, you and Damien are giving him an enema, not me!"

"Hells bells, B. No way that's happening. I'll make him eat applesauce and put prune juice in his drink if I have to."

"I'm teasing. He'll be fine. Just watch him. He tends to get carried away. He'll eat the whole pan."

"We know. We got schooled on that the last time we made them. We let them cool without watching Austin. The pan looked like it'd been attacked by a pack of wolves when we went back. Now we make his separate. Besides, he doesn't like everything on his like we do. Just gobs of cheese."

"Thanks, Dom. I miss you guys. Hopefully, once the stress of school is behind me, we can get back to meeting up for dinner more often."

"You do what you need to. We're happy to help."

Ugh! This day can't end soon enough. I woke up cranky, knowing it's my least favorite time of the month. The stage just before Aunt Flo comes to visit where I'm moody, bloated, crampy, and horny as hell. My spirits lifted a bit after speaking with my crazy brother earlier. Yet now the hormones are taking over, and I just want to crawl under the covers with a hot tea. Working amongst perky twenty-year-old nurses and technicians who get their nails done and never have a hair out of place is the last place I need to be. Chocolate. I might manage to make it 'til the end of my shift with a few ibuprofen and eating my weight in chocolate.

Finishing up the low back x-ray on a gentleman practically twice my size, I let my team know I'm headed to the cafeteria. Jeff has the day off. I needed the candy man today, if only for the chocolate. I need to watch things with Jeff after the night at the club. He's one of the nicest guys I've ever met. There just isn't any chemistry, and the last thing I need is to start up something with someone in the very department I hope to be working. Plus, I'm not sure how Austin would integrate into a relationship with someone who already has children. That might be more stress than either of us could handle.

Arriving at the small cafeteria, I stroll amongst the options. The choices are limited, given it's after the close of the official lunch hour. The grill remains open, which suits me just fine. I try to eat healthy enough that I can allow something greasy once a month when I crave it most.

"Yes, ma'am. What can I get you?" the smiling chef asks from behind the counter.

"Hi. May I have a veggie burger and fries, please?"

"Sure. Everything on it?"

"Yes, please."

I give in to my thoughts as I await the preparation of my meal. It's so backward. Why is it when your pelvis feels like it is on strike, that's when I'm the most ravenous for some hot and dirty sex? If only this had started a week ago. *That was some of the best medicine on the planet*, I recall. I rub my thumb across my lower lip, picturing the Adonis that took me all night long. Sebastian Lee doesn't hold anything back when he has you in his clutches. And I enjoyed every single moment of that pounding.

"How's it going with Xane?" The brunette in front of me interrupts my thoughts as she speaks rather loudly with her co-worker.

"It's going okay." I can hear a faint giggle in her response. These two appear to be in their early twenties, I surmise.

"Have you slept with him yet? Gina, he's so hot. I'd love to be dating a firefighter."

"Yeah. He didn't waste any time making his desires known. I wanted to hold out, but he's so fucking hot."

"I wouldn't have been able to turn that down. He's like a gladiator. Gah! I bet he's fantastic in bed." The blonde nurse fans herself as she awaits Gina's reply. *Hell, I'm waiting on Gina's reply.*

"Well, he's no Sebastian Lee. But he was hot all the same."

Wait, what?

"Holy shit, Gina. You've slept with Dr. Lee? How did you manage that?"

Yes, Gina. How did you manage that? And when?

"Same as all the nurses, probably. I saw him out at a club one night and pretended I didn't have a clue who he was. It didn't take long. Had a few drinks, flirted with him for a bit, and we were off."

"You'll have to tell me where he hangs out so I can keep my eyes peeled," the brunette responds.

Feeling my stomach do backflips, I'm keenly aware it has nothing to do with hunger pangs or my premenstrual syndrome. I feel sick. I knew he had to be a player. But this is beyond what I'd imagined. The girls saunter off with their food, and I question whether I should tell the grillmaster to just toss my burger. The thought of eating suddenly makes me want to hurl. I feel myself become flushed and assess whether I should grab a ginger ale on my way to the register when I'm acutely aware of warm breath dusting over my nape.

"What's with the disappearing act, GG?" The magnetic, deep tone of his voice causing goosebumps and outrage in equal measure.

My spine stiffens at the intrusion, and I try to hold my tongue, so the recent conversation by one of his fan club members doesn't set me off. You don't want to argue with a woman who is preparing for Shark Week!

"Is there another man in your life? Is that why you're so quick to leave my bed?" He continues to prod, standing entirely too close.

Honestly, I should come with a warning label this time of the month. He better watch himself. I can feel steam beginning to blow from my ears. How dare he have this conversation here. I rotate my head slightly, trying to give him a sharp stare so he'll get the message to leave me alone. About that time, I notice the kind chef placing my veggie burger on the counter.

"Here you go, miss. Veggie burger loaded. I just need to get your fries."

"No need, thank you. I've lost my appetite," answering with a smile so this nice gentleman doesn't think my irritation is directed at him instead of the pompous ass behind me.

Picking up my plate, I can almost feel Sebastian inching closer. *Why is he even in this line? He can probably get a T-bone steak in that elusive doctors' lounge.*

"I just want to be prepared for next time. In case he follows you," he continues to whisper in my direction.

Spinning on my heel, trying to keep my food from careening to the floor, I give him the death glare. "Yes, there is another man. But you needn't worry, Dr. Lee. There won't be a next time," I blurt and walk swiftly toward the cashier. *Screw the ginger ale. I need tequila!* This whole plate is probably ending up in the trash anyway.

CHAPTER SEVENTEEN

Sebastian

What the hell? What on earth had changed enough to cause her to become so venomous? Granted, it's usually directed at something I've done or said. And often, I admit, it's probably warranted. Yet, I haven't interacted with her since we fell asleep together. I went from bopping her on the tip of her nose to awakening to find her gone. If anyone should be snarly, it's me.

Why can't I just pick up on the obvious clues? There's nothing about this scenario that says this is the woman I should try something with. Even if I had the first clue how to make a relationship work, this explosive tart could leave me in bits on the floor. For all of the serenity and focus she restores after a night in bed with her, I'd have to deal with the unknown. Who is this man she lives with? What does he have that I can't give her? Have I met my match, and she's walking away without a second glance? If I continue to pursue this, will I be the one left picking up the pieces? *What the hell is wrong with me? I don't need this.* Not to mention she's made it perfectly clear our liaisons are over.

I stomp back to the office, having completed a routine surgery with only a few minor glitches despite how riled up I'm feeling. What could

I have possibly done to cause such ire in Isabella? Had she seen me outside her home? She has her walls up everywhere except my bedroom. My mind swiftly flashes to a vision of her on her knees, in those fuck hot black heels, sucking me off. The thoughts quickly change to the uninhibited groans of ecstasy that fell from her pouty, swollen mouth as I pleasured her with my tongue. There were no walls constructed there. The way she unabashedly chases her desire is one of the qualities I find most appealing about her. The sight of her giving in to her orgasm is beyond physical. Her rapture is awe-inspiring. Picturing her snarky retort, I can hear her voice mock me. *There won't be a next time.*

This is more than Nick and Kat voodoo. This saucy little strumpet has me tied up in knots. To continue to think this thing with her is purely a physical attraction is a joke. There's so much more to this woman. But I've never chased anyone. And I'm certainly not going to start now.

Reaching my office, I practically throw myself into my chair and get about my work. I need to submerge myself in my patients, hit the gym, and maybe head out for a drink and a piece of ass. That should do it. I'll get a young, blonde, co-ed and fuck this out of my system. Someone the polar opposite of Bella. Two can play this game.

Bzzz. Bzzz.

"Hello," I answer my cell quickly, noticing it's Nick.

"Hey, Bas. Glad I caught you. Wanted to let you know the plans for Grace's party. We're having a few folks over next weekend. It's not going to be anything fancy. Just some close friends and family hanging out by the lake. I already looked. You aren't on-call, so don't give me some bullshit excuse for why you can't come."

"No, man. I'll come. I'm happy for you three."

"Well, good. It'll be Saturday afternoon, around four."

"Got it, Nick. I'll be there. Just promise you won't mention mine is a few days later."

"I don't know what your deal is with birthdays, Sebastian. But okay. We'll only sing Happy Birthday to Grace." I hear him chuckle into the line.

"Good. I have to go. I'll see ya."

"Okay. See ya, Bas."

Entering the date into my calendar, I reflect on Nick's little family. Nick, my sworn bachelor buddy for life, had fallen hard and fast for Kat. They married, and it wasn't long after they returned from their honeymoon that Grace's mother chose an adoption plan for her daughter. Now Nick has it all. His practice is thriving, they live in a beautiful home on the lake, and he couldn't be happier. Even his 'little brother,' Gavin, whom he met through the Big Brothers, Big Sisters Association, has practically become a member of their family.

I scratch at the stubble on my chin and consider how much Nick's life has changed since he declared he'd remain a lifelong bachelor. We'd competed at everything for so long, always focused on career and the next hot lay. Now he's got the brass ring, and I'm just the bitter rival.

Nick's divorce from Sophia was ugly. The only thing uglier was the fact his best pal hooked up with his soon-to-be ex. I admit I'm unsure if I'll ever forgive myself for that transgression. That dalliance wasn't my usual callous behavior with women. The guilt was immediate, and her self-serving ways were revealed early. There isn't enough room in my life for more than one self-righteous bitch. I'm keeping that title all to myself.

My thoughts continue to interrupt any attempt at productivity. While Sophia had been a challenge I'd lost to Nick, pursuing her was very different than the interest I have in Isabella. There's no doubt it was a sick fetish, allowing that tempestuous relationship to move into something sexual. It was the equivalent of a child wanting something that'd been denied by his parents, only to have it beckon him when they weren't looking. I would've never acted on it had Nick and Sophia still been in a committed relationship. Yet, I admit it. I should've never gone near her, divorce or not, and I appreciate that Nick could forgive me for my actions, even if I can't entirely forgive myself.

Yet, this desire to chase Isabella is primal. It's a want I can't contain. Having slept with her twice only deepens the longing for more. Wanting to know more about her is beginning to consume me. Who is this man she lives with, and what kind of relationship do they have?

Why is there no ring? If I was living with her, she'd have the biggest fucking rock I could find. *Wait. What the fuck am I saying?*

Bzzz. Bzzz.

I glance at the screen and see Sam's name flash on the screen. *Holy hell. What does he want now?*

"Yes," I answer without pretending to mask my continued agitation.

"Nice, Bas. I was calling at the bequest of our mother. She's having a dinner party and would like—"

"No," I blurt without waiting for him to complete the sentence.

"You didn't even—"

"Sam. I have absolutely no interest in participating in any sham dinner party she's planning. You know as well as I do, it's all for show. Our parents' marriage is all for show. Her happy, wealthy existence is all for show. And we're just her show ponies." Silence. All I can hear is his breath through the line and wonder if I should simply disconnect the call.

"You're right. I'll let her know you're unavailable."

"Sam?" I bark.

"Yes?"

"Why do you do it? You're a smart guy. You'd do much better to rid yourself of them and live your own life."

"Sebastian, I'm not made of the same stuff you are."

"Like fuck you aren't. You're just being lazy. Grow some damn balls and do something with your life."

"Watch it, Bas. Just because I didn't go off to medical school to become a hotshot surgeon doesn't mean I'm not doing something with my life."

"What're you doing? Last I heard, you were running from some bimbo or her husband."

"Listen. I only called to ask you to come to this dinner party because Mom asked me to. I know the vineyard isn't your thing, but I'm happy there. Sure, I probably need to consider making better choices about the women I see. I can't help that women find me attractive and throw themselves at me. I simply need to screen them better. But something tells me you aren't in a monogamous relationship, so spare me the lecture."

His words hit me like an anvil to the chest, and I picture Isabella smiling up at the man who greeted her in her doorway. He's right. I need to stop the holier than thou routine.

"Sorry. I just hate to see you under their thumb," I mutter.

"I'm not. I know the score. One day when I feel confident they won't come in and take all I've worked for, I'll try to make my mark on the vineyard. But, for now, it is what it is. I'm taking notes and saving it for later when I can run the place the way I want, once and for all."

"I'm sorry, Sam." I pause, trying to end this call better than the way it started. "When that day comes, I'll be first in line at the tasting table."

"Thanks, Bas. I appreciate that. I'll catch you later."

There's so much about Sam I'll probably never know. He shares only what he feels he needs to divulge at any given time. But given how we grew up, I understand how difficult it is to have relationships with people. Always questioning their honesty. Are they a manipulative cheater like my dad? Are they a self-serving, shallow bloodsucker like my mother? How do you develop a friendship or become truly intimate with a partner when you've been spawned from such a shallow gene pool?

Admitting defeat at accomplishing any more work tasks, I gather my things and decide to head out for the day. I can dictate on my charts remotely if needed. I want a good hard workout, a hot shower, and a scotch. *Preferably the scotch neat, with a pussy chaser.* There's no doubt, thinking about this infuriating radiology tech isn't getting me any closer to my goal.

I've changed into my running gear, and for some crazy reason, find myself in my car. My home has a gym, and I hold a separate membership to a private club with a personal trainer. Yet, I find myself driving toward Monument Avenue. There's only one reason I could be headed in this direction, and nothing about this makes any sense. *I've honestly lost my fucking mind.*

Looking at the clock on the car's dash, I notice it's 4:30 p.m. It won't be long before the streets are overcrowded with people returning home for the day. I have no idea how long Isabella's scheduled to work today, but given she was in the cafeteria at 1:30 p.m. for lunch, she's probably working the early shift. They typically disburse around 3:00 p.m. from what I recall from shift changes on the hospital floor.

I pull into a space near where I parked to stalk her the other night. Letting out a heavy exhale, I drag my hands down my face in awe of my ridiculous behavior. *What the fuck is wrong with me?* I stand from my car, coming around behind the trunk to stretch my quads in preparation for a run. I could run anywhere, so how will I explain why I'm here if I do bump into her? I'll tell her a little white lie. I'm training for the Monument Avenue 10K. The race takes place down this gorgeous tree-lined avenue every fall. Runners from all over the world travel to Richmond to participate in the race. I've never run it in the past, *but I could. That's my story, and I'm sticking to it.*

I honestly want to see her 'roommate,' but I can't sit here in my car stalking them in broad daylight. And what good would any of that do? At least if I see Bella, I can confront her. Ask her what had her more irritated than usual with me earlier.

I begin jogging at a slow but steady pace. It wasn't that long ago I'd run every morning. Yet I started to find it played with my head. I'd question why some days I could run for miles while others I was winded after the briefest of jogs. A good brisk run used to clear my head, prepping me for a better, more intuned day in the OR. However, the last time I ran, I nearly required crutches afterward. I'm turning thirty-seven, not eighty-seven. Are all of the years of my high-octane lifestyle catching up with me? God, maybe I'm starting to have a midlife crisis. But instead of wanting to buy a red sports car or a motorcycle, I'm questioning what all of these suckers around me have. Have and probably no longer appreciate. A beautiful woman in their bed, night after night. The same beautiful woman versus the revolving door of bevies I've entertained until now. *Well, until her.*

I can feel my pulse thumping within my chest. I've done this loop multiple times now. Not sure what on earth I think I'm accomplishing here beyond bringing on a heart attack. I haven't been tracking how far I've run, distracted by looking for her car or any movement around her door. I slow my pace so I can check my pulse and the time. It's 5:40 p.m. It's been a while since I've run that long, but it certainly shouldn't be making me winded or my heart pound like I'm a couch potato. Have I been drinking too much? Maybe it's too much cheese. I need to get my cholesterol checked. *Maybe I am having a heart attack.*

Shaking my head at how ridiculous my life has become, I slowly head toward my car. My hair and body are soaked, I'm panting like a wounded animal, and I discover I have about ten blocks before I can sit down as I can barely make out my vehicle in the distance. Ambling the expanse with my hands on my hips, I try to catch my breath as I notice a couple come around the corner from a home a few blocks ahead of me. They're holding hands. The male is tall and thin, and the female looks Just. Like. Isabella. The picture of Nick and Kat holding hands, all goo-goo eyed at each other, flashes in my mind, pouring gas on this irrational fire.

My pace picks up, my curiosity piqued. I try to control my composure, not wanting to look like the maniac I've apparently turned into. If they turn, I need to act casual. *Hey, Isabella, fancy seeing you here... Isabella? Wow, do you live out here? Or... Just out for a run, I was considering the Monument Avenue 10K, and look who I run into... Good Lord, man. What has happened to you?*

The closer I get, it appears her boyfriend is young. Jeez, is Isabella a cougar? What interest would she have in me if she's living with a young stud? At least I can keep up in the bedroom without looking like a heart attack is about to happen, unlike this excuse for a workout. I notice Bella look lovingly up at her mate, and my insanity becomes unleashed. *Oh, hell, who am I kidding? I haven't been sane for days.*

"Isabella?" I shout, only a few blocks from them now. I watch as she turns to me with a questioning look, which instantly turns to what? Anger? Fear?

Her pace picks up as well, and she's practically dragging her boyfriend toward the steps of their home. What am I doing? Just because she likes them young... scratch that. Just because she likes someone else, that doesn't give me the right to ruin it for them. *You've seen what you need to see here, Sebastian. Go home before her boyfriend starts asking questions.*

I slow my pace, trying to do the right thing. But I'm possessed with the need to get a good look at him. This man she runs home to.

"Go in the house, Austin." I hear ahead of me.

"But—"

"Just go in the house, please," she barks.

"Okay, Mom." I hear as he turns in my direction briefly.

"Mom?" I question in shock at the base of her steps, undoubtedly louder and more curt than it should've come out. That's the last thing I was expecting to hear.

Isabella delivers a scowl the likes of which I've never seen, just as she slams the door. I hear the clunk of a heavy deadbolt latch into place and realize this conversation is over.

CHAPTER EIGHTEEN

Isabella

What the hell just happened? He just happened to be jogging outside my door? Did he have his driver follow me home when I left? I don't recall seeing anyone, but this guy has money, and I'm sure there are ways to get whatever he wants.

But, why? Why on earth would this rich, stupidly handsome playboy need to know where I live? Is it because he isn't the one calling all the shots?

"Mom?" Austin's voice breaks through my hysteria.

"Yeah, honey."

"Was that a bad man?"

"No, Austin. That was no one."

"Why was he calling your name?"

"I work with him at the hospital. But, he's no one. Don't worry, okay. Let me get your dinner. It's late." Trying to think quickly on my feet to something that would both comfort and instantly distract him from the current situation, I fire back, "How about grilled cheese for dinner?"

"Yes. I like grilled cheese, Mom."

"I'll make it if you promise to eat some fruit and a small salad. Now go wash up for me, okay," I coax.

"Yes, Mom." There's a slight pause before he says, "I hate salad." Then he heads toward the washroom.

Chuckling at my stoic boy, I grab the skillet and go in search of bread, butter, and cheese. *Thank God he isn't lactose intolerant. I don't know what I'd do.* I find lettuce and ingredients for a small fruit salad in the crisper. At least that diverted his attention away from our uninvited guest. Taking great care not to lop off a fingertip as I'm aggressively chopping away at bananas, apples, and oranges, I can't help but fume at Sebastian's facial expression when he overheard Austin. He'd sneered the word mom, mocking Austin, and appeared horrified. The memory makes my heart lurch.

Sadly, I'm used to this. Not quite this in your face with other men, however. I don't know why it's harder coming from Sebastian. There should be no surprise that the playboy surgeon would be repulsed by a single mom. He didn't want anything from me beyond taking me to pound town. Well, that destination can be checked off his bucket list, and he can now move on to some other willing, what? Hospital employee? *Gah!* How could I have been so stupid? Going back over there and throwing myself at his stupid sexy self. The sweet way he teased my dimples and held me after our ravenous night of unbridled sex was just part of his seduction package, I suppose. His one night, and let's move along seduction package.

But if he's truly a one-and-done kind of guy, why was he at my house? Monument Avenue's a big road with large, beautiful trees and historic homes dotted up and down. I guess it's not that much of a stretch to think he decided to run somewhere beautiful. But my particular portion of this expansive road? I mean, what are the odds, really?

I scrape the chopped morsels of overripe fruit into a bowl and begin spreading butter on the first slice of bread. It's evident I'm taking my irritation out on the innocent pieces of dough as they start to crumble with my overzealous application of butter. Dropping the bread and knife onto the counter, I place my head in my hands. Why am I letting this guy get to me? It's not like I was here pining for him. I mean, sure, he's hot as hell and can back up his prowess with the best orgasms I've ever had. But this is purely physical. I've known it from the start. Yet, the way I felt lying in his bed, wrapped up in those strong, corded arms, started to play with my head each time. I fully expected him to push me out the door as soon as the deed was done. Instead, he pulled me into him and held me so tight. The feeling caused an ache in my chest. Both times, I felt an identical squeeze of longing I had to push away as I crawled out of his bed.

I'm not stupid. I'm lonely. It's only natural for a woman who's been alone this long to want more. It has nothing to do with him. His pheromones just do something to my brain. I guess that's why I started to panic. Yes, I needed to get home to my son. But honestly, the clench of my heart in reaction to his embrace was disturbing. Each time he'd nuzzle his nose into my hair, it was like turning a worn key into a locked door. A doorway that could only lead to heartache. I need to invest in a padlock for that sucker and keep my head on straight. It's painfully obvious he isn't interested in someone like me. I again shudder at the reminder of Sebastian's obvious displeasure when he heard Austin. What's worse, if I ever did decide to enter a healthy relationship with someone… well, Sebastian Lee has completely ruined sex for me with anyone else. Because there's no doubt, he's set the bar higher than any other man could reach.

Grabbing a fresh piece of bread, I try to apply the now softer butter more gingerly before dropping it into the sizzling pan. I retrieve the remaining items we'll need for dinner and finish the grilled cheese before calling Austin to the table. Wiping the remaining butter from my fingers with a dish towel, I walk toward my son's room to see what he's up to. Peeking in the door, I find he has his sketch pad lying on his beanbag chair to guide him as he lightly mimics the drawing with a charcoal pencil on the wall. Tilting my head to take it in, I all but shrug my shoulders, knowing I haven't a clue where he's going with this one.

"Do you want to eat in here or at the table?" I interrupt.

"Can we eat here, Mom?"

"Sure, Austin. I'll make a tray." Returning to the kitchen, I gather our dinner and two glasses of water and return to his room. "Just don't wait too long to eat. Grilled cheese isn't very good cold."

His appreciation for warm cheese apparently gets his attention as he quickly puts down his pencil and comes to stand beside me. "Do I have to eat the salad, Mom?"

"Yes, Austin. You can't live on cheese alone." I take a crunchy bite and let the soothing taste of butter and cheese melt on my tongue before I swallow. "Going to give me a hint what this one's going to be?" I ask, pointing my elbow toward the wall.

"Falling leaves," he replies between bites. "I like all of the colors," he adds.

"Oh, I can't wait to see that one." I smile, taking another succulent bite. I tilt my head, taking in the primitive drawings. Ah, now that he's shared his direction, these do look like leaves. I watch as my son lovingly considers his drawing and devours the remainder of his sandwich in two big bites. *Yeah, who needs a man? I've got all I need right here.*

Sebastian

"Jesus," I shout as the cold water hits my skin. Still distracted by the constant replay of the evening's events in my head, I step back from the jets until the temperature can warm up. Between the exhausting jog and the uncomfortable run-in with Isabella, I couldn't wait to get a hot shower and clear my head. Turning up the heat a bit more, I tilt my head back to allow the spray to pound into my scalp. How did that interaction turn so hostile?

Mom? Hell, I'm sure the stunned look on my face had her thinking it was directed at her son. I'd been so fixated on who the man was she ran home to, I never considered it was a child. Not that he looks like a child. *Fuck, I thought she was a cougar.*

He must be a late teen. From what little I could gather, he almost seemed Gavin's age. He's a little taller than Gavin. His hair color matched his mother's, yet the rest not so much. He's tall, thin, and appeared to have blue eyes in the short glimpse of him I managed.

What's more, he seemed reserved. Despite holding the hand of a woman who resembled a human grenade, he was calm and collected as he answered her respectively and went into the house.

Scrubbing the suds from my hair, I shake my head and turn off the water. Reaching for a thick towel, I make quick work of drying off and finding a T-shirt and shorts before heading to the bar. Tonight's entrée will be of the liquid variety.

Pouring two fingers of scotch, I slump into my leather recliner and take a sip. This whole situation with Isabella has been a cluster fuck of epic proportions. Taking another sip and allowing it to burn my senses to a more alert state, I consider recent events. I was cocky enough to think I could still get her back in my bed after her pronouncement in the cafeteria. The 'other man' was the only thing standing in my way. Challenge accepted.

It suddenly dawns on me that there could still be *another man*. Was her husband in the house waiting for them? Yet, after seeing her with her son this evening, I have a greater sense of calm regarding who she's been running home to. While it's possible someone is waiting in the wings, I'm no longer preoccupied with that. I don't get the feeling Isabella is the cheating type. She appears to take her commitments seriously. I think she returned to me for the pleasure of it. Because she could.

It's obvious how good we are together. Hell, she came to my house and walked right in, taking what she wanted. Not that I minded one damn bit. But it's clear, this isn't one-sided. Maybe her libido is as revved and ready to go as mine is. Yet, this isn't just her body and the hot sex for me. I've never chased after anyone before. So why did I want her to stay? Hell, letting her leave the club the night we met didn't seem like an option. I was almost fanatical about taking her home with me.

If Isabella Potter is my crack, I don't want to go to rehab. I just want another hit. Another snarky smirk in my direction. One more half-smile that pushes her dimples into high gear. I've been in full control practically my whole life. But I've never been happier than when that petite powerhouse barged into my home and started barking at me.

Chuckling at the memory of her telling me to zip it, I swirl the scotch in my glass before taking another sip. As the sting of the alcohol brings clarity to my predicament, it hits me with full force. I want to know her. I like the feeling I could be a better man with her around. Sure, we haven't had much interaction beyond the physical, but her presence does something to me. It's changed me somehow.

It's horrendous to confess that my disrespectful behavior in the OR would probably still be occurring if she hadn't put me in my place. And I wouldn't have entertained a rebuttal from anyone else. Their conversation would've been discontinued on the spot. I recoil at the knowledge of my selfish arrogance but know beyond a shadow of a doubt, it's true. Isabella has been my wake-up call. None of this would've happened if she was just a booty call.

From our explosive reintroduction after surgery to the interaction outside her steps this evening, the writing should be on the wall. Move along, Sebastian. Yet, I don't want to leave. I'm every bit as drawn to her now as I was at the bar the very first night. Hell, I'm not father material. I'm not even boyfriend material. But this damn woman makes me want to consider stupid shit. Maybe it is the sex. Looking down into my empty glass, I consider. *Maybe it's all the scotch.*

CHAPTER NINETEEN

Isabella

Rolling over to the sound of my alarm, I fling my arm over to the phone and smack the screen, hoping it will silence the horrendous noise. I don't think I slept a wink. I tossed and turned until 2:00 a.m. when I finally lamented and got up to take a Benadryl and a glass of milk. The last look at my clock read 3:40 a.m. This is going to be a long day.

I admit the worry over my finals is causing unrest, but this sleepless night was all courtesy of one Sebastian Lee. I need to shake this off. I've gotten used to my existence the way it is. Just because I got a couple of hot nights with someone dreamy, I shouldn't let his rejection affect me more than any other man's. If only I could stop replaying that moment of tenderness when he looked at me like I was somehow different.

Grabbing my robe, I head for coffee. I need to get to work and focus on something tangible. My finals are quickly approaching, and I need to do whatever I can to secure that spot in radiology that is due to open. I'll plow through work and grab the ingredients I need to make a stellar first birthday cake for Grace and a little smash cake she can have all to herself. Pictures of a one-year-old celebrating their birthday covered in frosting are priceless. I wonder how long until Nick and Kat welcome another little one into their life. They're such a special couple. *Is it wrong to feel a little jealous?*

Quickly making a half pot of morning blend, I pour a cup and transfer the remainder into a travel mug to bring to work. I just need to shower and check on Austin before I leave. I'm sure he'll be busy drawing… what was it, leaves? I giggle at the anticipation of his wall looking like Monument Avenue covered in multicolored foliage. Our house will match, inside and out.

"Hey, B. How you holding up?" Donovan greets me from around the corner of the ER.

"I'm a little stressed. I think I'm letting finals get the best of me."

"Oh, you've got this. Don't stress it. Plus, it'll be behind you in no time. Then you can focus on life again. Hang out with us Potter boys and maybe meet someone," Donovan adds.

I recoil a bit at his remark. "Yeah, don't think I'm going to entertain that for a while. I've got to get my career on track before I worry about adding anyone into the mix. Besides, Austin and I are doing just fine on our own."

My eyes connect with Donovan's, and he shoots me an apprehensive look. He's smart. He's never pushed me to talk about my relationships or lack thereof. But I know he wants the best for Austin and me. I reach over and give his hand a gentle squeeze. He's such a good man.

"We're okay," I whisper. *Maybe if I keep telling myself, I'll believe it's true.*

Sebastian

Well, this day is off to a great start. I practically took a header out of the shower this morning, landing directly onto my bent knee. I can walk but bearing weight for any length of time on my wounded limb is uncomfortable and distracting. I can only imagine how adding this to the stressors of late will affect my performance in the operating room.

I discover too late that walking toward the physicians' lounge for a cup of coffee is a mistake. Between the constant throbbing of my knee and the neoprene knee brace I'm wearing, my gait resembles a drunk pirate as I drag my leg behind me. If I'd slept better, maybe I wouldn't need this coffee. Vowing to cut the bullshit and wash that damn pillowcase with Isabella's scent still clinging to it, I hope that'll be one less thing to torture me during the night. Instead of her perfume conjuring scenes from our sexathons, all I see is her enraged expression in front of her home.

"Hey, Bas. How are you?" Nick asks as I enter.

"How do you get any work done? You're in here all the time. Is Kat here?" I laugh.

"No. I get plenty done peg leg. What did you do to yourself?"

"Not hiding it well, huh? This getting old shit is for the birds. Just a stupid fall. It'll be okay, but it hurts like a motherfucker when I have to stand too long."

"Well, good thing you aren't a surgeon or anything. You have many cases lined up?"

"Three today."

"Ouch." I watch him stirring his coffee out of the corner of my eye as my cup begins to fill with aromatic, dark liquid. "Is that the only thing bothering you?"

"What do you mean?"

"Something seems off with you."

"I don't know, man. I'm struggling in the OR. I blame it on stress. My sojourns abroad to decompress were helping for a while, but I need to get my shit together. My mind was completely distracted when I fell." I shake my head at the event.

"Come on, Bas. It could've just been a freak accident. Give yourself a break. Your cases are a lot more demanding than mine. That kind of constant stress would be hard on anyone."

"I don't know. I think I'm going to call Kendal."

"Kendal Kramer, the neuropsychiatrist?"

"Yeah. We went out years ago. I respect her."

"You mean you fucked her and decided to still speak afterward," he adds sarcastically.

"Whatever. You haven't even been married a year, Nick. Don't act like I'm the only guy in this room that was focused on getting his dick wet without taking names." I shoot him a quick glare before continuing. "I've got way too much shit in my head, questioning where my future's headed. It's diverting focus from my work. Maybe she can shed some light on it. All I know is something has to change. I can't keep living like this."

Glancing at his watch, Nick grimaces. "Damn, I have to go. Hey, let's grab a drink for your birthday. I know it's mid-week, but we won't stay out late. I miss you, man. I want to hear more about what's going on when we're not in a rush."

"Sure. That'd be great."

Nick heads for the door and swiftly spins before pulling it open. "You're coming to the house Saturday, right?"

"Yes," I groan sarcastically. "See ya." Grabbing my coffee cup, I cover it carefully with a plastic lid before heading back down the long corridor. Don't need to add second-degree burns to my list of injuries. I'll give Kendal a call once I return to the office. Perhaps I should also reach out to my personal trainer. He'd mentioned there was a yoga instructor who did private lessons. I found yoga and meditation helpful on a recent trip to Fiji, but once I returned home and joined a class, it was torture. I couldn't immerse myself in the therapeutic elements of the class with hot, sexy women in skin-tight yoga pants contorting themselves into delicious positions all around me. By the end of the class, it was like ladies' night at the club the way they all flocked to the only male in the room. Returning to that class definitely wouldn't help my distractability.

Limping back to my office from the OR, my leg feels like it weighs a hundred pounds. I'm off tomorrow and need to ice and elevate it all day. I'm working and on-call on Friday, so I need to rest in preparation for any emergency cases which might leave me standing all day. *When the fuck did I start feeling so damn old?*

Continuing down the hallway, I pass the atrium and notice Isabella sitting at a small black, wrought iron table in the courtyard. She's holding a book and eating a salad. Her gorgeous brown locks are blowing around her beautiful face, and I can't help but stare.

Realizing I've stopped walking and am openly gawking at her, I try to put one foot in front of the other just as Isabella's eyes connect with mine, and her expression of quiet contemplation turns to scorn. I watch as she lifts her book to cover her reddening face. There's no confusing that dismissal. My head drops slightly as I hobble back to my office and decide I need to get that appointment with Kendal sooner rather than later. My brain is a torrent of confusion. I don't know who I am anymore. When my life was centered around work and a new piece of ass every week, I didn't have to contend with any of this.

∽

Bzzz. Bzzz.

"Hello?" I answer, not looking at my phone screen in my current muddled state.

"Hi, Sebastian. It's Kendal. I got a message you were trying to reach me."

"Thanks for calling me back so quickly. I'm not sure if you can help me. I'm happy to speak with your receptionist to make an appointment but wanted to reach out to you first."

"I'm happy to help if I can. Is something wrong?"

"Well, I've noticed over the last few years my focus has been declining. This has become evident in the OR, which is not at all helpful." I give an uncomfortable laugh. Sharing my struggles with anyone other than Nick isn't something I'm accustomed to. "I've tried introducing meditation, yoga, workouts… I even noticed some improvement with taking rejuvenating trips to peaceful destinations several times a year, but these things have become be less beneficial.

I'm sure it's the stress of the job and the overcrowding in my head." I again laugh.

"Well, your job is certainly demanding. And the type of work you perform requires a great deal of precision. Why don't you come by this afternoon? My last appointment is scheduled for three-thirty. I'm happy to see you afterward if that'll work for you."

"That'd be great. Thank you. I honestly don't know if there's anything you can do to help, but I'd like to find some way to ease the amount of pressure I'm under. I love my job. But I don't want to risk making a mistake that could affect one of my patients long-term. Or get me sued."

"No, I understand completely. I'll see you this afternoon. It was nice to hear from you, Sebastian. Even if it's under these circumstances," she adds. Her sultry voice takes me back to our one night together. Kendal is beautiful. She's a successful, intelligent, and sexy blonde. If I had been interested in pursuing something more than a one-night stand, we could've made quite the power couple. While she's only a few years younger, she's completely focused on her career as well. Or at least she was at the time of our hot evening together.

We've stayed in touch, but it's been purely professional. I try not to make a habit of sleeping with women I know. Yet, this particular evening had caught me off guard. Kendal had been attending a dinner lecture hosted by a colleague on a medication approved for the treatment of numbness. Neuropathy is an area treated by both orthopedists and neurologists alike. We chatted over dinner, enjoyed a glass of wine at the bar following the lecture, and after giving in to the flirty, hungry looks she'd been sending me all night, I accepted her invitation for a nightcap at her home. The only thing we drank once we got there was each other.

Kendal is sweet and engaging. She can easily keep my attention during conversations. She's fuck hot and knows how to please in the bedroom. Yet, there was never any pull toward taking it further for me. Not saying I wouldn't have minded a repeat performance of that night. However, my work was and is my priority.

Kendal reached out a few times over the following months. She never pushed for more or acted offended I didn't offer. Maybe I should've considered a relationship with her. A bond with a like-minded professional who could please me in the bedroom but not distract me from my priorities could be just the right fit. Sadly, I doubt I can even handle that kind of relationship. Not to mention, how likely is it I'd find a woman who is *that like-minded*? Would they eventually want more? Would the relationship precipitously bring nothing but arguing and disappointment when they realized they were never going to be the priority?

"Dr. Lee? Your three o'clock appointment is here," Rebecca says from the doorway.

What the hell? "I thought my last patient of the day was at 2:00?"

"Originally, it was. I know you don't like to have them run too late when you have multiple OR cases during the day. But you told me to add this one on."

I give her a perplexed expression, knowing she's probably right, given how distracted I've been lately.

"It's Mr. Hansen. A postoperative follow-up of a tendon repair you performed," she replies with trepidation.

"Oh, of course. I'm sorry, Rebecca. I completely forgot. I missed his initial post-op appointment because I was away. We added him on at the last minute. Thank you."

Unsure why my mood has suddenly brightened, I carefully stand from my chair. I don't know what it is about this old guy that gives me such peace. And direction. I don't take kindly to unsolicited advice from anyone. Yet, from our first meeting, I've been drawn to him. His openness. His words are genuine and without judgment.

Walking into exam room two, I smile as I meet the shining steel gray eyes of my new favorite patient. "Mr. Hansen." I extend my hand. "It's good to see you." I become aware of an abrupt change in his facial expression.

"What did you do to yourself, son?"

"Oh, that. Stupid accident. Just being careless. I've been distracted," I reassure.

"You sure you don't need to see a doctor?" He winks, the smile returning to his face.

"I'll be fine. Just need to get off of it later. It's the least of my worries."

"Hmmm. What else is bothering you?"

I find myself grabbing the chair beside him and lowering down into it before I realize I've done it. "I'm still struggling with my focus. I'm getting there. I've recruited some help to get it worked out. I don't want to go back to my old behavior," I respond, still feeling a little self-conscious about my explosive rant in front of this kind man.

"Do you mind my asking what you do for fun?"

"Fun?" I'm taken aback by his line of questioning. "I don't understand."

"That's kind of what I figured. I did the same thing for years. Only concentrating on one thing. Life's too short. I think you'll find once you make room for things that bring you joy outside of the operating room, the rest may improve. If it doesn't, you'll be none the worse for wear."

I feel the corner of my mouth curl a bit. *I should be paying him for this appointment instead of the other way around.* "Thank you. You're probably right. I have been trying to work out, meditate… but it's all with an end goal in mind. Nothing for the joy of it." I give him a full smile before continuing. "Now, let me see that hand."

Returning to my office after wishing Mr. Hansen well, I recline back in my desk chair and shake my head at the unexpected lift in my mood. Shifting my focus out of my window, I take in the many trees that dot the hospital grounds. Maple trees, Bradford Pears, and Crepe Myrtles are planted along the walkways, with tall pines growing along the small pond to the far corner of the complex. Many of their leaves have already begun to turn the rich colors of fall. Some decorate the manicured lawn below while others rustle in the breeze in transition, awaiting their turn to tumble. A lone maple leaf, deep purple in hue, dangles precariously in the wind on a tree nearest my vantage point. Will it hold on a while longer or make it's decent? Will it end up carried away on an adventure of a lifetime or swept into a trash bin? I can feel a lump lodged in my throat as the leaf suddenly feels like a metaphor for my life.

Staring out at the scene in front of me, Mr. Hansen's words haunt me. "Don't end up old and alone like me."

CHAPTER TWENTY

Sebastian

Rolling over in bed, I stare at the clock. It's 10:30 a.m. The last consult of the evening ended up in the operating room until 3:00 a.m. I haven't had a call shift run that late in a long time. At least the cases yesterday were straightforward, and everything went smoothly for a change.

I already feel I've made the right move speaking with Kendal. She was quiet and contemplative as I laid out my concerns. I know I can be a little too cerebral for some people, but she *is* a neurologist. If anyone can handle my concerns for my overcrowded brain and poor focus, it's Kendal.

Pushing up onto my elbows, I consider the week ahead. She's ordered some tests as a routine screening portion of my evaluation and has given me some books to look at to consider limiting my stressors. I need to delve deeper into meditation. Still surprised I went there with her, I laid it all out regarding my fears of letting someone into my life. Kendal's words about opening up to a relationship have carried with me since our appointment. She felt I should consider seeing a counselor to address my underlying issues with commitment, particularly in light of my poor role models. Not sure I'm interested in adding psychotherapy to my routine.

I was shocked that an uber professional like herself would've tossed her career focus to the side in place of a committed relationship. She immediately corrected me, saying it wasn't an either-or scenario. That this could actually improve my focus, having my stress levels under better control. I'd buy this if there were any guarantees in life about women. But after witnessing the tumultuous lifestyle shared by my parents, I didn't want to risk inviting more chaos into my life in my attempts to diminish my tension-filled existence.

There was a point I considered this was self-serving on Kendal's part, as the gleam in her eye and the tight hug I received upon entering her office instantly had me on guard. Yet, once I sat down and noticed the giant rock on her hand, I discovered I was being both egotistical and paranoid. For all intents and purposes, married life has only improved her career. Not that I'm considering a trip to the altar, but it appears to have served her well.

Swinging my legs over the side of the bed, I rub my left knee instinctively. It's still incredibly sore. There've been too many long hours on my feet on the harsh tiles of the hospital floor in the last few days. I need to ice it this morning before heading out for the day.

Luckily, I have nowhere to be until this afternoon when I head to the lake to join Grace's birthday celebration. *What the hell do you get a one-year-old for a birthday gift?* I guess I'll just head to the toy store and see if someone can assist me. Knowing Nick and Kat, that child wants for nothing. They're incredible parents, and she's one lucky little girl to have them.

Having taken twice as long to make it from my bedroom to my kitchen as usual, I pour a cup of congratulatory coffee for arriving in one piece. Shaking my head, I take a sip of the rich Columbian brew and look about my home. It's silent. The space is beautiful but often wasted by the lack of inhabitants. The far wall of the great room houses a stone fireplace that steals your attention as you walk in. Taking another tentative sip of the hot liquid, my eyes flick over to the glass wall at the back of the den. It's comprised of a collapsible set of sliding glass doors that open up onto a luxurious heated pool and jacuzzi. The pool surround is a light-colored flagstone that draws your eye to the deep blue water in the center. A small door opens to the left of the jacuzzi that allows for changing and managing wet towels, and an expansive, well-manicured lawn sits at the rear. It's not lost on me how incredibly blessed I am. I've worked hard for this life, but is it really living when a home designed for memory-making sits empty much of the day? *Empty... now there's a word.*

Forcing my thoughts away from the negative, I make the longer-than-usual trip back toward my bedroom to shower and change. I'll elevate my leg and read a little after I get cleaned up, and pick up a gift for Grace on the way to Nick's. As I reach the shower, a thought comes to mind. Maybe I should stop by the vineyard on the way and pick up a few bottles for the party. I'm not interested in a run-in with Sam or my parents, but given it's a Saturday, it's unlikely either of them would be there.

Standing under the rush of hot water, I feel my shoulders begin to relax. I can kick back with a good glass of wine in an Adirondack chair with Nick and his family and enjoy his lake view for the evening. No more stress. It's going to be a good evening.

Isabella

"How's it look?" I ask, knowing full well Austin only has eyes for the sugary confection and not the appearance of this Supergirl birthday cake I've created for little Grace. She's been a fighter since she appeared in this world as a preemie, and her nickname, Super G, suits her.

"It looks good, Mom."

"You're the artist in the family, but it didn't turn out half bad, huh?" I smack the top of his hand as he reaches out to pinch off a piece of sweet buttercream from the bottom edge of the red, blue, and yellow cake. "Here," I say as I hand him a small container that houses the remains of the icing I used in making the smash cake Grace will get all to herself.

"Thanks, Mom," he says as he carries the bowl to his room.

"We're going to have to leave here in about an hour, Austin. Please don't get covered in paint before we go." *Or frosting for that matter*, I think to myself. Grabbing the white cake box from the table, I carefully slide the cake inside before doing the same with the smaller one. Now that the project is complete, I lick the sweet frosting from my fingertips before wiping my hands on my kitchen towel. Placing my purse with the directions to Nick and Kat's home by the cakes, I head to the bedroom to change. It's about an hour's drive, according to Katarina. They couldn't have picked a more beautiful day. She said the party was just close friends and family, nothing too big. I'm so grateful she invited Austin and me to join them. We don't get to share much social time with anyone outside my extended family.

"Hey." Popping my head into Austin's room on the way to my own, I say, "Why don't you grab a few things you want to take with you and put them in your backpack? They live on the lake, and you might find something you'd like to sketch while you're there."

Austin sits a little taller in his chair at this revelation. "Oh, good." As he stands to collect his prized possessions, I make my way to my room. Grabbing a pair of jeans and a light sweater, I head toward the bathroom. It's nice that the weather has cooled down a little. Between working in the hospital and the high heat and humidity of Virginia living, I was starting to keep my locks in a permanent messy bun or ponytail. It'll be nice to literally let my hair down with my new friends at their home today.

An hour and a half later, and we've arrived at Nick and Kat's gorgeous lake home. It's like something out of a fairy tale. Even Austin's face is bright with excitement as we pull up the tree-lined drive and see the shoreline in the distance.

"I can see the water, Mom."

"Isn't it beautiful, Austin?"

"Yes. I bet Bailey would like it here."

Bailey has taken Austin with her to sketch and paint at a local park on several occasions. She typically paints while he sketches, given his aversion to painting on an easel. But according to Bailey, Austin loves to sketch and reproduce the beauty of Mother Nature's bounty through his own unique lens.

"Hey."

I can hear Kat's cheerful voice as I close the car door. I look up to see Nick and Kat coming down the front porch steps in our direction. Kat is carrying little Grace and stops to introduce her to Austin.

"Thanks again for making her cake and coming all of this way," Nick greets as he engulfs me in a hug. This man is so dreamy. He's the perfect package of smart, sexy, sweet, and surgeon all in one. My mind instantly travels to another sexy surgeon I know, and my smile withers a bit.

"I'm so thankful you included us in your celebration. Do you mind helping me carry the cakes into the house?"

"Of course," he replies, beaming like the proud papa he is.

I receive a hug from Katarina and 'Super G,' and we all head up the porch steps into their incredible home. It's a perfect lake house built of rich wood and topped with a green metal roof. I can just imagine sitting curled up in a cozy chair by the fire as rain pelts the tin above. The back of the home comprises several large bay windows that open onto the incredible view below.

"Ma'am? Can I go down there?" Recognizing Austin's voice, I turn to see him pointing to the grassy area along the bank of the lake below.

"Of course, Austin. But please, call me Kat."

"Yes, ma'am. I mean, Kat." He hurriedly opens the back door to the deck, and I watch him as he descends, holding his backpack tightly in his hands.

"Isabella, this is my dad, Garrett," Nick interrupts.

"I've heard a lot about your propensity for making sweet treats, young lady." Garrett takes me in for a hug before I can extend my hand. He's as charming as his son.

"Well, reserve your opinion for when you taste it. I'm used to making cakes for underdeveloped palates." I giggle. "Most of mine are for the young crowd who are easily impressed with candy toppings."

"Who wouldn't be impressed with that?" Garrett laughs.

"And this is..." I look over to Nick, who suddenly appears

confused. "I was going to introduce you to my little brother. Well, let me correct. He's like an adoptive little brother I mentor with The Big Brothers, Big Sisters Association in town. But he appears to have taken off." I watch as Nick wanders about the large room and peers out the window. "Oh, there he is."

Coming closer, I notice a dark-haired teen sitting next to Austin under a tall pine tree facing the water. My hand instantly springs to cover my mouth as I feel tears well in my eyes.

"Isabella, are you okay?" Nick asks quietly, resting his hand on my back.

"Yes, I'm sorry," I splutter. Dabbing at my eyes, I try to get myself together. "Other than my brothers and my sister, Austin doesn't have any friends. He prefers to keep close to the house and surround himself with his art. He loves to sketch and paint. Almost near obsession. It can be off-putting to some people." I leave out *including his father*. "I've honestly never seen him in a casual environment where he was spending time with another young man his age. How old is Gavin?"

"He just turned sixteen. How about Austin?"

"He's seventeen," I say quietly, still in shock at this joyful surprise.

"Gavin's a good kid. His mother works a lot, and he never had a real relationship with his father."

"It appears they already have a lot in common," I respond quietly, continuing to watch them through the glass. I feel more unshed tears collect as I witness Austin showing Gavin the sketches in his prized book.

"I do need to warn you, though."

My gaze instantly flicks in his direction, wondering what this kind kid could need a forewarning about. It's apparent to anyone who meets Austin that he's a unique, socially awkward young man. There's no way this could be lost on this young man. Yet he continues to sit with him, seemingly in an ongoing conversation.

"Gavin has a mouth on him. I'm working on it the best I can, but there's never any filter with that kid. Just be prepared if Austin starts repeating any of his mess!"

"Oh, ha! I can't imagine Austin would do that. He's honestly almost too polite. It would be crazy to hear him talk like another teen."

"Take that back quick, Isabella." He laughs. "Keep him polite." I note the proud stare he sends Gavin's way as he shakes his head at his *little brother's* antics.

"We're here." I hear shouted in unison from the front door. Looking in that direction, I see several adults and two children coming our way.

"Hey, guys," Kat greets. "Come over here, Jenna, Luke. I want you to meet someone." I watch as Kat bends down to their eye level. "You remember that incredible candy cake you had for your birthday, Jenna? This nice lady right here made that for you. This is Isabella."

"Wow. Your cake rocked!" Luke exclaims.

"Is Super G's cake going to be covered in candy too?" Jenna asks.

"No. I didn't want her to choke on anything. But I put extra sugar in the frosting. It's over on the counter if you want to take a peek." I point in the direction of the two-tier cake in primary colors with a cape made of bright red fondant draping down the back and a big blue triangle adorned on the top, with Super G inscribed in the center.

"Whoa. This is awesome," Jenna declares.

I feel an arm slide around me and can't help but hug Kat back. "Isabella, this is my mom, dad, and sister, Rachel."

I greet her smiling family only briefly before her mother is reaching for Grace. I have to keep from staring at Kat's sister. The girl is absolutely beautiful. I mean, Kat is stunning with her tall, thin stature and long dark hair. Yet, her confidence and personality are honestly her most glowing features. But there's a timeless beauty about Rachel. She stands about five-six and has light brown hair with golden highlights, big brown eyes, and a radiant smile.

"Dad, can you help me with the grill? Hey, everyone. We've got chairs set up outside if you want to hang out by the lake. I set up corn hole down by the water if Luke and Jenna want to play—"

I laugh as the two kids race past Nick before he's completed his sentence. Following the crowd outside, I find a chair. Kat walks over with a glass of lemonade, offering it to me as she sits down beside me.

"This place is enchanted, Kat. Honestly, it feels almost magical."

"I know. The first time Nick brought me here, I felt the same way. Plus, he proposed to me here."

"What? I didn't know that. Are there plans to bring another child into the family?"

"You could say that." She smiles coyly as if she's guarding a secret. "We can't have children naturally. It's adoption or surrogacy for us, so it isn't as spontaneous."

For a moment, I'm speechless. It never occurred to me they couldn't have children biologically. I'd heard the story of Grace's birth and thought they were just at the right place at the right time to adopt her. "I'm sure when the right situation presents itself, you'll know."

"Yes. There's a lot of faith involved in this journey. But I wouldn't trade anything if it meant we didn't have Grace in our lives."

"You two look awfully serious over here," Nick says as he bends down to kiss his wife. "Did someone forget this is a party?"

"We were just sharing mom stories." Kat winks at me.

"Would you like to share your newest one?" Nick asks her. I adjust myself in my seat, feeling excited about being on the inside scoop of possible good news.

"Why not, babe?" Kat shrugs her shoulders and stands to wrap her arm around her devoted husband.

Nick gathers everyone around and shares they have some news. I can see everyone looking at the happy couple with hopeful anticipation. Katarina's mom is beaming from ear to ear.

"Dinner will be ready in ten minutes," Nick announces.

"What?" Kat's mom shrieks. "You had me thinking there was another grandbaby coming my way."

"Okay, that too," Nick says.

The group erupts into cheers, and Nick tries to use his hands to gesture everyone to quiet down so he can continue delivering their fantastic news.

"We received a call from the adoption agency yesterday that we'd been matched with a mother who is early in her pregnancy but wanting to have an open adoption similar to what we have with Katrina for Grace. She's in college and isn't prepared to parent, and we're excited to share the opportunity with her." Nick squeezes Kat to his side, placing a loving kiss on her temple.

I feel tears flood my face in response to their incredible news. I'm just thrilled for them. Them and this amazing young woman who gets to join their family. Because there's no doubt, the way these two love the important people in their lives, she'll become one of them instantly. I turn my head to see Austin is sketching in his pad, looking up occasionally to take in the space around him. Gavin is steadily talking, once in a while pointing at something Austin has drawn. Yep, magical.

I've eaten my fill of bratwurst and picnic sides and have thoroughly enjoyed my afternoon. Austin had two cheeseburgers, go figure. The kids are running about the yard, being chased by Gavin when Katarina approaches.

"Hey, would you mind helping me bring out the cakes, plates, and candles? I wanted everyone's food to settle before we dove into your luscious cake."

"Of course." I stand and follow her inside. "It's been a wonderful party, Kat. I can't thank you enough for inviting Austin and me to come."

"I'm secretly hoping this has guaranteed cakes for all our family's future events." She giggles.

"You can count on it. Especially if they happen in this delightful place."

"Well, I wish you could've met my best friend, Olivia. She's in New York doing an off-Broadway play. I've got the big cake. Do you mind grabbing the little paper plates over there on the counter when you bring her smash cake down? I already know we're going to have to take her dress off and put on a onesie to let her dig into that thing. She's going to wear it." She laughs.

"That's the whole point! I'll see you down there." I turn and reach for the plates. They have little Supergirl emblems on them, making me smile.

"Hey, sorry I'm late. I got caught up at the vineyard and—"

Turning toward the voice that's clearly not Katarina's, I gulp in a gust of air, feeling the plates fall to the floor as I look up into the deep blue orbs of the playboy surgeon who's tortured my thoughts.

CHAPTER TWENTY-ONE

Sebastian

"Hi," I croak out. My throat is suddenly hoarse. Why am I so parched?

"Hi." I notice her reply is as dry as my mouth feels.

Watching her as she stoops to pick up the fallen paper plates, I realize she's avoiding eye contact with me. Unable to stop myself, I bend and reach out to help her, only to grab her hand. She halts her movements momentarily before jerking her hand away from me.

"I didn't realize you'd be here," I offer. Perhaps I'm becoming paranoid that she's discovered my recent stalking. Or maybe I just want an in.

"It's fine. Luckily, the plates all landed right side up. I just need to get this cake out there."

"Please, let me help."

"No, I have it."

"Bella, can we please stop for a minute and clear the air. I'm sorry about the other day. I need you to understand…" I pause to gather my thoughts. "I was still reeling from the heated conversation in the cafeteria, and then I see you come around the corner, holding a man's hand. Curiosity got the better of me. I thought that was your boyfriend."

She gives me a stern look like she's thinking, *what kind of dumbass are you?*

"Honestly, from where I was standing, I couldn't tell. It wasn't until you told him to go into the house, and I heard him refer to you as 'Mom' that I realized he was your child. Changing gears that quickly simply threw me for a loop. My tone had nothing to do with you being a mother or him being your child."

Isabella continues to gather the remaining plates and stands without any acknowledgment of what I've said. I'm not sure what more I can do to plead my case.

"He's tall." Pause. "How old is he?"

I watch as her eyes finally connect with mine, and I can immediately sense a protective nature in her gaze. "He's seventeen. He obviously gets his height from his father."

It's at this point, I recall there's never been any discussion about whether her son is, in fact, the 'other man' or if there is a significant other in the picture. "Is he here?"

"Who?"

"Your son's father?" I ask hesitantly.

"No."

"Is he at home?"

"Yes, in New York. Austin hasn't seen his father since he was young."

"Oh, I'm sorry."

"Don't be. We're better off without him. Now if you'll excuse—"

Reaching for her hand, I try once more, "Bella, please. Can't we—"

"Hey, everything ok—"

I turn to see Katarina in the doorway with a shocked expression. It isn't until this moment that I realize I'm still holding onto Isabella's hand. Dropping it quickly, I observe a half-smile creep across Kat's features. *Hell, I'm definitely getting the third degree for this later.*

"Sorry, Kat. I dropped the plates, and Sebastian walked in about that time and offered to help clean them up. I'll get this right down there." Isabella places the plates under her arm and grabs the small cake before hurriedly heading for the door.

"Bas?"

"What?" I toss back sarcastically.

"Do you two know each other?"

"We work at the same hospital. It's not that big of a place, Katarina. You know that."

"Okay. Say what you will. But you two looked awful serious when I walked in."

"We've had a few shaky interactions. I was trying to smooth things over."

"Oh, lord, did you upset her at work?"

"Kat? Are you bringing that onesie down? I don't want Grace to sit here in just her diaper, it's a little chilly with the breeze." I hear Nick yell.

"Yeah, Kat. Get your daughter some clothes," I jab.

"Yeah, yeah," She laughs, walking away from me. I know full and well this is just the beginning of this conversation.

Opening a bottle of the Merlot I brought from the vineyard, I grab a few wine glasses from the shelf and head down the steps to join the others. Most of the women are making goo-goo noises at Grace in her highchair. A small boy is playing cornhole by himself, slinging bean bags at the wooden board and running to grab them for another turn immediately after each attempt. Off to the right, I see Gavin. *Man, I love that kid.* Walking toward them, wine glass in hand, I give Gavin a quick wave.

"Hey, Gav. How've you been?"

"Better than a pig in shit. How've you been, Dr. Lee?" *This kid.*

"Not *that* good." I laugh. "Who's your friend?"

"Oh, this is Austin."

I simultaneously recognize the name and the back of the teen's head. He hasn't looked up since I joined them. "Nice to meet you, Austin."

He looks up briefly but doesn't make eye contact. "Yes, sir." Continuing to draw on the large pad in front of him, I can't help but peer down at his work. It's intricate and quite impressive.

"Hey, I gotta take a piss. I'll be back later, Austin."

"'Kay. Bye," he responds.

"Do you mind if I sit down?" I ask cautiously, unsure of what Isabella may have told him after our interaction the other evening.

"No, sir."

Lowering myself to the ground, I attempt to keep a bit of distance between us until I have a better grasp of what he's been told. I lean my back against the rough bark of the tree, stretch out my sore leg, and turn my head to watch him sketch. "You're really talented." I'm met with silence. Is it me, or is he simply shy? "You have a gift." More silence. I look out onto the water and take a sip of my wine. Austin continues to work diligently on his artwork, not appearing the least bit bothered by my presence.

Our interactions haven't been engaging enough to judge, but I get the feeling Austin isn't your typical teen. Maybe he's bashful around new people. Unable to stand the tension any longer, I push forward. "Do you know who I am?"

"You're no one," he answers flatly as he continues to draw.

Trying not to splutter my wine at his response, I ask, "I'm sorry, what was that?"

"You're no one."

I attempt to gather my words when Austin swiftly interrupts. "I asked Mom who you were. She said you were no one."

I feel a sharp sting in my chest. Why should I care if that's how I was introduced? I'm sure she simply wanted to keep me out of her son's life. Rubbing my chest wall to dull the disturbing sensation there, I decide to continue on.

"My name is Sebastian. I work with your mom. I'm sorry if I startled you the other night."

"It's okay."

Not sure I'm getting anywhere here, I look back over at his work. It's honestly quite advanced for a teenager. The shading technique he uses to give shadows to the imagery on the page is quite appealing. "Are those leaves?"

Austin suddenly stops sketching and looks in my direction. "Yes. I like how different they are. This pile here..." he points with his pencil to a large pile of leaves in different shades of gray, "remind me of a crowd of people. All different, but the same."

Wow. I wasn't expecting this. "Do you only draw landscapes?"

"Mostly. I paint too. I don't draw people very well."

There's a certain cadence to his speech that causes me to think he has a spectrum disorder such as Autism or Asperger's. He could certainly have Asperger's as he appears very intelligent yet, I'm not trained well enough on these types of disorders to know for sure.

"Well, I think—"

"Austin, it's time for cake. Why don't you put that away for now and come and have some?"

"Okay, Mom."

Looking up at Isabella, I try to make eye contact with her but find she's staring out at the water with an unreadable expression on her face. "Austin's very talented."

"Yes, he is," she says, looking down at her son with a proud smile.

"I bet he gets that from his mother."

"Mom can't draw stick people," Austin quickly interjects.

"You're right." She laughs. "I tell him he gets his talent from his aunt Bailey."

"Ah, the sister from the club?"

I hear a guarded chuckle from her before she confirms, "Yes. That'd be the one."

"Come on, guys. She'll turn two before we sing *Happy Birthday* if you don't get up here," Kat yells. Damn, I'm really going to hear about *this* later.

Pushing from the ground, it takes some effort to bear most of my weight on my left leg so I don't collapse back onto the ground like an invalid. I'm trying to hide the lingering discomfort there. I don't want any attention taken away from Nick's family today. Not sure why I thought sitting my clumsy ass down on the ground was a good idea. The need to be on eye level with this young man overtook my judgment, I guess. Holding on to the tree with my left hand, I attempt to bend to retrieve my wine glass when Austin reaches for it, carefully handing it to me.

"Thank you," I respond as I watch him and his beautiful mother walk ahead of me. There's so much reverence in her glances toward him. I guess that's to be expected of a single mother. Yet, from the tales I've heard of Gavin's absentee mom, it isn't universal. Hell, I was raised in a two-parent family, and neither ever looked at me like that.

Finding an empty seat near the back of this gathering, I lower myself and take another sip of wine. This isn't the group I was expecting. Granted, many of their friends work in medicine, fire, or law enforcement, so their jobs may have been a factor. Normally, there's quite the collection of attendees when they're out. I hadn't realized Isabella was in their inner circle. But I'm grateful for the chance to clear the air all the same.

Isabella

Watching Grace covered in frosting brings back bittersweet memories. How can it be seventeen years since Austin was doing the same? Looking at him, watching her, I notice the cringe on his face. He doesn't care for messy things. Strange for someone so attracted to painting.

Austin is meticulous about his art. He sketches first, reproduces on his 'canvas,' and then sets upon painting his outline. He'll occasionally get frustrated when things don't go the way he wants. We've had to paint over his work so he can start over more times than I care to count. But if it'll settle the unrest and allow him to proceed, that is what we will do.

Although I'm surrounded by loving people all here to share their love of Grace and her doting parents, I feel an uneasiness. It's as if I can feel Sebastian's stare placing warmth against my skin. I need to protect myself. We have undeniable chemistry. But as much as I appreciate his attempts to clear the air, there's no arguing his lifestyle. If there was any doubt, the giggly girls in front of me in the cafeteria line have brought that to the forefront. I try to remind myself of this fact whenever I get lost in thoughts of the naughtier moments we've enjoyed together. I'd love to think things could be different, but I've lived through enough storms to know when to avoid treacherous waters. And regardless of an occasional sunny day, sharks are still dangerous.

The crowd disburses to eat cake after Katarina hands slices to everyone. I laugh as the kids devour the icing, leaving much of the vanilla cake on their plates as they return to running about the yard. I move in to collect dirty plates and notice Sebastian out of the corner of my eye. He's bending down to talk to Jenna and Luke with a mouthwatering smile across his stupid sexy face. God, that man is sinfully beautiful. *Just look away, Isabella.*

He stands to his full height and walks down to the water, a slight limp evident. *He probably hurt himself with an overzealous nurse from the hospital.* This has me picturing him on top of me, bronze chest glistening in sweat. I quickly shake those thoughts away and refocus on my task.

After cleaning up the remaining plates and utensils, I observe Austin pacing a bit. This is the longest we've been outside his comfort zone in quite some time. I think he's enjoyed himself here, but the crowd of people and festivities may be causing some anxiety. Deciding to gather our things and head out, I stroll over to give goodbyes to our friends before departing.

As we make our way around the house to the car, I hear young voices yelling Austin's name and turn. Watching Jenna and Luke run up to him with broad smiles on their faces, they hand him large handfuls of... leaves. They aren't dry and crumbly, but colorful, intact, distinctly different leaves. My eyes flick to Austin's, which are bright and shiny, as is his expression. I know he's excited about this gift.

"Thank you," he says to both of them as he gathers his precious cargo against his chest. "Mom, look at these great leaves."

"Yes, Austin. They're beautiful. Thanks, kids." I open the car trunk and ask Austin to place the leaves inside. "Son, could you try not to get those all over your floor at home?"

"Yes, Mom. I won't get them all over the floor."

Giving him a quick hug before he heads toward the passenger side door, I look up before heading to the driver's seat and lock eyes with

Sebastian. This was his work. I know it. I'm choosing to believe this was a kind gesture and nothing more. I refuse to believe he'd try to get to me through my son. He raises his hand to wave goodbye, and I give him an appreciative smile in return. Just guard your feelings, Isabella. This shark has bitten many a woman. You've had your fun, just let him be.

CHAPTER TWENTY-TWO

Sebastian

"Hey, man. Is seven o'clock, okay?" I hear Nick ask through the phone line.

"Sure, I'll meet you at the pub." Hanging up the phone, I let out a heavy sigh. Why does thirty-seven suddenly feel so old? I didn't think I'd be suffering a midlife crisis until at least my forties. Having finished my last patient appointment of the day, I grab my keys and head for the door. Maybe a quick dip in the jacuzzi to loosen my muscles would help before I go out for the evening.

The drive home seems longer than usual, taking in the splendor of fall's arrival. Since meeting Austin and witnessing his talent for interpreting nature, I've admittedly looked at the local landscape differently. I've come to appreciate each leaf has a unique fingerprint versus seeing it as a dying piece of foliage. It's clear Austin looks at the world through a special prism. His art is well developed for such a young soul. It occurs to me he might enjoy meeting Mr. Hansen and seeing his artwork if he hasn't already. I'm sure Isabella has provided him with opportunities to grow his natural talent.

Pulling into my drive, I'm taken aback at seeing a stray dog sitting atop my steps. He doesn't appear to be the typical malnourished, disheveled beast that wanders about from time to time, but moreover, a well-groomed, well cared for Labrador retriever. As I park and come closer, I'm surprised to find he's not skittish but sits wagging his tail in apparent expectation. His coat is shiny, a deep chocolate brown, and while he wears a navy-blue collar, there's no identifying tag present.

"Hey, fella. Where'd you come from?"

I reach out to rub his soft head, and his tail begins to wag faster still. It's a temperate day, thus, he isn't panting or appearing dehydrated from prolonged heat exposure. I'm not letting some stray into my immaculate home. I've never owned a pet, nor do I have the patience to start now. Looking around, I wonder if he could've wandered from a neighbor's home. I open the door and observe as the lab sits calmly, never attempting to dart inside. He appears well trained. I give the dog a wave and attempt to direct him back to whence he came and head for my bedroom to change out of my suit and tie.

After a few laps in the pool and a long soak in the hot tub, I'm relaxing with an ice-cold lager and a meat and cheese plate my chef has left for me. Looking at the rolled meats of pastrami and prosciutto on the tray, my mind returns to Fido. Strolling to the front door, I peer out of the peephole to find he's no longer sitting on the porch. Odd. Hopefully, he's returned home safe and sound.

"Bas, over here," Nick yells over the music and boisterous patrons at the bar. He's seated at a table for four instead of at a barstool as we usually do.

Reaching over to pat him on the shoulder, I lower myself into the seat across from him.

"I got you a celebratory scotch," he adds as he raises his glass in a toast.

Clinking his glass, I take a sip. "Thanks, man. I don't mind if I do."

"Where's your lovely wife? Home with Grace?"

"No, she's out with a friend for dinner. So, fill me in. Everything going okay with Kendal? You didn't hook up with her again, did you?"

"No. I needed sunglasses for the bling on her finger. Apparently, married life has only helped her career." I watch as one brow rises, the universal sign for I told you so. "Yeah, yeah. You married folks are all in some kind of club. Is there a commission that gets paid out for recruiting holdouts?"

"Nah, man. I just want you to be happy. I fought it so long. I don't want to see you miss out on a chance to have something meaningful in your life."

"What's not meaningful? I have a successful career, own a nice home, and travel where I want when I want. I have plenty of puss—"

"I know," he interrupts. "If that's still working for you, I'm not judging. For me, it came to a point where I wanted more. Random hookups didn't do it for me anymore. If I kept fighting my fear of where it'd all end up, I would've never taken a chance with Kat. It just sounded like from our conversation the other day, you might be at a crossroads."

"I don't know, Nick. I think I've been going full steam ahead with my career for so long it's catching up with me, that's all. I need order. Routine. I've had some chaotic surgeries recently at St. Luke's. Mistakes occasionally happen at other locations, but not like there. It's starting to make me paranoid of a bad outcome before I even begin." I watch as Nick waves the waitress over and asks for a menu and another round of drinks.

"What'll you have, Bas. It's on me."

"I'll take the surf and turf, medium rare with a side of asparagus."

"Would you like a side salad, sir?" the lovely young blonde asks with a twinkle in her eye.

"No, thank you." I place my menu down. "I hate salad."

Nick chuckles from across the table. "I'll take the salad and a filet, medium-rare. Thank you," he adds, handing her his menu. I notice the waitress takes her time gathering it from him, despite the platinum band on his finger. However, Nick doesn't give her a second glance. She's appealing, but I feel no interest in pursuing her as I might've in the not-so-distant past. Was Nick right? Was I not interested in these young women like I used to be because I secretly wanted more?

"Hey, there you are. We decided there was nothing we really wanted on that menu and came here for a burger and some fries," Katarina blurts, dropping down into the seat next to her husband, giving him a quick peck on the cheek.

I look up, shocked to see an equally stunned Isabella standing beside our table. Something tells me this was all Katarina's doing. Glancing in her direction, I see a smile dancing in her deep brown eyes and a slight shrug of her shoulders.

"Sit down, Bella. You know Sebastian, right?" Kat directs. She doesn't even try to hide her menacing grin now.

For fucks sake.

Isabella sits down wordlessly beside me. The not-so-subtle set up apparent to all at this table. I'm not complaining, but I don't like that she appears to be here under duress.

Undeterred by our silence, Katarina flags down the waitress and places her order, and encourages Isabella to do the same. A John Legend ballad begins playing in the background, and I watch as Kat jumps to her feet, tugging on her husband's arm.

"Come on, Nick," she coos.

"Happy wife, happy life." He laughs as he stands from his seat. From the smile on his face, this dance isn't as troublesome as he lets on.

The silence is now deafening.

"Would you like to dance?" I ask, looking in her direction. She's wearing a black shift dress which hugs her beautifully. Her hair is down in soft waves. Her makeup is natural, jewelry minimal.

"No, thank you," she replies, never making eye contact.

Bzzz. Bzzz.

Looking down at my phone, I grimace, seeing my mother's name.

"I'm sorry, I have to take this," I advise as I stand from my chair. There's no need for an audience for this phone call. "Hello."

"Happy birthday, Sebastian." My mother's voice is chipper. I immediately wonder if she's made this call with someone within earshot.

"Thank you," I answer flatly.

"I'm sorry you missed the dinner party."

I refrain from replying because she knows full well I have no interest in participating in that charade.

"Are you at least doing something nice for your birthday?"

I turn to look back at my table, Isabella gazing back at me questioningly.

"Yes, thank you. We were just sitting down to dinner."

"We?"

"Mother."

"Okay, okay. Well, I'll let you get back to her."

"Thank you. I appreciate the call," I respond, hanging up before she can add anything more to this meaningless conversation.

"Sorry. My mother," I share as I return to my seat. I'm not sure why I feel the need to clear the air but don't want her mind imagining who the woman on the other end of the line was.

"That was an awfully short call. I hope everything's okay."

"That's the only way to have a conversation with my parents," I respond, looking in her direction. I continue to look at her in profile until she looks up, wanting her dark eyes connected with mine. "I'm happy to see you," I add, trying to give her my most genuine smile.

Her look is guarded. Is she as nervous about me as I am about her? Is she feeling the desire for *more* but fighting it too?

"Your steak, sir," the blonde states as she slides my meal in front of me. She places Nick's steak at his place and grimaces as he returns to the table with Katarina in tow. "Your meals should be out shortly, ladies." She turns and heads away.

Katarina pulls a shaved carrot slice from Nick's salad and begins to chew before picking up her water. She's watching Isabella with a questioning look. No woman as feisty and independent as Isabella is going to put up with Kat's shenanigans.

The waitress returns a few moments later with the girls' entrees, and we eat, making polite superficial banter throughout the rest of the meal. It's starting to feel forced and uncomfortable. It's an odd dichotomy, wanting to be near her but not knowing what to say to break the tension. We clearly communicate better with our clothes off.

After a quick trip to the restroom, I decide to finish off my drink and head home for the night, letting Isabella off easily when I suddenly feel her soft hand rest atop mine beneath the table. My eyes flick to her instantly. *Real smooth, Bas. Did you forget the matchmaker across the table is probably watching your every move?*

"I wouldn't mind that dance now. If you're still offering," Isabella says, her dimples now coming back out to play.

"Sure." I stand, surprised, placing my hand at her lower back as we walk toward the dance floor. I make a concentrated effort not to look at the love birds across the table and focus instead on my good fortune.

A few other couples are swaying to an Ed Sheeran tune once we arrive. I can't tell you the name of the song, but I'm grateful all the same that I'm able to end this awkward night holding her close for a few moments. Wrapping my arms around her petite frame, I pull her into me and drop my chin to her temple.

"Thank you," I whisper. Inhaling her sweet scent, I close my eyes and enjoy her warmth. I sense my heart rate has picked up a little with her near. *What the hell is this woman doing to me?*

"A little birdie told me it's your birthday." I hear beneath me. *Ah, it's a pity dance.*

"A little Kat, you mean."

"Well…"

I let my hands drift lower, resting on the small of her back as she sways softly with me in time to the music.

"Why don't you like to make a big deal about your birthday?"

"Besides the fact, I'm a grown man, and we don't tend to wear tiaras and declare a whole week is needed to celebrate surviving another year?" I chuckle.

"Yeah, besides that." She giggles.

"I don't know. When I grew up, I was jealous of my classmates. Their mothers would bake cakes or cupcakes and deliver them to the school to help them celebrate their big day," I say, shaking my head at the memory.

Before I can continue, Isabella interrupts. "What, your mom didn't get you a cake for your birthday?"

"No, I got a cake. It was usually a multi-tiered cake, like something you'd see on a baking contest. At a catered party with a bunch of people I didn't know. Whatever would impress the Joneses." It was never about me. I knew that even from a young age. "Those other mothers went out of their way to make their kids feel special. My mother phoned it in," I continue. *Why am I telling her this?* "I know, poor little rich kid. It's stupid."

"No, it's not stupid. What kid wouldn't want to feel special on his birthday?" She answers with more passion than I was expecting, given our earlier flat conversation.

I feel her rest her cheek against my chest, and a familiar warmth spreads through me. "Thank you. I can tell you're a really good mother to Austin."

"Thanks. He's my everything."

I hold her a little tighter as the song nears the end, much sooner than I'd like. As the music changes to something more upbeat, I woefully pull away as we head back to a vacated table. We both stand transfixed momentarily, trying to make sense of the situation.

"Do you think they went to the restroom?" Isabella asks.

"Knowing those two, they probably went for a quickie."

"Hi, your friends said to tell you they had to run," the waitress advises.

"Oh, gosh. I hope little Grace is okay," Isabella says nervously.

"Um, it's probably not my place. But they were laughing, so I think there was another reason they left," the blonde continues, her eyes darting back and forth between us in a silent attempt to share her opinion on the situation.

"Did you and Kat drive separately?" I ask her.

"No." She laughs, seeming shocked.

"Let me drive you home. Charlie's around the corner." Katarina's meddling knows no bounds. I usher Isabella out, again unable to prevent placing my hand at the small of her back, desperately wanting to keep touching her. We approach the curb, and she gives me a questioning look."

"What's the matter, GG?" I ask carefully as I look down into her big brown eyes.

"Do you have any plans? For your birthday, I mean."

"I have a stripper coming by the house later."

"Jeez, I should've known," she huffs.

Grabbing her little body against mine, I push my lips against her ear. "I had planned to go home and jerk off to thoughts of you," I admit.

Spinning on her heel, she looks at me, eyes wide.

"What? Did you want me to lie?"

Her cheeks turn deliciously pink, and she turns away from me as she notices Charlie pulling up to the curb.

I open the rear door for her, and she slides in, making room for me to join her without needing to walk around the vehicle.

"Where to, sir?"

"His place," Isabella answers.

I look over, unable to hide my surprise.

"Well, do you want your gift or not?"

CHAPTER TWENTY-THREE

Sebastian

We've barely made it inside before we're frantically pulling each others' clothes off. Reaching behind her, I grab her zipper and gingerly lower it, so I don't ruin her dress in my haste to get it off of her. I barely manage to get it halfway down before I'm pulling her dress over her head by the hem.

I feel her fingers pulling at my buttons. I can't fight this untamable desire to feel her skin on mine and forcefully pull the front of my shirt open, buttons pinging against the marble countertop and hardwood floor. Clutching her body against mine, I nibble at the nape of her neck as I feel the soft swell of her breasts brush against my pecs. Reaching behind her, I pop the clasp of her bra and take a step back to watch her tits plunge free.

"God, you're beautiful," I moan as I drop my mouth to her soft mounds.

"Sebastian?" she whimpers against my tight pull on her nipples. On second thought, that sounded more like a question than a moan.

"Yeah, baby?"

"I know it's your birthday, but can I—?"

"Anything."

"Anything?"

"God, I'd give you anything right now?" I groan as I continue to nibble and lick on her creamy skin, my dick at full mast and ready for more.

"Can I tie you up?"

What the fuck? I certainly wasn't expecting that. "Um, what?"

"Please?" She's standing here, topless, wearing only the tiniest black laced panties and black heels, hair mussed, dark eyes wide and hopeful. Jesus, if she asked me to marry her right now, I'd have a hard time saying no.

"You're not going to leave me like that when you run off this time, are you?"

Giggling, she quickly answers, "No." Throwing her arms around my neck, she kisses my throat.

"If I ask you to untie me, will you?"

"Yes. I promise."

Looking into her shining eyes, her deep dimples winking at me, I pull down my boxers, step out and lift her into my arms before briskly carrying her to my room.

"I don't bring women here, Bella. I don't really have any kinky shit."

"Can we just use a couple of neckties?"

"Why do you want to do thi—?"

"Please, Bas?"

I toss her onto the bed, her giggle echoing behind me as I stride to the closet to grab the first two ties I can get my hands on. Truth be told, I'd let this woman do anything she wanted to me. Returning to the bed, I find her sitting on all fours, biting her bottom lip.

"Hell, you're going to make me come just looking at you if you keep that up."

I watch as the saucy minx just shrugs her shoulders at me and points at the bed.

"I only brought two."

"That's enough." She smiles. "Arms up, birthday boy."

Smiling from ear to ear, I make a mental note to thank Katarina for her meddlesome behavior. I couldn't have hoped for a better evening. A tug of the soft satin cloth against my wrist reminds me I'm at her mercy. As she reaches over me, I bite her left nipple and quickly lick the tip, hoping I haven't given her ammunition to do something worse in retaliation. This plays with my thoughts momentarily. Considering how mercurial her moods have been lately, I quickly take stock of whether I've done anything else recently that could be setting me up for a very embarrassing payback.

As if she's read my mind, the little tart leans over me and whispers, "Don't be scared. I'm not going to hurt you." Before I can react, she has stuck out her sweet pink tongue and is dragging it over my lips. God, I've never wanted to kiss anyone so much in my life. Yet, before my tongue can join the party, she's retreated to sit between my legs. I watch as she spreads her thighs wide, pulling her tiny panties to the side, and starts to rub little circles about her swollen pink nub.

I can't control the groan that escapes. Watching her pleasure herself for me, my hands restrained over my head, has my dick bobbing in an attempt to get near her. Her fingers dart inside her swollen, pink flesh, and her hips rock back and forth before she throws her head back.

"Jesus, Bella. You're killing me." My cock is literally weeping as precum sits atop the head of my eager dick.

She lies back, her feet resting on either side of my hips, and slowly peels off her tiny panties. Instead of dropping them off the side of the bed, she flings them so they land on my chest. The scent of her arousal pushing me further over the edge. Her fingers are now spreading her flesh wide, her wet center on display for me as she teases and rubs her wet pussy. The sounds are starting to cause me to break.

"GG, please?"

My heart rate picks up as I watch her change positions and crawl up beside me. She licks and nibbles on my nipples before reaching for the nightstand. Her eyes widen mischievously as she reaches inside. I'm expecting to see a foil packet, but instead, see she's retrieved the little bottle of potion from Bali along with a condom.

She leans back on her heels, placing a few drops of the lotion in her hands and rubbing them together before sliding her hands up and down my length.

A heady groan rumbles through my chest just before I feel the same intense warmth coat my balls. I'm practically hyperventilating as I feel her hot wet tongue glide up and down my shaft before she envelopes me for a long suck.

"Oh, fuck."

I feel her release me with a pop just before her tongue darts out to tease my swollen, aching balls. Her magical tongue continues to propel me closer and closer to my release as she strokes my cock. With a firm but gentle squeeze to the head of my dick, her tongue teases at the sensitive flesh between my balls and my ass, and I almost come undone.

"Fuck, GG. If you don't get that pretty little pussy on my dick, when I get loose from here, I'm going to pound you right through this damn—" I'm interrupted by the sensation of the condom being carefully placed onto my thick shaft and practically weep with joy. *Please don't let me blow my load before she's even on me.*

Bella climbs up the bed, straddling me before directing my almost painful cock into her tight heat. Her hips shimmy from side to side as she lowers herself onto me, and I can't keep from growling out my intense pleasure. I know she has to adjust, but this pace is torture. After a few moments of rocking, I note a smile cross her features as her body opens up to take me in, and she carefully glides her body down until she's fully seated on my cock.

"Holy—" I have to close my eyes, the sensation so intense if I see her naked body undulating over me like a porn star, I'm going to come. Feeling I have better control, I slowly open them to behold this beautiful woman, chasing her pleasure on top of me. As hot as this is, I can't last like this. I need to—

"Baby, untie me. Please?"

Isabella continues to rock her hips backward and forward, her fingers teasing her clit as she rides me.

"God, GG, please?"

Stretching her body forward, she reaches to untie one wrist and then the other, again her nipples too tempting not to bite as they bounce in front of my lips.

Feeling my hands now free, I flip her onto her back, throw her legs up over my shoulders and begin pounding into her like my life depends on it. Angling my hips, I attempt to strike her swollen clit with each thrust.

"Sebastian." I hear bounce about the room. My name on her lips, causing my balls to draw up.

"I'm going to fill that pussy so full of come, you little tease. Is that what you want?"

"Yes!"

My climax has begun. I only hope hers is close because there's no holding back now. I'm growling animalistic sounds of lust into her ear as I fuck her mercilessly.

Her nails dig into my ass just as I feel the first spurt of seed shoot into the condom. "Bella," I moan as I empty into her. Her beautiful cries of pleasure surround me as my body jerks within her.

Completely spent, I'm almost unable to move as I feel my heart rate slowly return to normal. Continuing to place tender kisses on her throat, I slowly move us onto our sides to withdraw and remove the condom. Carefully placing it beside the bed, I roll back to her. Pulling her against me, so that her cheek is nuzzled against my chest, I slowly stroke her hair and back. I've never felt so in tune with another person. This has to be more than sex. This connection is too intense to be merely physical. Feeling my breath returning to normal, I place kisses on her temple as I run my fingers through her wild mane.

Her gentle breath dances over my skin, and I start to wonder if she's awake.

"Stay with me?" I whisper into her hair. The words should startle me, that I've said them out loud. Yet, there's no use denying I want her here.

"I can't."

I want to reassure her, but I admit I'm disappointed.

"Austin's with my brothers. I'm already going to be facing an inquisition when I arrive. They were supposed to be watching him so I could cram for my final exam. But Kat called, and I gave in to a *girl's* night." I feel chuckling against my chest and know she's called Kat on her matchmaking, just as I have.

"It's okay, GG. Austin comes first. I understand. This has still been the best birthday I could've asked for," I say, kissing her temple once more. And it's the truth. Unable to fight it any longer, knowing all too well she can show herself out, I succumb to the beckoning sleep brought on by high dollar scotch, post-orgasm fatigue, and the magic of Isabella.

CHAPTER TWENTY-FOUR

Sebastian

As my body senses the arrival of dawn, I roll onto my side and inhale what I know is only lingering remains of Isabella's scent on my pillow. Opening my eyes, I confirm she's gone. My regular morning erection still holding out hope she might have accidentally fallen asleep.

Clank.

I jolt up from bed. What? Did she stay? My heart rate picks up as I spring from the room and come down the hall toward the kitchen. As I round the corner, I come face to face with Sam.

"Jesus, put that thing away before you hurt somebody." He laughs, cracking an egg into a frying pan.

"Jealous?"

"Whatever."

I grab the conveniently deposited clothing off of the floor from the night before and don my boxers before my irritation at the man in front of me returns front and center.

"Why the hell are you here?"

"I thought you were expecting me. Door was open."

I recall the events of last night. We were in a bit of a rush. I could see where that could've happened.

"Why would I have been expecting you? Never mind." I walk past him to start the coffee and catch the array of food items spread about the counter. Hmmm, something tells me these are mine. "Don't you have a kitchen?"

"Long story…"

"Yeah, I'm really not interested."

"So, who's your little friend?" he asks while flipping the fried egg gently in the pan.

"Who?"

"Oh, don't play dumb with me, Bas. I saw her leave."

"I instantly recall where our clothes were lying, and I look back at him, my face red with anger that he could've seen her naked due to his lack of respect for my privacy.

"Don't worry. I didn't see anything. I was trying to sleep on your couch when I heard her heels on the floor. I didn't want to freak her out by letting her see me or risk waking you up if she shouted. I only caught the back of her as she went out of the door. She was fully dressed."

Well, that's a relief. I feel eyes on me and glance up to see him staring at me in anticipation. I hunch my shoulders, attempting to look nonchalant, I'm sure I'm failing miserably. "What? She was a birthday present." Try as I might, I cannot keep the grin off of my damn face.

"What happened to not bringing women back to your place? Ooooh, she's a prostitute?"

"No," I bark before I can think better of it.

"Cool your jets, Bas. I don't mean any disrespect. I'm just needling you after the lecture I got the other day."

Rubbing the nape of my neck, I'm not ready for this conversation.

"That woman is more than a birthday present, and you know it." He lifts a fried egg carefully from the pan and places it onto a plate. "I haven't seen you smile like that since—"

"Don't!" I snarl.

He drops the other fried egg onto the plate, and I take it from him, grab the toast already sitting in the toaster, and walk toward the island to eat.

"You're welcome," he mutters before reaching for two more eggs. "All joking aside, Bas. I hope this girl works out for you. You deserve it."

"Thanks. You know what I really deserve? A damn phone call before you come over here. Scratch that. Just don't come over here."

"Real nice, big brother."

"If I finally wake up with a woman in my bed, and we stroll out here to get some coffee, the last thing I need is your sorry ass joining in."

"*Finally?* I didn't know this was a struggle for you."

"Shut up." I finish off my breakfast and grab my coffee to take to my bedroom. "Can you lock the door on your way out?" I shout as I return down the hall.

I have a few of the scheduled tests Kendal ordered later this morning; thus my office patients will not begin until 1:00 p.m. I open the garage door to take the recycling to the curb when I notice the chocolate lab has returned. Lying on the front porch, he sits up once he sees me.

What is up with this dog?

As I pull the recycling can down the drive, the Labrador retriever joins me. "I don't have anything for you, pup." I place the can at the edge of the curb and turn back, the dog hot on my heels. Could someone have moved and left this dog behind? I wonder if I should reach out to the local police station. As I return to the garage, the dog follows dutifully behind me.

"No, buddy. You can't come in here. This is a dog-free zone."

He tilts his head as if he is trying to comprehend what I'm saying.

He's a beautiful dog. Reaching out, I rub his head and watch as he instantly lies down, rolling onto his back for me to rub his belly. "Shame, fella. If I was going to attempt a relationship, you'd probably be the only kind I could handle. But I'm worried I'd even screw that up, and then where would you be?"

Heading into the house, I close the garage door and look for my keys.

~

Pulling into the garage, I open the door and marvel at the abrupt change in weather. Work wasn't bad today. I had a short day, got the blood tests and imaging done Kendal had ordered, and was able to leave the hospital at a decent hour. It was clear and sunny when I left work, but torrential downpours started midway home. I'd had a craving for pasta from Luigi's, yet with this weather, I didn't want to contend with running in and out of buildings carrying to-go food containers. So I opted to see what the personal chef may have left me.

Opening the fridge, I see another charcuterie tray, a fruit bowl, and what appears to be some sort of pesto pasta salad. Retrieving the items, I place them on the kitchen island as a large clap of thunder rumbles through the house. Not long after, I hear something at the door and wonder if perhaps, Isabella has returned. Walking briskly to the doorway, I grab for the door handle and notice that dog has returned and is sitting curled up by the door, soaking wet and shivering.

Oh, good grief. Turning to grab some kitchen towels, I run back and dry off the shivering mutt and usher him inside. It isn't that cold out, but he is soaking wet. The dog follows me into the kitchen and sits beside the kitchen island as if he's awaiting direction.

"I don't know what you want from me. I'm the last house you should be coming to thinking someone's going to give you treats or take you for walks."

Again, with the head tilt. Undeterred by my rant, he lies down, resting his chin upon his paws.

Should I call the police and ask if anyone has reported a lost pet? Maybe I should take him to the pound? Hell, I'm not going back out in this mess. Looking down at the now sleeping dog, I decide one night won't hurt. I'll just keep him in the garage for one night.

Washing up, I return to my meal and notice Boomerang is now looking at my tray of meats with wide eyes. *Hell. When's the last time this poor dog has eaten?* Is it healthy to give a dog deli meat?

I run my hand down my face and reach for my cell phone. "Hey, Charlie. I hate to ask you to do this in this weather. Is there any chance you can pick up some dog food?" Pause. "No, I didn't get a dog. I have a stray who's been hanging around the house. I haven't figured out where he comes from, but he just keeps coming back here. I'm unsure if he's eaten. I'll try to find a place for him tomorrow, but for tonight, I'm just going to let him stay in the garage."

"I can head out right now, Dr. Lee."

"No, no, Charlie. Wait until the weather calms down first. I don't want you getting into an accident over some dog food."

"Okay. What kind of dog is it?"

"It's a chocolate lab. Why? Any idea who it might belong to?"

"Nah. I just didn't know if it needed little fluffy dog food or big dog food." He laughs.

Lord, I didn't even think about that.

An hour later, Charlie comes to the door with a large bag of food. "Charlie, this will feed him for a month."

"Well, I didn't know how long he was staying."

"One night. That's how long he's staying."

Charlie squats down to pat the dog, and again, Boomerang rolls on his back, waiting for his belly to be rubbed. "This dog's got to belong to someone. He's too well cared for."

"I think so too, but I contacted the police who don't have any inquiries into missing dogs. They recommended I take him to the pound."

I watch as Charlie scrunches up his face, mimicking my thoughts on the matter. "Don't they put them down or something if no one comes to get them?"

"Hell, man. Don't tell me that shit."

"I'm just saying."

Another large clap of thunder is heard outside the house, and the dog looks up. God, his big brown eyes are almost as hypnotic as Isabella's. I guess it's no surprise I'm caving to his staying overnight. I mean I've named the dog for God's sake. The dog puts his head back onto his paws as if acknowledging his place.

"Let me know if you need me to take him out or anything, sir."

"What? Dogs don't pee in the rain?"

"Nah, I meant for a walk. I'm sure if he's got to go, he'll go rain or shine."

"Well, he's not staying long enough for me to worry with a dog walker, Charlie."

"Okay." He laughs.

Good lord. What've I gotten myself into here? Women and dogs in my house? The train's come off of the tracks here.

Isabella

Dragging my weary bones into the house, I deposit the milk and bread on the counter before going to check on Austin. I've been working more evening shifts lately, and I tend to worry a little more, as Margaret is usually in bed at this hour. I know Austin will knock loudly or call me if there's an issue. But I still can't help but worry all the same.

Poking my head in the doorway of Austin's room, I realize the day has caught up with him as he's completely crashed for the night. I turn to the right, taking in the brilliantly majestic fall colors painted on the wall. It's breathtaking. The mural is still in process, but it's glorious. The detail with which he's painted the individual leaves is incredible. They truly resemble the ones Luke and Jenna plucked off of the ground for him.

Suddenly, it dawns on me, he's actually kept his word. I fully expected to see the leaves all over his bedroom floor. I try to be flexible with his process of painting on our walls but dragging a rake into the house to clean those up was where I needed to draw the line. Smiling, I start to back out of the bedroom doorway when something catches my eye. Looking closer, I see them. They're all in his bed. He's lying on those darn leaves. *Ugh. I hope there weren't any spiders in there.*

I don't have the heart to wake him up tonight. And he didn't make a mess on the floor, so... I head back to the kitchen, shaking my head. I place the milk in the refrigerator and head toward the bathroom for a quick shower before bed.

Placing my nightclothes on the counter, I start the water. Feeling the hot spray hit my skin, I relax into the steamy liquid and give thanks for the week past and the one to come. I've had two interviews for the opening in the radiology department. I'm a little apprehensive about the job as it's a busy emergency department and they'd prefer someone with experience. However, given my references from Jeff and the other supervising technicians, things still seem hopeful.

I apply the eucalyptus mint body wash over my skin and inhale the relaxing scent. Looking down, I shake my head and laugh. If someone could see me now. There are distinct bite marks around both of my nipples. I guess after he let me tie him up on his birthday instead of offering to let him do the same to me, it's only fair. Gah! Every night with him is better than the one before. And it isn't simply the sex. I'm clear on that now. The way he held me, stroking my hair and my back. It was so tender. I was chastising myself almost immediately for allowing myself to consider he could be treating me that way. But when he asked me to stay, I knew it was real. If only Austin had been with Bailey, I would have stayed.

Arriving at the house to pick up Austin was awkward. I don't like lying to anyone, particularly my family. They were generous enough to watch my child so I could study, and instead, I went out for dinner and then home with Sebastian for an evening of hot and kinky. Luckily, there were no bite marks above the collarbone. Regardless of love bites giving me away, I think they suspected something was up. I'm thirty-seven years old, for gosh sakes. They can't possibly think I'm celibate. Needless to say, I said as little as possible, grabbed Austin, and got the hell out of there.

Drying myself off, I slip my nightgown over my head and blush as the silky material brushes across the bruised peaks of my breasts. The replaying of that night has taken up permanent residence in my head.

I have two days left before my exam. I need a good night's sleep tonight. The plan is to study in the a.m. and put in a good evening's work tomorrow, so I can spend Tuesday studying for my exam. No more focusing on Sebastian's hot body. I've got this.

CHAPTER TWENTY-FIVE

Isabella

"Thank you. I really appreciate this. Goodbye."

I can't believe it. I got the job. Well, contingent on passing my final exams, I have the radiology tech job. *No pressure.* The interviews apparently went well, and all the recommendations from the guys in the department certainly helped.

I shouldn't be worried about this exam. I'm smart. I've applied myself and studied hard. There's no reason to think I won't pass. But it's a big deal. So it's normal to be worried.

"Austin, I just got a call from the hospital. If I pass my exam on Wednesday, I'll be able to work there. Isn't that great?"

"Yeah, Mom."

"Okay, you check in with Margaret and let me know if you need anything. I'm off tomorrow to study, and then if I pass the exam, we're going to celebrate. Just you and me, buddy." Turning, I head for the door. Barely making it two steps, I see a young delivery man walking up toward me.

"Hi. Ms. Potter?"

"Yes."

"I have a package for you."

Looking down, I notice another package from Amazon and assume it's probably for more of the charcoal sketch pencils.

"Thank you."

I quickly head back into the house. "Austin. There's a package by the door," I yell. I try not to laugh when he scurries to the front room to check it out. My child is only quick when he's checking on the mail, in a hurry to get to the bathroom, or being called to dinner for something covered in cheese.

~

"Jeff, she said I all but have the job. I just need to pass my exam, and it's mine."

"Isabella, that's fantastic. I know that exam is going to be nothing for you. You've got this."

"Thanks, Jeff. I feel like I should be fine. But you know how it is when you're facing something important like this. Your mind can play tricks with you." Pushing the large portable x-ray machine toward the front of the ER, I stop in my tracks when I see Damian standing in full firefighter turn-out gear beside the ambulance bay doors. "Hey, Jeff. That's my brother. I'll be right back." Walking swiftly over to him, I approach cautiously. Is he hurt?

"Hey, what are you doing here?" I ask nervously.

"B, I came to see you."

"Is Austin okay?"

"Of course. I just wanted to hug you before your big day on Wednesday. I know you're going to want to concentrate on cramming tomorrow, and Bailey will have Austin."

"That's so sweet of you, Damien. But you wished me luck the other night," I say, rubbing his arm.

"I know, but that was after ribbing you for nearly twenty minutes about where you'd been all night. You never ask us to help, and when you do, we give you the business. I'm sorry. You're a grown woman. What you do on your time is your business."

I can't help but look at him in shock.

"I'm serious. I'm sorry. Now, give me a hug so I can get back on the truck and go. We were out in the area and had to stop and get our drug box changed out from an earlier call."

Enveloping him in a bear hug, I smile up at him. "You're so sweet. Thank you for thinking of me, D. I'm nervous but pretty confident I can do it. I'll let you know as soon as I hear the results.

"You better, we're all cheering you on." He bops me on the nose and turns to stride out of the door. The gesture takes me back to when Sebastian did the same. Suddenly, I wish I was getting a good luck hug from him.

Giggling, I turn back to Jeff. "Okay, sorry about that. I always get worried something has happened when they show up unannounced."

"You're fine. Now, let's make sure today you think about any questions you may have before your exam. Whether it's about completing an x-ray or something on your test."

"Thanks, Jeff."

Sebastian

Well, this day has started with a bang. I've had a crap morning in the OR. At both hospitals. I was only scheduled to be in surgery at Mary Immaculate, however, there was an add-on in the early afternoon at St. Luke's.

The first surgery was pretty straightforward, however, the surgical assistant was new, and many of the usual surgical tools were replaced with something I wasn't as comfortable with. This made the handoff of instrumentation clumsy at best. I lived in fear of something falling onto the floor.

At St. Luke's, fall on the floor, it did. Not just one, but two surgical instruments. This caused delay and more agitation. I'm starting to think I can't make it through a simple procedure without it occurring.

As if this wasn't bad enough, I dropped by the emergency room to see if I could catch Nick and Kat together and instead see Isabella all over a damn firefighter. I'd been trying to locate Nick. He was on call today and not in his office. Living on the lake, I wondered if they might be interested in taking this dog off of my hands if I can't find a home for it.

I've been beating myself up about it. I have no claim to Isabella. I need to shit or get off the pot. I know this is relatively new territory for me, but I need to just make a decision or risk losing that girl to someone who has the balls to go after what he wants. I used to be the king of accepting a challenge. So what was it about this that had me so afraid? My only painful rejection by a female had occurred almost seventeen years ago. I needed to man up.

Searching the ER, I'd come up short. Heading for my car, I send a text to Nick.

4:35 p.m.
Bas: Hey, tried to catch you. You weren't in your office or in the ER. Give me a shout if you get a chance.

I walk toward my car and head for home. It's ridiculous that while I'm trying to find a home for Boomerang, I'm equally excited to see that damned dog after the day I've had.

Thirty minutes later, I return home and park the car in the garage. As I enter, it's eerily quiet. I walk the hallways, calling Boomerang. I don't know what possessed me to name the damn thing, except I didn't want to keep calling him Dog.

As I come out of my bedroom, I see Sam sitting on a chaise lounge by the pool. "Hey, have you seen a dog?"

"A brown one? Yeah, why?"

"Because he's not here."

"*You* have a dog?"

"No. He's a stray. Where is he?"

"I don't know."

"What do you mean, you don't know? You just asked if I meant 'the brown one,' and he's suddenly not here?"

"I came in and realized I left something in my car. So I went back to get it, and when I came back to the front door, he was standing in the yard. He kept tilting his head, looking at me funny."

Ha, I'd think he was crazy if I hadn't seen the dog do the same thing myself. I wave my hand in a *keep-going* motion.

"That's it."

"What's it?"

"That's where I saw the dog," Sam states slowly, enunciating each syllable like I'm a dunce.

"So he just ran off?"

"I don't know. He was in the yard, and then he wasn't. So I guess so."

I'm suddenly hit with an overwhelming sense of disappointment. I have no idea why, as I've never entertained having a dog. Just in the twenty-four hours since he's been here, I've had to clean up small piles of dog hair that he'd shed all over my expensive rugs and hardwood floors. Not to mention, he probably belongs to someone.

Looking at Sam cuts through the thoughts of the dog and his whereabouts, and it quickly dawns on me... "Why are you back here? You're like a runny nose in winter. I can't get rid of you."

"Where's the love?"

"You know me, I love better from a distance."

"Isn't that the damn truth? I honestly just wanted a soak in the jacuzzi. I think I threw my back out."

"Fucking someone or running from them?"

"Uh, both?"

"Oh, for fucks sake, Sam."

"Well, once I got here, I didn't want to strip down naked and get in your jacuzzi if your lady friend might be coming by. Wouldn't want her to realize she was with the wrong Lee brother. So I decided to wait 'til you got here. Mighty polite of me, huh?"

"Get out."

"Awe, come on, man."

"Sam, it's been a shit evening on top of a shit day. I'm taking a shower, having a scotch, eating my weight in cheese, and going to bed. In that order. I don't care if you get in the jacuzzi, but please lock the door on your way out and don't come back here without calling me first."

Storming down the hallway, I head for the bedroom. I'm about to disrobe when my phone starts to vibrate in my pocket.

"Hello," I snarl.

"Hi. Sebastian? It's Kendal. Could you come by my office Friday morning? I want to go over a few things with you."

CHAPTER TWENTY-SIX

Sebastian

The hits just keep on rolling.

Meandering back toward the office, my irritation is at an all-time high. I arrived at Kendal's office as scheduled to find she'd been pulled into an emergent surgery for a head bleed. It's hard to act haughty when you're in the company of a neurosurgeon. But they're usually condescending enough for both of us.

When I inquired into rescheduling, I was advised by the receptionist she had instructions from Kendal to schedule a few more tests before we meet again. Like hell that's happening. I'm not doing anything else until I meet with Kendal in person and find out where she's going with this million-dollar workup. I mean, are these tests more psychology or neurology driven?

Kendal has always been into holistic medicine. She uses an integrative approach, not discounting traditional science but embracing new techniques to heal the body naturally. There was a time I was worried it could tarnish her career, as many of the physicians at St. Luke's stand behind a well-researched, evidence-based approach to treatment. I'm willing to consider holistic measures to get my mind on track in the OR. Especially after the way the surgeries have been going lately. But my expertise is highly sought after. I only have so much room in my schedule for tedious studies. Hell, this workup will cause more stress than I had when I started.

Bzzz. Bzzz.

"Hello?"

"Dr. Lee?

"Yes?"

"It's Ava. Nick asked if I could reach out to you. They've had a family emergency, and he's on-call for the ER. He doesn't think he'll be long, but as it so happens, he received a call at the worst possible time. He asked if I could reach out to you to see if there was any chance you could help him out and see what the consult is about, and he'll be here as soon as he can."

"Sure, Ava. Is everything okay?"

"I think so. I'm sure he'll fill you in once he's back. I don't know all of the details, but it didn't sound like it was anything too serious."

This all sounds cryptic. But there's little I wouldn't do for my friend and his family. Walking toward the ER, I approach the nurses' station to check in and see if I can locate the consult in question.

"Hi, Dr. Lee." Nurse Bobbi smiles coyly at me.

"Hello. I'm looking for the orthopedic consult that was placed to Dr. Barnes. I apologize, I don't have any details. He was pulled away, and I offered to evaluate them."

"Oh, sure. Let me find out who called you." She continues to bat her eyes playfully at me, and I have to prevent my eye roll. No sense pissing off everyone in my wake today.

Looking about the busy area, I observe several patients who appear critical, on ventilators and the like. The entire area is awash with the chirping of monitors, call bells dinging, and various phones ringing. A few patients sit quietly on their stretchers, looking at their phones. To my left, I notice Donovan Grant in one of the rooms, seated in a chair and holding the hand of an elderly woman as he speaks to her. I can only imagine the number of uncomfortable conversations he must endure on a daily basis.

"Dr. Lee? It was Dr. Silver who called in the consult. He's in the physicians' work area."

"Thank you," I offer as I stroll past her toward Dr. Silver.

"Dr. Lee. I wasn't expecting to see you today. I heard you're covering for Dr. Barnes."

"Yes. What've you got?"

"I have a little old lady who has a foreign body stuck around her thumb. We haven't got a clue how to remove it. How great to have a hand surgeon here?"

Is he fucking with me? It's rare that an emergency room provider can't find a way to remove a foreign body unless it needs to go to the OR. "Is this a surgical case?"

"I don't think so. But I can't figure out how to remove it, so I guess it could come to that—"

"Dr. Silver, your patient in room nine isn't doing well. Her blood pressure is dropping." A nurse appears with a harried look about her.

"If you'll excuse me, Dr. Lee. The patient is Mrs. Hickson in room seventeen," he adds before exiting the area.

I locate room seventeen and knock on the door and find an elderly black female seated on the stretcher, her face appearing downcast. Her husband is at her bedside, wearing a similar expression.

"Hi. I'm Dr. Sebastian Lee. I'm a hand specialist. Dr. Silver advised you had a—"

Mrs. Hickson holds up her right hand, which appears to be holding a pair of kitchen shears.

Confusion sets in. How is this a problem? I was expecting a ring or something small and tightly compressed about a digit. These kitchen shears are just dangling from her fingers.

"She was trying to cut open a bottle of superglue. But she must have hit the top of it because it dripped straight down onto her fingertips, and now her thumb and forefinger are glued together, and we can't get them apart."

Taking a closer look at her hand, the pads of her fingers are firmly glued in place, and the scissors dangle between them. "Well, we probably just need some acetone or something to get them apart."

"We've tried all that. We've soaked it in nail polish remover and even tried rocking a knife slowly back and forth over the glue to try to separate them, but I'm worried about cutting her fingers because she's on a blood thinner for her heart."

Well, hell. I don't have time for this ridiculousness. There's got to be a way the doctors here can figure out how to get her fingers apart because she definitely isn't undergoing a needless surgical procedure at her age, on blood thinners, no less. After completing a cursory evaluation, I excuse myself to meet with Dr. Silver.

"Yes, I've met Mrs. Hickson and her husband. She's not a surgical candidate, and this is not something I have the time or inclination to contend with. I would contact the pharmacy and see if there is anything else they would recommend and consider getting some bolt cutters to remove the scissors."

"Well, that's unfortunate. I didn't think she'd need surgery but hoped you could get her fingers apart. I guess I'll have to use a scalpel."

"You'll do no such thing. The woman is on blood thinners," I huff. "Hell, let me make a phone call." I sit at the desk and call the hospital operator, requesting the inpatient pharmacist.

"Hello? This is Poppy."

"Hi. This is Sebastian Lee. I've responded to a consult by the ER staff for a woman who has superglued her fingers together. Apparently, they've tried soaking in acetone without improvement. This woman is on blood thinners, so I'd like to avoid anything invasive in our attempts to separate her fingers."

"Oh, I understand. Would you mind giving me just a minute, Dr. Lee? I want to check on something."

"Sure, so long as it won't take too long." I sit on hold for what seems like an hour. For as much money as this hospital takes in, why they can't get better hold music is a mystery.

"Dr. Lee?"

"Yes."

"So, I think I've found something which might work. I can bring it right up if that'll help."

"Absolutely. Thank you." I hang up the phone, grateful St. Luke's employs one competent individual on their staff who is working today.

Moments later, I notice a beautiful blonde with a long white lab coat approach. She's carrying the largest tub of petroleum jelly I've ever seen.

"Dr. Lee?"

"Yes. I take it you're Poppy?"

"Yes. What gave it away?" She laughs, her bright blue eyes twinkling.

How have I never seen this woman before? I guess they keep the pharmacists locked away like mad scientists, creating life-saving potions in their lair.

"So, from what I researched, there's no quick fix for this situation. I would recommend you have the patient alternate between soaking their fingers in the acetone and the petroleum jelly and gently try to pry their fingers apart. In all the years I've worked here, I've never heard of a case like this. But I think it could work."

"Well, you've worked harder at coming up with a solution than anyone, including me." I wink. I suddenly feel an odd sensation in my chest. This beautiful girl feels off-limits. I have no relationship with Isabella preventing me from flirting or pursuing someone else. But the thought she could do the same doesn't sit well. Poppy is clearly attractive, but the regular pull to pursue more isn't there.

"I'll check back in to see how it went," she says, winking back as she spins and returns the way she came.

I carry the oversized tub of goo back to Mrs. Hickson's room and explain what we're going to try. Suddenly, this quiet, sweet woman starts to tear up. I watch as her husband reassures her. *Hell, did I say something to upset her?* I look to Mr. Hickson, unsure of what's happened. I would've thought a plan of action that didn't involve a surgical procedure would be a relief.

"She hates anyone making a fuss over her. She's just upset that she's put all of you out over something so foolish."

My heart falls, hearing this and seeing her downtrodden expression. I grab the chair closest and take her scissor-clad hand into mine. "Mrs. Hickson. Freak accidents happen all of the time. I'd be without a job if there weren't kind people like you giving me a purpose in life," I tease.

A small smile seems to curl her lips. If she only knew of the foolish mistakes I've made in the OR of late. Don't think I'll share that and break any confidence she may have in my ability to free her.

"I'm going to go and let your nurse know the plan. How about you help her out and hit your call bell once you've soaked for thirty minutes? Then she can clean that off and try the acetone again. I'll come back later and check on you. In the meantime, you can gently try to pull the fingers apart, but not too aggressively. You know how easily you bleed."

"Yes, sir. Thank you," she responds with renewed hope on her face.

I fill nurse Holly in on the plan and tell her to contact me if she needs me. Heading for the office, I look at my watch and realize the time. Shaking my head at what this consult has done to my appointments for the day, I estimate I'll be about an hour behind unless someone cancels. As I reach the end of the hall, I see two familiar bodies in a tight embrace. *What the hell?*

Stopping in my tracks, I see Jeff with a huge smile on his face as he holds Isabella firmly against him. *Why is he always touching her?* I have no right, but I'm livid. This possessiveness I feel for her is unsettling. Why in the hell did I think I could consider a relationship with someone if this is how unhinged I become at the thought of someone touching them?

I immediately turn and walk in the direction I came. I need a different exit from this department. If I don't put some distance between Jeff and me, I'm libel to rip his arms off.

Several hours later, I return to the ER to check in on Mrs. Hickson. The *one* day no one cancels their clinic appointment. As expected, I ran about an hour late the entire afternoon. Let's just hope this sweet woman has had success.

I come around the nurses' station toward Mrs. Hickson's room, and

I'm hit with uproarious cheers and laughter. As I walk toward her doorway, I see her hugging Dr. Silver.

"Oh, thank you. Thank you, Dr. Silver. I'm so grateful my fingers are free without surgery or bleeding. That stuff really worked."

Are you shitting me? That asshole gave up on her and just happened to be in her vicinity when what we tried worked. Yet, he's acting like her knight in shining armor. I spin on my heel, ready to be done with this day. Everyone's getting hugs but Sebastian today. *Maybe I should've pursued Poppy. She looked the giving sort.*

I make it down the long corridor toward the physicians' parking lot when none other than Isabella approaches. Feeling jealous of Jeff's ability to hug her in public, I consider just walking away and pretending I haven't seen her.

"Hi." I hear from her direction.

"Ms. Potter," I greet flatly.

"I'm excited I got to see you today. I have some—"

Bzzz. Bzzz.

Witnessing Kendal's name on the screen, I hold a finger up to Isabella as I gruffly answer the phone.

"Sebastian. I'm sorry I was detained this morning. I'm happy to meet with you on Monday. I'd like to sit down with you in person to go over what he have so far and plan where to go from here."

"Monday? I'm not waiting until Monday," I spit.

"I'm sorry. I've already left for the day. I had an unavoidable appointment and will be out of the office for the next few days. I don't want to have this conversation over the phone, Sebastian."

"This is incredibly unprofessional. If this turns out to be a bunch of holistic bullshit—" I cut myself off before she fires me as a patient due to my uncontained anger. "I'm already under a lot of pressure. This isn't doing anything to help the matter."

"I understand. Just hang in there a few more days. I'll see you, Monday."

Hanging up, I look up and discover Isabella is still standing before me. I must look like an ogre. I can feel the heat radiating from my angry face.

"Sebastian. Is there something I can do?" she asks, her hands grasping tightly to her to-go container from the cafeteria.

Suddenly, all I can think is that I want the hug Jeff received earlier. A myriad of emotions is catching up with me. This long, disappointing day, pulling me into its undertow. My life seemed so ordered before meeting her. Sure, I'd had the occasional tough day in the OR, but nothing like the days of late. Could this woman be contributing to my downfall? My possessiveness and uneasy want for more quietly playing like background music during the rest of my day. I'm not cut out for this.

"No." It is the only safe reply I can muster.

"Are you sure? I want to help," she adds as she starts to reach for my hand.

"I don't need any more help, good girl. I'm better off on my own," I declare and abruptly turn toward my car and the solitude of home.

CHAPTER TWENTY-SEVEN

Isabella

Driving home, I hate admitting I allowed Sebastian to steal my glory today. I'd been so excited throughout the day. Finding out I'd passed my exam and secured a full-time job had me floating on air. Not only was I relieved that all of the hard work had paid off, but I was proud of myself. I'd accomplished a lot. Any single mother successfully going after what's important to her while simultaneously setting a great example for her child deserves to shout it from the rooftops.

I know for someone like Sebastian, my news is small potatoes. But it started to seem he cared about me. The tender way he asked me to stay the other night... was that just for more sex in the morning? It had felt like more.

Yet witnessing Sebastian's reaction during his phone call, my joy became shrouded in concern. His behavior wasn't his usual brusque dismissal of incompetence. I couldn't completely follow his conversation. It wasn't right to eavesdrop. But he didn't walk away. He was the one lifting his finger in the air in the 'give me a minute' salute. Sure, initially, I was a bit offended by his behavior. Yet, after hearing part of that conversation, the irritation I felt was replaced with worry. *Is he okay?*

Sitting at the stoplight, the bold red beacon has me halting my current worries and changing gears. Was that a dismissal? Had he, in no uncertain terms, tried to tell me that he wasn't interested in me any longer? What had he said? "I don't need any more help, good girl. I'm better off on my own."

And what is it with the good girl routine? I know that's how he sees me, or so he said. But for heaven's sake, I extended our one-night stand. I turned up on his doorstep and marched my way in like I was taking no prisoners just to later spend his birthday doing just that. He was at my disposal that night, all tied up and at my mercy. In what way was this good girl behavior?

Is he referring to my life with Austin? He had no idea I was a single mother when he gave me that ridiculous nickname. *I'd like to show him how bad I can be!*

Bzzz. Bzzz.

Looking down, I see Katarina's name flash on my phone screen.

"Hey," I greet excitedly. Thank goodness. I know this conversation will go a lot better than the one I just had.

"Hi, Isabella. Sorry, it took so long to call you back. It's been a day."

"You okay?"

"Yes. We got a call from our attorney about the adoption. There were some concerns the biological mother needed to address. We had to agree to the conditions and sign some paperwork so she wouldn't consider another couple."

"Oh, Kat. She can do that?"

"Yes. Adoption is a huge test of faith. It's not the mothers' fault for wanting to be clear about their priorities. They want what's best for their children. That's typically why they make an adoption plan. Because they can't give their child what they feel is best. You can either react to their concerns in fear, thinking of them as manipulative, or you can respond in love, appreciating what a tremendous sacrifice they're making."

"Katarina, you're such a strong person. I can't imagine how

difficult this has to be for the two of you. I know you put on a brave face, but you've got to be under a great deal of stress."

"Thanks, Isabella. You're right. Even though I'm trying to keep a healthy mindset about the whole process, it's anxiety-provoking. It's easier with Grace here. I try to focus on her. We didn't have time to think about it with her adoption." She laughs. "Enough about me. What was your news? I so hope it's what I think it is."

"I passed. I passed my exam and have accepted a full-time position in the radiology department at St. Luke's."

"Oh, I'm so happy for you. You deserve this. What're you planning to do to mark the occasion? Maybe you and Sebastian can celebrate *you* this time." She giggles into the phone. I laugh at how this girl set me up, telling me it was Sebastian's birthday and to at least offer him a dance in the pub if I couldn't give him one of the lap variety.

"What?" I try to sound shocked, but after their disappearing act the other night, this is pointless. "I think Austin and I might get take-out from Luigi's."

"Have you told him?"

"Who, Austin?"

"No, Sebastian, you goof."

"Kat, we don't really have that kind of relationship. Hell, we don't have any kind of relationship. I don't even have his phone number. We've hooked up a few times, but it's really only physical between us."

"I'm calling bullshit, Isabella. I saw the way the two of you were looking at each other. Hell, Nick and I left early because watching the two of you together on the dance floor was getting us too hot and bothered. I've never seen him like that with a woman. Ever."

"Whatever. He made it clear he isn't interested in more."

"What do you mean?"

"I tried to tell him my news as he was heading out for the night. We got interrupted by a phone call that he didn't sound happy about. Then he basically told me he didn't need a good girl like me."

"You're kidding?"

"No. I tried to chalk it up to him being in a bad mood, but thinking back, I saw him in the ER earlier, and he was flirting with someone."

"Isabella, that's just Bas. He's overly charismatic with everyone."

"No, this seemed different. She was gorgeous. I saw him wink at her. It needled at me most of the afternoon. I tried to focus on my happy news, but after that interaction later… well, he is a playboy. I'm sure I was just one more notch—"

"I don't buy it for a second, B. Nick even sees it. He said he's never seen Bas like he is with you."

"You only saw us together a couple of times, Kat."

"I know. But, I think Sebastian confided in Nick. I didn't press. But Nick seems to think Sebastian has it bad for you."

My cheeks warm at the thought. I'm not sure why. I mean, why should I care if someone who is so dismissive is interested in me? *But I do.* As much as I should run screaming in the other direction, I can't fight how I feel when we're together. I'm kidding myself if I think this is purely physical.

"I don't know what made him snap, Kat. The last time we were together, he was so different. Maybe it's wishful thinking."

"Isabella, you've proven you can tackle anything you put your mind to. I know you've protected your heart for a long time. It isn't just you. You have Austin to think about. But I think Sebastian needs a push."

I don't mind pushing. But for what? Is this how it'll always be with him? Up one hill and down another? Always trying to prove my worth? Fighting for my place in his world? Yet I had to acknowledge, I'd been the one running out on him. Never staying because my priority was Austin. I had no right to judge. But the dismissal earlier today didn't feel like it was for a noble cause. This didn't feel like he was putting someone else's needs above his own. This felt selfish. Like he'd decided. *The End.*

Katarina continues, "Men like Nick and Sebastian are used to being in control. They aren't going to let anyone or anything come between something or someone they want. I've seen it. Nick and Bas are a lot alike. They'll move heaven and earth to get what they want if they feel it's being taken away."

"Well, he can find that challenge with some coed or nurse at the hospital. I'm too old for those games, Katarina."

"I agree. They love a challenge. But this is different. Nick pulled out all of the stops for me. I almost missed out because I was protecting myself. But getting hurt won't leave you any worse off than where you are now. I'm just saying, think about it. If there could be something special between you, don't fight it."

"I'm not sure it's up to me."

"But it is. Okay, I've got to feed Grace. You go pick up Luigi's. Have a long soak in a hot bubble bath with a TL Swan book and think about what I said. You're every bit as strong as one of her characters. If they can slay their men, you can too."

"You're crazy." I laugh.

"Maybe. But when you're ready, give me a call. You're going to need your girl tribe for this one, but I'm ready."

Sitting in the corner chair in Austin's room, I rub my belly as he paints. Luigi's hit the spot. Now I'm celebrating with a fruity glass of chianti and enjoying the show before taking a soak in a hot bubble bath.

This painting makes me a little sad. Not because of what he's depicting, but because it's honestly one of my favorite "Austin originals," and the thought of painting over it makes me heartsick. If only I could get the Potter boys to carefully cut out that wall and build a new one.

I observe Austin as he stands back from his work, head tilted to the side, inspecting. I can feel my defenses rise. This stance occurs frequently before he announces he needs to start again. Trying not to let my mind entertain such a deplorable thought, I try to spot what has him so fixated. I can barely make out the smudge around one leaf in the upper right-hand corner. Please don't let that bring this masterpiece down.

Closing my eyes, I take a deep inhale of my delicious tangy wine before taking another sip.

"Fuck it."

My wine sprays about the room as I splutter on the remaining beverage lingering in my throat.

"Austin?"

"What?"

"What did you just say?"

"Fuck it."

"Where did you hear that?"

"Gavin says, sometimes you just have to say fuck it."

Holy shit. Nick wasn't kidding. "Well, I'm not used to your words being as colorful as your art. Maybe keep that language to a minimum and only in the house, okay?"

"Okay, Mom."

"Austin?"

"What?"

"*Why* did you say that?"

"That leaf is bothering me. I was sketching at the lake, and that happened, and Gavin said I shouldn't throw away the whole picture because one spot bothers me. He said, sometimes you just have to say fuck it and make it work."

Shaking my head, I had to agree with Gavin. "I think there's some wisdom to that, Austin. I'd hate to see this mural get painted over. It's one of my favorites."

"Me too, Mom."

It's late. I have an early day tomorrow, but I'm feeling restless. The soak in the tub was nice while it lasted, but my mind kept drifting to a certain surgeon. I can't shake the feeling something is off. He just didn't seem like himself. The irritability at whomever he was speaking with seemed more like fear.

I've replayed the limited conversation in my head again and again. Does he have a patient who's in a bad way? Is he consulting someone who isn't being timely with their recommendations or treatment? Or is this more personal? Whatever's happening, I choose to believe that's what has him pulling away. Not me.

I can't continue to pretend that our electricity is only physical. I've never been with any man who makes me feel the way he does. Even when things were good with Rick, before medical school, he was always self-serving. My mind drifts to when I dared to ask Sebastian if I could tie him up. Never in a million years did I think he'd let me. That night was beyond anything I've read or dreamt about. The only thing better was afterward, lying in his arms. For all of his bravado, he's so sweet and tender. God, how I wish I could've stayed with him longer.

Lying here, picturing his deep blue eyes, his strong arms, and the way his dimple pops when he smiles at me, I can't get the grin off of my face. Hell, I'm all in. I'm falling for this loser.

I sit up in bed and grab my phone.

10:35 p.m.
Isabella: Hey Kat, sorry for the late hour. I've been thinking. You're right. I want it all. I don't have a girl tribe. It's just me and my sister, Bailey… and you. If you'll help me.

10:38 p.m.
Katarina
Katarina: Hell yeah, I'm in! I have a plan. Do you work tomorrow night?

10:40 p.m.
Isabella: No. I'm off at 3.

10:43 p.m.
Katarina Barnes
Katarina: Great! Can you come to the lake house? You're welcome to bring Austin. He may need to hang with Nick. And bring your sister. We'll need reinforcements.

Holy hell, what is she up to now?

10:46 p.m.
Isabella: I can ask my brothers if Austin can stay with them. If not, I'll bring him along. Thank you.

10:49 p.m.
Katarina Barnes
Katarina: Don't thank me yet 😂

CHAPTER TWENTY-EIGHT

Isabella

"I don't know about this, Kat." I look up at her and her sister, Rachel, my eyes wide in shock while Bailey laughs behind me.

"I'm telling you, Isabella. This will work," Kat says in total seriousness. She's holding up a see-through mesh bodysuit with bright gold stars, which are sewn strategically over the breasts like built-in pasties. *What the hell have I gotten myself into with this girl?*

"I think you should go for it, B. I'm here for you, sis."

"Uh, shut it, Bailes. Why did I bring you again?"

"Moral support?" She shrugs her shoulders, unable to keep the smirk off of her face.

"Awe, come on, B. It'll be fun," Kat cajoles, her sister now covering her face at Kat's antics.

"Fun for who? Are you wearing one of these?"

"Been there, done that." Rachel laughs.

"What?" I ask, confused.

"Nothing. Ignore her. I rode rescue with this tart who danced at a local strip club. I've since met the owner, who's actually a decent guy. I made a few phone calls and tada!"

"Tada, what? He let you have some costumes?"

"Um, no." She's wincing at me now, her shoulders pulled tightly up to her ears. *What on earth is she getting me into?*

"He's letting you dance," she blurts out before stepping far enough away I can't hurt her.

"Dance? Like letting me use the place after hours?"

"Um, no."

"Okay, spill it, Katarina," I blurt over the uncontrolled laughter of Rachel and Bailey.

"He's going to have an amateur night. He said he does it once in a while, and he'd be thrilled to have you on stage."

"What? Oh, no! There's no way I'm doing that!"

"Awe, come on, B. You can do this," Bailey encourages.

"I'm not stripping on stage in front of a bunch of strange men."

"Is that the part that's bothering you? The strange men?" Bailey laughs.

"Isabella," Kat cajoles, grabbing my arms firmly in her grip to make a point. "You're a beautiful woman. I've seen you dance. You just need to put yourself out there. Enjoy it. Live a little. You mark my words. If Sebastian Lee sees you parading your assets for a bunch of screaming men, he'll lose his shit!"

Standing there wordless, blinking at Katarina, I try to absorb what she's saying. How is *this* the plan?

"Think of it like a wet T-shirt contest," Bailey teases.

Spinning to give her the death glare, Kat interrupts, pulling me back to look in her direction.

"It's nothing like that. You'll have hot pants and a jacket on. You can flash him at the end if you want, but those stars are pretty big. No one is seeing anything with those on there. We'll work on the dance here, so you'll have something to concentrate on while you're on stage. I'm telling you, this is going to work."

Frozen to this spot on the floor, I can hear the words coming from her mouth but am trying to assess whether I'm actually awake. That this is a real conversation and not a hallucination. I look at these girls, mouth agape, like I've completely lost my mind. I cannot believe I'm even considering this.

"Okay, we've got no time for dawdling. Let's get this show on the road," Kat says, walking over to her phone.

"Literally," Bailey says, snickering.

"Bailey, you need to help with this dance. We're all going to be at the end of the catwalk cheering you on and doing the dance. So you can mimic us if you get nervous."

"It'll be like we're the dance instructors at Jenna's dance recital." Rachel claps. "Except I won't give you a carnation and a pack of Skittles when you're done." Rachel and Bailey start to laugh, and I again give them the stink eye.

"The key is to get out of your head. Just enjoy doing something crazy for once," Katarina says, cueing Demi Lovato on her cell. As the opening chords to "Confident" pour out of her blue tooth speakers, she stands in front of me and starts to dance. "I'm just going to see what works, and then we can piece it together, okay?"

"Ha, yeah, okay." I'm shaking my head back and forth, trying to wake up from this crazy dream.

It's late. I'm so glad the boys kept Austin at home with them tonight. I'm going to get up early and head back to get him in the morning. I may just fall asleep right here on this floor.

We've all been dancing, laughing, and drinking for the better part of the evening. Every now and then, Nick sneaks down to the basement to catch a good laugh. I'll be mortified when I see him when this ridiculous show occurs, but I'm going to do as Kat suggested and just focus on them.

"I think we've come a long way, ladies," Kat slurs. We're all lying in a circle, on our backs, staring up at the ceiling.

"We did a good job," Rachel adds.

"The margaritas helped," I chime in, round-robin style, each of us adding something as we go clockwise around the circle.

"Yeah, they were my favorite part." Bailey breaks out into a fit of laughter. This is the way much of this evening has gone. Will I even remember any of this when it's time for this show to occur? *Oh, yeah. When exactly is this show supposed to occur?*

"Um, Kat?"

"Yeah, B?"

"When is this show supposed to happen?"

I quickly notice, it's eerily quiet. God, did she fall asleep that fast?

"What?" Bailey squeals, laughing so hard I can see her arms across her abdomen to steady herself. *What did I miss?*

"What's so funny?" I ask nervously.

"She said tomorrow," Rachel whisper-yells before joining Bailey in hysterics.

"What? Tomorrow?"

"I knew you'd chicken out otherwise. The more time you had to think about it, the more time to back out." Kat just shrugs her shoulders like, *no biggie.*

"Kat?" I blurt.

"Yes?"

"Are you crazy?"

"I think we've established that several times over," Rachel guffaws.

"Listen. We'll meet at my place in town. We'll have a few drinks to take the edge off, help you get dressed and take you to Daddy Rabbits. Nick will come later with Sebastian."

"Holy shit, there's no—" I'm cut off when Katarina grabs my arm.

"There is a way. You're a rock star, Isabella. You're going to strut down that catwalk like you own the place. Every guy in there is going to be yelling for you and throwing money your way. Just soak up the admiration. If you get nervous, you look at us. But you're going to own that fucking stage. Then, you'll own him. Mark my words, B. He'll be putty in your dirty little hands."

It's showtime. I'm a hot mess. I've had a few drinks, but not so many I can't manage these black stilettos. My hair is blown out, with soft dark waves cascading over my shoulders. I'm wearing this mesh bodysuit that literally only covers about four inches of space around my nipples. Sure, they're shaped like stars, so there's the illusion of coverage. The black leather jacket and black hot pants make me feel a little better. I guess I could've been dancing in a thong.

Katarina is sitting in the backseat of her SUV with me, trying to calm my nerves while Rachel drives. We hit a pothole in the road, and I nearly jump out of my seat.

"Holy hell, please don't get us pulled over on the way there. I'll never be able to explain this getup."

"Just relax, B. You look hot," Bailey says with a wide grin. "I'm so proud of you. Hell, I want to dance for someone now."

"It's not someone. It's someones!" I bellow.

"You're going to be great. If you get nervous, try and focus on one person. Tease them a little. It'll only further your cause with Sebastian," Kat encourages.

"How do you know he'll be there?"

"Oh, he'll be there. Trust me. Nick will make sure of it. He's rooting for the two of you."

About that time, I feel the car turn and look up to see a dingy gray building with a neon hot pink sign overhead that reads Daddy Rabbits. *Oh, good lord, what am I doing here?*

We exit the vehicle, and I can't help but look around, feeling completely conspicuous. Kat grabs my hand and rubs my back as we head for the door. I'm so anxious it feels like an out-of-body experience. I'm not really listening to the conversations around me, just trying to convince myself it's one night and no one is going to get hurt. If *this* doesn't dispel the whole good girl image Sebastian has for me, nothing will. And if I dance my ass off, and he's still not willing to put himself out there, then screw him!

I follow along behind Katarina and a staff member as they show us to the back room. Rachel and Bailey wave goodbye and look for seats. As we enter the back room, I quickly turn to Kat.

"I feel like I'm going to be sick. I don't think I can do this."

"You're going to be fine, B."

Before I have a chance to say anything more, a platinum blonde with her hair teased wildly upon her head approaches. Her breasts are quite large for her slender frame.

"Isabella, this is Crystal. We go way back." Kat smiles at the girl who's only looking at me.

"Honey, you're beautiful. Tiny little thing. They're going to love you."

"Wow, you think so?"

"I've worked here a long time. You need to just enjoy yourself out there. If you don't let your nerves get you, they're going to be eating out of your hand."

I take a deep breath and follow along behind them as we enter a very small area with multiple mirrors, clothing, and props everywhere. Several women are milling about. Most are wearing next to nothing. Heck, compared to these girls, I look like I'm going to a church picnic.

"Okay, you'll be up in about twenty minutes. They'll come to get you, and you'll climb up those stairs to the curtained area. We have your music cued and ready to go."

"Holy shit. This is really happening," I mutter.

"I'll stay here with you until you head up the stairs, then I'll make my way out front, so the first thing you see when the curtain goes up is your girl tribe." Kat beams.

"Okay. I'd say thank you for checking this off of my bucket list, but I'm pretty sure in a million years this wouldn't have been on there."

"Too bad," Crystal answers quickly. " 'Cause once you do it, you'll wonder why you never thought to do it before. It's electric. Having that many men worshipping you."

Yeah, whatever. Let's just get this over with.

"You're up," a voice says from behind me, and I notice Kat's nervous expression as she pulls me in for a hug.

"You got this, B. I'm so proud of you. Try to have fun out there," she says, placing a kiss on my cheek before turning to dart out of the room.

I start to make my way up the narrow, metal stairway and pray my stomach contents will not be the headliner this evening. As I get to the top of the steps, I note an X on the floor constructed of white tape and assume that's where I need to stand. Assuming the position we rehearsed at Kat's house, I try to calm my shaking limbs. How the hell is this going to look sexy? I'm going to look like I'm having a seizure if this trembling keeps up.

There is no time to contemplate this any longer, as the familiar notes of "Confident" by Demi Lovato begin to play and the makeshift black curtain begins to rise. I can see in my periphery, the room is dimmer than when we entered. There are flashing lights swirling overhead to the beat of the music. *Focus, Isabella. Focus.*

Almost immediately, I see my tribe jumping up and down at the end of the stage. To their right sits Nick with a huge smile on his face. To his right sits one Sebastian Lee. He's deep into his phone, paying no attention to what's happening around him. *Is he texting someone for a hook-up later?*

My eyes connect with Katarina, who's waving her hands about like she's trying to land a jet plane. I'm sure she's trying to get me back on track. I slowly walk forward, swinging my hips as we practiced. I'd like to think I look sexy, but my knees feel like they're still knocking together. My eyes trail back over to Sebastian, who's still deep into his phone. Enough of this, I'll spend the whole dang song doing this if I don't focus on Kat and the girls.

I watch Kat and the girls and start to relax a bit. The moves we practiced start to come back like second nature, and I feel myself swing a little more provocatively, the crowd around me cheering in response. I hate to say it, but Crystal was right. It's electric to think these men are all focused on me with rapt applause. Feeding on this, I'm able to get into the act more.

Feeling a little daring, I recall what Kat had said. Focus on someone in the crowd. I turn to a male about my age who's standing to the left of the stage. The song is at a part of the chorus where I can improvise a little. Grabbing his tie, I bend at my hips, so my ass is on full display and reach over to muss his hair. Holy shit, the smile this guy's giving me.

It's about this time that I turn my head to the side and notice Sebastian has looked up from his phone and is staring at my ass. There's a perplexing look on his face. Has he not figured out it's me?

Deciding to go all in, I throw caution to the wind and shake my backside briefly before standing to my full height.

As I turn toward the crowd, there's no mistaking who's dancing on this stage now. It's all but confirmed as steam practically pores from his ears as he mouths, "What. The. Fuck?"

CHAPTER TWENTY-NINE

Sebastian

"What. The. Fuck?"

Gathering my senses, I take in the crowd. They're all on their feet, clapping and throwing money at Isabella while that Demi Lovato song plays loudly overhead. To my right, I see Katarina and two other girls on their feet, jumping up and down. This has Kat written all over it. But, how on earth did my good girl get roped into this? My eyes flick beside me to Nick. He's wearing a shit-eating grin that covers every square inch of his face. *Jesus*. Why should it bother me he's looking at her dancing in that outfit when every other guy here is ogling her?

I'm so fucking pissed right now. It's all I can do to stay in this damn seat. But I'm not leaving her here with this den of vipers, even if Nick and Kat are here with her. Hell, I'm certain they got her into this mess in the first place.

Looking back at her, I find her on all fours in front of a man holding a bill out to her. *What the ever-loving hell? Is she...* I watch as the man folds it in half and tucks it between her tits. She's squeezing them together with her arms, the globes elevated above her black corset, those stupid gold stars barely covering her nipples. *I swear to God if I get my hands on her…*

Isabella raises to her full height, keeping her arms crossed in front of her, accentuating her breasts. Dipping her chin to her chest, I watch in amazement as she retrieves the bill with her teeth before plucking it in my direction. She haughtily turns and starts to shimmy that perky little ass up the catwalk.

With her back to the crowd, she starts to drop her leather jacket behind her. Shifting in my seat, I feel like a cougar ready to pounce. There's only a tiny bit of black corset seen along with that see-through thing as she drops the jacket lower. Abruptly, the jacket returns to her shoulders. *Thank fuck.* The music seems to be building to a high point when suddenly, Isabella's right arm is fully extended, her corset dangling from her fingers.

The crowd goes wild. I'm apparently on my feet without thinking when Nick places his hand on my shoulder, pulling me down to my chair with a thud. Giving him the 'what the hell' look, he just shakes his head and points to the stage. *I'm hanging by a fucking thread here.*

It's about this time, Isabella's face turns to the side, her back still to the audience, and she mouths the words to the song. Our eyes connect as she repeats the words, "You had me underrated." Quickly, she spins around and rips her jacket open, revealing nothing but a pair of tiny black hot pants and that fucking see-through thing, her glorious tits covered in only the tiniest pieces of gold, shiny fabric. The entire crowd is on their feet, screaming for her.

That's it! Before I can think better of it, I've catapulted onto the stage and charged at her, dipping my right shoulder enough to scoop her tiny, lush body over my shoulder in a fireman's carry. I make it about four steps down the catwalk toward the back of the club before smacking her ass. *I'm proud of myself. That's three steps more than I anticipated.*

"Ouch!" I hear yelled above me.

"Shut it, GG," I shout. I've got to get her the hell out of here. Thank god, I'd been texting Charlie to meet me out front. There was zero interest in watching this show. I had no idea why Nick dragged me to this place until Miss hot pants showed up on stage. Little did I know how quick an exit I really needed to make.

As I plow through the back door, the cool night air hits me, and I realize her legs and backside must be cold, given how little she's wearing. I reach up and smack her other ass cheek as I walk to the town car.

"Ouch!"

"Just trying to keep your ass warm," I snarl.

Charlie jumps quickly from his seat to come around to the back door. Something tells me this is to get a better glimpse of what kind of madness I've gotten myself into. I toss Bella into the back seat before he can get a good look at her attire, or lack thereof.

"Where to, sir?"

Hell, he thinks I picked up a random stripper? Really? "Home, Charlie."

He gives me a look of total confusion as I slide into the seat beside my tiny dancer and shut the door. She's lying on her side, looking a little nervous. She should be.

Looking forward momentarily, I see the moment Charlie has figured out who's in the car with me. He still looks puzzled, but I can see the relief washing over his face. *No, I haven't started bringing strippers home.* Reaching for the button that controls the privacy screen, I raise it before looking back down at my dream girl gone wild. *What am I going to do with you?*

"You want to be a bad girl?" Slowly, I unbuckle my belt, needing the full effect. I slide the length of it dramatically from the loops of my suit pants and watch as her eyes widen. I've never taken this girl for being into any type of BDSM beyond spanking. I have no intention of marring that beautiful porcelain skin, but she doesn't need to know that.

She visibly gulps as she watches intently.

"On your knees, GG."

She carefully adjusts herself, sitting upright briefly before sliding onto the floor and positioning herself between my legs.

"Pull it out."

I sit back, watching her do my bidding. I'm still so pissed off, I can barely see straight. Maybe a distraction will help. Her nimble fingers work quickly at my pants before she tugs my pants and boxers down vigorously. Lifting my hips, I allow her better access. *Well, I am a gentleman.*

Bella makes quick work of moving my slacks out of her way before she cups my balls and begins to stroke my dick. I've been hard since the first slap of her ass, knowing I planned to punish her for this display. Nothing she did on stage had me turned on. Exposing her beautiful body to others only served to enrage me. The possession I felt when she was with Jeff was nothing compared to that moment.

Her sweet tongue darts out to tease my opening, and a small hiss escapes. I need to control this better. She doesn't deserve to be rewarded for her actions tonight. "Harder, GG. And don't you even think about touching yourself or rubbing those soft thighs together. This is all about me. Do you understand?"

Her dark brown eyes flick up to meet mine as she nods, all while continuing to devour me. Her tongue trails up and down my engorged shaft, occasionally dropping lower to give my balls some attention. *Hell, this woman.* It's taking control not to let her see how much I'm enjoying her efforts. As she continues to stroke and lick, my mind flashes to that ridiculous stunt with the dollar bill in her tits.

"Get up," I bark. Grabbing her by the shoulders, I fling her onto the seat. Pushing her shoulders back, so she's lying flat against the leather, I reach into her jacket and grab ahold of the sorry excuse for a top and rip it down the center. Watching her eyes widen, I climb over her, straddling her chest with my knees. "Squeeze those tits for me, good girl."

She appears confused until I slide my needy dick between the soft mounds of flesh and place my hands over hers, demonstrating exactly what I want from her. Once she's holding them firmly against my cock, I reach over her to the window and brace myself as I fuck her tits.

"Oh, Bas, please," she whimpers. *It's working. I want her all revved up and nowhere to go.*

Isabella

"What's the matter, GG? You wet? Feeling needy?" Sebastian continues to aggressively slide his cock between my breasts, the visual both depraved and decadent. "You need my cock, don't you?"

"Yes, please."

"Should've thought about that before you pulled that stunt earlier," he quips.

I'm dying here. My swollen, achy sex is throbbing. I refuse to believe he'll leave me wanting like this all night. Perhaps if I can hasten his climax, he'll be more forgiving. Dropping my chin down, I flick my tongue against his crown with each upstroke.

"Fuck." I hear above me as he quickly pulls away from me.

What? I thought he'd like that. Watching him closely, my mouth waters as he vigorously strokes his hard length over me. The lust in his eyes is intensifying my need for him. Maybe he won't notice if I bring my thighs together underneath him.

Sebastian starts to grunt as he tugs harder at his shaft. God, I've never seen anything hotter in my life. The rapture taking over his face is carnal. I grip my breasts, pushing them together for him, and tease my nipples, hoping he won't think this is self-gratification. This is all for him.

The grunting turns animalistic as ropes of thick white come are deposited across my breasts. His breathing is labored, but this doesn't appear due to his orgasm. This feels different somehow. Looking down on me, his deep blue eyes almost seem to penetrate my soul.

Dipping his finger into the milky substance lying on my quivering breasts, I watch in stunned amazement as he begins to trail his finger along my collar bone. Is he marking me? With precision, he alternates dipping his finger and returning to his work. Looking down at my chest as he pulls his finger away for the last time, I can see it in the dim lighting.

MINE

～

We arrive at Sebastian's home, and as Charlie opens the door, Bas is quick to cover me and pull me into his chest as he pulls my leather jacket around me and works his way to the door. Lifting me into his arms, I hear a slight "thank you" directed at Charlie before he carries me up the stairs.

Once inside, he wastes no time walking down the hallway to his bedroom. Stepping into the bathroom, he flicks on the light and deposits me on the counter before reaching in to start the water. He removes his clothing and turns to undress me before picking me up and carrying me into the shower. I'm unsure if this is part of his whole possessive routine he has going on or if he can sense my adrenalin starting to take over. I'm not sure I could stand on my own two feet right now if I tried. The only thing keeping me alert is the overbearing need to be touched. My body is thrumming. It's unnerving how turned on I am.

I feel his hands sliding up and down my wet, shaky body. This is only building my frustration. Particularly when he allows his soap-covered hand to graze my swollen flesh. But these caresses are few and far between. More of a tease than a relief.

The shower is over far too quickly. He grabs for a towel and dries me off, wrapping it around me before reaching for one for himself. After he's toweled off, he lifts me and heads for his room. I'm deposited onto his bed, and he lies down on his back beside me. There's no effort to reach for me or touch my skin. *Holy hell. He's really going to leave me like this.*

Sebastian places his arms behind his head, staring up at the ceiling. I'm torn between lust and loathing right now, loathing beginning to take the lead.

"You can get yourself off now if you need to."

What the hell?

"I'm still too fucking pissed off to get you there, but if you need my cock, you know where the condoms are."

Part of me wants to storm out of here, but the larger part is horny as hell. Plus, I have to admit, I started this with this ridiculous plan of Kat's to bring out my alpha male tonight. Ridiculous or not, she was right about the effect this would have on Sebastian. And there's nowhere else I want to be besides here with this domineering sex god.

I climb over him, straddling him and leaning to the side to retrieve a condom from the drawer. *At least he was nice enough to get hard for me again.* My eyes connect with his as I roll the condom down his swollen length. *If this is what he needs to feel like he's in charge, that's okay by me.* I got what I wanted out of this situation.

Raising on my knees, I line myself up with him and slowly sink down. I notice his eyes close as my body accepts him fully. *Mr. Bigshot.* Knowing this will not take me long, I begin undulating on top of him. Rocking back and forth, I reach down and stroke my swollen, achy clit while Bas lies motionless underneath me, his arms still folded under his head. *Whatever.* The intensity is building in my core. Pushing up further onto my knees, I lift up and drop myself down onto him, eliciting a grunt. The pleasure begins to spike, and I drop back onto his cock again and again. I'm so close now that my whole body is beginning to shake.

I suddenly feel his hands cupping my ass, lifting me up as he thrusts into me from below. The nonsensical moaning coming from my lips must sound like I'm speaking in tongues. I'm so turned on, my adrenalin coursing through my veins. I don't know how I'm still upright.

The familiar pull of my groin is there, signaling my orgasm has been detonated. I lean forward slightly, allowing enough friction to strike my clit as he thrusts up into me that I go off like a rocket. "Sebastian," I cry out, my entire body quivering in its release.

Despite my quaking, I can feel his fingers dig into my ass as he thrusts one last time and empties into me. I want to see his face, but I cannot hold my eyes open. I'm so completely spent. White spots cloud my eyes, and I can feel his strong hands pulling me down onto his chest.

As his corded arms wrap tightly around my back, I can feel tender kisses on my scalp as I continue to tremble.

"Shhh," he whispers, stroking my back and my hair. "My bad girl had a big day." I hear the slightest chuckle from him and know we've turned a corner, back to where we always end up after whatever games have led us to this point.

"What now?" I ask, wondering where we stand but honestly too mentally and physically fatigued to care anymore tonight.

"Well, one thing's for certain. You're going to be here when I wake up, that's for damn sure." He's quiet for a moment, then I hear him ask sweetly, "Is Austin okay without you tonight?"

Gah. This man. "Yes. Good thing, too. I'm too tired to leave."

"Now, you tell me. I should have tried harder before."

CHAPTER THIRTY

Isabella

The morning sun breaks through the expensive drapes adorning the windows on the far wall as my eyes blink open. My mind is completely unfocused. It takes me a minute to understand what's happening around me. I'm lying on my side, a firm, warm body wrapped around me. He's gone from shark to octopus, his limbs circled about me like tentacles. My head is lying half on a luxurious pillow and half on Sebastian's outstretched right arm. As my eyes travel down the corded, bronzed skin dusted in dark hair, I try to make out what's in his hand. *Is that a condom?*

I blink a few more times, trying to examine it closer. Was he ready for another round when I fell unconscious? Did he fall asleep with that thing in his hand? About that time, I notice his hand wiggle. As he adjusts his position behind me, I can feel his hard cock resting against my ass. Again, with the hand wiggle.

"What're you doing?" I laugh.

"Waiting for you to wake up and put it on me."

"Oh, my god, have you been holding that thing in your hand all night?"

"No. Had it tucked under my pillow." He chuckles. "Now get it on me, GG. I've been waiting for this moment for a long time."

Giggling, I tear open the condom wrapper as he lifts my left leg and drapes it over his. His hips start to glide back and forth behind me, stroking my swollen flesh in its attempt to get his length close enough I can place the condom on him. "I didn't know morning sex was your thing."

"It's not."

"What?"

"I've never had it before."

"What? How is that possible?"

"Easy. I've never spent the night with anyone."

"No one?" I'm flabbergasted. How has this playboy made it this many years without this?

"Well, I had a girlfriend back in high school. But we never spent the night together. I left for college by the time she'd moved out of her mom's house. So, you're the first."

There's no chance to respond to this unbelievable conversation before he's gone from sliding his cock through my folds to angling my hips and plunging deep inside me.

"Fuck. You're so warm and wet." He reaches forward, grasping my left breast as he strokes his cock in and out of me. "All of this instant access to your body. I'll never think of morning wood the same way," he mumbles in my ear as he shifts his hand back to pull my left leg wider over his before picking up speed.

I start to pant, needing him to touch me. Just as I reach for his hand, he moves it, so he's cupping my mound, thrumming my clit with the pad of his finger in time with his thrusts. My head drops back against his shoulder as he fuels my desire with his talented fingers.

"Come for me, GG. I want to feel your pussy convulsing on my cock."

"Oh, Bas. Please. Harder. I need it harder."

I'm quickly flipped onto my stomach, my thighs spread wide as he lifts my hips and starts to pound into me. His muscular right hand snakes around me, teasing my swollen nub as he bucks wildly, the sound of his balls slapping my skin making me quiver.

"You're mine. You're mine," he grunts over me as he pounds relentlessly into me. "Say it," he growls.

"Yes. Yours. Only yours."

"Fuck, GG."

The sound of his pleasure has mine crashing down around me. I let out a loud scream into the pillow as he lets out a guttural moan and holds himself deep. I can feel my body shuddering around him, so incredibly intense. Turning my head toward the window, I watch as he carefully lowers himself onto me.

"My new favorite thing," he hums into my hair.

"Hmmm?" I still can't form words.

"Sliding my dick into my girl first thing in the morning."

"You're so romantic, Dr. Lee."

"Aren't I, though?" I feel a playful thwack against my ass. "Now, catch your breath. Because I intend to have another round in the shower before I eat you for breakfast."

Looking at my watch, I grimace. "I can't believe it's already nine."

"Where does the time go?" Sebastian asks, looking like the cat that ate the canary. He's sitting on a barstool, sipping his overpriced coffee.

"Well, I'm glad you had a good morning, sir." I walk over to where he's leaning on the newly christened countertop and kiss his cheek before heading for the door.

"I like the outfit." He laughs.

I'm wearing one of his T-shirts over my black hot pants from last night, tied in a knot at my hip so I don't trip over the damn thing. "Are you sure Charlie doesn't mind giving me a lift home? I can always call an Uber," I tease, knowing full well he'd never let me ride with anyone but Charlie, dressed like this.

"Shut up. Now when can I see you?"

"What?"

"Can you come back over tonight?"

"Bas, I haven't seen Austin in two nights."

"Well, can I come over to your place then?"

Is he for real? "Really?"

"Sure. What's for dinner?"

"Ha, you're in luck. Leftovers."

"I eat leftovers. What're we having?"

Shaking my head, I reply, "Luigi's. Hope you like baked spaghetti with extra cheese. We ordered too much celebrating the other night and have a ton left."

"Celebrating what?" He looks at me, appearing concerned.

"I passed my finals. And I'm going to be working at St. Luke's full time."

Sebastian jumps up from his stool, scooping me into his manly arms, making me giggle. "Baby, that's fantastic. Congratulations." He stops, looking serious. "Shit. Was that what you were trying to tell me the other day?"

"Yeah," I whisper, not wanting to go back there.

"Was that why Jeff was hugging you earlier?"

"You saw that?" No wonder that day was such a shit show.

"Yeah. Sorry. That whole day sucked."

"Well, don't do that anymore. I wanted to help. I'll have you know that whole amateur night was your fault."

Recognition is evident in his features. "I'm sorry, Bella."

"Don't be. I really enjoyed it. I think I might—"

"Not ever going to happen. You hear me."

Waving at my possessive man, I thank the heavens above that Kat had a plan.

Knock, Knock.

I walk toward the front door, a little pep in my step. Swinging the door open, I greet my dinner guest. "Well, hello. Come on in."

Sebastian enters the house, dressed in dark jeans and a Henley. As handsome as he is dressed in suits or scrubs, this version might be my favorite. I doubt there have been many women who've seen him this way from what he's described. I rather enjoy feeling uniquely his.

"These are for you," he says, pulling a small bouquet of sunflowers from behind him.

"Bas, they're beautiful." I'm speechless. I'm still bowled over that he wanted to see me again so soon, much less be willing to enjoy leftovers at my home with my son. This is more than I could've hoped for with this guarded man.

I notice he looks around briefly before coming closer and pulling me into his side. "I missed you today."

"I've barely been gone," I tease.

"I'm going to fuck this up. You know that, right?"

"Well, let's just enjoy it until you do," I say, poking him in the stomach.

"Austin, come and say hi," I yell as I try to reach over the refrigerator for a vase. I don't know why I insist on keeping them here. I can never reach them. Out of the corner of my eye, I see Sebastian start in my direction at the same time Austin comes into view.

Sebastian stops walking, almost looking concerned about how to interact with Austin. Austin's on autopilot, however, heading in my direction. He reaches up easily into the cabinet and pulls out the vase we use regularly.

"Thanks," I say, rubbing his arm. "Say hi to Sebastian, please. He's joining us for dinner."

"Hi," Austin directs to Bas.

"Hi," Bas returns. Boy, this should be some stimulating dinner conversation.

"What're we having for dinner?" Austin asks.

"Leftover Luigi's spaghetti."

"With lots of cheese?"

"Yes, Austin. Plenty of cheese."

"Can I go now?"

"Sure, honey."

Turning to Sebastian, I see he has a blank expression. From what I've gathered about his history with women, this must be a little overwhelming for him right now. "You okay?"

"Yeah, why?"

Walking to him, I wrap my arms around him and feel him relax against me. "This means a lot to me. That you'd try. That you'd spend time with both of us here."

Bending down, he kisses me on the nose. "I want to be here."

"I'm going to put the leftovers in the oven to heat up. Why don't we open a bottle of wine, and you can see the show?"

"I think I've had enough of your shows for a while."

Laughing, I pour him a glass before doing the same for myself. "Not that kind of show." Handing him a glass of Sangria, I add a few berries I've rinsed from the fridge. He smiles in my direction and follows me down the hall to Austin's room. As we walk in, I hear an audible gasp. *Oh, hell, here we go.* Turning to redirect him outside of Austin's room so that I can explain the situation better, I watch as he steps around me. Stepping back a few paces, his mouth falls open in awe. This isn't the usual expression I see when I have to explain Austin's proclivities to people. He looks totally and completely enthralled with what's before him.

Sebastian drags his hand down his face before reaching behind his nape. "This is utterly incredible."

Austin turns around, facing Sebastian. "You like the leaves?"

"Austin, they're phenomenal. That you took that sketch at the lake and created… this."

My eyes well with tears, the pride in my son is overwhelming in this moment. Abruptly, Sebastian's facial expression changes as he examines the wall more closely. Turning to me, he looks alarmed. *What on earth?*

"I don't understand. What do you do when he's finished?"

"Take a picture," I say, shrugging my shoulders.

He looks at me in horror. *Yeah, welcome to my world, buddy.* "You can't possibly paint over this."

I just nod at him feeling sad at the thought of its eventual demise.

"There has to be another way. Perhaps we could build a large structure that could be nailed into the wall? The painting could be removed, and a fresh canvas applied when he's finished?"

The only word I heard was *we.* "I'm sorry, I didn't catch that."

Sebastian repeats his thoughts, and I answer, "He doesn't like painting on canvas that's sitting on an easel. It's too restricting."

"Austin, you don't mind painting on canvas so long as it covers the whole wall, do you?"

"No."

"We would just have to pull the structure away once each piece was done to remove it from the housing and prepare it for the next."

There's that *we* again. *Don't get ahead of yourself, Bella. He's just a thinker. He's simply thinking out loud. Solving a challenge.* I turn and sit in my usual seat, watching Sebastian fully absorb the painting in front of him.

"I have a friend you'd enjoy meeting, Austin. Mr. Hansen. He's an incredible painter. He likes painting nature, land, and seascapes." Turning to me, he continues, "You know him, Bella."

"Me?"

"Yeah. Well, you didn't actually meet him, I guess. He was the patient in the OR the day I... well..."

Sebastian's cheeks turn pink, and his eyes are downcast. His embarrassment clues me in immediately.

"Ah, yes. So you're friends now?" I tease.

"Yes. Well, I hope so anyway. He's an amazing man. I bet he'd be impressed with your work, Austin."

Austin's completely unphased by this and continues the fine detail work on the leaf he's constructing.

In the distance, I hear the oven timer. "Are you going to be okay here?" I try to mouth to Bas before exiting the room. I don't want him to become overwhelmed his first night with us.

"Can I steal your front-row seat?" he teases.

"Sure. Dinner should be ready soon. I just have to finish the salad."

"I hate salad," Austin says to the wall. Shaking my head, I look to Sebastian, who's beaming.

"What?"

"I love this kid."

∾

"Thank you for dinner." Sebastian looks over his shoulder to make sure the coast is clear before coming closer to place a kiss on my temple.

"You're welcome."

"Would you go out for dinner with me?"

"You didn't get enough to eat?" I laugh.

"No. I meant, on a date."

"Uh, sure. I'd love to go out with you. I just have to see about Austin."

"I understand. Tomorrow night, then?"

"Bas, you're going to get sick of me."

"Not possible," he says, turning for the door. "I'll pick you up at seven."

Sebastian

I pull into my drive with a feeling of calm I can't explain. How had I been afraid of this for so long? The contentment I felt, sitting at that tiny table eating leftover spaghetti with her and her son, was mystifying. Normally, I'd blame it on the post-sex high I felt whenever I was with her. And sure, morning sex lived up to the hype. But this was different, and I damn well knew it.

I felt at home there. And I didn't feel at home anywhere. There were times I wasn't entirely relaxed in my own space. But there was a peace that enveloped me in her home. The brownstone was smaller than I expected, being a duplex. The furnishings were nice but dated. It wasn't the lavish surroundings I was accustomed to. Yet, I felt more like myself there than I had in a long time.

Shaking my head at this revelation, I look up in time to notice Boomerang is lying on my front porch. As if he senses my eyes on him, he sits up and begins to wag his tail. Well, holy hell. This day just gets better and better.

I park the car in the garage and immediately walk out to find him standing on the sidewalk, tail flying through the air. "Hey, buddy."

He runs over to me and sits as if waiting for something.

"Where've you been?" Bending down, I pet his head and scratch behind his ears. "I missed you." As I continue to stroke his fur, it dawns on me that's the second time I've said that today. Before this, I doubt I've ever felt that way about anyone except Nick when we were arguing. "You hungry?"

I stand to my full height and watch as he follows me to the door. Today has been a good day. Maybe Nick and Kendal are right. If I keep this up, my performance in the OR should be back to normal in no time.

CHAPTER THIRTY-ONE

Isabella

"Holy crap!" Looking at my watch, I see it's 6:55 p.m. Where's the time gone? Looking at my bed now covered in almost everything I own, I think I have my answer.

Why am I so anxious about this date? I've not only been completely uninhibited with him but practically the whole town after my little show. I've settled on a knee-length, deep purple wrap dress. I have no idea where we're going, but this should be acceptable anywhere. I'm wearing minimal jewelry, my hair down, and my makeup natural.

Thankfully, I didn't even have to finish my question when I asked Bailey if she could watch Austin tonight. She couldn't stop giggling about how right Katarina had been. I can't wait until Bailey has the opportunity to meet *The man God created just for her*, as she puts it. I'll be her girl tribe whenever she needs it. Although, let's hope it never needs to go as far as mine did.

Knock, knock.

Good lord, my nerves... Grabbing my clutch, I walk to the door. Opening it, I peer up at the incredibly beautiful man before me. "Hi."

"Hi," he responds, leaning in to place a kiss on my cheek. It dawns on me he still has yet to kiss my mouth. But, maybe after our date? Offering his arm, he continues, "You look beautiful, GG. Are you ready?"

"Yes. Where are you taking me?"

"Is Julep's okay?"

"Oh, I've always wanted to go there," I answer, unable to contain my smile. Julep's is a highly-rated fine dining restaurant in downtown Richmond that specializes in Southern cuisine. It's located in a restored, historic building and continuously receives fantastic reviews.

As we approach the car, Charlie opens the door for me. "Good evening, miss."

"Hi, Charlie. Please call me Bella."

He offers a polite smile, and I scoot onto the seat as Sebastian walks around the back of the town car before joining me on the other side.

Without haste, we're headed to our destination. I feel a warm blush hit my cheeks as Sebastian leans into me, placing a kiss on my neck as he grabs my hand in his. I feel like Cinderella. *Please don't let this experience end at midnight.*

We don't say much in the car, just occasionally smiling at one another. The newness of this must be weighing on him. I need to find a way to reassure him I don't need to be wined and dined. He already has me. But, one date couldn't hurt. Right?

The car travels down the one-way streets of downtown and slows as Julep's comes into view. Sebastian lifts my hand to his mouth just before he exits the vehicle. A few moments later, my door opens, and I take his hand. This all feels a bit much for me too right now.

As we walk toward the entrance of the restaurant, I see the ironwork over the door and smile. This is going to be great. "Bas?"

"Yeah, baby?"

"Thank you."

He smiles down at me before lifting our joined hands and bopping the tip of my nose with his index finger. Escorting me inside, he greets the hostess and gives his name as I take in the establishment. It's beautiful. The restaurant appears to be on two floors, as there is a wrought iron spiral staircase that ascends from the center of the ground level. The restaurant is dimly lit with beautiful flowers and candles in the center of each table. There's a slight hum of voices as conversations occur over their meal. The walls are rich mahogany, and chairs of a similar hue are placed about tables adorned in cream linen coverings.

"Right this way," the hostess directs, and simultaneously, Sebastian's warm hand rests on my lower back. My skin practically sizzles from the contact.

We're seated at a corner table with a clear view of the restaurant. Everything about this place screams romance. Suddenly, it dawns on me. Is this where he takes women when he's seducing them?

"Have you been here before?" I ask tentatively. Do I really want to know the answer?

"Yes, many times." He smiles back at me.

Ugh. Just let it go, Bella. He's here with you now.

The waiter takes our drink order and returns with water and a bottle of wine. He begins to open it when Sebastian interrupts. "Do you mind?"

"No, sir."

Sebastian takes the bottle from him and skillfully removes the cork. I watch as he pours a small sip for me. My eyes lock with his as he smiles at me, waiting for me to taste. I bring the glass to my nose and inhale the crisp, fruity notes. Allowing a few drops of the wine to hit my tongue, I close my eyes to enjoy the flavor and smile.

"Thank you," Sebastian says to the waiter, dismissing him.

"You're awfully skilled at this," I share.

"I should be. I grew up with it."

"What do you mean?"

"My family owns a vineyard. My brother still works there. It wasn't my calling, but I appreciate that it taught me to value a good wine."

"Wow." I pause, trying to find my words. Our relationship is so backward. "I feel like I know nothing about you."

"That's my fault, GG. I've kept people at a distance. But I want to let you in. It's just going to take me some time to get used to all of this."

"I understand," I say, smiling warmly at his confession. The magnitude of the evening is making me feel a bit overwhelmed. "I'm going to visit the ladies' room. I'll be right back, Sebastian."

Bas stands, pulling my chair back for me, and I turn to walk away.

Looking in the mirror, I grin at the girl looking back at me. Enjoy this, Bella. Enjoy him. Everything doesn't always have to be so serious. We've enjoyed casual conversation and flirting, and the best scallops I've ever tasted. Sebastian's been a polite, cordial companion. I've found it a little surprising that we could enjoy this much time together with our clothes on.

As I make my way back to the table, I notice an incredibly beautiful statuesque blonde walking toward me with a knowing smirk. Why does she look so familiar? Was she just at the table with Sebastian? My eyes immediately jump from her to him, and his expression is telling. They were together just now. Is she one of his many conquests? Had he brought *her* here before? *Gah, don't ruin this for yourself, Isabella. You know he has a past. Let it go.*

As I approach the table, Sebastian immediately stands to pull out my chair. I decide to take the high road and ignore any concerns I have about that woman. For all I know, it's paranoia out to get me.

"Would you think me a total cad if I didn't want to stay for coffee and dessert?"

My stomach flips, my mind instantly convinced he needs to get me home so he can meet up with the blonde later.

"No. It's okay. I've had plenty, thank you." I can't keep the nervous edge from my voice.

Suddenly, I feel his warm hand under the table, sliding up my thigh. "Because I'm damn sure there's nothing here that's as sweet as what's under that dress."

I gasp, not at his provocative words but at his reassurance this night is all for me. That this incredibly sexy, successful man wants to be with me. His hand quickly moves to my chin, lifting my face to meet his.

"What is it, baby? Did I do something to upset you?" He looks genuinely concerned.

"No. That's not it." I pause. "I guess it's going to take me some time to get used to all of this too."

~

In the days that follow, I try to stay focused on what's directly in front of me. My new job, my son, and my willingness to trust again. It's been a few evenings since our date, and I admit, I miss Sebastian terribly when we're apart. I guess this is how it is at the beginning of a relationship. So excited to see the other. I need to pace myself.

"Quitting time," Jeff yells out.

"I thought seven o'clock would never get here," I reply. Jeff has an odd expression on his face as he looks over my shoulder.

Following his gaze, I notice Sebastian in the doorway. "Ms. Potter. Can I see you for a moment?"

Unable to control my smile, I quickly stand. "Certainly, Dr. Lee." Following him around the corner to a more private area in this fifty-bed emergency room, he looks down at me and smiles.

"How's my girl?"

"Better now. I miss you."

"Yeah?" I watch as he stands tall, adjusting his expensive gray silk tie. "Any chance you and Austin are free for dinner tomorrow night?"

"Both of us? We don't go out much, Sebastian. Austin prefers to eat at home."

"I meant my place. I wanted to do something to celebrate your achievements. I'm sorry it took me so long."

This man. My heart is thumping in my chest at his kind gesture. Reaching out to him, I touch his arm. "We'd love to. Thank you. You really don't have to do all of that for me. Just knowing you're happy for me is enough."

"Nonsense. I want to do it. Can you come by around six? You could bring suits if you want to hit the pool. It's heated."

Of course, it is. "No, not this time. Austin isn't big into swimming. But thank you. We'll see you at six."

He gives me a sexy wink and walks down the hallway, and I try to wipe the dimple popping grin from my face before returning to Jeff. I'm not sure how I'd explain that.

~

"Come on in," Sebastian greets as we stand on the porch alongside a beautiful chocolate lab that's facing the door like he's hitched a ride on this party invite.

"I think we have an unexpected guest." I laugh, looking down at the well-behaved pup.

"Ah, that's Boom."

"How did I not know you had a dog?"

"I don't. Boomerang just keeps showing up here. He's kind of made himself at home. And I guess I kinda let him." He stops for a moment and then narrows his eyes playfully. "Sounds like someone else I know." He winks.

"What are we having for dinner?" Austin asks, surprising me.

I watch as Sebastian rubs his hands together in excitement, a look of utter glee on his face. "Well, we're celebrating your mom passing her exam and getting her new job, but I picked out the dinner for you and me."

I look at him curiously. *What is he up to?*

Bas leads Austin toward the kitchen island and spreads his arms wide to demonstrate the display of food choices like Vanna White on Wheel of Fortune. "We'll eat at the table, but I've got everything here warming up. There's cheese fondue to start and chocolate fondue to end."

Austin notices the large bowl of melty cheese, and his eyes spring wide. "What's fondue?"

"Only the best thing ever invented." Sebastian picks up a metal skewer, stabs a piece of crusty bread with it, then gently dips it into the cheese and hands it to Austin.

Austin looks at it briefly and then pops it into his mouth. "I like fondue," he quickly utters with a mouth full of cheesy bread.

Sebastian is wearing a proud smile, and I just shake my head. "Please tell me you have a salad to go with it, at least."

"Why would I go and ruin dinner with that? I have some fruit slices and vegetables we can dip in the cheese, bud. We don't need no stinkin' salad." Sebastian's got a grin the size of Texas on his face as he speaks to my cheese-loving son.

Austin's face lights up, the twinkling in his eyes, giving away his joy. That Sebastian would go out of his way to find something he knew would please him is the best gift anyone could give me.

Sebastian gives us a brief tour of his place. It's like a luxury resort. The pool and jacuzzi out back are worthy of a magazine cover. The gourmet kitchen, the home gym, and lavish furnishings... it's otherworldly to think people live like this every day. Returning to the kitchen, he reaches for a bottle of red wine and pours a glass, handing it to me. "I think you'll like this one, GG."

"Her name is Isabella. Why do you call her GG?"

"It's just a nickname."

"What does it mean?"

I inwardly groan. This is so awkward.

"She's a generous girl, Austin," he says without missing a beat. "She does nice things for people and makes them happy," he says, appearing sincere. I can't speak. My heart is so full. I need to face it. I'm falling hard for this man. I've never been happier. I take a sip of wine to try to distract my whirling emotions.

"Sit down, and I'll bring everything over," he directs to both of us.

Austin and I take a seat, and I watch as Boomerang sits quietly beside Austin. He carefully reaches over, patting the dog's head.

We spend the next hour laughing, devouring our food, and enjoying all this night has to offer. I keep hearing an odd sound beneath the table and look down to see Boomerang licking at Austin's hand. Sebastian catches on and looks down at Boom, who is sitting between the two of them. I can hear the dog licking his lips.

"Don't feed the dog from the table, Austin. I don't want him to start begging."

"I'm not."

Sebastian looks back down and laughs, prompting me to do the same. Austin has a few droplets of cheese on his pants. The temptation is more than this sweet dog can handle.

"I like Boomerang," Austin says between two cheesy morsels.

"Well, I think you're his new best friend," Bas belts out. Sebastian stands, grabs the cheese and chocolate fondue pots from the table, and makes his way to the kitchen sink.

I have to stifle a laugh. Austin looks defeated. The best meal of his life is coming to a close.

"This special occasion calls for two desserts," Sebastian hails as he lowers a plate of something almost unrecognizable onto the table.

Austin and I blink slowly, staring at the dessert in front of us. It looks like the cupcakes my son decorated as a child. The vanilla cake has crumbled into the icing, which is covered in haphazard candy sprinkles.

"My first time," Bas says, looking embarrassed. "Clearly, you need to make all of the cakes from now on, but this party deserved cake."

Instantly, my mind harkens back to the conversation on the dance floor where Sebastian shared why he didn't enjoy birthdays. That his mother never made the effort to make them personal. She didn't take the time to make him feel special. My eyes begin to fill with unshed tears, and I have to cover my mouth to prevent crying out. This man truly cares for me. There isn't a doubt in my mind. It's as clear as the ugly cupcakes on that plate.

"Don't cry, Mom. I bet they still taste good."

Sebastian and I break out laughing, and I encourage Austin to pick his favorite. I try to eat my misshapen cupcake without becoming emotional, but it's difficult. Looking across the table at these two beautiful men covered in sprinkles and icing, a dog named Boomerang sitting in wait, my cup runneth over.

CHAPTER THIRTY-TWO

Sebastian

"I'm happy for you, man. You know if you ever need anything, you can count on me. Even if I did have to get involved with that crazy super glue consult in the ER that day."

"Thanks," Nick replies, tilting his beer back. "Adoption is a daunting process. There are so many what-ifs. But, I'm learning that's just life in general." He takes another swig from the amber bottle. "I swear I didn't know Silver was on duty when I asked Ava to call you." He chuckles.

"That guy's a tool," I reply quickly. "I get more bullshit consults when he's on."

"Well, don't get Kat started. She says he's lazy as fuck. He's always pawning his work off on her."

"Short-dicked fucker. There has to be something to cause someone to act that way. Karma will get him." I laugh. Considering my condescending behavior over the last few years, maybe I have to consider that she's been visiting me in the OR lately.

I look out onto the dance floor and see Kat and Bella dancing, huge smiles plastered on their faces. "I still haven't forgiven you for that stunt you and Kat pulled."

"Forgiven us? Hell, you should be thanking us. I'd given up thinking I'd ever see you with the same woman twice." I notice he grimaces in response to my facial expression.

"Nick—"

"Don't, Bas. Honestly. It's behind us. And from what you've said, it was a one and done with Sophia. You gotta let this go. I have."

Lifting the alcohol to my lips, I try to soothe the ache of regret with the burn of the top-shelf Scotch. I wish I could let go of my self-loathing over hooking up with his ex-wife.

"It's nice to see you happy, Bas. You deserve this."

"Yeah. It's kinda taken me by surprise. I just don't want to hurt her, and I know it's inevitable."

"Don't put that shit out there. Just do the right thing by her."

"What if the right thing isn't me?"

The music shifts and a Shawn Mendes song begins. Looking at the girls, they're giggling and really getting into the beat. I can see Isabella's dimples from here. Even from this distance, they've cast their spell on me.

"Come on," I say to Nick as I rise from my chair.

"You're kidding me? You hate dancing." He guffaws behind me. "Holy fuck, man. You've got it bad."

"Shut up." I laugh, smacking him in the chest as we approach my tiny dancer and the Dirty Librarian. Reaching out, I grab Bella's arm, pulling her into me as she spins with wild abandon. Looking over to Nick and Kat, they're wrapped around one another as she wiggles in front of him.

Isabella looks up at me, mouthing the words to "There's Nothing Holdin' me back" with her dimples so deep from the strain of her smile, you could plant seeds there. My heart catches at her joyful expression, and I have to get control of myself. My skin could crack from the strain of the smiles she puts on my face.

Sliding my open palm down the front of her face, causing fits of laughter, I try to dispel the bewitchment she's weaving. I'm falling so fucking hard for this woman it's scary. I'm man enough to admit I've never felt this way for another human being. This has all happened so fast. There's no way this is love. But it's more than I've ever let myself feel before.

Watching her radiance emit from her like beams of light, I decide I need to invest in a little sunscreen. I can't give away my whole heart this fast. I need to protect myself. Baby steps.

~

"Sebastian, I'm sorry I've put you through this battery of tests, but it was necessary. I know it has been frustrating and time-consuming, but it needed to happen." Kendal's voice is clear and confident through the phone, and I try to contain my sudden worry.

"Can we meet?" I ask.

"Yes, I promise I'll fit you in this afternoon. If you can come after office hours, I'll stay, and we'll go over everything."

"Okay. I'll be there at four-thirty. See you then." Hanging up the call, my trepidation is at an all-time high. Maybe I'm reading too much into this, but I've been in this profession long enough to know she would've told me if everything looked normal.

I have a light afternoon. I'd recently started looking into another sojourn when the issues in the OR had begun to amp up. I'd been thinking about going to Tulum, Mexico, and had briefly considered asking Bella to join me. Yet, I need to take this time to concentrate on meditation and relaxation, not her. Plus, I don't know that she's willing to leave Austin that long, and I haven't gotten a feel for how he'd do with international travel. God, that kid's stolen a piece of my heart. He's the bonus prize in this relationship for sure.

My last patient of the day is scheduled at 3:00 p.m., and I need to get a better look at their images. Walking toward the radiology department, it dawns on me, I don't know Bella's schedule. Hell, I still don't even have her damn number. There have been multiple times I was tempted to ask for it but worried I'd go off the deep end if I had instant access to her. I'd be begging to see her or sexting her like a horny teenager seven days a week.

Entering the small, dark ER radiology room where she normally works, I'm pleasantly surprised when I find her sitting alone, looking at the computer screen. Sneaking up behind her, I whisper, "How's my girl?"

Isabella jumps at my presence, and I lean back and laugh. "Holy crap, Bas. Don't sneak up on me like that."

"Sorry. Hey, can you pull up Ms. Jackson's CT of her hand? I know you do x-rays, but since you're here..."

"Sure." She winks.

I lean over the back of her chair as she enters the information, looking through the machine for the right image. As I inhale her scent, I nuzzle her hair and give the side of her neck a flick of my tongue.

"Bas," she scolds.

"Hmmm?" I sneak my hands across her lower belly, caressing her groin through her scrub pants.

"Bas, someone could come in here."

"You're right." I immediately pull my hands away and laugh when I hear her exhale in disappointment.

"Come with me," I urge.

"What?"

"It'll only be a minute. Just tell them you went to the bathroom or something."

"Where are we going?"

"Just come with me," I repeat. She follows along behind me as I push through the doors connecting to the main radiology department. I walk briskly down the hall, feeling her on my heels. I try to look at my phone, so it appears there's nothing to see between the two of us. Spotting the angiography suite, I check the door. It's locked, but I have a key. Opening it quickly, I push the door open to allow her entry.

"What are we—"

"Shhh," I say, grabbing her hand and pulling her along behind me to an area I've used in the past to review films and dictate notes when I knew the area was closed for the day and needed the quiet. Turning to her, I lift and place her on the counter in front of several large monitors, displaying films from procedures performed earlier in the day. I waste no time dipping my hand into her scrubs. "Hell, you're already wet for me."

"Bas," she groans.

"You've got to be quiet, baby." I drop to my knees and pull her scrub pants down. Looking up at her shocked face, I see the panic there. "I've got you, GG. I swear. It's fine." Another look crosses her features, and I immediately know what she's thinking. "No. I've never done this with anyone else."

She visibly relaxes until I pull her panties to the side and swipe my tongue through her swollen, wet folds. "Oh, my god, Bas."

"GG. No one's going to find us unless you keep squealing like that." I laugh.

"Sorry. Please continue." She giggles back.

Resuming my delicious assault on her pussy, I suck and finger fuck her until I feel like she's close to the edge. Sure, I'd normally relish the idea of her coming all over my face, but I have work to get back to, and this is risky enough.

Her moans and continuous whimpering are making me unravel. My dick is so hard, it could rip right through my trousers. Standing to my full height, looking down at Bella's glassy lust-filled orbs, I lower my zipper, pull out my needy cock, and plunge deeply into her.

A loud gasp escapes her, and I have to reach up momentarily to cover her mouth as I hold onto the counter with my other hand and continue to plow into her. As the monitors start to shake, I make a mental note to control my thrusts, so they don't all come crashing down to the floor.

"Fuck. You're the best medicine, Bella. I was having a shit day, and then you," I groan quietly, panting into her ear. "Fucking come for me, GG," I beg.

Isabella leans forward, biting into my starched white dress shirt as her orgasm tears through her. I can feel her pussy convulsing around me, prompting my release.

I groan louder than I must've realized, Bella's hand flying up to cover my mouth as I empty into her. I was so engrossed in her body and its reaction to our encounter, I'd forgotten where I was for a moment. Leaning into her, I try to calm my breathing.

"Bas?"

"Yeah," I pant.

"Do you have a handkerchief or something I can clean up with?"

"What?" Hell, I didn't check to see if it was that time of the month, but obviously, there's no tampon—

It suddenly hits me. We didn't use a fucking condom. What the hell has happened to me? I thought I'd crossed the finish line quickly because she was so revved up, and we were in public. "Are you on the pill?"

"No," she whispers, sounding nervous.

"Fuck." I sigh. I reach into my pocket for my handkerchief and hand it to her. I should offer to clean her up. This is all my doing, but all of the peace that connecting with her usually brings is now shattered by the revelation I could've gotten her pregnant. "Come on. I have to lock up. Let's get you back."

We both take another look, ensuring we're dressed and cleaned up before exiting the suite and turning the key.

"I've got to go," I say before walking away.

"Sebastian." She stops me. "Please. Don't do this."

Walking over to her, I lean in and place a kiss on her temple before I turn and walk toward my office.

"I'm sorry, Sebastian," Kendal says quietly.

"Thanks," I reply. "I need to go. There are some things I need to take care of," I mumble as I turn and head for the door.

Walking the distance back to my office, I retrieve my phone. My first inclination is to call Bella. Yet, I recall I still don't have her number. I think about contacting Nick, but I'm not ready for that conversation. So I do what seems like the next obvious choice.

"Hi. This is Sebastian. I'm glad you're still in. I need to meet with you."

"Sure. What's going on, Sebastian?"

"I'm handing in my resignation."

I've stirred the entire evening. I know this has to be done, but it's killing me. Out of all of this, why is this where I'm struggling most?

I spent the early evening making arrangements for my departure. I guess the trip to Tulum is coming a little sooner than I'd anticipated. I need this time. It may be selfish, but I have to handle this the right way.

Standing in the dim porch light, I hear soft footsteps pad across the floor. I know she's checking the peephole because that's my good girl. She's smart. She'll be okay.

"Bas. What are you doing here?"

"I wanted to see you. I know it's late."

Isabella is wearing a long pink nightgown under a matching satin robe. Her dark hair tumbles over her shoulders. She looks like an angel.

Stepping into her, I pull her tightly against me.

"It's okay. I'm sorry things got so tense. I should've said something before it went that far."

I don't have the heart to correct her. "Is Austin asleep?"

"Yeah. He has a routine. He's usually down for the night once his light goes off."

"Can I stay?" I whisper into her hair.

"There's no morning sex happening, Bas."

"No, no. I just want to hold you, Bella. It's been a long day."

She steps back, allowing me further into her home, and I gaze about the place. Unlike my den, hers is covered in pictures of Austin and who I assume are various family members. She does have some brilliant pieces of artwork hanging. I was too nervous to look at them when I was here for dinner. Walking closer, I inspect the pieces.

"Austin?"

"Yep. We take pictures before we paint over them, and I blow up the ones I love most."

"He's incredibly gifted, GG."

"I think so too. But it's hard to be objective when it's your son." I feel her rub my arm and look down at her. "Is there anything you need? Water?"

"No, I'm good."

Taking my hand, she heads to her room, and I begin unbuttoning my shirt. I drape everything over a cozy chair in the corner of her room and take in the small space. The room is easily a third of the size of mine. Austin's is the larger of the two bedrooms. There's no en suite bath, but she has a queen-sized bed, and the furnishings are nice. Again, multiple prized family photos adorn her dresser and nightstand. The room is everything I would expect from Isabella. Beautiful, functional, no fuss. Turning back to Bella, I notice she's removed her robe and sits on the edge of the bed wearing only her dusky pink nightgown. It has thin spaghetti straps and cascades over her beautiful skin loosely. Her breasts are full against the confines of the top of the gown, and her firm nipples are evident through the material. But her beauty is all I see. Her body doesn't elicit lust but love. I'm totally and completely in love with this woman. I've never been more sure of anything.

Holding her hand out to me, she says quietly, "Come to bed, Sebastian."

Entering the far side of the bed wearing only my boxer briefs, I slide in until I'm curled against her. She leans to her side, clicks off the lamp, and reclines back into my chest.

We lie still in the dark for a while until my curiosity gets the best of me.

"GG?"

"Yeah?"

"Can I ask you something without upsetting you?"

"Yes," she answers timidly.

"Is Austin on the spectrum?"

"Yes."

"Is it Asperger's? I don't have a lot of experience, but he's so smart."

"No. He has Autism. He's very high functioning, so I can see why you'd think that."

"How did he learn to paint like that?"

"He's been painting since he was small. The sketching started later. I had him enrolled in a private Christian school where the art teacher had a real fondness for him. She found ways to help him, despite his limitations."

"Well, I don't see any limits now. He could go anywhere with his talent. I'd be honored to have an Austin Potter original hanging in my home."

"Lind."

"What?"

"Austin's last name is Lind. I took my maiden name back after the divorce, but his father's last name is Lind."

Why does that name sound so familiar? "That name. I've heard it before. It's not common."

"You may have worked with him. His dad. He's a cardiologist. He worked at St. Luke's briefly after college before moving to New York."

"Your ex-husband is Richard Lind?"

"Yes. He's great with hearts... unless it's his wife or son's that's on the line."

"Bella, I'm sorry." I'm acutely aware mine is breaking. This girl has suffered so much heartache already. *Why did I come here?*

"We were high school sweethearts. I put him through medical school. Then he left."

"Did he run off with his nurse?" So cliché, but I need to know.

"No. He didn't leave for anyone else. He just didn't want us."

What the hell?

"I think he fell out of love with me before Austin came along. He may have thought a baby would bring us closer, but he wasn't interested in parenting a unique child. I'm glad he walked away. We're better off without him."

A dull ache develops in my chest. She's the strongest woman I know. She deserves so much better than this.

"Sebastian, about this afternoon—"

"I don't want to talk about it, Bella. Please?"

"Would it be that bad if I got pregnant?" she practically whispers.

"Yes. Yes, it would be that bad. Now, drop it."

The space suddenly grows quiet. The very last thing our situation needs is a baby. I know I've hurt her. What's more, it's just the beginning.

CHAPTER THIRTY-THREE

Isabella

My eyes blink open, and I know before I roll over, he's gone. I couldn't sleep. I have no idea what time I finally dozed off. The way we ended our night was painful. He was so adamant about not wanting a baby with me. Was he worried we could have another special needs child or was it being tied to me that caused him concern?

Turning to lie on my back, I stretch my arm over the sheets and find they're still warm. Springing up in the bed, I realize he can't be long gone. Looking at the bedside clock, it reads 6:45 a.m. I jump up, run to my closet for a pair of jeans and a T-shirt and throw a hoodie over my head. I quickly visit the bathroom to brush my teeth and hair and then find a pair of shoes in the den.

"Austin?" I ask quietly into his opened door.

"Yeah, Mom," his tired voice returns.

"I've got to run out for a bit. I won't be long. Call me if you need anything. Otherwise, I'll be back soon."

"Are you getting donuts?"

"Sure," I toss back. Maybe if this conversation with Sebastian doesn't go well, I can at least drown my sorrows in coffee and donuts.

Running down the front steps, I race for my car. I have an ominous feeling about this. Something didn't feel right last night. Not only did he look awful when he came to the door, but when had he ever sought me out to only sleep? There was no snark. No reaction to my obvious arousal last night. Was he having second thoughts about trying a relationship with me? It didn't seem Austin was a barrier, or at least, I hadn't thought so until I brought up the subject of more children.

Looking at the speedometer, I notice the needle is sitting at 60mph. Hell, I don't need a ticket or to end up dead. Making a mental note to watch my driving a little more carefully, I let up on the gas. My mind is reeling, so I decide to turn on some music to distract myself. I'll deal with whatever happens when I speak with him. But I'm not going to live my life in limbo, wondering what's going on. We're adults. If he's no longer interested, he needs to just say it to my face.

Flipping through the stations, nothing is playing but commercials and love songs. Neither are helping the turmoil I'm in. I reach his subdivision, and my heart rate escalates. Thank god I have the day off. I'm practically manic. I don't know how I could work after this discussion, good or bad.

As I reach his drive, I turn in slowly. It dawns on me, I may not be able to tell if he's here. He frequently parks in his garage, and I don't know until he opens the door if he's home. He could've had an early case in the OR, and I'm making more of this than—

I immediately pull my foot off of the gas and let my car coast to the side of the drive as it rolls to a stop. His shiny black town car is parked in front of his porch with the trunk open and several suitcases placed behind. I sit behind the wheel, stunned. He's leaving and couldn't even tell me goodbye? Is this a work trip? There's no way he wouldn't have known this last night, not with having his bags packed at this early hour.

Charlie descends the steps, carrying another large suitcase and Boomerang on a leash. I watch as the dog jumps into the front seat, and Charlie places all of the bags in the trunk. Suddenly, Sebastian is at the top of the steps. My heart stops. He's leaving. *Do I run to him? Ask him not to go?* I grab the handle as he turns to his front door. Exiting my car, I watch carefully for clues as to what to do. I assume he's locking his door and assess whether I should call out to him until I see him extend his arm to a tall, statuesque blonde. The same tall, statuesque blonde from Julep's the other night.

I feel tears start to collect in my eyes as I watch him escort her down the steps. Charlie stands, holding the door open for them, and I watch as Sebastian gets in first while she stands at the door speaking with Charlie. My heart feels like it's being torn in two. How could this man have come to me last night? Come to hold me in my home, just to go to her. Not just go to her but go away with her.

As if she's heard my thoughts, our eyes connect, and the same smirk present from the night in the restaurant reappears on her face just before she slinks down into the backseat, and Charlie closes the door.

I can't stop the tears from pouring down my face. How could I have been so wrong about someone? I realize I'm frozen in place, staring in their direction when I make eye contact with Charlie, who's wearing a disenchanted expression. He tilts his chin in my direction as if he's sending his apologies the only way he knows how.

Climbing back into my car, I swiftly recall they'll need to come in this direction to leave. I quickly back out the way I entered and make it down the road a safe distance before I bury my face in my hands and cry.

Sebastian

"Well played, Sebastian. However, did you know she'd be here?" Sophia asks, sitting in the seat next to me.

"I wasn't sure. But I suspected she might." I leave out because she's a beautiful, strong human being who'll fight for the people she loves, even to her own detriment. *Unlike you.* "Thank you for coming on such short notice."

"I have to admit I was surprised to see your name on my phone last night. You seemed so cozy with her at the restaurant. Did she wait a while before sinking her claws in?"

"It's not like that, Sophia."

"You know I'm free if you'd like some company on your getaway. Where are you headed?"

"Minnesota."

"Minnesota? What on earth? It'll be cold there. What happened to all of your tropical destinations? What's in Minnesota?"

"The Mayo Clinic."

"Ah, you have a new job."

"No, Sophia. I have MS."

The car is suddenly deathly quiet. It isn't until I see Charlie's concerned eyes reflected back at me in the rearview mirror that I realize I've had this conversation with the partition down. Turning, I peer out the window. I don't need anyone's pity right now. Hell, that's one thing I don't have to worry about with Sophia.

It disgusts me that I had to put this plan into action, but there was no other choice. I know how strong-willed Isabella is. She stripped at that club to call my bluff. She'd never let me walk away if she thought she could fix this. But in the end, I'd have nothing to lose and everything to gain. She'd be the one giving up everything. And I couldn't do that to her.

I let my guard down with her time and time again. There was no doubt after seeing the look on her face when I placed those ridiculous cupcakes on the table. She knows. She knows how much I care for her. I can't let her give up any more of her life for the people she holds dear. I won't be one more burden. She deserves so much more. So does Austin.

As we continue to drive toward Sophia's home, I replay the conversation with Kendal in my mind.

"It's MS, Sebastian. There were clues in some of the things you mentioned, and the tests weren't conclusive until the MRI came back. But, there's no doubt that's why you were having issues. It wasn't the stress, although I'm sure that wasn't helping," she'd said.

"But I'd go months and have no trouble, thinking the trips abroad or intense meditation had controlled my stress."

"You have a relapsing-remitting form of multiple sclerosis. Your symptoms probably began slowly, appearing to just be clumsiness or generalized weakness.

Initially, these episodes occur every few years with no symptoms in between. Yet, they can escalate to a more progressive form of MS down the road. I'm not sure where you are right now. I think if you look back, you may be able to connect the dots. Your numbness and weakness have been mild compared to many of the cases I've seen. Optimistically, this is an indication we've caught it early, but there's no guarantee. I honestly hoped I'd be proven wrong about this."

"Yeah, you and me both," I'd muttered.

"This isn't a death sentence, Sebastian. You have a lot of life ahead of you. You're young and healthy and can lead a very productive life."

"It's a death sentence for my career, though, isn't it?" There's no way I can continue to operate knowing my limitations could cause long-term damage to a patient. It's only by the grace of God I'd managed to avoid causing a catastrophic outcome due to my undiagnosed condition.

"Well, I'm afraid you may need to look at that. You have a very specialized practice. You could consider teaching or work in the clinic. Or manage rehabilitative physical medicine."

"Kendal, you know that's not me."

"Yes, Sebastian. You always were an adrenalin junkie. I'm sorry. I know there's a lot to consider."

"And none of it good."

"Could I give you one piece of advice? From one friend to another?"

"Sure."

"There's a lot more to this life than your career. You've accomplished a lot. Seek out treatment options that will help you live your best life. Make sound decisions regarding your career, but don't live your life focused on what could happen."

"Thanks. I just need to let all of this sink in."

Pulling up in front of Sophia's stately two-story brick home, I thank her again before watching her exit the car. Before Charlie can close the door, she bends down once more.

"Take care of yourself, Bas. If you need anything, please call. Honestly. I know what you think of me, but I'd be happy to help if you needed it."

"Thanks. I appreciate that. I'll be in touch," I say, raising a hand to wave goodbye.

Returning to the driver's seat, Charlie looks to the right before pulling away from the curb then stops short. "Sir?"

"Yes?"

"Is there anything I can do for you?"

"No," I answer harshly. I appreciate what he's trying to do. But I can't handle that right now.

We proceed to the airport, making it to the gate within twenty-five minutes of leaving Sophia's home. I shake Charlie's hand after he hands my bags off to the curbside check-in, hoping he understands my gruff attitude isn't personal.

"Any idea when you'll be back?"

"No. I'll try to give you plenty of notice. I'll still be paying you the same wage, so either enjoy a side hustle or take that vacation you've been putting off."

Charlie opens the front passenger door, and Boomerang hops out. I've never traveled with a dog before. This will be different. Bending down in front of him, I scratch his ears.

"It's just you and me, Boom. You ready for this?" *Hell, I hope one of us is.*

I've been in Minnesota for several weeks, and the time has been busy with appointments and therapy sessions. I've learned that I'm likely in the beginning stages of a relapse, thus, I should anticipate these symptoms getting worse before they get better. Once it passes, I may have several years before another occurrence strikes. However, there's no one size fits all to MS. Only time will tell.

I'm blessed to have the financial means to tackle this head-on. I'm taking both a holistic and scientific approach to treatment, hoping it will all benefit me in the long run. The folks I'm working with believe my use of meditation and yoga has only benefitted me. They also strongly recommend a good exercise routine. Thus, I'll have to continue to work more regularly with my personal trainer once I return.

Minnesota has its benefits. Beyond The Mayo Clinic, its many lakes and parks make it a great place to live. When it's not thirty degrees below zero. I plan to travel somewhere tropical when the hard winter weather strikes.

Boomerang loves it here too. He gets lots of walks and enjoys swimming in the lake. In the short time we've been here, I've managed to locate a top-notch veterinarian who referred us to a kennel that trains service dogs. They've been working with Boomerang. They typically only train pups, but the trainer put Boom through the paces and was shocked at how well he's done. He feels he can qualify for whatever I need. I just need to locate a private nurse who's willing to travel with me, and I'll be all set. I know I can't run from my problems. But until this relapse is over, I plan to see the world and try to come up with a plan for my future.

As much as I loved my career, there's no question I can't continue to put a patient at risk, given what I now know. I'll have to consider whether a career change is in order or whether I'll simply retire early and focus on other pursuits.

I've sent an email to Nick advising that the stress was compromising my work and that I needed to take a step back before something catastrophic happened to one of my patients. We'd spoken enough about it before I left, so this should appease him until I can explain more. I hate keeping him at arm's length, but I can't risk anything I tell him going from Kat to Bella. I need my girl mad enough at me that she'll move on and not look back.

In the quiet hours when Boom and I sit on the porch of our lake house rental, my mind always returns to her. This beautiful, strong woman that I was blessed to know, even for such a short time. I have no doubt she'd insist on giving up more of herself to be with me. It's not vanity. it's just who she is. Forever putting the people she cares about before her own wants and needs.

She's spent the majority of her adult life taking a back seat to her child. If she became pregnant with my son or daughter, she'd have the full weight of that on her shoulders as I don't know what my future holds. If she wants more children, I can't ask her to give that up on top of everything else. I can't sit and watch her spend her days being caretaker to her adult Autistic son, our child, and me. She deserves so much more.

She was so excited about graduating and finally working in her chosen career after all of these years. She put her first husband through school just to have him run out on them. Well, I wasn't going to be another man in her life looking to take advantage. She and Austin will always be my priority. Even if she doesn't know it.

CHAPTER THIRTY-FOUR

Sebastian

It's been two months since I left home. I spent just shy of a month in Minnesota before the cooler weather pushed me toward a warmer climate. I packed up Boomerang, and off we flew to Tulum. Mexico was gorgeous. The sea, sand, and warm climate were what my body needed. Can't say it did anything for my soul. I fear that may be irrevocably broken.

I'd found a nurse who fit the bill. She's old enough to be my mother but strong enough to deal with me. She's a fiery redhead I refer to as Nurse Nancy. While she doesn't interfere in my life choices, she doesn't put up with my shit and gets things done. If I have a solemn day where I want to skip exercising, she'll drive me crazy until I get my ass in gear. It's a good thing, considering things have only gotten worse since I left Minnesota.

My weakness has progressed. I don't know how long this relapse will last, but I'm currently at the disposal of braces for mobility. I use the wheelchair when I'm alone, conserving my energy. But try to make short trips with the braces to get out once in a while. I've gotten used to the pitiful glances. The worst is when I get the come hither glances and watch them quickly look away when they see me needing the braces to stand. Not that it matters. There's no interest in other women. But you develop some thick skin when you go from being a playboy to an invalid.

All women aren't this judgmental. But in my travels, the women I meet are not looking to saddle themselves to someone needy. They're on vacation from their troubles. They don't need to collect a new one as a souvenir. I know of one woman who'd never dismiss me. But I blew that.

I've been second-guessing my decision to leave Bella without an explanation. I know deep down what I'm doing is best, but I harken it to someone deciding they no longer want chemo to fight their cancer. How do you walk away, knowing the only life you've ever really known depends on what you're leaving behind? Yet, in my case, continuing to expose Bella to my weaknesses wouldn't hurt me as much as it would slowly destroy her. It's too much to ask.

But God, I miss her. I miss her so much it's physically painful. I've tried to rub the spot in the center of my chest where it feels my heart has been ripped out to the point I'm probably losing chest hair. Lying in bed, I can almost feel her in my arms. *I'm starting to lose it.*

We've almost reached our destination. We left Tulum, driving toward Cancun to board a cruise ship. I'll be able to see more of the world, even if it's from my veranda. I've always enjoyed the water and think this could be good for me. The ship will have a gym, a spa, and a doctor available if needed. It'll break up the depression that has started to settle in.

Arriving at the cruise terminal, it's wall-to-wall chaos. Thank god Nancy is with me. There's no way I could manage this on my own. As we maneuver the check-in system and get Boom cleared to board the ship, I pray this will bring me some much-needed peace.

The last few nights have haunted me. I haven't slept well. My mood must really be deteriorating as Boomerang is continually placing his head in my lap, looking up at me with those sorrow-filled eyes as if he's trying to reassure me. I already feel so alone, what would've become of me had this loyal canine not invaded my life?

Bzzz. Bzzz.

I notice Nick's name on my screen and quickly answer the call before we board, and I no longer have easy access to people on the mainland.

"Hey, Nick. Glad you called when you did. I'm boarding a cruise ship in Cancun and probably won't have service for a week or so."

"Ah, partying on the high seas, are you?"

I drop my head, not wanting to lie to my friend any longer.

"Bas? Did I lose you?"

"No, give me a sec, will you?"

"Sure."

"Nancy, I'm going to take a call for a minute. Then we can board."

"Nick?"

"Yeah?"

"There's something I need to tell you."

Thirty minutes later, we board the ship. I'm glad I chose to use the power chair for this jaunt, as I would've been completely wiped out by the time I managed the terminal boarding process with the braces.

Checking in to my suite, Nancy advises she's right next door if I need anything. What I need is a nap. I set my phone alarm to rise in time for dinner and get Boom settled in for our departure.

～

"Are you okay, Sebastian?"

Nancy's voice has interrupted my trance, and I look up from my perch on the veranda. It's where I've spent the majority of this cruise. Alone. Watching the world go by without being a part of it.

"I'm fine. I'm just disappointed. I'd hoped this trip would bring me some peace." I have to admit, I feel even more removed from the world around me.

"Can I get you something?"

"Would you mind bringing me a cup of tea?"

"Of course, Sebastian. I'll be right back." I watch as Nancy steps inside the stateroom, leaving me to my thoughts. *Tea? When the hell did I start drinking tea?* Looking down at the small metal table beside me, I try to make room for when she returns. Moving Pride and Prejudice out of the way, I snicker. *Been reading too much of this. It's rubbing off on me.* I've been unable to read much more of this book since coming here. Hell, since leaving her. There are just too many damn passages where Fitzwilliam fucking Darcy keeps screwing up his chance with Elizabeth Bennet. It's like the universe has equated my relationship with Bella to this historical romance for all to see.

Returning with my tea, Nancy places it on the open spot beside me. Boomerang's head pops up as he lies here beside me to see if there's anything for him. "Is there somewhere else you're considering traveling, or are you thinking of heading back home?"

"I'm not ready for home, Nancy. I think I'd like to go to Italy. Have you been? If you need to get back, I can try and make—"

"No. Sebastian, I'm committed to this job. To you. Don't worry yourself about that. I've always wanted to go to Italy."

"Good. I'd primarily like to stay by the sea. Sorrento, Naples, Capri, the Amalfi Coast. But we could take in Rome if that's what you'd like." I reach down to pat Boom's head unconsciously. This magnetic mutt has brought more comfort than anything the Mayo clinic has given me.

"You're very kind, Sebastian. You go where your heart takes you. I'm happy to sightsee wherever we end up."

If we were going where my heart takes me, we'd be headed to Monument Avenue.

~

It's been ten days. I've loved being in Italy, but the loneliness just has a new zip code. The people here are wonderful. The food is incredible. And the views of the deep blue sea are magical. But they all feel two-dimensional. As if a part of my puzzle is missing. Parts, actually. I miss Austin almost as much as I miss his mother.

Sitting on the balcony of my hotel room, I'm brought back into the present as I feel my phone vibrate in my pocket. Reaching for it quickly, I see Nick's name on the screen.

"Hey, Nick. How are you?"

"I'm good. How are you?"

"I'm okay.

"Bas?"

"Yeah?"

"Come home."

Dropping my head at his words, I know he's right. I'm just not ready. If I came home now, I'd only go to her. I'd be left with my tail between my legs when she sent me away for what I did to her. "Nick, I'm hoping to gain a little more strength before I come back. It's beautiful here. If I can't get around, at least I can eat my weight in pasta and look out at the sea."

"Okay, man. We just miss you. We can help."

"I know." I start to end the call when my willpower breaks. "Nick?"

"Yeah, Bas."

"Is she okay?"

"She's getting there. The first few months were hard. We didn't know what to say. But she's gone through all five stages of grief now and landed on acceptance."

Dropping my head once more, I know it's for the best. Part of me wants to know if she's moved on to someone else, but I have no right to ask after the way I treated her. "Thanks, Nick. I feel better knowing you guys are looking out for her and Austin."

"It doesn't have to be this way, Bas."

"Yes, it does. I have to go."

It's been a few days since my call with Nick. I don't hear much from the outside world, so I'm surprised when my phone starts jumping on the table. I manage to drag my weary body from the jacuzzi, although I probably look like an injured mammal. It takes some stealthy maneuvering on my part to reach my cell before the call goes to voicemail, but I accomplish it without ending up on the ground.

"Hello?" I pant into the phone.

"Hello. Is this Sebastian Lee?"

"Yes. May I ask who's calling?" Why does this voice sound so familiar?

"Yes, of course. I hope you'll pardon the intrusion. But one of your colleagues was kind enough to share your cell number with me. I was concerned when I tried to make an appointment and was told you were no longer working with the practice. This is Eugene Hansen."

My spirits perk up for the first time in months at hearing his name. I sit a little taller in my chair. "Mr. Hansen, it's so good of you to call. Is your hand doing okay?"

"It's doing fine, son. I'm back to painting, and it's all because of you. But I was calling to check on you."

"Me?"

"Well, after our recent conversations, I admit I've developed a fondness for you. You remind me so much of myself at your age. So driven and determined, sometimes unknowingly to your disadvantage. It didn't make sense to me that you'd up and quit without sending a letter to your patients advising them where they could find you."

"I'm sorry for that, Mr. Hansen. I resigned without moving my practice. I probably should've sent letters regardless, as a courtesy. I apologize. Things have been... difficult." Sharing my recent predicament with this man is making me feel emotional. I don't know why I feel so drawn to him.

"Is it okay to ask if you're all right?"

"Of course, sir. I'm just adjusting to a new way of life." *Hell, just tell him, Bas.* "I was diagnosed with MS. I honestly didn't know at the time of your surgery, Mr. Hansen. Once the diagnosis was made, I resigned before I could risk making any mistakes that could cause a bad outcome to any of my patients."

"I'm not worried about that, Sebastian. I'm worried about you."

Suddenly, the damn has broken. I can feel tears I've kept pent up for years start to fall. Tears for having someone care enough to do what my parents should've done, tears for waiting so long to allow myself to connect with anyone in a real way, tears for all I've lost. I'm so overwhelmed by the kindness of this man, I'm not sure I can continue this conversation. I hope he can't hear my spluttering.

"Sebastian, where are you?"

"I'm in Italy. Sorrento at the moment."

"Ah, I bet it's beautiful there."

"Yes, sir. It is."

"Would you mind terribly if I came for a visit?"

Sitting up taller, I adjust the phone to my ear. "I'm sorry, what did you say?"

"I've never traveled much and always wanted to see Italy. Will you be there long enough I could pay you a visit?"

I can barely contain my excitement at the prospect. "I'd love that, sir. I have no plans to leave anytime soon."

"Well, let this old man make some plans. I'm hoping to bring my lady friend along. We've come quite a long way since I saw you last."

"Wow, that's wonderful. I'm really happy for you."

"I'll call you with our travel arrangements. I look forward to seeing you."

Well, what do you know about that?

You'd think I was awaiting the arrival of Santa Claus. I'm so worked up. Mr. Hansen and his lady friend should be here any time now. Perhaps this excitement is merely needing to see someone other than nameless passersby on the street. Or possibly Nurse Nancy has pushed me to the brink with her "Get up and out of this house" routine. But, I know deep down it's because I've come to think of Eugene Hansen as a father figure.

I check the kitchen and smile when I note the antipasto tray in the refrigerator and the premade pasta I ordered for their visit. I'm anxious to finally meet his girlfriend. Eugene located a villa not far from where I'm renting so he and his girlfriend can spend a week in Sorrento before traveling to Florence, Rome, and Tuscany. He'd said they anticipated an extra week there before returning to the states. I could only imagine the landscapes he'd paint after visiting the picturesque cities in Italy.

Seated in my favorite chair overlooking the water, I try to calm my excitement, stroking Boomerang's head as I wait. I hear a knock at the door, and Nancy heads in that direction as I try to gather my braces and stand to greet them. As the door opens and she greets him, I see him standing alone, wearing an expression I can't decipher as he stares back at me. It's not pity.

"Sebastian. Thank you for having me," he says as he approaches with a warm smile.

"I'm honored you came," I reply. We stand in momentary silence, the emotions causing a tightness in my chest.

"Would it be all right if I gave you a hug?"

"Of course," I respond, trying to keep it together. As this kind old soul gathers me into his fatherly embrace, I can feel tears start to well. *Get it together, Bas. Don't blubber all over him.* "Please, sit." I direct toward the chairs behind me to give me a moment to collect myself. "Where's your girl?"

"Ah. I asked her if we could have a few moments alone before she joined us. She found a beautiful spot out back to sit and read. I hope that's okay."

"Certainly." I watch as Boomerang walks over to sit beside him, and Mr. Hansen strokes his coat, giving him an almost knowing look. "Do you have pets, Mr. Hansen?"

"Yes. I have a black lab that looks much like this one. She's kept me company for many years. They have such a kind spirit about them. Like they can sense your struggles."

"You're right. I've never had a pet before Boom came along." This dog has gotten me through a lot in the last few months.

"Boom?"

"Ha. Yeah. He just showed up on my doorstep one day and kept coming back. So I named him Boomerang."

"Ah, I like it," he says, scratching behind Boomerang's ears.

"I'm thrilled to hear you're painting again. I can imagine this country will give you a lot of inspiration."

"No doubt."

"I mentioned your work to a young man I met recently. He's incredibly gifted. He's a teenager but possesses a vision I haven't witnessed in many seasoned artists," I add proudly. "He gravitates toward land and seascapes as you do. I wish I could've introduced you before this happened."

"What's stopping you from introducing us now?"

Turning my head, I try to find words to explain the situation so he might understand. "I was seeing his mother before I was diagnosed."

"Jesus, Sebastian. She left you when she found out you had MS?"

"No," I blurt. "I left her."

He gives me a sharp, perplexed look as if I'm speaking another language.

"Isabella is a single mother to a teen son with Autism. He's very high functioning but nonetheless has required all of her time and devotion. She's an incredible mother and has devoted her life to him. I couldn't ask her to now be a caregiver to me as well." I watch as he silently stares. "She mentioned wanting to have another child. She'd be juggling the care for all of us on her own." He continues to sit wordlessly, listening. "She just graduated from school and has started working for the first time since putting her husband through medical school years ago. I couldn't let my situation keep her from having the things she's worked so hard for. And if she wants to marry and have a family, I don't want to stand in her way."

He continues to stroke Boomerang's fur for a few more moments before patting him on the head. "May I be frank with you, son?"

"Of course."

"That wasn't your choice to make."

"What do you mean?"

"This woman sounds like a very independent, intelligent, resourceful person who has thrived despite her circumstances."

I smile at this statement, unable to deny that Bella Potter is just that.

"It wasn't your place to decide for her what she should choose to handle. She's had enough things decided for her in her life. And it sounds as if she's risen to meet each challenge. Do you love her, Sebastian?"

"Yes," I answer without hesitation.

"Do you think she feels the same?"

I consider the night she asked if it would be that bad if she were to get pregnant and know. This woman would never bring another child into the world if she didn't feel the same. She wasn't looking to parent alone. I know it.

"Yes," I admit, feeling crushed that I couldn't have seen this more clearly before.

"Sebastian, you are fortunate to have means. You already appear to have reliable help," he states as he looks over his shoulder toward Nancy. "You can certainly afford a nanny if children came along. Stop being a martyr. You're scared. Don't destroy what could be something beautiful because you're afraid of what could happen."

"I think I've already done that."

"What do you mean?"

There's no way I'm telling him about the rouse with Sophia. I can't even repeat what I did out loud, I'm so disgusted with myself. "Let's just say, I'm not sure she'll ever speak to me again after the way I ended things."

"Well, that's too bad. But if you love her, don't you owe it to her to at least give it a shot?"

I drag my hand down my face in frustration, knowing he's right but unsure what I could possibly do to get my spirited, strong-willed girl to forgive me.

"Just think about it, son. If this is something you truly want, pray on it. The universe will send you clues if you're on the right path. Just be open with her." He chuckles. "And begging doesn't hurt."

Knock, knock.

Looking up from our deep conversation, I see Nancy greeting a beautiful older blonde woman at the door. She looks to be about my mother's age. Before I can stand to greet her, Boomerang charges for the door. *Holy crap. He's never done this before.* If he runs out, how will I ever find him?

"Boom!" I yell, trying to stop him. Making it to my feet, I quickly hobble over, my braces clanking hard against the tile in my haste. Mr. Hansen is by my side, probably realizing my concern to catch Boomerang before he either darts out the door or attacks this poor woman.

"Boston, sit," she whispers as I get closer.

"Sebastian, meet Sarah Beth." Sara Beth is now crouched on the ground, Boomerang licking her face as she laughs.

"Wow. I've never seen him respond like that to anyone. He's normally much better behaved. Down, Boom."

Sarah Beth stands, taking Mr. Hansen's hand as they return to the den where we were just seated. Boomerang trails closely behind. As everyone takes a seat and Nancy offers to bring everyone lemonade, I look on in bewilderment as the two of them look at each other as if they're silently communicating.

"I need to confess something, Sebastian," Mr. Hansen says.

Unease hits as he looks back at Sarah Beth.

"We may have been a little underhanded, but it was for your own good." Sarah Beth giggles by his side, and I'm completely flummoxed. "Boomerang is our grandson."

"What?" I choke out.

"My black lab is Boomerang's mother. I got her through Sarah Beth years ago. She works with service animals, and Stella didn't cut the mustard." He laughs.

"Stella is sweet and so smart, but I didn't get ahold of her until she was older than we normally start training. I was able to hold onto her, and I could see over time that Gene needed her more than I did."

"I'm sorry, I'm confused. How did this happen?"

"Well, I started training Boston a while ago, and we were scheduled to have him matched with a young man who unfortunately passed away before the training was complete. It was terribly sad. But Gene mentioned meeting you. He said after some of your conversations, he felt bringing you and Boston together might be as beneficial for you as having Stella had been for him."

"I know it was sneaky. It was easier than I expected to find your address, and so we arranged to have Boomerang pay you a few visits."

Stunned, I sit staring at these two amazing people. Again, I try not to give in to my overwhelming emotions. That this amazing couple would do this for me. I've never experienced anything like this. It's suitable that Boom would be their grandchild. Because these incredible people feel like the parents I always wished I'd had.

Boomerang walks over to me as if sensing the overpowering

sentiment which now engulfs me. Placing his big head in my lap, he looks up at me with those sweet big brown eyes. Rubbing his soft head with both of my hands, I speak to the sneaky addition to my life. "Boston, huh?" His chosen name, reminding me of Bella and Austin when I hear it. *The universe will send you clues if you're on the right path.* I hear Mr. Hansen's words repeat in my head.

"When you two head back to the states, would you mind terribly if Nancy, Boomerang, and I accompanied you?"

"We'd love that." Gene smiles back at me, holding Sarah Beth's hand in his.

Boomerang walks over to her, and I take a sip of my lemonade, feeling more at peace than I have since before the MS diagnosis. "So, Eugene's your first name? Not sure how I missed that on your medical records." I chuckle.

Laughter escapes as he winks at me and replies, "Hell, so maybe that's the real reason for the pen name."

CHAPTER THIRTY-FIVE

Isabella

Acceptance. I've gone through all five stages of grief, and I've finally made it to the last.

Denial was tough. The first stage took me longer than it should have. I'd beaten myself up about allowing this man to enter my heart, knowing he was such a playboy. How could I have overlooked the way our relationship started? Why was I so dense to deny what was clearly plain for anyone to see? Sebastian Lee wasn't the relationship type. It was merely a challenge. Once I hinted I was okay with more, he ran.

Anger lasted much longer. At times, I feel I'm still stuck there. I'm angry at myself as well, but mostly him. That he could come to my home, spend time with me, and my son, just to drive off with her. I'm angry that the thought of my becoming pregnant could've repulsed him so. Was it the worry that we could have another child with special needs? It's not lost on me that having a child at my age comes with certain risks. Down Syndrome for one. But I can't help wondering if it was the thought of being tied to me that upset him. I'm not going back there. I've had enough of these questions torturing me night after night when Rick left. The thing I'm the angriest about. Those damn cupcakes!

I allowed myself to believe he loved me. Those god-awful-looking things had touched me so. And for what? He had to know he already had me at that point. What reason could there have been to get my hopes up with those pitiful-looking things?

Next in the grief process was bargaining. This phase didn't last long because this proud Irish girl isn't begging for any man. Ever! He was the coward who couldn't stay and have a grown-up conversation. He can suck it.

Depression enveloped me like my favorite hoodie. I wore it to bed, and it stayed on all day. I'm sure some of it remains to this day. But it's been months since I've seen or heard from him, so I need to let it go. It's a good thing I never had his number. I'm sure during this time, I would've texted just to have the chance at knowing he was okay. My mind would play tricks on me, thinking there had to be some other explanation for his leaving. But I remember that morning he climbed into his car with his tall beauty queen companion. Had she told him she'd seen me?

I'd tried hard to contain my grief. I didn't know how much of an impact Sebastian's brief interactions had on Austin. I didn't want him concerned seeing me so devastated. I stupidly thought I was hiding my despair well until I brought dinner into Austin's room one night just to drop the tray on the floor when I saw he was painstakingly covering every vibrant leaf on his beautiful mural in white paint.

"Austin! What're you doing? I didn't even get a picture of this one. It was my favorite," I cried.

"I don't want to look at it anymore."

His words made tears spill from my eyes. How could I have let anyone do this to him? This was worse than the men who weren't interested in continuing a relationship with me after meeting Austin. They never pretended to care.

In the days that followed, we picked up the pieces of our lives and tried to move on. Austin began painting a seascape on the wall. This wasn't a serene lake stream, but a bold turbulent blue sea. I'd never seen him paint anything quite like it before. I'm not sure what inspired this project, but he seemed more settled than he'd been when he painted over the leaves, so I was glad for the diversion.

I'd picked up some extra shifts at work. I knew I could potentially bump into Sebastian there, but I tried to stay in the radiology department and packed my meals. I needed to keep my mind busy, and that chaotic ER didn't allow for the downtime I had at home.

It wasn't until a few weeks later that I'd heard through the grapevine that Sebastian had quit. I was shocked. Yet he'd been managing a large caseload between the two hospitals, so maybe he'd decided it was best to stick with one. One that didn't employ the likes of me.

I considered asking Katarina if she knew what was going on, but I didn't trust myself not to give in to any schemes she may come up with if I showed I wanted a chance to get in touch with him. I wasn't going to bargain to have him back in my life. But I admit, the chance to hear from him in some way still pulled at my heartstrings. Even if I was so mad at him, I could spit nails.

Knock, knock.

Hmmm. That's odd. I put down my cup of tea next to my tattered copy of Pride and Prejudice and head for the door. I don't want to read any more of that dribble anyway. Elizabeth is way too good for the likes of Mr. Darcy, and she knows it!

I note it's 9:00 p.m. on my watch. Who'd be coming by unannounced at this hour? Looking into the peephole, I gasp. *Holy hell?*

Opening the door partway, I greet my unwelcome guest. "Yes?"

"Hi, Isabella? I apologize for the late hour. May I come in?" the familiar blonde dressed immaculately in designer clothing asks from my porch.

"What could you possibly have to say to me that I should allow you into my home?" I sneer.

"Please? I won't stay long. I'm trying to do the right thing here."

The mystery behind her visit and this statement has me opening the door the rest of the way before I've completely considered the implications. "My son is still awake. You can come in, but I ask that we keep our voices down and if he enters, you not say anything that will upset him."

"Yes. Of course," she answers, walking past me into the den. Thank heavens I broke from my grief long enough to straighten the place up this morning. Had she come yesterday and found the Ben and Jerry's containers and pizza boxes strewn about, I wouldn't be able to mask my current mood.

"Have a seat." I point toward the den. I'd offer her a drink, but *fuck no.*

"My name is Sophia. Sophia Barnes," she says knowingly. Still unsure why she's here or if I need to prepare myself that Sebastian was upset about my questioning children because he already has one on the way with her, I clasp my hands tightly in my lap and wait for her to continue.

"I've known Sebastian a very long time. We're friends. Nothing more." She stops as if this is supposed to mean something to me. I cannot picture that suave Sebastian Lee could simply be friends with any woman, much less one that looks like Barbie.

"Sebastian is a proud man. I don't know all of the details, but he's been hurt before and hasn't let himself get close to any woman since. Hell, I even tried at one point. When he called and asked me to meet him at his place to pretend to be going away with him, I thought he'd acquired a clinger he couldn't get rid of."

My face starts to heat at this conversation. How dare she come into my home and accuse me of being a woman that would degrade herself to such tactics. Sure, I was there when they left, but not for the reasons she's describing.

"Please, don't get upset. It wasn't until I was in the car, and he explained, that I understood fully. He cares a great deal about you. In his own ridiculous way, he was doing what he thought was best."

I look at her, completely baffled by this conversation. How could this charade have been for the best, particularly if he really does care for me? Is this where she drops the bomb about their love child?

"Sebastian has MS. Multiple sclerosis. He was told the day before he left. He immediately quit his job for fear of hurting someone during surgery because of his condition. And he ran out on you for fear of hurting you."

My eyes immediately well with tears. "I don't—"

"I don't know much. He was headed to the Mayo Clinic the day you saw the two of us. I've reached out a few times to check on him. His symptoms have progressed, but he has a private-duty nurse with him to help. The last I spoke with him, he was in Europe. I think he's trying to figure out how to deal with all this."

Sitting silently, I stare down at my hands, trying to picture my larger-than-life man so weak he'd require the help of a nurse. I can't help but remain a little skeptical about this news.

"He's a good person, Isabella. I had the definite feeling he was leaving to protect you, not to harm you. He's having to face a lot of changes. His career was everything to him. I'm sure, knowing Sebastian, he's doing a lot of soul searching over there."

A tear tumbles down my cheek. I'm still angry with how he's handled this. That he couldn't talk to me. But my heart breaks for all he's struggling with on his own. "Why did you come here? You didn't have to tell me any of this."

"I know. It's self-serving on my part. I need to make some changes in my life. I need my karma cleaned." She laughs. Putting a more serious look to her features, she continues, "I've struggled with this. Sebastian is my friend, and I feel like I'm breaking his confidence coming here. But he's only hurting himself. It's none of my business, but I felt like you needed to know."

"Mom?"

I jump from my seat, startled at Austin's intrusion. *How much has he heard?*

"Austin, honey. I'm sorry if we disturbed you. This is Sophia. She was just leaving." I hate that I'm being rude, but I don't have it in me to pretend we're friends. Even if she didn't have to go out of her way to share this information with me. Karma cleanse or not.

"Yes. I have to be going. It was nice to meet you, Austin." Sophia holds her hand out to him, and Austin awkwardly grabs and shakes. Her eyes give away a questioning glance as she lets go of his hand and smiles back at me as if this has shed more light on things for her. She gracefully glides to the door like a Hollywood starlet and turns back as she grasps the handle. "Thank you for seeing me," she says as she closes the door behind her.

"Is everything okay?" Austin asks.

"Yes. It's fine. You finish up what you're doing for the night and head to bed. I have a long day tomorrow.

"You have to work?"

"Yes, I'm working a lot this week. And with the snowy weather, I need to leave extra early to make it on time. Have you got everything you need for the week? With me working so much, I left some extra food in the fridge for Margaret to help you heat up. Do you need more pencils or sketch pads?"

"I've got two more, but I'd like to order some more."

"Okay, Austin. I'll order two more packs of pencils and a three-pack of your favorite sketch pads from my phone before I go to bed. They'll probably be here in a day or two. Don't start checking the mailbox until then." I laugh, knowing he'll wear out the carpet if I don't give him a very distinct time frame for delivery. "Good night."

"Good night, Mom."

Heading to my room, I decide to take a hot shower before bed. I need to let my tears fall in a safe place, so Austin won't see. I may be mad at Bas for leaving us the way he did, but not enough that I don't need to acknowledge the sorrow I feel for all he's going through. Whether I've fallen in love with him or not, I don't think I could ever trust him enough to let him in again after pulling a stunt like that.

Sebastian

Home sweet home. *Or is it?* This place feels emptier than it did before I left. I feel more alone here than when I was out there, watching the world move on without me. There's something about knowing how close she is that has me feeling raw. Looking out the glass doors onto the pool deck and snow-covered grass beyond, I concede it could be the abrupt change in weather that has me feeling this bleak. But I know it's her.

Gene and Sarah Beth had been great company for Nancy and me as we returned home to the states. They kept my thoughts distracted from Bella and focused on the positives. After all these years, I had these amazing people in my life that I considered stand-in parents for the ones who'd let me down. I had found the perfect combination of ballbuster and benevolence in Nurse Nancy. And Boomerang was the companion I needed to teach me I was capable of managing at least one relationship successfully.

Knock, knock.

Standing from my chair, I grab my braces to steady myself before heading to the door. The long travel home from Italy had exacerbated my weakness. I pray this relapse will be over soon, and I can try to take advantage of some new therapies to prevent future relapses from coming as often or as intense.

"Hey, come in." It's odd greeting my brother this way, given his penchant for breaking and entering.

"Fuck, Bas. I heard what you said on the phone. But I didn't realize it was this bad," Sam says, not moving from the porch.

"Thanks. You're a ray of sunshine."

Stepping through the doorway, he follows me into the den. "Shit, Bas. I'm sorry. How are you holding up?"

"I've had a few months for it to sink in. I guess I'm as good as you'd expect."

"Have you told Mom and Dad?"

"Why would I do that? Hell, I haven't seen them in years. What good would it do?"

"I don't know. I just thought they should know."

"Well, tell 'em if you want. I don't care. It's not like Mom is going to come running over here to dote on me. Unless she has something to gain from it, I'll never hear another word about it." I can picture her repeatedly dropping my name at a multiple sclerosis charity gala and shudder. I leave out I have new parents and don't need her anyway, but even I think I sound a little nuts considering the thought.

"Yeah. Maybe you're right."

"How's your girl dealing with it?" Sam asks, concerned.

"My girl?"

"You know… your birthday girl?"

"Oh, she's not in the picture anymore."

"Hell, Sebastian. That was really insensitive of me."

I find this perplexing. It isn't near as offensive as half the stuff he asks. "What was?"

"Your dick probably doesn't work anymore, huh?"

"Oh, for fuck's sake, Sam. My dick works just fine." Not that it's seen any action from anyone but my hand. There's no one else for me but her, and I know it.

"Thank god. I mean, I don't even want to think what would happen if *my* soldier wouldn't salute.

"Can you please?' I huff in disgust. How had my affliction with MS been reduced to this?

"Sorry." He winces. "So if your third leg is working better than the other two…" he points to my legs as if to make a point, "why don't you give your birthday girl a call? She could at least put a smile on your damn face."

Flicking him my middle finger, I shake my head at his one-track mind. "I blew that situation. And anyway, I don't have her number."

"Well, that's too bad. I'd never seen you look so happy. I would've tried to chase her down— Oh, sorry. I would've walked carefully with my braces and given her the whole Tiny Tim routine."

"What the hell are you talking about?"

"You know, hobble on over and let her feel sorry for you. She'll take one look at you and want to make you feel better," he says, waggling his brows.

"I seriously think they dropped you on your head when you were born."

It's at this time that the universe decides to step in and save me when Nancy enters the kitchen. "Hi, you must be Sebastian's brother. You two look so much alike."

I grimace at the statement as Sam walks over to shake her hand. "Hi, I'm Sam. Who are you?"

"I'm Nancy. Your brother's nurse." She turns to put a few things into cabinets and looks into the fridge. "It looks like your chef was here. There's a gorgeous charcuterie tray in here."

"Yeah. I'm not hungry."

"You'll eat something and get in the gym, young man. We aren't playing the moping game today." My eyes narrow at her. I'm used to this type of scolding from her in private, but not with an audience, brother or not. "I'm sorry. I hate to see how your good mood from the other day has diminished. Is there anything I can do?"

"No," I mutter.

"You could get Charlie to find out where his girl lives," Sam says.

"Shut up, Sam!"

"His girl?" Nancy quickly interrupts.

"Yeah. She can put a smile on his face."

What the ever-loving hell is happening here? I've barely considered this thought before Nancy is walking toward the front door. *Where is she going?*

She swings the door open, and almost as if he's heard us speaking of him, Charlie walks in with Boomerang.

"Man, this dog loves the snow. He can't get enough of it." Charlie laughs, stomping his shoes on the mat by the front door.

"Charlie, do you know where Sebastian's girl lives?" Nancy asks.

"What the fuck?" I bellow.

Charlie looks over at me, stunned by the outburst but continues despite it.

"Yes, ma'am."

"Well, what are you waiting for, Sebastian? Go over there," Sam joins the circus.

"Ya'll have lost your minds. I'm not going over there. I'm going to my room." I stalk past them and fling myself onto my bed once I finally reach a space devoid of meddlers.

I've lain in this same spot for hours, staring up at the ceiling, thinking of nothing but what a dumbass I've been to have destroyed my relationship with Bella. I miss her so god damn much it hurts. I'd think I was hollow inside if it weren't for the constant dull ache that sits in my chest whenever I think of her.

Sitting up, I rub the back of my neck. What would I even say to her? If I saw her again, I would treat it as I did the meeting in the atrium at the hospital. The day I apologized to her for my horrendous behavior, not expecting anything in return. Simply hoping for forgiveness.

This must be the thought that propels me as I head into my closet and find a pair of boots. Sitting on my ottoman, I slide the Timberlands on and scold myself for considering this. I should at least have a plan instead of going over there unhinged. But I know with the way I've been feeling, there's no stopping me now.

Heading for the garage, I try to go slow so as not to bring any attention to my movements. I don't need Nancy or anyone else asking where I'm going. I'm a little nervous about driving, only because I haven't attempted it since my weakness progressed, but I wouldn't put myself behind the wheel of a car if I thought I could harm someone— even for Bella.

I manage to enter the garage unnoticed and slide myself into the driver's seat after placing my braces in the back seat. As the garage door opens, it hits me. I'd completely forgotten about the ice and snow on the roads. My reaction time is a little slower than usual, but I just need to go slow and take it easy.

Twenty minutes later, I'm blessed to find an open spot near the curb that'll allow me to pull up without parallel parking. It's not late, yet even at 6:30 p.m., the skies are completely dark. I turn off the ignition and carefully exit the vehicle and attempt to retrieve my braces from the back seat. The snowplows have been here recently as all of the snow is pushed in steep peaks against the curb. Staying upright in this mess would be an act worthy of a performance artist even if I didn't have MS.

Looking up the sidewalk toward Bella's door, my heart is in my throat. I don't want to contemplate what returning to my car dejected will feel like. I need to think positively. The minute this thought leaves me, my feet fly out from under me as my brace hits the ice. As if it's in slow motion, my body is suddenly flying through the air like the Saturday morning cartoon characters I remember as a child, before colliding with the hard ground below. There's no laugh track for this show. This could be disastrous.

Lying here, looking up at the night's sky, I wonder how long I might lie here before anyone sees me. Have Bella and Austin hunkered down for the night? Most of the neighboring houses look quiet, their porch lights lit as if they've welcomed the end of their day. I could catch pneumonia and die out here. I let go of my remaining brace and attempt to reach into my pocket for my phone until I realize I've left it in the car. *Fuck. Why had I thought this was a good idea?*

Suddenly, I hear a noise and try to focus on the source. I don't need to scare anyone and cause them to fall as well. I hear footsteps shuffling until they stop. Turning my head, I don't see anyone and close my eyes. I'm soaked down to my boxers. Should I start screaming? Maybe someone will hear me and come out. Or if they call the police, at least they can help me get up. *Jesus, what has happened to my life?*

Opening my eyes, hoping the universe will 'send me a sign,' I find Austin standing over top of me. My eyes instantly well with tears at the sight. I know this has nothing to do with being found. It's all him. God, I've missed this kid.

Before I can speak, he's reaching down to lift me up. I clutch my braces as he helps to steady me. Hell, this kid is strong. Wordlessly, he helps me to get my bearings and walks me toward the steps. I stop, taking in the ice-covered things, wondering how I'll maneuver them after what just happened. Maybe I should sit down and—

"Hold on to me," Austin says as he unexpectedly grabs me by the side. I grab onto the railing with my right hand and hold onto Austin's neck and shoulders with my left. Slow and steady, we manage the stairs one by one until he opens the door and helps me get to the couch.

In a flash, he runs out of the room and comes back with a towel. "I'll be right back." With this, he darts out the front door and returns, holding a package. "My pencils came," he says, a familiar shine in his eyes. Placing them on the kitchen table, he returns to me and sits down on the floor beside me, helping me remove my boots. I can feel myself getting emotional again. Why did no one tell me MS was going to make me start crying like a baby at the drop of a hat.

Austin meticulously helps to get me out of my wet clothes and leaves me sitting in wet boxers on the couch while he again darts out of the room. Moments later, he returns with a T-shirt and sweatpants. I put the pants on and hesitate briefly before pulling the oversized green T-shirt overhead that reads 'I'm into Fitness.' A picture of a large taco is noted in the center. Underneath it reads 'Fit'ness taco in my mouth.' Laughing, I pull it over my head as Austin tries to assist me.

I start to speak when my legs are yanked from under me, and I'm pivoted to lie lengthwise on the couch. He grabs a blanket from the chair next to the fireplace, and I immediately sense Isabella's scent. I lift it to my nose and inhale like it's the very oxygen I need to breathe.

"You need to say sorry," Austin blurts. "To Mom. You need to say sorry."

"I will. I promise." My mouth goes dry. "I know. Buddy, I really am sorry."

Abruptly, he walks over, bends down, and kisses me on the head. "It'll all be okay once you say sorry." He walks away, leaving me to sit and think about my current predicament.

If only you're right, Austin. Something tells me it isn't going to be that easy.

CHAPTER THIRTY-SIX

Sebastian

As I look at my watch, I realize it's been an hour of sitting here fretting about Isabella's arrival. My boxers are wet, and my nerves are shot, but the thought of seeing her is keeping me rooted to this spot. Well, that and the fact, I could die out there.

Suddenly, I hear a key enter the lock of the front door, and my whole body is on red alert. *Holy shit, I wasn't this nervous before my first surgery.*

Sitting up, I try to take a deep breath and prepare myself. The door opens, bringing a chill, and I pray it's due to the weather. Isabella has her hands full, juggling grocery bags as she enters, and quickly turns to close the door before making eye contact with me. Taking a few steps over to the kitchen, she drops the bags and turns before our eyes meet, her mouth hanging ajar. She takes two steps in my direction, deep worry lines crossing her brow before she stops in her tracks as if recalling all I've done. I watch as she stands a little taller, crossing her arms about her chest. *God, I love this woman.*

"What are you doing here?"

"He says sorry, Mom," Austin blurts as he rapidly enters the space.

"What's for dinner?"

"Grilled cheese and soup," she answers, never taking her eyes off of me.

"My pencils came."

My beauty now turns, grabbing Austin by the arms and smiling at him. "Oh, I'm glad." The smile she gives him makes my heart thump harder. I can't believe I'm finally here, with her.

"Let me get the groceries unpacked, and I'll start working on your dinner."

Austin leaves the room, and I watch as she turns to the grocery bags like I was just a mirage.

"Bella?"

"Don't." She spins to face me. "I don't know why you're here, but you can leave the way you came." It's now, she takes in my appearance. I can see by the way she scrunches up her sweet little nose and tilts her head to the side, she realizes I'm wearing her son's clothing. But in true Isabella style, she turns back to her work and continues putting away groceries, grabbing a pan to make her son's dinner.

Sitting here, I'm not entirely sure what to do. I don't want to argue with her in front of Austin. But I can't leave here without talking to her. I guess I just sit here quietly and hope the opportunity presents itself.

Examining my hands in a way I've never done before, I try to distract my thoughts so my nerves will calm the fuck down.

After what seems like an eternity, Isabella leaves the kitchen without so much as a glance in my direction. I notice she has soup on the stovetop, but nothing else is cooking. God, this is maddening.

A little while later, Bella returns, having showered and changed into leggings and an oversized hoodie. I'm dying over here. I want to go to her. To hold her and tell her I'll do anything if she'll only give me one more chance. I attempt to rotate my body on the couch to face her when she turns to place two plates on the table and calls Austin's name. They sit at the table and begin eating. I feel like I'm in a Christmas Carol, visiting people I've wronged, watching them from afar. Like I'm completely invisible.

My heart hurts. Why did I come here? What did I think I'd accomplish? I'll wait until Austin leaves the room and make my apologies and try to get back to the car. If I could just get to my phone, I could ask Charlie to come and get me.

My thoughts are quickly interrupted as Bella stands from the table and leaves the room. Have I upset her? Austin looks in my direction, but his face is unreadable. He stands from his seat, walks over to the stove, and looks as if he is grabbing seconds when he turns and brings a sandwich to me.

"Thanks, buddy. I don't want to upset your mom. I think I should go."

"No. You haven't said sorry yet. Don't go. I'll get her."

I attempt to stop him, but he's too quick for me. I consider leaving before she returns, but I've been there, done that, and have the scars to prove it. I can't walk out on her again without an explanation and think there will ever be a chance at forgiveness.

Holding the sandwich Austin has gifted me, lovingly made by Bella for her son, I find I can't eat with this lump in my throat. I have nowhere to place it, as he didn't give me a plate. My eyes dart from the sandwich to the beautiful brunette who's now standing in front of me, and I practically jump.

"Austin said you had something you needed to say."

"Bella, I..." My mouth is so dry. How will she ever believe I'm sincere if I'm begging forgiveness while holding this grilled cheese? "Would you mind?" I hand her the sandwich, and she rolls her eyes at me as she carries it over to the kitchen table. "GG, I'm sorry. Please, please believe how sorry I am."

"Oh, I know how sorry you are." She's so mad. I have this coming. *Just take it like a man, Sebastian.*

"I know I went about this all wrong, but I was trying to do the right thing by you."

"Ah, leaving town with a blonde just hours after you were in my bed. Not even a note to say goodbye. That was doing the right thing?"

"No. You're right. I handled all of this poorly. I was trying to protect you. You've given your whole life to others. You put your ex through medical school just to watch him leave. You've devoted your adult life to caring for your child. I couldn't saddle you with this too. I found out the day I came here that I have MS. I quit my job before I could hurt a patient who was seeking help from me—"

"Then you quit me. You quit us. Not just me and you, Austin too."

I'm a little taken aback that she isn't shocked to find out I have multiple sclerosis. Is she that mad she isn't fazed? "I know that's the way it seemed, but I couldn't risk you giving up more of your life to care for me. You'd just graduated from your program and were starting a job you love. You were asking about babies, and I didn't know how I was going to take care of myself, much less an infant. I couldn't let you take on everything yourself."

"That's not your decision to make, Sebastian."

"I know." I drop my head in shame. Gene was right on the money. "But none of that with her was real. I staged that whole situation with Sophia, so you'd be mad enough to move on and not look back. I wanted you to have a full life."

"But that's the problem, Sebastian. It was real. You walked out on us without a word. You weren't concerned for our feelings when you left. The hurt you left behind was very real," Isabella murmurs as a single tear tumbles down her beautiful face. *What the hell have I done?*

Turning her face away from me, she swipes at her tear and lifts her chin. God, I'm so in love with this proud creature. "Are you okay?" She sniffles.

"Baby, I'll never be okay if I can't figure out a way for you to forgive me. I can live with this," I say, pointing to my braces. "I can't live without you."

I see her take in the braces, and her face softens a bit. "Why are you wearing Austin's clothes?"

"I fell in the snow and couldn't get up. He helped me in and even got me out of the wet stuff."

A look of shock takes over her features, but I still can't tell if I'm out of the woods. "Can I stay?"

"What?"

"Can I stay here?"

"On the couch? Sure, if that's what you want. It's been a really long day for me. I'm going to bed. You can show yourself out in the morning," she says, spinning on her heel and walking toward her room.

I'm unsure how I feel at the moment. She hasn't turned me away, so there's that. She hasn't forgiven me, but I'm still here. Austin appears to have forgiven me, so I'll take that as a win and hope tomorrow will bring her around. I'm not sure how I'll sleep lying on this couch so close to her, but I'd rather be here in this house with the two of them than anywhere else in the world right now. I'll take whatever she'll give me.

Looking at my watch, it reads 10:10 p.m. I can't believe, after all this time, my boxers still feel wet. I grab my braces from the floor and head for the bathroom. Stopping by the kitchen table, I take a few bites of the now cold cheese sandwich and throw the rest in the trash before cleaning up the kitchen. I slowly make my way down the hall to the bathroom and notice Bella's door is cracked. She's lying on her side, her back to the door. I've never wanted to go to someone so much in my life, but I know now isn't the time. I meander down the hallway a bit farther and notice Austin is in bed, eyes closed, but the light is still on in his room. Dying of curiosity, I decide to peek inside to see how the leaf mural turned out and gasp.

The brown and burgundy leaves are now gone and in its place is a wall of vibrant blue waves. The rolling water has a circular appearance to it, reminiscent of Van Gogh's 'Starry Night' painting. Looking back toward Austin, I verify he's asleep before I carefully come closer to the wall. To the untrained eye, the painting appears to depict a turbulent sea with a brown-haired mermaid seated in the upper left-hand corner and a sailboat tossing about the sea to the right. Yet, as I examine the mermaid more closely, my breath hitches.

The woman sits in profile, one single tear tumbling from her eye toward the water down below. This is an ocean of tears. Of Bella's tears. Looking more closely at the sailboat, I realize it isn't a boat at all, but a seagull whose wings appear broken, hanging down by its sides. How could he have known? What torment has this young man watched me put his mother through?

I swiftly turn toward the bathroom, praying I won't awaken them in my haste and barely make it inside before I drop myself onto the closed commode lid to collect myself. I love these two people beyond anything I've ever known. I feel physically sick that I've hurt them this way. How will I ever be able to show them how incredibly sorry I am? I may have walked away that morning with good intentions, but I left my heart here in this home and proceeded to destroy theirs.

∾

"Good morning." I hear above me. Opening my eyes, I find Austin holding out a bowl to me.

"Good morning, bud. What's that?"

"Breakfast."

Taking the bowl from him, I notice what appears to be a sugary cereal of some sort with a splash of milk.

"It's Captain Crunch. It's my favorite. Mom won't let me use the stove when she's gone."

"Thanks, Austin. It looks great."

He takes a seat across from me and digs into his cereal. My heart is so full of love for this crazy, talented kid. As difficult as last night was, I need to take this as a sign from the universe. We're all hurting. But I've never been more sure of anything. We belong together.

"Where's Boomerang?"

"He's at the house." All of a sudden, it hits me. I snuck out like a thief in the night and didn't leave so much as a note. "Austin, I need your help. I left my cell phone in my car. I'm afraid to attempt getting it without another fall. Do you think you could get it for me? I want to let my nurse know I won't be there for a few days."

"Sure. Where are you going?"

"What do you mean?"

"If you aren't going to be home. Where are you going?"

"I'm going to be here with you and your mom." I almost drop my bowl of Captain Crunch as what resembles a smile dots Austin's face.

He jumps from his seat abruptly. "Where are your keys?"

∾

"Thanks, Charlie," I say, taking the overnight bag from him.

"No problem, sir. Although I dig the T-shirt."

"Haha. I'll ask Austin if you can borrow it," I tease. "Please tell Nancy I'm in good hands for a few days. I'll get back to exercising and all that rot once I can get things settled here."

I sling my bag over my shoulder and carefully amble toward the bathroom. It's a bit of a struggle maneuvering the shower without a seat. I sit carefully on the side of the tub until I can manage to get myself safely to a standing position and then take the quickest shower of my life. As much as I love being in this home, the bathroom situation is not designed for someone with circumstances like mine.

Exiting the bathroom almost an hour later, I drag myself over to Austin's room and knock on the door. "Hey, can I come in?"

"Yes," he says, seated on his bed diligently sketching in his pad.

As I drop myself into the soft chair in the corner, I point to the wall. "I'm sorry, Austin."

He stops drawing and looks up at me. "I know."

"I never meant to hurt you."

He nods and continues sketching.

"I'm sorry I didn't get to see the leaves get finished. What are you working on now?"

"Nothing much. Just snow and wind. They're hard to draw."

"Austin, have you ever traveled anywhere with your mom? Like on vacation?"

"Not really. We've gone to the beach."

"Would you be nervous to go on a plane or a boat?"

"I don't know. I don't like crowded places."

Considering this a moment, I wonder if he'd be willing to do a cruise if we weren't subjected to a crowd. I might have to look into this. I shake my head, realizing I've definitely gotten ahead of myself. *She's barely speaking to you.*

We spend the rest of the afternoon chatting as I watch him draw, feeling more at peace than I can recall. Excusing myself, I go to the den to sprawl out on the couch and attempt a nap, given how poorly I slept the night before.

I awake to the sound of pans clanging together in the kitchen and rub my eyes. What time is it? Looking down, I notice it's 8:15 p.m. *Hell, I've slept all afternoon.*

"There's leftover macaroni and cheese and green beans in the fridge. Good night," Bella says, walking swiftly away from me. I try to get her attention, but she's gone in a flash. *Fuck. I waited all day to see her, and now she's gone.* She offered me food, though. That's a good sign, right?

I am a bit hungry. The neighbor who came by earlier in the day seemed startled to see me until Austin introduced me as his friend. She helped him sort out lunch, but I wasn't about to ask her to make me anything. In hindsight, I should've asked Charlie to bring me something, but food hasn't been at the top of my priority list. I could always look for another bowl of Captain Crunch if I got that hungry.

I make my way to the kitchen and heat up the leftovers Bella has offered. The warm gooey cheese hits the spot, lifting my spirits. I decide to head down the hall to the restroom and potentially say goodnight to Austin.

Once I've changed into lounge pants and a white cotton T-shirt, I wish Austin a goodnight and start to make my way back to the front room when I notice Bella is lying on her side, facing me in that unforgettable pink satin nightgown I remember so well. I stop in my tracks and watch as she lifts the covers. My heart is in my throat as she slowly brings herself to the edge of the bed and stands. My mouth goes dry as she carefully slinks in my direction. God, this woman. As she makes her way toward me, I look into her deep brown eyes just before the door closes, and I hear the latch click shut.

Dropping my head, I make my way back to the den, cursing myself. *What did I think was going to happen?*

Night after night, I take up residency on the couch and pray things will get better between us. I fear if I leave, she'll never let me back in. I attempt to surprise her by ordering Luigi's take-out tonight, so she won't have to cook when she comes home. Austin is excited he'll be getting baked spaghetti.

Charlie drops by around 7:10 p.m. with our take-out order, Boomerang in tow. When I tell Austin he has a visitor, his face lights up the way he does when he's happy. I tell him we'll have to wait on spaghetti until his mom comes home, and we set the table for the three of us in anticipation of her arrival.

Bella arrives twenty minutes later, appearing surprised but not overly happy about my gesture. Is she completely sick of me now? She hasn't asked me to leave.

"You two go ahead and eat. I'm going to change," she says and hurries down the hall.

I hate eating without her, but if I hold Austin back from this spaghetti much longer, there will be hell to pay. Opening the containers, I spoon an oversized serving for Austin and one for myself and place them on the table. I turn to him with a plate of salad and watch the shine in his eyes dim. "I know. I'm not happy about it either, but you know this will make your mom happy," I say.

About that time, Bella steps back into the main room, looking beautiful. She's dressed in a short black cocktail dress wearing shiny black heels, holding a small clutch. She walks over to Austin and kisses him on the head before turning to grab her coat.

"You're leaving?"

"Yes. I have plans."

"I got us dinner."

"No one asked you to. Austin, if you need anything, Margaret said she'll be home all night."

"I'm right fucking here," I bark.

"Mom doesn't like fucking," Austin says.

I abruptly stop myself from correcting him, that she does, in fact, like fucking, knowing that could get me kicked out for good. "Where are you going?" My voice is admittedly too loud.

"It's none of your business."

I look back at her, my mouth hanging wide open. I'm speechless.

"No one asked you to come here, Sebastian."

I can feel steam pour from my ears I'm so hot. Nearly snapping the chair in half as I watch her exit, I ask Austin, "Do you know where she's going?"

"I think she has another date."

I quickly make it to the door in time to see Jeff open the car door for her. *Fuck me.*

CHAPTER THIRTY-SEVEN

Sebastian

It's been over two hours since Bella left. I tried to hang out with Austin in his room, but my anger was getting the best of me, and I just needed to be alone. I considered searching her place for alcohol or calling Charlie to make a scotch delivery, but Austin is here. Even if Margaret would be available all night, I couldn't do that.

I opt instead for a shower. This will easily kill an hour. My initial attempts to get into the shower are fruitless. I'm so fucking livid it's causing me to be unsafe. I finally lower myself into the bathtub and bathe that way, letting the shower water hit my head from above to rinse the shampoo from my hair when I'm done.

Trying to get out of the tub is a whole other challenge. *Hell, I may die in here.* I lay my head back on the porcelain and stare up at the ceiling. Is this pointless? Should I just call Charlie and head home once she returns? How much torture can I live with? She's made her point. I've tried to apologize. If I ever make it out of this tub alive, I need to go before I say something else in front of Austin I might regret.

After multiple attempts, I manage to get myself to the edge of the tub and up onto my two feet. I'm exhausted. I hope I have enough energy to make it back to the bed... I mean, couch. Stumbling down the hall, I notice Austin's gone to bed before I could tell him goodnight. Looking at him brings a smile to my face, despite the shitty night I've had.

I slowly clomp down the hall with my braces, stopping to gather my strength just outside Bella's bedroom door when I notice she's already home and in bed. Suddenly, she rolls over in my direction. I can't even look at her. Did Jeff kiss her goodnight? *Fuck, I've never even kissed her goodnight.* My anger starts to bubble over, and I forcefully pick up my feet, heading back to the front room when I hear her.

"Bas?"

I stop. Waiting for more, I force myself to look straight ahead. I'm tired of her fucking with me.

"Sebastian?" I hear again. This time she sounds as if she's crying. I quickly turn her way to find she's holding the covers out for me. Please tell me this is really happening. I clumsily drag my feet in her direction, waiting for the other shoe to drop. Fuck, I'm probably working the whole Tiny Tim routine, just like Sam suggested, but in this moment, I don't care.

"I'm sorry."

Sorry for what? Has she been sleeping with him? Are they an item now? Standing here, waiting for more information before I lose it, she continues.

"I shouldn't have hurt you like that. It was wrong. Please come here so I can talk to you."

I tentatively lower myself to sit at the edge of her bed. I can't touch her until I know more. I'm too angry right now and would rather call Charlie and head home than say or do something else I can't take back. "Did you sleep with him?"

"No. It was just a date."

"Austin said another date. How long have you two been going out?"

"Only one other time. I needed to move on. He's so nice that I knew he'd never do anything to hurt me."

Her statement feels like a blow to the chest. But she's right. I've known all along he's the safe bet. "Do you have feelings for him?" I ask, a little worried about the answer.

"No." Reaching for my hand, she pulls it to her sweet lips and kisses my knuckles. I can feel my breath catch. I've missed this woman so much, but I'm afraid to let my guard down. "I'm afraid to trust you again. You really hurt me."

"I know, GG. I'd do anything to take it back. I'm sorry. You were all I thought about. Wanting to come home to you and make everything right again."

"Bas? Can you do something for me?"

"Anything."

"Will you shut the door?"

I knew it. I'm being dismissed again. Picking up her soft hand, I raise it to my lips. I need to taste her sweet skin one last time before I leave. Standing slowly, I feel as if my battery has run dry. I anticipate I have enough energy to make it back to the front room, but I'm unsure if I'll have enough to make it down the steps if I attempt leaving tonight. As I make it through the doorway, Bella calls after me.

"No, Bas. I just wanted you to shut the door," she says, pointing toward Austin's room. "Stay with me? Please?"

My heart suddenly begins to race, and I feel as if I just got a jump start from a kind passerby. I enter the room, shutting and locking the door behind me, and clomp over to her like a baby foal up on all four legs for the first time.

Landing on the bed with a thud, Bella giggles as she slides over to make room for me. *If that didn't turn her on*, I snort to myself. "I should've had that song "I'm Sexy and I Know It" playing." I laugh. Dropping my braces to the side of the bed, I lie down and turn on my side, facing her. "GG?"

"Yes?"

"Are we going to be okay?" She looks at me with her big brown eyes shining, a small smile popping her left dimple. I can't even wait for an answer. Reaching to cup her cheeks, I place my lips over hers and groan. The heady feel of her mouth on mine after all of this time is better than anything I could've imagined. Her lips are soft and sweet.

But, it's beyond physical. It's a connection. Giving myself to her in a way I've never allowed with anyone else.

My tongue swipes through her lips, and I kiss her as if I'm making up for every night we were apart. Our tongues dance as I push my fingers through her hair, wanting to anchor her to me forever. Her mouth is decadent, delicious. I don't want this to ever stop.

Bella's arms slide around my back and pull me into her, and I tilt her head slightly to deepen our kiss. My heart is racing in my chest, and it's not because I'm in her bed. It's not from the kisses I waited entirely too long to enjoy. It's knowing there's a chance. This beautiful woman is giving me a chance, after all I've done.

Isabella

I can't wait a moment longer. I need to touch him. I've missed him so much. Grabbing at the hem of his T-shirt, I lift it over his head and toss it to the end of the bed. Pushing him down to lie on his back, so he isn't using any more energy than necessary, I glide my hands down his chest. He's not as muscular as he was when he left, yet I can still feel the ridges of his abdominal muscles as I trace them with my fingertips.

I'm surprised when he doesn't reach for me in return, but the look of pure joy on his face reassures me everything is okay. I reach up to lower my spaghetti straps and lift my gown over my head to join his shirt at the end of the bed.

Sebastian's eyes sparkle as he reaches for my breasts, cupping them and teasing my nipples under his gentle touch. This isn't the wild, unbridled sex of the past. He's tender and sweet, and I appreciate the moment after all we've endured. "Kiss me again, GG," he says softly.

Straddling him, I bend down to kiss his big, beautiful lips. I alternate kisses and nibbling at his lower lip, stroking his stubble. His five o'clock shadow has practically morphed into a full beard. But he's just as sexy as ever.

Sebastian looks at me with lust, and I realize I've been grinding myself against his hardening cock while we kiss.

Reaching down, I slide back and stroke him within his boxers until he lets out a low moan. Lowering his boxer briefs, I stand to remove my panties before climbing back on top of him. I bend down for another kiss as I feel him arch into me, his stiff length gliding up and down against my wet center.

He moves his hand down to my mound and teases my opening as we kiss. "God, GG. I've missed you so much. Not just your body but fucking everything about you." I can feel him exhale against my ear as he continues to stroke my flesh. "You're so wet. I can't wait to slide inside you, baby."

Sitting up, I cup my breasts, circling my nipples with my index fingers the way he likes. I can feel him arch up into me again and know neither of us will make it much longer. I attempt to swing my leg off of him, so I can go to my closet to obtain a condom when he clamps his hands down onto my hips with a look of desperation on his face.

"What's the matter?"

"Where are you going?"

"I need to get a condom."

"Bella, I haven't been with anyone since I left. I swear."

"I believe you, Bas. I haven't either, but I'm not on the pill," I try to reassure him.

"Baby, I'm all in. If you want babies, we'll hire a nanny. I've already got a private nurse. I don't want you to be burdened by making a life with me. But I need you with me so I'll do anything to make this work."

I sit still on his lap, my eyes blinking in shock.

"GG, please. I don't want anything between us anymore. I love you. I love you so fucking much it makes me crazy being apart. If you aren't ready and want to use one, that's fine. I'm okay with whatever you want. But know I'm never leaving again. If you want babies, I'll knock you up as often as you'll let me."

"Oh, lord."

"I'm serious. You and Austin mean everything to me. I hate what I did to you. I only wanted the best for you. I just thought you deserved better than me."

My eyes fill with unshed tears, and I reach down to stroke his beautiful face before kissing him again. Looking into his deep blue eyes, I try to absorb his words.

"What's the matter, Bella?"

We sit quietly, looking at each other for a moment before I try to break the serious mood. "I'm just trying to figure out what you did with Sebastian." I laugh, wiping away my tears.

"Shut up," he says, smacking my ass. "Now be a good girl and suck my cock."

"Ah, and he's back."

Sliding down, I wrap my hand around his hard length and glide it up and down until I see precum sitting atop the head. I dart my tongue out and hear him hiss above me. Continuing to tease his opening, I flick my tongue along the underside of his shaft before taking him fully into my throat.

"Oh, sweet Jesus, Bella."

His groans of pleasure only spur me on, and I continue to suck and tug at his engorged cock until he begs me to mount him.

Straddling him again, I line him up with my opening and slowly shift my hips back and forth to open myself up for him. After a few moments, my body seems to relax, and I'm able to slide down his length completely. This time it's me that lets out a groan of pleasure as I undulate on top of him.

"You're so warm and wet. I've dreamt of this for so long. Thrusting my dick into your tight pussy." He reaches forward and flicks my clit with his thumb. "Night after night, jerking myself off, dreaming of those beautiful tits bouncing for me while feeling you fluttering around my fat cock."

I'm trying not to cry out and wake Austin, but this man is making me crazy.

"You're mine, Bella."

"Yes."

"From here on out, you're mine."

"Oh, Bas, I'm…"

"That's it, GG. It's right there." Sebastian picks up his pace, rubbing and flicking my bundle of nerves with precision.

Rocking my body over his, I'm so close to the edge. I slam my body down onto his cock and hear his shaky exhale and know he's right there with me. Dropping down once more, I feel my limbs grow tight around him.

Unexpectedly, Sebastian's fingers are now digging into my ass, tilting my pelvis so that each buck of my hips causes delicious friction against my clit.

"Fuck, GG. Fuck."

The feel of his body pulsating inside me has me free-falling into my orgasm. I tumble forward as my body contracts around him. This euphoria is more than I can handle and remain upright. Abruptly, he's turning my head to the side, engulfing me in a kiss.

Pulling back, he whispers against my mouth, "I love you, Bella."

"And I love you," I reply, returning a kiss to his waiting lips. Resting my face against his chest, I close my eyes and exhale, overwhelmed at everything I'm feeling. Tears start to trickle from my eyes before I realize the intensity of my emotions.

"Baby? What is it?"

"I wanted to come to you. To beg Kat to tell me where you were and come to you. But my pride wouldn't let me after what you did. I was so worried. My heart so wounded at knowing you were going through this alone."

"I hate what I did to you. But I would've rather had you hate me than be hurting," he says, wiping my tears from my eyes. "I wish they hadn't told you."

"Who?"

"Nick and Kat. I held off telling Nick for a long time because I didn't want them to upset you."

"They didn't tell me. Sophia did."

Sebastian shifts in the bed, looking stunned.

"She said she needed her karma cleaned."

Shaking his head, he pulls me into him, kissing me on my head. "That she does. Maybe there's hope for her yet."

CHAPTER THIRTY-EIGHT

Isabella

"Good morning."

Rolling over, I see the handsome face of my love smiling back at me. "I was afraid I'd wake up, and none of this would be real."

"Yeah. I kind of thought the same thing when I opened my eyes this morning. I didn't want to wake you but had to squeeze you a little tighter to make sure it wasn't my imagination." He places sweet kisses on the side of my neck and nuzzles my hair. "Did you sleep okay?"

"Best sleep in months." I giggle.

"GG? Can I ask you something?"

Twisting my torso so I'm completely facing him now, I run my hand through the inky hair that's fallen into his piercing deep blue eyes. "I hope from here on out we can ask each other anything."

"Why did you let me stay?"

"What do you mean?"

"You were so mad. But night after night, instead of throwing my ass out on the street, you let me stay."

Biting my lip, I can't help but laugh. "Sometimes you just have to say fuck it."

"What?" he chuckles. Bopping me on my nose, he dips his head to the nape of my neck and playfully sinks his teeth in.

"Ouch." I laugh.

"That's the most romantic thing you've ever said to me. My sweet little—"

Knock, knock.

We both freeze. *Holy crap.*

"Mom?"

"Yeah, buddy."

"Sebastian isn't here. He left."

Pushing back from Sebastian, I hold my finger up to my lips to shush him and grab my nightgown from the end of the bed. Walking to the door, I try to calm Austin. "Hey, bud. I'll be right out. I'll meet you in the kitchen."

Rotating to Sebastian, I cross my arms over my chest. "Just to be clear. Is this happening? We're going to make a go of this? Because I wasn't the only one hurt when you left."

I watch as his face turns solemn, and he sits himself up. "I know, GG. I'm sorry. Yes. I meant what I said last night. I need you two crazies in my life. What can I do?"

"Well, I'm going to try and find a way to explain things. I've never had a man stay the night with him here. We haven't had a lot of conversations about this type of thing. This could be all kinds of awkward."

I open the door and make my way to the kitchen. Austin is sitting at the table with a bowl of Captain Crunch in front of him. Giving him a quick peck on the head, I grab the coffee pot and fill it with water. "Austin. I have something I need to talk to you about."

"Is Sebastian okay?"

Placing the carafe in the coffee maker, I scoop the last of the fragrant grounds into the top of the appliance, turn it on, and sit down at the table. "He's fine. Sebastian slept in my room last night."

There's a change in his facial expression, but I'm unsure whether this is confusion or relief.

"I care a lot about Sebastian," I say.

As if his ears were burning, Bas comes into the room and slowly lowers himself into the chair beside Austin. "Hey, bud."

Austin's eyes flick from me to Bas and back again.

"Sometimes when a man and a woman care about each other, they sleep in the same bed." Holding my breath, I attempt to prepare myself for further questions.

"Like the mom and the dad on that movie the other night, when you said we should change the channel?"

Sebastian looks over at me with one side of his mouth raised in a knowing grin.

"Yeah, kinda like that."

The room gets quiet, and Sebastian reaches for my hand, seeming happy to let me take the lead on this. I'm glad none of this has him running for the hills. Yet.

I watch as Austin turns to look at Bas. "Does this mean you're going to be my dad now?"

Holy crap, so much for that. This might be more reality than Sebastian is—

"I'd be honored to be your dad, buddy. I love you *and* your mom. I'm sorry I hurt you guys when I left. I didn't handle the news about my illness well. I shouldn't have done that to you."

Astonished, I gawk at him. That he could share the magnitude of his feelings for me last night was one thing. But for this man to say these things to Austin, without provocation, is more than I could've hoped for. The tears are back, and this one is a gusher. Covering my face with my hands, I try to regain control.

Tugging on my arm, Sebastian pulls me to him, and I sit in his lap as he holds me close. As his warm hand strokes my hair and my back, he places a gentle kiss on my temple. "Austin. I'd like to set up an art space for you at my house. Turn one of the guest rooms into your art room and maybe put a connecting door between it and a room you can use to sleep if you stay over there sometimes. I like it here, but your bathroom is going to be the death of me."

A chuckle escapes when I think of how difficult it's probably been maneuvering that small space in his current condition. Yet, he never complained and refused to leave us.

"I'd like to build a wall where we can remove your art after you finish instead of painting over it. Your art is too beautiful to destroy. It should be shared."

"Okay," Austin says, scooping a large spoonful of cereal into his mouth like these conversations happen every day.

"I also want to see if we can try to take some trips together. We could start off with a few short car trips close to home and progress to train or cruise travel. We'll work our way up to flying. But, I want you to see the world. There's so much more out there for you to explore. And a lot of great new things to paint."

"Okay." He abruptly stands from his chair, places his bowl into the sink, and makes his way back to his room.

"Well, I think that went well," Bas says.

Squeezing his beautiful sexy face, I plant my lips over his and kiss him tenderly. "I'm so in love with you, Sebastian Lee."

"Thank god. I'd hate to have to tell Austin to just forget all that."

                            ∽

Sebastian
Six Months Later

"Austin, look over there." I point in the direction of a bald eagle sitting atop a tall Spruce tree.

He quickly turns his binoculars and then lowers them when he can't focus them quickly enough. Austin has seemed more excited and receptive to his surroundings since boarding this cruise than I've ever witnessed. At first, I was worried it was anxiety due to the crowd size during check-in and the muster drill. But in hindsight, I think it's more at the experience being so new.

I contacted the cruise line to advise them Austin has some special needs, and they've been nothing but accommodating. It doesn't hurt that I've booked the largest suite on the ship. He has his own space, and the stateroom attendants have provided a place for Austin to draw and even paint a little if he so desires. I've told him, no painting on walls on this trip. I don't want to get banned from returning.

Alaska's provided the perfect backdrop for our first cruise. I'm thrilled I could walk onboard the ship without the use of braces or a cane. My strength has gradually returned over the last few months, and I'm back to working out, yoga, meditation, and reducing my stress through lots and lots of hot sex with my devoted girl.

Sitting on the veranda, there's been a notable drop in temperature since we departed Vancouver. Bella steps outside, pulling a wrap around her shoulders before sitting down in my lap. We could've taken a cruise to a warmer climate, but I'm feeling better and thought this would be a more exciting backdrop for Austin's creativity. The days of drinking by the pool and checking out my next conquest are over.

I gaze over my companions and can't stop the megawatt smile that crosses my face. How things have changed. No longer am I the shark looking to claim his next mate. No more successful surgical career. No longer do I live an ordered life, preferring instead to let Bella steer this ship.

I'm also no longer watching the world go by without being a part of it. I'm surrounded by a dog that sheds, a child who paints on walls, and a woman who tells me how things are going to be. My whole world is sitting right here with me, and I wouldn't have it any other way.

The End.

THANK YOU FOR READING

And if there were things about Bas and Bella's story you are still curious to know, stay tuned… an extended epilogue is in their future.

Keep reading for an excerpt of My Best Shot, releasing spring 2022 https://geni.us/7rP7VrA

And for readers just starting with The Bitter Rival, a snippet from Deprivation, Book One in The Deprivation Trilogy, is also included.

It has been my dream to share the many characters taking up residence in my mind. I hope you enjoy their adventures as much as I have enjoyed putting them to paper. Without you, I could not continue to live this dream.

To obtain more information on my current books, upcoming work, and special offers please visit my webpage: www.authorlmfox.com

Visit me on Facebook at AuthorLMFox and my readers' group, Layla's Fox Den, as well as on Instagram @authorlmfox, Twitter @authorlmfox and TikTok @authorlmfox

PLAY LIST

Wobble, V.I.C.
Wow, Post Malone**Bad Habits**, Ed Sheeran
Kings & Queens, Ava Max
New Rules, Dua Lipa
All of Me, John Legend
Perfect, Ed Sheeran
Bad Things, Meiko
Hot n Cold, Katy Perry
Bad Habits, Ed Sheeran
Confident, Demi Lovato
There's Nothing Holdin` Me Back, Shawn Mendes
Lost Without You, Freya Ridings
The Story, Brandi Carlile
Too Good at Goodbyes, Kurt Hugo Schneider & Alicia Moffet
You Mean the World to Me, Freya Ridings
The Last Word, Frances
Sexy and I Know It, LMFAO

ACKNOWLEDGMENTS

I cannot thank TL Swan enough for starting me on this journey. I had hit burnout long before COVID made its way into the world. Healthcare workers are a tough breed, but we're still human all the same. Watching so many suffer alone was depressing. When I was off work, I would attempt to lose myself in books. Then one night out of the blue, there was a post from my favorite author encouraging anyone listening to follow their dreams. It was as if that very day she took my hand and walked me into the light. All of the 'what ifs' suddenly seemed possible. To have someone you idolize inspire you in this way is a gift I'll treasure forever. The Bitter Rival is technically the sixth book I've written since that fateful day. I'll always be grateful for the push I needed to follow my bliss. If I can do this, so can you! I'll shout it from the rooftops. If there's a dream locked deep down in your soul, don't let one more day pass you by. Make it happen. You've got this!

I also need to sincerely thank the many Indie Authors I've met along the way that have continued to lift me up. I appreciate your time and generosity more than you know.

Thank you to my team! I would be lost without the amazing work of my editors and formatter, Kelly, Cheree, and Shari. I'm so thankful to Wander Aguiar for his photographic genius and Hang Le for her creative vision. Working with all of you is honestly a dream come true. To Jo and the team at GMB, thank you for everything you do to get my work out there. And Linda and your incredible team at Foreword, I thank heaven for your guidance and incredible patience. I don't know what I'd do without you. And to my sweet, dedicated PA, Ashley, thank you for keeping me afloat.

Thank you so much to my beta and ARC readers! You were the first

I trusted to share my books, and I so appreciate your time, honest feedback, and encouragement. Denise, Laura, Siri, Rita, and Kelly, you've been a constant source of encouragement and direction. A special thank you to Kelly, for her experience with individuals living with Autism. Having your input with Austin's character means a great deal to me! I'll never know how to adequately thank my incredible ARC readers. Between the constant motivation, the beautiful edits and reviews… you guys are such a gift!

I want to send a special note of thanks to all of the Fox Cubs in Layla's Fox Den, my Facebook Author group, as well as the followers on my Facebook, Instagram, Twitter, and TikTok pages. Your posts continue to motivate me, and I truly appreciate all of you.

Ultimately, I'd have never completed this book without the endless love and continued support of my husband and kids. I thank you from the bottom of my heart for giving me the alone time to create. I love you all so very much.

AN EXCERPT FROM MOONSHOT

Mick

"We'll see you back in two weeks," the receptionist tells the older gentleman, handing him a small appointment card.

"Thanks, Joanie. See you then," he waves as he and his wife walk out the clinic doors.

Looking down at my watch, it's now 12:25 p.m. My ass has officially fallen asleep in this brutally hard metal chair. I've been sitting here for over an hour. Initially surrounded by patients of all ages, I gaze about the waiting room and discover only one person remains. That person would be me. A twenty-seven-year-old ex-baseball player turned medical device salesman, who again finds the torturous thoughts of what might've been to be his only companion. I turn, looking toward the receptionist, Joanie, as I push my black horn-rimmed glasses back up my nose.

"Hang tight, Michael. I'll check again for you. Thank you for always being so patient," the sweet older brunette encourages. She gets up from her seat after flashing an embarrassed smile in my direction.

Normally I'd bring a book or something to work on while I sit here. Of all of the offices I visit, this one's the one that always leaves me hanging. But it's a part of the job I've come to accept.

"I don't have time to deal with some sales guy today. It's been a busy morning and I want to grab some lunch. I'm sorry he had an appointment, but no one asked me. Get Ava to see him."

I overhear the unmistakable sound of Dr. Stark's arrogant voice. Dr. Joseph Stark is an orthopedic surgeon specializing in shoulders at Central Virginia Orthopedics. In his mid-thirties, he's intelligent, educated, certainly skilled in the OR, and one pompous asshole. Every interaction I've ever had with this man has been condescending. It doesn't matter that I'm also a trained professional, here to do a job. *We are all beneath him.*

I've worked with FlexPath for over a year now. The work isn't bad, as far as sales jobs go. I do quite a bit of traveling, but for the most part my product sells itself. Our company supplies partial knee replacement hardware to the hospitals who perform these operations. This product has found wide appeal with surgeons in my area. I'm rarely needed to answer questions, but the high dollar item requires regular visitation to the hospitals to ensure they have the correct stock on hand as well as routine calls on the orthopedic clinics to address any concerns. When I first started with the company, I'd occasionally scrub into surgeries where the device was utilized to answer any questions. However, this is no longer necessary as the procedure has become more routine. I typically visit each office once a month, however, the busier practices I try to call on every other week.

This was never my dream. I didn't wake up in high school one morning dying to sell prosthetic parts. The only thing on my mind back then was chasing a childhood dream. I was going to be a major league baseball player.

I'd played ball my whole life and was fortunate to receive a college scholarship to join the baseball team at my local University. I was studying business when I began my college career, but my primary goal was always to get signed with a major league team after graduation. This hope crumbled the end of my freshman year when I blew out my shoulder. Batter's shoulder they called it. Well, whatever it was, it tore my dreams apart and I've been trying to pick up the pieces ever since.

"Ava should be out in just a minute," Joanie advises as she leans into the receptionist window.

"Thanks Joanie. I appreciate it. I know they're busy."

Ava. Now there's a silver lining to this wasted hour and numb ass. Ava, or *Elsa* as I've named her in my dreams, is a Nordic beauty. She's tall, thin, pale skinned with almost platinum blonde hair and ice blue eyes. Yet, more striking than her physical beauty is her personality. Her external Elsa vibe may be icy cold, but her nature is warm and endearing. She's never without a bright smile and appears genuine in her conversations. Her persona is a glaring contrast to the self-important, conceited surgeons in this office. Even some of the other physician assistants can be a little haughty at times, truth be told. But never Ava.

I've spent many a night fantasizing about her. I'm attractive, fit, and financially secure but I'm sure I'm no match for the highly educated, successful surgeons with impressive bank accounts she's surrounded by daily. I make a decent living but I'm fully aware I'm a salesman with a bachelor's degree. I've considered returning to school to obtain my MBA, but I don't really enjoy business. Not too motivating when you're only contemplating this feat to keep up with the Joneses, so to speak. My job is okay and I keep baseball in my blood coaching a local little league team. The only thing missing from my life is a woman. But that ship has sailed. When my baseball career went up in smoke, so did my girl. As much as I'd love the chance to date someone as beautiful and kind as Ava, I'm not willing to risk another letdown. Losing my girlfriend of five years and my dream of playing in the big leagues was enough for this decade.

I meet plenty of attractive women in my travels. I'm on the road at least twice a week and am thankful to still have plenty of options for occasional company. There hasn't been anyone who's tempted me into anything beyond one night. But, if anyone could…

"Hi, Michael. It's good to see you." I look up to the blonde-haired beauty and try to keep my cool.

Preorder here: https://geni.us/7rP7VrA

ENJOY A SNIPPET FROM

DEPRIVATION, BOOK ONE IN THE
DEPRIVATION TRILOGY

Present Day
Kat

Rolling away from the harsh sunlight, I squint at the clock. It's 6:29 a.m. Bolting upright, I realize my day is once again starting with a bang. I rarely sleep well. When I do manage to get some shuteye, it's usually short-lived as I frequently awaken from nightmares. Occasionally, I'm able to get back to sleep. However, this time, I've slept through my alarm. I need to brush my teeth, take a four-minute shower, braid my hair, and make it to work within the next thirty minutes.

Running into the bathroom, I jump as my toasty feet hit the harsh, cold tiles. My awakening is nearly complete as I turn on the water and my tepid skin meets the frigid spray. *Holy crap!* I dart through the shower, running shampoo and body wash onto me like it's a cheap car wash, then quickly jump out to dry off and don my scrubs for work. *Ugh, no time for coffee. Please let this shift go better than the last.*

As I drive the fifteen-minute commute to work, I reflect on my chaotic morning. Rubbing my eyes of any remaining debris Mr.

Sandman left behind, I try to recall anything specific about my most recent nightmare. *Nope, not a thing.* After a while, they all run together. I can't remember the last time I've gotten more than three to four hours of sleep.

It isn't like I have PTSD. No one's ever attacked or abused me physically. How have I developed constant nightmares and insomnia from years of bad boyfriends? I'm sure something's wrong with me. I know I should find a therapist, but how would I explain my reason for being there? "Hi. I'm Katarina Kelly and I'm having nightmares from the ghosts of my past relationships?" Granted, I could win an award for worst dating life ever, but enough to cause years of this? There's a reason I've avoided dating over the last three years. Quickly, I do the mental math and realize it's probably closer to four. Oh well, three or four, it doesn't matter, Gabe was the last and biggest dickwad in a string of many and I'm not going there again. Lonely or not, I'm better off this way.

As I pull into the physicians' parking lot with mere moments to spare before the start of my shift, I spot one remaining open space. Knowing I need to grab my bag and run once this car is in park, I quickly turn toward my destination. I make a harsh left into the parking spot, throw my gear shift into park, and open the door like I'm a contestant on *The Amazing Race*. Grabbing my work bag, I pull it swiftly from the back seat, close my door, and look up to see a car idling behind mine. As if everything else in the world has ceased to exist, I watch as the driver's window rolls down and the operator of the vehicle leans out.

My mouth goes dry, and I stop breathing momentarily as I take him in. *Jeez, this guy is like something out of a Hollywood movie.* He has gorgeous, tousled dark blond hair worthy of a photo shoot, movie star aviators sitting atop his straight nose, and the sexiest stubble covering his firm, square jaw. I watch as a sneer becomes evident despite the sunglasses.

"Nice. You almost took me out trying to steal that spot out from under me, Mario Andretti," he says, the angry timbre of his voice breaking through my stupor.

What? There wasn't another car waiting for this spot. I instantly feel my cheeks turn pink in embarrassment. Realizing I don't have time for this, I decide to avoid a car lot confrontation, return his menacing glare, and abruptly sprint for the ER doors.

Available on Amazon: https://geni.us/qVoIg6

ADDITIONAL TITLES BY LM FOX

The Deprivation Trilogy, Book One:

Deprivation

The Deprivation Trilogy, Book Two:

Fractured

The Deprivation Trilogy, Book Three:

Stronger

Upcoming Titles:

Moon Shot

(Anticipated release: spring 2022)

My Best Shot

(Anticipated release: March, 31, 2022)

Mr. Second Best

(Anticipated release: summer 2022)

Deprived No More, The Deprivation Trilogy: Epilogue (Anticipated release: 2022)

ABOUT THE AUTHOR

Born and raised in Virginia, LM Fox currently lives in a suburb of Richmond with her husband, three kids, and a chocolate lab.

Her pastimes are traveling to new and favorite places, trying new foods, a swoony book with either a good cup of tea or coffee, margaritas on special occasions, and watching her kids participate in a variety of sports.

She has spent the majority of her adult life working in emergency medicine and her books are written in this setting. Her main characters are typically in the medical field, EMS, fire, and/or law enforcement. She enjoys writing angsty, contemporary romance about headstrong, independent heroines you can't help but love and the hot alpha men who fall hard for them.

www.authorlmfox.com

Printed in Great Britain
by Amazon

86754975R00202